The Florida Saga

Robert James Connors

Published by Plumeria Press

The Florida Saga
Copyright © 2022 Robert James Connors

Publisher's Cataloging-in-Publication data

Names: Connors, Robert James, author.
Title: The Florida saga / Robert James Connors.
  Description: Lake Wales, FL: Plumeria Publishing, 2022.
Identifiers: ISBN: 978-1-959296-00-3 (hardcover) 978-1-959296-03-4 (paperback) | 978-1-959296-02-7 (epub)
  Subjects: LCSH Florida--History--To 1565--Fiction. | Prehistoric peoples--Florida--Fiction. | Prehistoric peoples--America--Fiction. | Indians of North America--First contact with Europeans--Fiction. | Indians of North America--Florida--Fiction. | Florida--History--Fiction. | BISAC FICTION / Historical / Ancient | FICTION / Indigenous
Classification: LCC PS3603.O552 F67 2022 | DDC 813.6--dc23
Publisher's Cataloging-in-Publication data

Copyright © 2022 Robert James Connors
All rights reserved. No part of this publication may be reproduced, stored in a retrieval system, or transmitted in any form by any means, whether electronic, mechanical, recording, photo-copying, or any other method, with the sole exception of review excerpts of no more than sixty words, without the specific written permission of the copyright owner. For such permission, please contact Robert James Connors at rconnorsresearch@gmail.com and include "Reprint Permission" in the subject line.
Plumeria Publishing
3311 Harbor Beach Drive, Lake Wales, FL 33859

Author's Note:

This book is a work of fiction, based upon documented events. All pre-Columbian characters are, of necessity, fictional. Non-historical characters are the product of the writer's imagination. Any resemblance to actual persons, places, or things, companies, or firms is coincidental and may not be relied upon.

In later chapters, the individuals central to significant occurrences and events are generally historical figures of importance. For the most part, with respect for their individuality, they are described as seen through the eyes of fictional central or supporting characters. I have included a chronological list of historical figures in the order mentioned at the end of the book.

The locations described in this book are real, including the hidden island, the sacred hill, and the Father of the Forest.

On the Cover: Osceola, from an 1838 portrait by Edward Curtis

Dedicated to all those who love their homes,
remember the things that made them special,
and work to preserve them for future generations.

Other titles by Robert James Connors

Historical Fiction

For Salt and Sand (included - Book One)

And Still They Came (included - Book Two)

Science Fiction

Encounter at Cloud Ranch

Non-Fiction

Romancing Through Italy

Upcoming Historical Non-Fiction

Olmsted's Lake Wales

Preface: A Few Words about the Setting

The long natural history of Florida and that of the earth, often escapes the grasp of human imagination. Our planet was once a fiery world of volcanism. As the surface of the young planet, although itself many miles thick, shifted and wrinkled under the relentless force of the currents spinning within her liquid heart, the cooling plates of continental crust collided and were crushed into mountains by their immense inertia. In their reluctant divorces, they also left behind the yawning emptiness that became the seabeds. The process has repeated like an erratic dance across the face of the earth, from pole to equator and on to pole again, for four billion years.

It was only late in that vast span of time that primitive life forms began to emerge from the seas and slowly adapt to colonize the land. Only a hundred million years ago, the Appalachian Mountains were perhaps the highest on earth, towering miles into the sky. Then, as the pressures that had created them ceased, they stopped rising and began to slowly erode, surrendering their mineral riches to the power of water and wind. The mountains cast their detritus and the rivers cut into the soils and carried them in their floods to the sea. There they were further refined to sand as coastal currents bore them southward and eastward. Distributed by the tides, they were deposited in broad alluvial plains upon the skeletons of the many prehistoric creatures which had lived in the warm equatorial waters.

Beneath the weight of the sands, a vast portion of the sea floor slowly subsided. In time, the billions of bits of sand and shells and the organic remains of trillions of creatures solidified under immense pressure into a massive block of porous limestone, the Florida platform.

The sun warmed the shallow waters. Fish of a thousand kinds swam in the sea and the bottom was covered with varieties of corals, their colorful and fantastic shapes growing and changing, perhaps an inch in a hundred years. The continental plate which bore

Florida drifted slowly north with the creep of the earth's crust, moving across the equator from a place far to the south.

Sixty-five million years ago, a great asteroid struck Mexico's Yucatan Peninsula, only a few hundred miles from Florida. The impact pierced deeply into the earth's crust, buckling it, and casting out vast amounts of debris. The entire planet was left in a cold shadow as a dense layer of dust remained suspended in the upper atmosphere. The dinosaurs and most of the forests died and so did the coral formations under the sea, buried beneath layers of sand and mud. Then as the atmosphere slowly cleared and the light returned, the corals regenerated, new kingdoms of mineral growth crowning the graveyard of the old, reaching toward the sun.

The place that would become Florida remained mostly submerged for tens of millions more years. Above the surface, fabulous and complex new life forms emerged, flourished, and became extinct as climate and conditions changed, but in the shallow sea the deposition of shells and corals continued almost without interruption for fifty thousand centuries, building layer upon layer.

Ten million years before the arrival of humans, Florida was still not yet a place at all, but remained a shallow seabed to the south of the vast, changing continent. Throughout the forces of nature were at work shaping the conditions that would create this amazing land of springs and caverns, forests and wetlands, beaches, and dunes. Forced upwards by the pressures of the earth's crust, the land that would become Florida was at times exposed and the limestone was cut by flowing water. Then those channels were again hidden beneath the tidal sands.

As the lands that would become North America moved northward, cold winds swept the vast expanse of continent. Sheets of ice began to spread southward, and the seas shrank. Eventually the floor of the great coral sea rose higher, emerging above the waves and exposing the sands that had smothered the reefs. The wind and the sea soon sculpted them into great dunes and hills. Seeds borne by birds and tides began to take root on the new lands, which slowly grew as the winters grew colder. Fish filled the waters and birds the skies. As the ice retreated the seas advanced, ocean currents passed to the north and much of present-day Florida became a large island.

In time, the waters again retreated, and the island was reconnected to the lands to the north. Eventually a vast, cold desert formed, stretching two thousand miles from the Atlantic to the distant Pacific along the shore of the remnant Gulf of Mexico. Strange animals evolved and prospered there, adapted to the harsh climate. Great herds of mastodon filled the plains while giant sloths and saber-toothed cats wandered the forests. Gigantic armadillos, tiny horses, bison, elk, fierce dire wolves, and vast flocks of birds filled this strange new world.

Creatures great and small roamed the arid uplands, while forests thrived along rivers and clung to low places. Underfoot, lizards and tortoises burrowed in the sand. Plants, too, adapted to the harsh, dry climate. Cactus and scrub plants grew where once the sea had reigned, and stunted oaks with curled, moisture-conserving leaves replaced forests of ferns. As the ice retreated again the desert was drowned under the waters of the Gulf of Mexico, and Florida's creatures were separated from their kin far to the west.

Below the surface, the great deposits of limestone had begun to change as well. Rains fell and percolated rapidly through the sands, filling the caverns below them and slowly dissolving the limestone under their constant flow. The sands and lime rock became a vast reservoir. As the seas again slowly rose, the pressure of denser salt water forced the vast lens of fresh water to rise. Fresh water sprang from every low place, and basins filled with rainwater carved new rivers in their search for outlets to the sea. Fragile limestone caverns began to collapse, creating vast sinkholes that swallowed miles of surface. Thousands of solution lakes formed in the resulting depressions.

Then, following a unique wanderlust that came with its large brain and incipient curiosity, a new species appeared in North America. It was into this strange new world that humans began to spread, adapt, and discover. Bipedal, armed, and intelligent, humans were to reshape the fate of nearly every other species present in this hemisphere.

The Objects

BOOK ONE
FOR SALT AND SAND

Booker's Box 1
The Forked Stick 3
The White Stone 10
The Shell 29
The Feather 70
The Gold Frog 73
The Ring 83
The Bone 106
The Blue Cloth 112
The Nail 114
The Dried Corn 129
The Half-penny 148
The Chain 156
The Crucifix 158

BOOK TWO
AND STILL THEY CAME

The Trail Map	203
The Lucky Horseshoe	255
The Horn of Coral	296
The Broken Eggshell	310
The Slide Rule	340
The Rivet	363
The Canvas Patch	379
The Suffrage Pin	390
The Black Stone	404
The Carved Bird	411
The Cypress Knee	425
The Rusted Nail	428
The Stock Certificate	449
The Tin Cup	454
The Brass Shell Casing	484
The Flag	490
The Medal	503
The Transistor Radio	506

Booker's Box

AS SHE PULLED THE HEAVY WOODEN BOX from beneath her bed, Nana-Marie gave me a mysterious smile. "Do you want to hear some stories?" she asked me. Coming from my favorite great-grandmother, that question could only be followed by some fun. I was five years old and loved story times. I grinned, nodded, and climbed into her lap in her old over-stuffed chair as she began to pull the first object from her box of surprises.

"This chest is full of stories," she told me. "It can tell us all about where you came from and all the people that helped send you here. A long time ago, before there were cars or airplanes, my great-grandfather came here on a horse. This place was just forests, full of wild animals and dangers, but he was very brave..." she would begin. Always I would sit attentively, my normal youthful restlessness temporarily lulled by the melodic tones of her voice and the wonderful pictures she would paint of the adventures of days gone by.

Some of my earliest memories were of afternoons spent perusing the box with my great-grandmother, choosing an interesting object from its dark corners or small cloth bags. Each stone, bone, pocket-knife, ring, glass bead, watch, feather, tooth, or bit of fur seemed to have a fabulous tale connected to it. Someone, somewhere in the past, had owned or been connected to each object and to me. Nana-Marie had tailored the stories to suit my childhood imagination and nurture my interest in the things of the past.

"What's this one?" I had asked my great-grandmother one afternoon when I was six years old. I sat cross-legged on the floor and pointed at an old horseshoe that lay in the bottom of the heavy wooden box at her feet. Of the dozens of mysterious objects in the box, it was the heavy lump of metal that had caught my young eye.

"That belonged to your great grandfather, August Booker," she told me. "I never got to meet him, but he had a wonderful life, even though it didn't start out so great. By the time he was an old man, he had seen many marvelous things and had raised a beautiful family that made a big difference in the world..."

Many days my mother and grandmother would also join us and sometimes they would ask questions or offer comments about the connections to other family members or events of the distant past. I was seven when Nana-Marie died. It was then that my grandmother explained to me that all the objects in the box, and all the stories I had been told, were but parts of the same story. Eventually I came to grasp the long but fragile threads that connected the people who had lived here thousands of years ago with those who live here today.

My grandmother became the keeper of the box and later began to share the stories it held with my own children. I watched their eyes widen, as mine had, at the encounter with the bear, or the story of the great hurricane.

Now many years have passed and I, too, am growing old, but the stories told by the box live on. It is now my time to share them, not only with my children and grandchildren, but with you, and with other parents and grandparents, so that they, too, can understand and appreciate how our place in the world came to be as it is. In this way, those events will always be as fresh and real as the people who lived them.

BOOK ONE
FOR SALT AND SAND

The Forked Stick
20,000 Years Ago

NA'PA'AN STRETCHED CAUTIOUSLY to his full height, rising above the waist-high grasses to sweep his piercing gaze across the terrain before him. Far above him a hawk circled lazily, but a low rumble from his stomach reminded him of his purpose. He had not eaten more than a mouthful in two days. The fast-shrinking food reserves of his small group were being saved for the nursing mothers. His own hunger would wait for success at the hunt, but he knew that several more days without food would leave the hunters too weakened to continue. The entire tribe faced starvation, a fate which had been met by other wandering bands on these desolate plains.

The low knoll upon which he stood offered the only place where a man might gain an overview of the terrain and any sight of distant herds. Like a magnet it had drawn him and his companions, a small band who climbed its stony slope in single file, breaking a path through the tall grass and brush.

At the summit they paused in a silent group, seven pairs of eyes scanning the plains beyond, looking for signs of game. A grey overcast hid the sun, muting the details they hoped to discern. The only movement was a solitary vulture, which banked and swooped low, perhaps to eye an old carcass picked clean long ago. It slid gracefully across the sky in search of its next meal. Below its flight a broken line of stunted trees marked the course of a stream.

At last summer had thawed the ice in these southern plains and allowed the earth to offer up its flowering glory. Ahead of them, a series of low ridges rippled with the faint greens and browns of summer's tall grasses. Small birds flitted among the delicate stems seeking insects, and Na'pa'an's band kept constant watch for flocks of quail, pheasant, grouse, or other game birds that might be brought down by a flick of a dart. Wandering through these new lands sometimes brought such opportunities, as the animals here seemed quite naive and unafraid of humans, but their hunts had been unproductive.

Behind them in the distance they could see the slow progress of the remainder of their band of thirty. Women, children, and the elderly carried most of the tribe's possessions, or dragged them on simple slings made of poles, leaving furrows in the soft earth behind their stooped shoulders. Among them were his mother and younger sister. His father, older sister, and a brother had died over the past four years, victims of poor nutrition, cold, disease and exposure.

Na'pa'an had been born on these broad plains and was tall for his fifteen years at almost five feet. His hair, nearly jet black in its dark intensity, fell about his shoulders, draping over his rough cape of animal skins, which he wore with the fur inward, allowing the rain and snow to shed from the exposed hide. His legs were covered with similar wrappings of hide, tied about his waist with raw-hide strips to conserve precious heat and energy on this chilled summer afternoon. His feet were shod with simple moccasins, but in colder weather he would wear them in layers to fend off frostbite.

As evening came the band settled on a new campsite close to a small stream. There they found a sheltered spot behind a low ridge, but well above the water. A few stunted shrubs helped to break the wind, and a past flood had deposited a pile of sticks in a heap that would sustain their cooking fire. Even in their depleted state the group quickly set to work, methodically mounting the poles in a circle, and lashing them at the top to form a simple dome. A shallow ditch was scraped around the perimeter of the shelter. The fresh soils, cleared of stones, were cast between the poles to form a soft base for their sleeping mats. Over the top of their new home, they layered their large collection of well-worn animal hides, lapping them to shed any unexpected rain into their simple drainage system. A small central vent allowed smoke to escape.

Inside their dark communal shelter infants slept in simple sling hammocks, as couples nestled with their older children among their mounds of animal skins. On happier days a variety of meats would be roasted on a spit, which rested on the cut forks of two green saplings, but this evening none spoke of food, for that only made their hunger more acute. It was to be another long day before Na'pa'an might savor the meal that his growing body demanded.

The following morning the hunting party heard a commotion, the sound of a battle. They crept forward to see the cause. From the top of the next rise, they could see a distant mastodon, its enormous mass like a boulder moving among a field of pebbles. Yet as they watched, the "pebbles" also moved and struck, again and again, at their weakened prey. They were not stone at all, they knew, but a pack of wolves, perhaps as many as twenty. As great as was the power of the mastodon, they would wear it down as water wears away soft earth in a flood.

Perhaps sick or already dying, the mastodon had wandered far from its herd, where size and numbers gave it defense against the wolves and other predators. As they watched it repeatedly tried to charge through the encircling pack, stamping futilely toward the swifter canines, but each time, other wolves would attack its haunches, now red with blood from the wounds inflicted by their sharp teeth. Another wolf, even bolder, leapt upwards from its flank to its back, causing the mastodon to rear and shake to dislodge its enemy. It was a matter of time.

A mastodon would be a great prize, one that would normally be beyond their capabilities, but here was one all but finished. Yet the threat of an entire pack of wolves was not to be ignored or easily overcome. The party held their place and discussed their options as the fight unfolded in the distance. To their advantage, the wind was in their faces, and they could almost taste the scent of the heated confrontation. Neither wolves nor mastodon knew or cared that their battle was being observed.

When the gruesome fight had ended the tribe watched patiently as the pack began its well-earned feast. Na'pa'an knew as well as the elders that the wolves, once gorged, would be far easier to drive from the kill. They watched impatiently as the pack squabbled over the kill, the leaders taking the choice positions at the belly as the lesser animals satisfied themselves by gnawing at the trunk or legs. It was difficult to watch the wolves feed while subduing the rumbles in their own empty stomachs.

After an hour they advanced, the hunters reinforced by the older men and young boys, forming a line of spear points as they moved as a body. The wolves quickly sighted them and reacted with confusion. Their unexpected approach unnerved them, but they growled in defiance as they paced around their kill.

Carefully each man pulled a dart and atlatl from their quiver. The atlatl was a "throwing stick" that cradled the deadly dart. Each the length of a man's arm, they amplified the arm's power and range. The dart, made of sharpened wood or bone, fitted over the small hook at the back of the atlatl. Releasing only at the top of the arc, the extra length allowed it to carry great distances at impressive speed.

As the wolves began to summon the courage to defend their kill the men launched as one and a small shower of darts fell among the dodging pack. Two of their number howled in pain and the show of courage was broken. They fled, still snarling their defiance, to the top of the next rise, from where they watched the men quickly surround the steaming carcass.

Working quickly, the men began using their stone blades to cut the mastodon into workable pieces, careful to protect the nearly intact hide. By the time the women and children arrived at the scene and set up their shelter, the animal was being swiftly processed. It was two days before the wolves gave up their attempts to regain their prize and left to seek other game.

The following days were spent cooking, gorging their famished bodies, and listening to tales of their tribal history. Several large chunks of meat roasted on a spit, turned occasionally by one of the watching women. Na'pa'an watched the fire dance, silhouetting the "Y" shape of the green sapling forks that held it, imprinting the shape in his mind as it had generations of other children. The fire-spit itself was split from the thigh bone of an antelope, its heat-hardened length black with the smoke of many fires.

That communal fire and the meals it provided were the symbol of tribal unity, the nurturing force that kept minor squabbles from becoming open hostility. A ruling from the elders ordering exile was tantamount to a death sentence unless a lone wanderer might be lucky enough to find and be accepted by another band. In these vast, empty spaces, that was a forlorn hope.

Their campsite for the following weeks was determined by their success in seizing the mastodon, and nothing would be wasted. By then, many hundreds of pounds of meat had been smoked over the cook-fires or salted in their precious and dwindling supply of salt, which they had scraped from the rocks around a warm desert spring. Bones were being worked into new tools and weapons. The hide was tautly stretched in the sunlight, and women had patiently scraped away the last shreds of flesh and sinew. It would make an excellent new roof for their home.

Fully modern humans, Na'pa'an and his fellow hunters were perhaps a million years removed from the primitive humans that first used fire, but they retained many of the physical characteristics of their more recent Asian ancestors, now also left many generations in the past. Those people had been seafarers, hugging the shores of the Pacific, or storm-blown to islands.

For over a hundred generations humans had migrated along the Pacific coast. Sped by the path of the sea, they were driven by the search for new food sources, or the insatiable human urge to learn what was around the next bend of the coast or over the next hill. Steadily, hunger and human curiosity had led them along those distant shores, advancing eastward toward North America.

The stories Na'pa'an heard from his elders gave wings to his thoughts, and in his youth he had often scratched pictures in the dirt, or upon stones, of the places and animals of his imagination. The mountains he had seen were mere hills, he was assured by his father, compared to those the people had left behind in his own childhood.

Na'pa'an tried to imagine the places the storytellers described in their vast skein of tales, which they guarded and memorized word for word through the generations. The stories were central to his life and that of the tribe, fulfilling their needs for both education and entertainment. The long saga of their people was taken to heart. and the memories of heroic acts and the overcoming of hardships gave them the will to persevere against the hardest experiences, as their ancestors had always done.

The death of a storyteller was a tragedy, worse than the loss of a chief, for they were those few able to carry them in their memories and repeat them in a great cycle that took many moons to complete, in the process teaching their younger counterparts. In the evenings by the fires, they spoke of ghosts and heroes, famine and cold, floods and fires. Always they were careful never to skip a story, for then it may be lost forever.

Storytellers kept account of their long history with the help of a lengthy and well-worn belt of small artifacts. Bone, shell, wood or stone, each piece represented an event in the story of their tribe. The belt had grown for countless hundreds of years and had many times been repaired as the circle of stories were told.

Only gradually had the search for game led their band to leave their coastal home and travel inland along the banks of westward-flowing rivers that pierced the mountains, and thus into the heart of the frosty continent of North America. There, besieged by the relentless advance of the glaciers and ice sheets, they had struggled to escape the ice and snow by following the migrating herds. Many had perished in the process, through famine or exposure. Na'pa'an and his fellows were survivors.

On their journey Na'pa'an and his people brought knowledge of edible herbs for food and medicine, and their simple technology. They made and used bone needles to sew the skins that made their clothing, and carried wooden spears as tall as a man, as well as the shorter darts that were launched using the atlatl. Sacks made from the stomach of an elk or other game served as handy storage containers for smoked meats, fish, or berries. Others held salt, or a special finely-powdered clay used to treat infections or eaten to cure internal illness. Simple woven baskets held herbs used for medicine, to ease pain, or treat wounds or illness. Others held plants used to dispel the gloomy moods of dark winter days, or to communicate with the spirit world around them. The plains through which he had traveled had been almost uniformly harsh and barren, save for tall grasses and shrubs. Long captive to the grinding sheets of ice, the earth had been swept clear of forests millennia before. The glaciers and ice sheets themselves, in places thousands of feet thick, had locked up more of the world's water, lowering the sea level and exposing almost a million square miles of dry land, shrinking the Gulf of Mexico to half its size. Yet the world he wandered upon would soon begin to tip into a period of warming. With the changing climate would come a new diversity of wildlife, much different from the woolly beasts that had long wandered the broad plains and grasslands.

Although he didn't think of himself in that way, Na'pa'an was a pioneer opening a new continent for the growing human race. The ages-long migration had come to its final stage, reaching at last the farthest corners of the earth. Eventually the land between the mountains would emerge as rich grasslands and forests. Bison, elk, antelope, and deer would spread to fill the growing habitat. That fact would assure the survival of the descendants of Na'pa'an for the coming millennia.

The White Stone
16,000 Years Ago

THE THIN CRESCENT MOON OF EVENING had long since set and the familiar and comforting green of the forest had been transformed into a realm of darkness. Although he did not normally fear darkness, now fear was thick, almost palpable to the young man. It clung to him, poured into him with each breath. As he lay flat upon his belly, motionless, the ants roamed over him, exploring, seeking anything edible. He could feel the sensation of their scurrying legs as they crawled upon his own, but he paid no attention. His focus was solely on silencing his own breathing and hearing everything he could not see.

A low voice carried to his ears. It was the voice of a stranger, but he could not hear the words. Strangers were dangerous and he was an invader, a trespasser in a strange place and his death seemed imminent.

He was not used to this feeling, the darkness, the danger. Fires and family, the security of the camp, that was what he knew, what he had breathed, what he had seen. But now, he was part of something he had longed for, an adventure. A chance to explore the wider world.

For days on end, the dense green of the forest had surrounded him and the blue of sky had often been reduced to a narrow sliver above his head. Sometimes even that had disappeared as the trees became an over-arching canopy, swallowing the sky and the light and leaving him in a nether world of semi-darkness. Every day of their travels he had seen things new and strange to him. Now his adventure had led to this.

Concealed among the undergrowth at the edge of the water, he listened carefully for the sound of other breathing, but could not discern it. Yet he knew he was not alone in his concealment. Nearby was his father, a man he trusted intensely, a man he honored. They feared very little, but both knew that of all the dangers they might encounter in these forests, the greatest was man. If they were seen by strangers, they might be forced to surrender and offer their hands in peace but understood that they might well be killed or enslaved. This night they would survive together, or they would die together.

The young man feared most because he had no name. He was known only as the son of his father. Without a name, he was mortal and if he died this day, his spirit would be wiped away. A lost soul soon forgotten in the lore of his people he would be doomed to wander unremembered through the afterworld. It was the most terrible thing he could imagine.

To escape from the terrors of this dark moment, the son filled his mind with memories of brighter times. He recalled the time when his father first took him away from the fires of camp and into the dark night. "You have now seen seven winters," his father had said to him. "In seven more winters, you will be a man. A man must see the world for what it is, not what he first thinks it is. To live you must know the whole world. Now you will learn to see. Sit here in this place and watch the skies until you see the world for what it is."

His father had left him alone there in that meadow, although he sensed that he must have remained near, hidden in the darkness. Silently the son had stared up into the night sky, trying to find something new, something different, that would show him the world his father spoke of.

Like every child, he had noticed the stars that provided the only light for many nights when the moon left the sky. They always stayed behind, and they had stayed behind this time. He gazed at the twinkling lights above, but they seemed resolute in their stillness, frozen and unmovable. For an hour more he sat, trying to stay alert, but saw nothing. Then suddenly he jerked himself upright. He had seen everything, without seeing it! Not a single thing had moved... yet the sky itself had moved! The stars, always cold and immobile, were moving above him. "If this is possible and I have not seen it before, what else do I see but not see?"

Since then, many months of watching the night sky had revealed to his eyes the center around which all revolved, and the presence of the wanderers, those few pinpoints that moved around among the others. Like hunters, his father had explained, they stalked the night skies in search of something. As he watched, he could begin to see the shapes of animals, the bison and the deer, the grouse and rabbit, emerge as patterns against the blackness. He learned to hear the wind speaking to the trees and understand the passing of the seasons, the retreat of the sun and its return. He began to understand the lessons of the earth.

Now seven winters more had passed and he was a man, yet when he opened his eyes, he could see only darkness, smell only the damp earth that chilled his face. He lay tense and silent as low voices drifted through the night. He tried to hold back the fear surrounding him and thought of the stars turning far above and stifled his breathing to a near halt.

Gripped tightly in his right hand he held a slender spear, poorly designed for facing a deadly fight with other men. In his left hand pressed close to his chest, he clutched a stone dagger, its edges patiently chipped and flaked to razor sharpness. He hoped that he would not have to use either weapon, for it would likely be his last act.

Through their tribe's ceaseless wandering the young man's small band knew well the sight of broad waters, vast glacial lakes and rivers left by the ice, teeming with trout, salmon, and other delicious fish. They knew the shaggy bison that roamed in growing numbers across the expanse of sun-warmed, treeless grasslands, where a few mastodons might also be found. Giant sloths weighed as much as four men. Camels, elk, antelope, primitive horses, and packs of fearsome dire wolves roamed the land. Although the northern lands had once been rich with game, scarcity was forcing them to look southward, with hope that new, unoccupied lands might lie this way.

They had occasionally encountered other tribes, extended families who had staked out their own territories, usually both summer and winter campsites within several hundred square miles of range. Some of these fellow wanderers were good trading partners, providing one commodity or another, or some prized decorative item that could be obtained for something currently in abundance. Most of the young people gained their mates from these other tribes, after careful discussion among the elders.

Some others, they had learned, were not to be trusted and coveted all that could be stolen or won in combat. These people they learned to avoid, for their small band was not strong enough to waste blood in warfare.

He thought back to their parting from the tribe. With a final backward glance, he had sought to capture a lasting memory of the family he was leaving behind. Some, he knew, expected that he would not return.

Although invisible in the darkness, the first light of the coming dawn would reveal the young man's face. He was tall for his tribe, with fine features that made him handsome to gaze upon. High cheekbones and a strong nose accented his face, which was framed by a thick shock of jet-black hair. His chest was broad and the muscles in his young arms, employed daily in paddling their heavy canoe, had gained with his exertions.

The sound of the strange voices slowly faded and yet for long minutes he refused to move, ignoring the biting of the insects, listening closely for any sound of danger. At last, when the buzzing of the insects had filled his ears so that little else was heard, he sensed motion to his right as his father slowly, ever so slowly, raised his head to peer toward the stream only a few paces away.

Eventually, the older man stood, signaling with a soft sound that the way was clear. They could move with caution to recover their own canoe and resume their trip down the river. Better to attempt travel with no more than stars for light than risk a fight with a large hunting party. Their canoe had been capsized and covered with brush that evening, well concealed as just another log in the water at the muddy bank of the stream.

The pre-dawn fog clung to his skin like a damp blanket, but the young man worked swiftly in the darkness. Silently he counted each of their personal items as he stowed it, saying nothing to his father, who kept watch for any return of danger. He blindly yet nimbly handled familiar shapes, knowing each one as well as his own fingers. Carefully he placed their few possessions into the primitive canoe and whispered that all was ready, then took his place at the bow.

They stayed completely silent as they drifted down the stream, crouched low and listening sharply for any sound beyond the call of an owl or the splash of a fish. They continued onward, knowing that if the hunting party that had just passed upstream came from a village on the riverbank ahead of them, their discovery would likely mean their deaths. The night was now their best friend as they glided through a strange, dimly lit land. It would be hours before they would rest again.

As the first glow of the dawn began to fade the stars they were far away from the strangers, the steady work with the paddles warming their bodies better than the assorted animal furs they wore over their own sun-browned skin.

Though they were not tall men, the two scouts shared a broad frame that spoke of power. The older was well muscled in his prime, used to such physical effort. He gazed cautiously and knowledgeably upon the passing forests which crowded around them. He seemed able to sense both danger and opportunity as though his life depended upon discerning each in turn. The younger, although strong, was not yet as powerful in his appearance. His dark eyes shone from his face and his teeth gleamed white when he smiled, as he was prone to do when he saw the otter at play in the river or heard the songs of birds in the branches above his head.

Soon they had passed far down the river and the sun had returned to rule the east. Its rays fanned across the sky, backlighting the scattered clouds, and shooting their pastel colors through the world. Although summer was fast approaching the morning air remained chilled, but they ignored the discomfort and kept their paddles at a steady, mile-eating rhythm. The dangers of their effort were stimulus to the young man, a heady opportunity to dare the fates and emerge the victor. If he was strong, he would earn a name and live forever.

As the rhythmic pace of the paddles moved them steadily toward the rising sun, two pairs of eyes continually scanned the vegetation ahead and around for any sign of human habitation, dangerous animals, or game. Two pairs of ears listened sharply for the familiar sounds of birds or the unwelcome sounds of other men.

The banks of the river were lined with cypress and sweet gum, loblolly and maple, their dark leaves and pale needles forming a thin barrier along the water's edge. Only occasionally did they note muddy banks, favored watering holes for unseen game and choice hunting places when the opportunity arose. They were used to roaming far to feed their family, and competition with other tribes for prime hunting grounds was the reason for their southward exploration. Yet danger was still close in their minds, and they would not risk delay this day.

The simple hollowed-log canoe glided quietly that day through the narrow ways of the stream and blazed its own path through the reeds which occasionally blocked their way.

With their extended family on the northern grounds, they had hunted bison and lived well for weeks afterward. They had faced a giant cave bear nearly three times a man's height and the older of the two occupants of the canoe wore about his neck the teeth and claws of the loser, symbols of his superior strength and manhood. That deed had given him his current name, Madaga-mako, which meant Bear-killer. He also wore souvenirs in a second form, that of the scars that streaked his face and shoulders. The younger man had looked with pride upon those marks since his childhood, for they had set his father above their tribe as a chief. Perhaps it had been the scars rendered by the slashing claws of the bear that had earned these two the responsibility of exploring far ahead of the tribe, seeking more-plentiful hunting grounds. Born to wander, they had passed beyond the edge of the known world.

Madaga-mako carefully scouted the way for the following band, leaving detailed messages in the form of small piles of carefully arranged pebbles at the foot of a chosen tree similar in size and shape to one that stood near their home camp. The symbol of their people, the forked tree offered a broad Y shape that represented the division of all things that were one: the day and night, earth and sky, man and woman. The spirit of the earth had made all things so. Always the tribe had used these trees as landmarks along streams, with the certainty that these forested lands would always provide another tree with the necessary peculiar shape. When they came upon the familiar shape of their tree, they marked their progress, using the few stones they carried for the purpose.

Madaga-mako placed the small stones in a pattern that told the date by the phase of the moon and their success in hunting. By arranging the pebbles of different sizes and colors into patterns, he could also let the tribe know if they had found danger, other people, game, fish, or even if they were ill or healthy. Colored stones helped communicate the location and type of game they had discovered nearby and other useful details of their journey. The scouts who led the tribe searched ahead for the trees and their pebble markers and the bits of news they displayed to the trained eye. They would not lose the trail.

As evening fell without seeing any further signs of other humans, the two made camp quietly on low ground, close to their canoe. Their dinner was only strips of salted meat and dried roots and berries, for they had taken no time to hunt for several days, nor to gather the nourishing greens or fresh roots from the woods around. They ate in virtual silence, then at last the father spoke.

"You have done well, my son. This is new land and now I think we may find what we seek."

"I think as you, my father," the young man replied. "The trees here are tall and the forests deep. I see many animals near the river, and they do not flee us. They do not know the sting of a spear. Here we will find plenty."

For another ten days they followed the river without a sign of other men and that was good. They scanned the shoreline constantly and marveled at the strange new plants and birds they saw. They had seen many deer, graceful creatures with magnificent racks of antlers wider than a man could reach, coming to the water to drink in the evening light. They had seen strange birds in plenty, along with the vast and familiar flocks that blocked the sun for hours. These birds they knew, for they had often hunted the tasty Passenger pigeons, knocking them from the air with thrown sticks and scrambling about to catch those that fell. When the flocks came to roost at night, they would crush trees with their weight and entire tracts of forest were left bent and broken. Hunters could approach the docile birds and take as many as they wished. Then, their people had plenty to eat.

In the forest and mountains of the north they found the waters filled with fish and these southern waters seemed just as plentiful. They spent part of one afternoon spearing the silver treasure, smoking them over a fire for future meals. In the north, they had been able to cache their kills in the ice, where they would be kept fresh for many days. In this new land without ice, they must learn new ways. Salt, they knew, was a valuable preservative and they had traded many good skins to friendly tribes before their journey to acquire a few small sacks of the mineral.

As the sun rose higher one clear morning and the low hills dropped behind, they slowed their paddles and drifted along with the current. The narrower stream had gathered waters to become a sluggish river, but the towering forests still lined the banks, hungry for new territory for their tangle of root and branch. The day wore on and the river gradually broadened into a wide waterway with dozens of intertwined passages. The current grew faint, and they set to work with the paddles once again. They sensed that they were approaching a large water body and increased their caution, hopeful that they would not encounter hostile people while caught in the open, without cover.

After the sun had reached its heights and begun its slow decent, they began to have the sensation that they were paddling upstream, rather than down. Quickly they assessed their position, but they had not turned. Other signs were strange, too, they realized. Shoreline plants were again changing and the familiar reeds had been left behind, replaced by banks of low trees. Madaga-mako sniffed the air and was puzzled. Knitting his furrowed brow, the older man hunched low over the prow of the narrow craft and behind him his son instantly mimicked his motion. He, too, had detected an unusual scent.

With a low guttural sound and a series of soft clucking noises, Madaga-mako informed his son of his feeling of trepidation. Slowly, without rising from their crouched positions, they coaxed the canoe into a thicket of bushes along the side of the stream. Instantly a cloud of insects rose to assail them through their coats of smeared mud and herbs, but the men did not react, staring instead at the distant reaches of the stream ahead.

From their position among the shoreline growth, they had a clear view for some distance, yet neither man could detect anything out of place. Madaga-mako continued to stare ahead, occasionally sniffing the air, searching for the source of the odor that seemed so foreign. A slight shift of the breeze brought it to him again: a faint, tantalizing scent from downstream. It was almost like the scent of food, he thought, or cooking, just a hint of something strange. They could not afford to leave their place of safety until all chance of danger had passed and so they waited while the sun continued its slow journey across the cloudless sky.

Then, suddenly, the odor was strong. It was all around them, filling their senses like the smell of a bear or other large hunter. The young man in the rear of the canoe felt a tingle run up his spine, understanding that they were facing something unknown even to his father, who knew everything about the land. For long minutes they sat without moving, but nothing happened.

Then, reaching slowly over the side of the canoe to slake his rising thirst, the young man made the most amazing discovery his people had made in many generations. Dipping his hand into the water, he brought it to his lips and quickly spit it out.

"Salt!" he said aloud, prompting a stunned reaction from the old chief. Slowly, Madaga-mako reached out and touched the cool surface, raised his fingers, and tasted salt water for the first time.

The tide had turned.

•

Before the sun set that day, Madaga-mako and his son made their camp on a low sand dune near the mouth of the river, having traveled over four hundred miles ahead of their wandering tribe. Together they inhaled the powerful smell of salt air and smiled as they listened to the new sound of large waves breaking on a sandy beach. They watched in trepidation as for hours the waters rose higher upon the beach and then fell once again, like slow breathing.

The two explorers could not know that they stood on the shores of a huge gulf, an arm of an even vaster ocean. They were unaware that they were the first men from the east to gaze upon those waters. They could not comprehend that, even as they stood on the shore of that gulf, the vast water they looked upon grew larger, fed by a thousand rivers, rising with the steady melting of the vast glaciers that shaped the surface of the land far to the north. The world was indeed larger and more complex than they could understand.

Neither Madaga-mako, already counted an old man at thirty-one summers, nor his son, considered a man of fourteen years, had ever seen such wondrous things as they saw that day. Strange new birds stalked the shore of water that had no end. Schools of new and wonderful fish leapt out of the water at their feet.

They had not known where they would go when they had moved ahead of the tribe, nor what they would find there. Now, as they watched the last glow of the sunset make way for a dazzling display of familiar stars, they understood the purpose of their journey. They had found a new home, away from the competition with the other tribes, far from the cold lands of the glaciers, under a warming sun.

The young man knew instinctively that the tribe's move to the land by the great salt water would bring many changes in his life. He sat and pondered them in the dying light of the evening, imagining the canoes drawn up on the banks of the broad water and the women busy preparing the meal. He wondered about the future and what it might hold for him. Would he become a great chief and lead his people to plenty? He could only hope and wait, as had his fathers before him. He could not imagine the new dangers that he would soon face, as alien as the new land itself.

"Son of Madaga-mako," said the older man, rising to his feet, "you have won a name. From this day you will be known as Danta-pako. It is a good name, I think."

The name meant "He who tasted salty water."

The young man did not move for a moment. Frozen in his crouch upon the sand, he felt a great warmth fill his heart and struggled to suppress the tears of joy that came to his eyes. He was a man. He would not die a forgotten one. He would be remembered always and have a place forever at the campfire, honored among his ancestors by the generations that would follow.

The young man rose solemnly and looked down. "Thank you, father," he replied, "I will carry this name proudly because you have given it to me."

With a steady grace, he lifted his face toward the stars and raised his arms heavenward.

Slowly he repeated his new name, so that the stars might hear and remember. "I am a man!" He knew then that this was his moment before the spirits of the world. Then with the stars as a million witnesses, he made his claim. "This land I have found for all our people, forever."

Although he could never know it, the man we might now call Danta-pako had earned for himself the honor of being the first human to set foot in what is now called Florida. From his place on the shore, he could not imagine the watery outline of the four-hundred-mile-long peninsula that lay before him, nor the new challenges it contained. He only knew that this new land was his discovery and that it might provide a chance for his people to prosper. They had found a home.

•

Six months later the reunited clan was encamped on a low knoll near both sea and river and learning about their new surroundings. Survival and the discovery of new food sources was their primary concern.

For Danta-pako himself, however, the change was even more pronounced. He was now treated with great deference by the women, who only months before had assigned him menial tasks.

Soon it was arranged that he would be wed to a woman of the tribe called Macombe, whose husband had died of an infected wound. Although she was much older than her new husband, there was no other man available in the small band and she was very pleased that she would not now be left alone. She also had a young daughter named Mara-si'i, so Danta-pako found himself with an instant family. It was considered a great honor to take a wife. He was pleased but knew that he had much to learn about being a husband as well.

The marriage was a simple ceremony witnessed by all the tribe. Even the children stood silently as the elders blessed the young couple and the children it was hoped they would bring to the light.

In the reverie after their ceremony, they were approached by the elderly woman called Mononoke, who had watched the ceremony from the door of her simple shelter. As she moved into the circle the children scattered to hide behind their parents, for they feared her as a witch, even though the elders recognized her abilities as a healer. When she stood before the young couple she bowed slightly, her hunched shoulders bending even lower.

"I have seen the story of things to be," she told them. "The spirits showed me that your children and their children will be many. There will be much sadness to come, but one, many lifetimes to come, will be a bird-woman. She will have wings and will rise above sadness and make the world new." She withdrew a white feather from her left sleeve and presented it to them. "Keep this," she said. "This is my gift to you."

With that pronouncement Mononoke retreated to her hut, leaving Macombe and Danta-pako standing in surprised silence. Neither could understand the strange prophesy, for no one could imagine a child with wings. At length they dismissed the story as the vivid imagination of an old woman.

The days flew by for the young chief and his tribe. Already since arriving in the new land three of the women had grown big with new life and all the people had a healthy glow that came from being well-fed. Macombe was among the women who would serve as mid-wives.

They adapted quickly to the life in the tidal lands, as if the steady rise and fall of the waters was ingrained deeply in their genes. Those movements were associated, they saw, with the travels of the moon through the skies, thus renewing knowledge lost after many generations removed from the sea. They saw large fish in plenty and several strange animals, plentiful sources for food. Most importantly, they saw no sign of other people.

By watching the shore birds Danta-pako and his companions learned to find shellfish in the warm waters of the sea which lapped nearby. Their reward was the addition of many new foods to their diets and the children grew rapidly and the adults added flesh to lean frames. The sea was filled with fish, which the women trapped in the shallows at low tide. The hunters had an easy time with the kills. Here was both the familiar game of the northern plains, like the bison, deer, camels, and horses, but also new and different species. Game was plentiful and easy to take. In summer, huge turtles climbed the dark beaches to lay their eggs. In winter, manatees filled the springs. All were naïve to the danger posed by these clever new predators.

Danta-pako was particularly pleased to find that the gigantic mastodons still roamed these lands in plenty. Few remained to the north, where men had long hunted them and their cousins the woolly mammoths. A single kill could provide the tribe with enough smoked meat to last through the winter. Watering holes in the forest made good places to lay traps for the giant creatures, waiting in the distance for the sound of their approach before attempting to surround the beasts. They used the massive tusks of the animals to make beautiful ornaments, the bones for needles and tools and the hides for new blankets and shelters.

They also found other familiar game, such as the slow-moving giant ground sloths and the agile peccaries that churned the soil in search of roots and grubs. Within months the small band had laid up generous stores of smoked, salted, and dried meats and fish, more than they had ever seen. So much food, in fact, that it became unnecessary, even burdensome, to travel as they had always done.

The men of the clan built a rough shelter of logs and branches covered with skins, not for a home, but as a cache for their food stores. Many nights the guards had to defend the camp against wolves or bears drawn by the scent of food.

After so many years of nomadic living in their portable shelter made of skins and poles, the tribe made no quick effort to change their traditions, but only when game grew scarcer did they bother to break their camp and wander on. Their low dome still provided adequate shelter from the rain. Around them the sounds of the forests lulled them to sleep, while young braves stood guard to ward off dangers.

Spring brought new flocks of birds from the south and many new discoveries by the hunters, who ranged farther afield. Each day, it seemed, they discovered that some new or familiar animal also lived in this strange new world. Some birds had no fear of men and would perch upon their fingers or heads and pluck curiously at their hair. The different types of great cats were familiar to the tribe, but the alligators and the small black bears were new.

Plants, too, were sources of surprise and new sources of critical vegetables and fruits to augment their diets. They found small plums that grew wild on the sandy inland. They learned about the edible hearts of certain palm trees, the seeds of the tall pines and the green salad plants that grew in the woods. Exploration also brought them to caverns within the lime-rock of the earth, many of which contained sources of fresh water, important in the arid, sandy lands.

Danta-pako now had plenty of time to search the streams and beaches for the large logs suitable for the painstaking burning, chipping, and shaping which would turn them into serviceable canoes. Many hours were spent in this way, while Macombe and Mara-si'i busied themselves with their friends, gathering the various new herbs and berries which they had discovered in the new land. Watching the animals closely and examining the bushes and trees gave them insight into which plants were safe to eat and which should be avoided. They lived easily and the daily rains of late summer had made the land lush with greenery.

The land was full of dangers new and old, and they took care in all things. All the people were concerned about the unknown hazards of their new home and kept their children close even as the men were forced to roam far in search of game. Ever vulnerable to painful death, they knew that a simple broken bone could become a life-long deformity. A small accident could lead to an infection that even their medicinal clay and herbs could not defeat.

Failing to recognize the dangers, two of the men of the tribe had wandered through the shallow waters and been cut by sharp stone or shell and suffered from terrible infections that burned them with fever. One died. Another was bitten by a poisonous snake, the first they had encountered of the aggressive serpents with the white mouths. He died in agony in a day. Their most powerful medicine men could do little against such dangers.

When winter returned the band was prepared. Though the deep snows came they did not last, melting before the warming sun. The winter was not so bitter as those they had known, and they were grateful for their new land. With the winter also came the blessing of vast flocks of waterfowl, settling on the bay in honking multitudes and filling the skies overhead with the whirring and whistling of their wings.

The men soon learned how to disguise the newly-finished large canoe with branches to conceal themselves and drift among the flocks of birds. There they could spear the birds or catch them with a simple snare device made of rawhide on a long stick.

In the spring the waters warmed, and they were able to bathe, taking care to stay in the soft sands and to wrap their feet before venturing into new areas. The women spent long hours trapping fish in a tidal pool which they closed off with stones, waiting until most of the water had drained away before gathering the silvery treasures into baskets with woven nets. Shellfish, too, were plentiful, not only oysters, but also mussels, clams, and occasional conchs.

Since the move to the bay, the tribe had grown by seven new children and the women of the tribe were very busy providing the care required by the youngsters. The men busied themselves with hunting, or making canoes, tools, and weapons from heavy shells. Carefully they wound strips of dried skins around the stout wooden handles, binding the heavy conch shells with their many points to make fine clubs to use for crushing the pulp of the roots of coontie plants. Their roots supplied the starchy paste they learned to cook to create long-lasting cakes that could sustain hunters for days in the woods.

The area continued to supply all their food needs, even as the tribe slowly grew in numbers. By observation and experimentation, they continued to learn about the native plants and had found many new kinds of edible berries. Time was spent tending to the wild blackberries found, guarding them against birds as the crop ripened. They also found many smaller animals which could be killed with their spears or darts. The men spent much time hunting far up the rivers and sometimes moved the entire tribe to join them in the broad, shallow interior valleys and they lived in plenty.

The years passed swiftly for the growing tribe and Danta-pako became a powerful chief. Soon he became the father of several more children, but always his favorite was his first, whom they called Buck. The boy grew tall and strong, not unlike his father, and the two were inseparable.

The days were all an adventure for Buck, who spent his free time wandering the beaches around the broad bay, spearing fish in the shallows, and gathering shells and other things he found there. In the eternal role of a child, he sought excitement and longed for new challenges to vary the daily routine. He grew stronger and taller, and many could see that he might well become a leader.

Each evening the tribal elders would gather after dinner and often discussed the results of the hunts, the signs of nature, the phases of the moon and the turning of the seasons. The shaman was responsible for marking the days of the year and carefully noted when the sun reached the solstice and began its long decline toward winter. He reported the passing of the wanderers among the stars, those bright lights which traveled slowly across the face of the sky. Special among them was the brightest which was in harvest months the evening star, and during the winter months became the morning star and helped to bring new warmth to the world.

The women of the tribe sat nearby and were often called upon to give guidance to the men, sharing their wisdom in the ways of family and their nature.

The elders thus marked the passing of the seasons and the passing of their fellows, even as they marked the birth of the children. They spoke of the fat years and the lean and the new plenty they had found. Always they looked to the future, to the seventh generation yet to come and considered how their decisions might affect those to follow. In their hunts they were careful never to kill the strongest animals, but took from the herds the old and weak, so that the animals, too, would prosper.

When Buck had seen eight winters his father took him hunting with the men, teaching him the ways of the wild animals and the birds of the air. He was at his side when Danta-pako led a hunting party to the sacred hill where they spent their summers, where the earth was red clay and the pines towered high above. Buck stood to take in the view of the land below for miles around.

"This land is your home, as far as you can see and all the land that lies between here and the sea, beyond the horizon," Danta-pako told Buck as they stood upon the hilltop looking toward the west. The sky was deep blue, and a thin crescent of moon hung in the sky, appearing only as the sun sank into the sea. Looking hard, Buck thought he might see the flash of orange sunlight upon those faraway waters.

"Take care that you learn well the ways of this land and teach them to your children, so they can teach their children," Danta-pako told him. "In this way those who follow will know our lives and we will live with them, even after we pass away into the mountains of the sky."

Buck looked solemnly at his father, who still stared toward the western horizon.

"I will do this, father. I will be a great chief someday, like you. I will be good for our people," he said firmly.

The years flowed steadily over the People of the Forked Tree. Danta-pako had time to ponder the wonders of the world around him. Often, he wandered from the camp alone at night, passing the watchers with a soft whistle. Then he would walk along the darkened shore of the water and many times gaze upwards at the stars he had studied as a child. Now he knew them well, turning in their never-ending cycles, marking the passages of the seasons. The morning star and the evening star marked the coming of the warmth and the cold. The great serpent that spun through the northern heavens moved through its nightly circle and he had long ago realized that it must continue through the hours of the sun, although hidden from his view, to reappear at the fading of the light.

He knew the wanderers, too, those few lights that were not fixed, that moved against the others, wandering through the background that never changed. These puzzled him most of all and he wondered if they were the lights of men, of hunters in the night sky. He knew they too had their rhythms, and the wise men could predict when they would appear. The sky, it seemed, was the greatest mystery of his life. If only, he thought, he could understand why it moved as it did and why those lights hovered above all below, unchanging while in his own skin he grew old and grey.

When many years had passed, Danta-pako one day called his son to his side. The wizened old chief had reached seventy-eight winters, more than any man of the tribe in recent memory. He looked long and hard at his son, still strong and in good health, a respected hunter and chief. He thought of their little band of wanderers, now grown to more than fifty and the prosperity they had enjoyed for many years.

"I have lived with our people for many winters," the old chief said at last. "I have seen our people grow from few into many." As he spoke, he thought of his mother, and his father, Madaga-mako, gone for many years.

"Soon I will go to see things told of by the father of my father. I will go to see the mountain of great snows and walk above the clouds. You will be chief for many more winters. Lead our people well and care for Mara-si'i until she comes to the land where all the fathers of fathers walk."

Buck stared at the old man in silence, noting the deep creases on his face and the still-keen light in his dark eyes. He had seen death, but still was not prepared to see his father leave on a journey with no return.

"Danta-pako, my father, I wish you to stay with my people, to guide us. I know that soon you must go, but my heart will walk with you until the end of the trail," he answered.

The old man gazed at his son, seeing the grey streaks in his long black hair and the signs of age upon his face.

"I know that you would have me stay," he said, "but your time with our people will pass away and you, too, must go. You are wise among our people and must stay to guide them while you may. My time is over, but travel with me a little way upon my journey and all will be well."

When three more days had passed, the old man called his beloved daughter to his side and gazed at her as he had his son, taking in every feature and line of her face, the sad smile, and the intense light in her solemn eyes.

"You are a good daughter and a good mother. You have done honor to the memory of your own mother, who loved you. I will think of you all my days," he told her, and a faint smile crossed his face.

"I will miss you, Danta-pako," she said and kissed him tenderly. In silence she lingered with him for several minutes, holding and stroking his withered hands, before rising and walking slowly away.

Then Danta-pako walked slowly down to the water's edge, where Buck waited with the fine cypress canoe the old man had patiently shaped so many years before. Together, they paddled slowly out across the broad bay,

His daughter stood for a long time watching them go. When at last they were lost in the distance, she walked slowly back to the camp to share the responsibility of watching over the children of the tribe. She stared at their young faces, so full of promise for the future, and wondered what a world they would meet.

"Now you children be good," she said at last, "and bring me some wood for the cooking fire."

The Shell

9,000 Years Ago

FLORIDA LAY UNDER A WARMING SUN while the generations of human experience swept over her. The ice age had ended and with the retreat of the glaciers, the rising seas began to flood much of what had been dry land. Florida's breadth shrank from four hundred miles to no more than two hundred, forcing humans and wildlife into smaller ranges. Gigantic springs poured forth millions of gallons of fresh water from deep within limestone caverns, forming lakes and rivers. The warming climate meant an end to regular winter snows and vegetation grew lush.

The descendants of Danta-pako prospered in their new land and varied their ways more closely to the environment. It had been many years since their family group had wandered, ranging thousands of miles over many generations following migrating deer, bison, mastodon, horses, and camels, but those stories were not forgotten. Elders could recite long tales of travel and hardship traveling along streams and rivers and a young man known as Gokosasso would listen for hours as they told the names and deeds of the fathers of their fathers. He knew how the tribes had come to this land and discovered the salt waters. He knew the land was their sustenance, the giver of life. He knew the ways of the ocelot, the panther, and the tiger, as well as those of the timid creatures that hid in the forests and grasses.

Sometimes on those starry nights as they sat around the cook fire embers, the elders told of how their ancestors had traveled through mountains and lived in ice caves, but for Gokosasso, and even the storytellers who had memorized the legends, it was difficult to imagine those things. His mind could not grasp the true size of mountains as high as the towering clouds that filled the summer skies, or the true depth of an ice-age winter. Yet it was better to take bold risks in search of game and great discoveries than to die starving with the women and children, Gokosasso thought. "Someday the chiefs will tell stories about the bravery of Gokosasso. I will be like Socomato, who saved all the tribe when a great flood came from the snow in the spring. The legends tell us that there are places far away where the snows stood as high as the mountains. If these places exist, I will see them some day," he thought.

Gokosasso knew many stories himself and had studied the writing of the bead-work, but always enjoyed the seemingly endless circle of stories the elders drew forth. Even the harsh reality of the vast, icy ranges of the Rocky Mountains, which his ancestors had crossed through low passes thousands of years before, had remained in the old stories.

He knew the stories about their former village by the big spring, which was now under the great water. That was understandable.

In the memories and stories of the tribe remained the knowledge that all the rivers moved to the sea and the sea slowly grew and had swallowed their tribe's former homes. Young men sometimes went there in their canoes where they could dive into the waters to pay respects to elders who had been put to rest there, to seek their blessings.

The water was now as deep as a tree was tall, but still the tribe marked the place where the sweet waters of the spring continued to flow, joining with the salty waters of the great sea. Someday, they thought, perhaps it will swallow all the world and that will be how the story of their people would end, in a great flood.

Gokosasso filled his days learning to hunt and fish, to feed the tribe and to skin and preserve the game they caught. His world was a predictable existence, where questions inevitably revolved around where the next hunt would occur. Left to the women were the routine tasks of gathering the various wild fruits, herbs and roots that provided the necessary balance to their diets.

Gokosasso's first adventure as a man was a week-long hunting expedition, which also allowed the hunters to wander farther afield and explore new lands. They had followed a river far upstream and reached an enormous spring where the waters emerged, clear and cold, from a deep artery flowing from the heart of the earth. Here the hunting was good.

Rising before the first light, they joined the men of the tribe in planning the day;s hunt, sending scouts ahead in the canoes or on foot to search for the slowly moving herds of camels, tapirs, sloth, horses, or occasional mastodons.

Moving against the wind, they would seek out the herds and design a plan of attack. The two dozen men and boys would move out along a broad front to attempt to encircle the herd. The young men would then drive the herd toward where the more experienced hunters would lie in wait.

On this day, as the group spread out through the dense underbrush, the hoped-for prey was a family of tapirs browsing in a clearing. Grey and plump, they used their long snouts to gather the sweet grasses. The day was fine and clear, and the dew still dampened the ground underfoot.

Gokosasso and his father Lowahee were part of the flanking movement, and circled quietly around the small herd, following a sluggish stream of black water, wary of alligators. Lowahee took the lead on the right bank, while Gokosasso followed his friend Lutaka'a, who was older and had a bit more experience.

With the practiced skill of experience, the older men led the way, gradually spreading out along their line, hoping to remain undetected by the tapirs until the critical moment when the signal would be given, and they would rush forward as one.

This day, however, there was more than one hunt underway, and other eyes watched from hiding as the men crept along the stream. The big cat, too, had been watching the tapirs, waiting for a chance to catch one unawares. Now it saw other game, though in a strange new form. It watched closely, intent on any chance at an easy kill. It spread its lithe form out on the ground and remained motionless. With a length of twelve feet, it was nearly a thousand pounds of muscle armed with two enormous dagger-like fangs. Sharp eyes and hearing made it the most-feared predator of the land.

Gokosasso moved silently, staying close to the ground, scrambling in a crouch under cover of the undergrowth. He sniffed the wind constantly, making sure that he stayed downwind of the tapirs, wary of any sudden shift in the breeze that would reveal the hunters.

The shrill shriek of terror from the man who moved only a short distance ahead of him split the stillness of the morning and startled Gokosasso from his concentration. He whirled as the herd of tapirs broke into a thundering run and saw the huge cat with his jaws locked upon the already-still form of his fellow hunter. Still firmly gripping his prey, the tiger snarled defiance at the young brave who faced him alone.

After only a split second of hesitation, Gokosasso, almost without thinking, moved deliberately toward the giant saber-toothed cat, moving in a trot to within an easy spear's throw. It snarled again, though the dim recesses of its feline brain registered a tiny doubt about this strange new creature. The tiger had expected it to flee like the tapirs. Now it approached him as if to challenge him for the kill.

Gokosasso eyed the big cat nervously. At nearly seven feet tall at the shoulder, it towered far above the slim young man and outweighed him almost ten to one. Yet he knew that he could not flee from battle with this giant. He took several strides toward the beast, raising his spear and making thrusting gestures. When it roared it dropped its victim and Gokosasso almost choked as he attempted to answer with a throaty scream of his own, but the thinness of his voice only reminded him of the improbability of the situation. He bit back his fear and hoped that help would arrive soon.

Suddenly, the big cat left its prey and leaped to meet the challenge. Gokosasso fought back a momentary panic as it sprang across the scant distance separating them. Stumbling back a step, the young hunter braced himself to meet the attack, planting the butt of his spear in the soft earth.

With a final bound, the monstrous beast was upon him and deftly Gokosasso aimed the crude sharpened-wood spear toward the cat's breast as he instinctively ducked to avoid its weight. The full impact of the charging, half-ton animal bowled him over in a fury, a huge paw sending him spinning ten feet against a log. He quickly rolled over and faced the cat in a crouch, keeping his bloodied body close to the log for the small protection it offered against the next charge.

The cat was already rushing toward him again when he saw it stagger, as if pulled up short. It took a swipe at him, but Gokosasso jumped back to avoid it. It was then that he saw the broken shaft of his spear protruding from the animal's throat near its collar bone. A spurt of blood showed him the wound was serious.

Enraged, the cat tried again to mount a charge toward the young hunter, who again jumped deftly away from the staggering animal. Then, staring dully at Gokosasso, it gave a final, gurgling roar and fell to the ground before him.

The cat had barely hit the earth when Lowahee charged into the clearing and quickly thrust his spear into its ribs near the beast's heart, making sure of the kill. Dazed, Gokosasso sat back on the log as the gathering hunters came running in from the woods around. After only a moment's hesitation, they took in what had happened and examined the huge beast sprawled across the grass.

Acknowledging the great service that had been done by the killing of the animal, they soon came forward to congratulate Gokosasso and Lowahee. The older man stood back and made it clear to all that it was his son who had made the kill and the shattered shaft of his spear was all the evidence the men needed to prove the fact.

Bleeding and in a state of shock, Gokosasso suddenly remembered the fallen hunter Lutaka'a and sprang forward to find him in the undergrowth. The others had not noticed their missing companion in the excitement. Quickly locating the other hunter, Gokosasso reached to him and saw the gaping tear at his throat and clasped his still form but detected no sign of life. Knowing only basic herbal remedies, such injuries were invariably fatal. Helplessly the group stared down at their dying friend while Gokosasso cradled his limp form. It was a feeling that they had come to know too well.

Standing, Gokosasso looked down at his own chest to examine the terrible slashes made by the huge claws in their glancing blow. Already his blood had run down his body and his legs were streaked with red. His head spun and his fall was broken by four pairs of hands. He was lifted lightly and carried back to the camp. Weak from loss of blood, he remembered nothing of his return down the river to the village, a man changed forever in the eyes of his companions.

For three days Gokosasso lay helpless on a crude mat of grass, while his mother tended to his wounds, cooling his fevered body with damp mosses, and wrapping him in thick robes to control the biting chills he suffered. He remained in his crude bed while the tribe gathered to light the funeral pyre of Lutaka'a and chant the ancient rhymes of the names of father and son, mother, and daughter, calling upon many generations of ancestors to receive their honored descendant into the land of the sky. Hearing the chants in the distance, Gokosasso wondered, in his delirious fever, if they were not for him, as he began a journey into the nether world. Yet the severe chills he suffered reminded him of his continued grasp on life.

When at last the fever broke and his strength began to return, Gokosasso began to think of all that had happened and sort the reality from the wild nightmares brought on by his fever. On the evening of the fourth day after the hunt, he rose and walked to visit the wizened chief of chiefs. He was the eldest of the tribe and had seen sixty winters, but his unsteady gait took little from his proud bearing.

Though most decisions were made by the council of all the chiefs, Matubu was the undisputed leader in the social affairs of the tribe. Although he had never had the honor of great achievement, his wise counsel and great years had earned him the respect of all the tribe. Now he rose to greet Gokosasso and offered him a place of honor before the fire.

The light of day was slowly fading from the sky and the evening meal was completed. The people of the tribe began to take their places, men around the fire, women in a larger circle around them. Standing, the old chief spoke in a loud voice, so that all the gathering tribe could be witness to what he said.

"You have killed the great tiger. You have become a chief," Matubu said. With that, he ceremoniously presented Gokosasso with the fangs of the great cat, almost as long as a man's forearm. "You have won the teeth and the skin of the tiger, so that all may know of your courage" he said loudly.

Then, while the entire tribe was gathered about them in silence, the old man bent and lifted a crude basket of woven reeds, stained dark with the blood of the great tiger. Holding it high in the air, he intoned as if from memory, "You shall own the bravery and strength of the tiger for all the days of your life. May our people prosper with you." Then he presented the basket to Gokosasso, who accepted it with studied reverence.

The young man knew that his next move would be most important and remembered as his first act as a chief. Turning, he carried the basket directly to the cutting block. Kneeling, he opened the basket and took from within the heart of the saber-toothed tiger, wrapped in a piece of skin from the cat. It had been smoked and salted to preserve it for this occasion. Unwrapping it slowly, he placed it on the stone and, after a brief pause of reverence, began to cut it with his crude shell blade. Then, with great ceremony, he walked around the circle of elders, placing one piece in the hands of each man. All were moved by his generosity, for the heart of the tiger was a most revered and powerful object.

When each of the men held a small piece of the heart in their hands, Gokosasso walked to the center of the circle and stood very near the brightly-flaming fire. Holding his own, largest piece of the heart over his head, he called out to the stars. "Together with my brothers, I will be brave and strong as the great cat, so our people will prosper," he said. Then he ate the heart of the cat, and the others did the same, savoring the strong, sweet and salty flavor that would give them great bravery and strength. Gokosasso was a chief and the world lay at his feet. In other ways, though, life had become much more complicated.

Soon he was married to a woman named Awinita and within a few years Gokosasso had fathered two sons and a daughter, but his favorite was his inquisitive eldest son, whom he called Beimota. Gokosasso also rose in the esteem of the tribe and was soon the most respected judge of disputes among the people. As such he became a senior chief and was the man to be trusted in any sort of crisis.

•

One winter afternoon by the bay, after a day spent drying and smoking meat from a successful hunt, Beimota came running into camp out of breath and rushed straight to his father, looking up at him with a wild expression on his face.

"They come!" he said. "Others come this way."

Gokosasso stared at the boy but quickly rose, grabbing his spear and calling to the other men.

"Show us," he said, and the child took off at a run, despite being already winded by the run he had just made.

Behind them, the women quickly buried the coals of the cooking fire in dry sand and hid all signs of the camp, withdrawing into the woods with the children. Their knowledge of the legends shared by the story-tellers, when strangers often meant danger, came tumbling back.

After running a short distance up the trail towards the bay, the child suddenly stopped short and turned toward the beach into the undergrowth. The following group of men mimicked him.

"They are there, on the water," he said, pointing. "Two canoes."

Gokosasso and the others looked ahead down the water, but at first could see nothing in the bay, with the afternoon sun shining on the water close at hand. After staring for a long moment, Gokosasso spotted them, two long, graceful canoes, with four men, moving toward the beach in the distance.

Gesturing to his men, Gokosasso led the group through the trees of the shoreline toward where the strangers were cautiously stepping ashore. Posting two men to watch at a safe distance and warn the women if necessary, he led the remaining men ahead and then split them into two groups, sending one around to approach the strangers from the other side.

Slowly they crept ahead until they were only a long stones-throw from the newcomers. Gokosasso pondered what to do next. He had never seen a stranger and he remembered from the old tales that many were very dangerous. Perhaps they should simply kill these men and save the risk, he thought. At his side, his son stared in amazement at the men.

"Let's go see them, father," Beimota suddenly suggested and Gokosasso looked down at him in surprise.

"What if they would kill us?" he asked.

"They are not here to make war on us, for they are too few. They explore as we explore, to find new game. We can tell them that this place is ours!" the boy answered flatly.

At this the chief thought a moment, then smiled. "You are right, my son, to say that they do not come to make war. We shall see, then, what brings other men to our land."

Looking back at the strangers, Gokosasso knew that they would soon meet the strangers anyway, since they had discovered footprints in the sandy shore and were talking excitedly among themselves.

Ordering the rest of the men to remain hidden, Gokosasso stepped forward onto the beach. His son would not be separated from him and followed like a shadow. The chief hailed the strangers in as commanding a voice as he could muster, to try to show confidence and strength.

The four visitors looked up, as if surprised to hear another human voice. Glancing from one to another, they stood for a moment before one stepped forward, leaving the others to stand by their canoes at the water's edge.

After only a few steps up the beach, the stranger stopped and set his weapon on the ground, facing Gokosasso with open palms. Gokosasso mimicked the gesture, taking a few steps toward the man before laying his spear upon the sand. Together the two men strode slowly toward one another and Gokosasso forgot for a moment that his son was still at his heels. Curiosity would not allow the boy to remain behind.

When the men were only a few feet apart, they stopped, eyeing each other closely. After a moment Gokosasso spoke in the guttural language of the tribe.

"What do you seek in our land?" he asked.

Immediately the other man's eyes brightened, and he answered in a crude approximation of the same dialect.

"You speak the tongue of the land-of-many-rivers," he said, pointing and gesturing. "We are your brothers of the north and we seek to trade many things."

Gokosasso understood some of what the other said but was still unsure of the purpose of the strangers' visit and knew he should be firm.

"This land is ours to hunt and the waters ours to fish. We have been many winters in this place and will not leave it. You are not of our people. What do you seek here?" he asked slowly, so that the stranger might better understand him.

Quickly the stranger, being experienced at diplomacy in his role as a trader, opened his pouch and produced an unusual flat stone, which he held out to Gokosasso.

"This is what I bring to you, to help you in your hunt," he said, calling upon all his knowledge of the dialect.

Gokosasso made no move to touch the gift, but in a flash his son ran ahead and snatched the object from the other man's hand.

"Get back, boy!" Gokosasso said sternly, but the lad was already marveling over the stone. The soft stone he knew from the hills was useless, but this was different.

"Look, father! It is sharp as a broken shell, but not of a shell," he said.

Gokosasso quickly took the stone from the boy's hand, examining it carefully while keeping one eye on the stranger. He saw the sharp edge with the strange fluting, the triangular point, and the curious notch on the shank. He could quickly see its value as a knife or scraper, or perhaps other uses.

"What is this stone?" he asked, intrigued now by the possibility of acquiring some.

"Boy, bring us my spear," the man requested, and in a moment it was retrieved from where it lay in the sand.

Looking closely at the weapon, Gokosasso saw the intricate lashings that held the long shank of the stone to the shaft of the wooden spear. The wood had been split to receive it and the craftsmanship was excellent. The chief was impressed. Hefting it in his hand, he balanced it and noted the satisfying weight the stone added. This would throw farther, and sink deeper, than any spear used by the tribe, he thought. The tribe had not had access to such stone since leaving the mountains and they had resorted to using such material as could be found in Florida.

Looking again to the trader for approval, the chief deftly flung the weapon high onto the beach. With a smile of approval, he turned to the trader.

The men of the tribe had been watching from concealment, but at this event began to step into the open and cautiously approach the traders. One ran ahead and retrieved the weapon and walked to return it to the chief, examining it closely. At this, the men gathered and began to talk in excited voices.

It was not long before the men of the tribe had gathered around the traders, who sealed the good will of the group by handing out a few gifts, including various colored stone beads and an ingenious and intricate necklace made of hollow bird bone.

It became clear to the men that the supply of tokens was not endless, yet they wished to know more about these strangers. Speaking with gestures and using the words understood by both groups, they talked as the sun traveled across the sky, sitting on the sand of the beach, the sun warming their skin against the cool afternoon.

They had traveled for an entire moon and seen no one, the traders told the tribe. They had believed they were the first in this new territory until they had seen the footprints of the hunters on the beach. Their people lived to the north of the land-of-many-rivers and there they returned each summer. Their work was rewarding, and they had traveled from the far north, where ice-mountains choked the river valleys and to the eastern sea, where huge waves crashed against the rocky shore. They had crossed green mountains and met many strange peoples.

Gradually, through their conversation, a sense of trust was built. They seemed not a bit war-like and carried only a few weapons. Their leader was a man called Etchemin, who told them that war was bad, and trade was good. This made sense to the men of the tribe and to Gokosasso.

At last, as the sun began to move into the western sky, the chief invited the strangers back to their camp to eat. The invitation was graciously accepted.

Walking up the beach, with the traders following in their canoes, the chief spoke quietly to his tribesmen. "These men bring us many good things and we must trade with caution. Make them welcome, but keep your guard," he said. He then sent his son ahead to tell the women to rebuild the fire and prepare a meal.

With the confidence of their superior numbers, they welcomed the strangers back to their campsite, though the traders, too, were cautious. They were soon greeted with a welcome meal of meats, fish, roasted oysters, greens, and small fruits. The visitors were especially grateful for the strange new fruits and greens, since they were most difficult to find in strange lands. They spent much of the evening dickering around the fire, while the women watched with deference from the shadows and kept the children from underfoot.

As the evening passed, the traders asked many questions. "Were there other tribes nearby?" No, they were told, they had seen only their own people, though the old stories of distant memories told of others.

"Were there many people in the land to the north?" they asked in return. Yes, they were told, many bands, some as numerous as the leaves of a tree. The men of the tribe were surprised and struggled to imagine such a village, even though their small community had grown to a several dozen.

As the evening progressed, the traders brought a variety of samples from their bags, but only one of each, with the promise that they could bring many more. It was a technique they had perfected over many trades, a skill that was passed from father to son. No greedy stranger chose to steal a single treasure, when many more could be earned through negotiation.

The traders made the tribe a gift of a sack of rice and exhibited spear, dart, and arrow points, which tempted the men of the tribe. A beautiful bow made of fine, strong wood brought much interest. Yet, when the traders repeatedly asked for objects to trade, the men were hard pressed. The tribe offered salt and dried fish, smoked meat, things of necessity for the traders, but the visitors sought goods to bring north. The traders seemed uninterested in the basketry of the women, or the primitive spears or canoes of the men, for in each case the strangers had better.

When the visitors brought out baskets of their own, made with obvious skill in a variety of patterns, Awinita overcame her timidity and came forward into the circle of firelight to see them. After examining one, she urged Gokosasso to trade for one of them. He was willing but had no object which the traders needed in return.

It was then that Beimota made his contribution to the family, for he had heard the conversation and thought about the many things the tribe used in their daily life. He dashed away and soon returned with two large conch shells and dropped them by the fire.

Immediately the traders stopped their conversations and began to examine the strange, horned surface of the giant shells and the beautiful, satiny interiors with their lustrous pink color dancing under the firelight. These, perhaps, they could use, as rare objects in the deep woods far to the north.

Then, to the surprise of everyone, the boy picked up one of the shells, which had a broken tip from his father's hammering. Putting it to his lips, he began to blow, sputtering at first, but then changing to a long, clear blast.

No one moved. The sound was unlike anything they had heard before. More than the call of wild animals, louder than the wind, it echoed across the water in the still of the night, a stillness unbroken by any spoken word.

The boy stood in the circle of firelight and his eyes traveled the stunned faces of the men. Had he done wrong? A momentary panic seemed to cross his face and he turned to his father, afraid of what he might say.

Gokosasso stood still and stared at the boy, as stunned as the others. How had this boy, his son, made this sound from the shell?

Suddenly the circle was a babble of excited voices and hands reached again to touch the shell that had made the sound, comparing it to the other. The traders seemed even more surprised at the reaction of their hosts to the feat of the child. They quickly fell to talking among themselves in a strange language.

After only a minute of this pandemonium, with the boy stammering answers to shouted questions, one of the traders suddenly stood, holding one of the conchs in his hand. The group fell silent.

"For these shells we will trade with you. One shell, one spearhead. How many shells have you?" he asked.

The strangers returned the next morning before they bid their farewell, promising to return with the desired goods. When the strangers had paddled their canoes out of sight across the bay, Gokosasso called the men of the tribe together.

"Before the traders return," he said, using the new word the strangers used to describe their people, "we must gather many of the shells. My son has shown us how to trade what we have in plenty, for what we need."

Then, calling his son into the circle of chiefs. He gazed at the young man, now twelve winters with the tribe, then spoke aloud.

"Today you have earned a new name. It was you who first saw the strangers far away, with the eyes of an eagle. It was you who first held the spearhead in your hand. It was you who learned the secret of the voice in the conch shell. You shall be called Remoweh, and you shall sit in the council of chiefs." The name meant "wise eagle," a very high honor.

The men of the tribe voiced their approval as one, with many adding commendations. The son of Gokosasso stood breathless for a moment. At length there was silence and he spoke.

"I am proud to be called Remoweh, a chief of the tribe of the long water. I will bring honor to my father and my mother and together with my people I will be strong." Makawee gazed upon the scene with pride. She felt herself a woman blessed by the universe.

•

With the new stone points, their atlatls were even more effective and hunting soon became even more successful. The men found they could bring down larger game from a longer distance with a more accurate throw. The points were recovered from the fallen game and could even be sharpened, if necessary, by flaking the stone carefully. The hunters were very pleased with their trade.

Awinita was happy for the great success the men had with their new spearheads, but she had ideas of her own. When she finally had a chance to be alone, she carefully began to disassemble the basket she had acquired from the traders, studying each of the intricate knots that made it so much stronger and more beautiful than the crude basketry she had learned as a child. She studied the strange materials, too and began to try to find new, finer materials to replace the reeds she had always used. Then, applying her new skills, Awinita began to make her own new baskets and taught her methods to the other women who had begun to watch her curiously. Green needles from the longleaf pines were supple but became rigid as they dried and gave the finished basketry fine detail. In the far north, they had no such material to work with, making her baskets unique.

By the time the traders returned the following winter, the tribe of the Forked Tree had gathered many of the showy conchs and many other beautiful shells from the waters of the bay and the gulf. Many shells they had strung together to make necklaces, which they adorned themselves with, in hopes of tempting the traders to larger purchases.

The new chief, Remoweh, had taught the others his skill at sounding the conch shells, so the first recognition of the returning traders brought forth a blast from a conch, which was soon answered by several others and the combined sounds of greeting echoed along the bay.

The traders were no less enthusiastic about the value of the conchs than they had been when they left and brought plenty of the new stone spear-points and scores of other tools. Now Gokosasso had a solid stone hammer and pestle and a strong chisel for carving, to replace the brittle conch shells.

The traders were especially curious about the new baskets that Awinita had designed, and she was proud when they offered to trade a stone hide scraper and a tiny stone drill for two of her fanciest baskets.

Of the four traders, one was a stranger, who had taken the place of another. At the feast that night, after a round of successful trading, this man began to tell tales of the lands far away. He spoke of the legends of heroic deeds and ice mountains that moved down valleys, pushing forests before them.

He told of the deeds of the fathers of fathers of men long dead, who had traveled many days in boats across the sea, out of sight of land. He told of the northern lights, of spirits that danced in the sky and places where water burst forth hot from the ground and flew into the sky, at the command of spirits of the underground.

Gokosasso marveled at these things and more, his mind drifting into worlds of his imagination, of places he would explore and great deeds he would do. Then, he looked at Awinita, huddled under a deer skin, her smiling eyes aglow in the firelight, with his son, Remoweh, sitting at her side and he knew that he could not leave them. "This is my land," he thought. "I cannot go yet."

Gokosasso's children were many and the family prospered as the generations passed. The land had given a rich yet simple life to her sons and daughters, who were the sons and daughters of Gokosasso and Awinita and those of a thousand generations of hopeful parents. Florida was theirs and, they knew, would remain so forever.

The encounter with the traders was a scene to be repeated many times. Far away across the breadth of the continent, other cultures were developing, trading, and enriching each other. Those people would become known as Arapahoe and Shawnee, Sioux and Cheyenne, Iroquois and Pawnee, Pequot and Coosa. Each had a distinct way of life, rich traditions and culture, and histories that made their people unique among those of the world. The Puebloan, Maya, Aztec, and Mississippian cultures encountered by the Europeans were not the first, but the last of the great native civilizations of the Americas.

7,000 Years Ago

ON A LATE-SUMMER DAY the afternoon warmth made the sea water inviting. It lapped gently upon the narrow strip of beach, but Tahumpka gave it little thought. Instead, he chipped patiently at the charred interior of an especially fine cypress log he had found while exploring up a quiet backwater. It had been left standing after a lightning fire and it had taken him a full day of patient chopping and digging to drop it to the ground and clear away the remains of branches.

Rolling the log into the water, he had struggled to pull it through the shallows to the beach, where he had built a fire of his own to burn away the thicker part of the wood. Now he was determined to turn it into a canoe. It would be the largest belonging to the tribe, and he was very proud of it, though only he could see, in his mind's eye, its final form.

Patiently Tahumpka shaved away the wood and char from the interior, using a large conch shell, conserving the valuable stone tools obtained by trade. The shell served as a chisel, which was struck with a heavy hammer made of wood. A thin wrapping of grasses cushioned the blows and protected the young man from the occasional chips of shell which flew from the conch. When the conch edge finally shattered, he turned it over in his hand to find a new, sharper edge and continued his work.

This day, as Tahumpka was hard at work on his new canoe, Yaholo appeared and stood for a time watching his son at work. He felt great pride in this young man, but he had little time for words. Today he had a strange apprehension.

Tahumpka stopped his work and stood to face his father, for he knew that the old chief would not stand and idly watch while work waited. Something was on his mind. Something important. They stood for a moment looking at one another without words. At last, the old chief spoke.

"My son, I have spoken with your mother, who speaks of your wife, Ahyoka. She is with child, and you will be a father," he said.

The words hung heavy in the air around Tahumpka, who was still in many ways a boy himself. He thought of his love for Ahyoka, which had grown still stronger since their pairing. He knew that his mother, Ma'coura, would also be proud and yet he felt a sudden chill and a shiver passed through his body.

"I am glad, father. It will be good," he said.

His father smiled a soft, gentle smile, such as the son had seldom seen, and a faraway look came into his eyes. Then, suddenly, it passed, and a worried look was on the old man's face.

"What is it, father?" Tahumpka asked him, studying his face. "There is more that you wish to say."

"Yes, my son. Today the signs change, and I do not understand."

Tahumpka turned slowly and stared at the sea. Gentle waves broke in steady succession on the sandy beach nearby. Dozens of small sand crabs scurried on the sand, yet no birds stopped to feast on them. Those in sight flew up the beach, strong strokes of their wings hurrying them on their way. Looking toward the land, he saw no sign of danger. A gentle breeze blew a few clouds along, yet there was no sign of the thunderstorms that had come every day throughout the summer. To the south and west, a veil of high cloud was cast across the sky, wispy tendrils beginning to dim the power of the warm sun.

Looking back at the beach, he again saw the sand crabs walking up the beach and over the low sand dunes. Even as he watched, he saw others emerge from their burrows to follow, forming small columns of marchers.

"This is strange. The crabs come out when the sun is high and leave the water," Tahumpka said softly.

"It is the same at the other river. Many crabs like the leaves of the trees and they too, leave the sands and seek the forests," his father answered.

Tahumpka stood quietly for a time, contemplating this. He was puzzled. "I do not know what these signs mean, father. I will watch and we will talk when the moon rises."

Yaholo nodded, turned, and walked slowly back down the beach toward the camp, his burden of doubt no lighter than when he came. Tahumpka watched him go and thought about the news he had received. To be a father was a good thing. He smiled to himself as he returned to his work.

Later that day Tahumpka stopped again to knock away the crabs that scuttled unafraid over anything in their path. Distracted from his work he looked up and noticed that the sea had built from small, gentle waves into an occasional large roller that broke onto the sand with a dull roar. Yet the glassy surface seemed peaceful and held no threat.

Scanning the sky, Tahumpka saw that the wind was stronger from the east and scattered clouds sailed steadily out to sea to the west. Far away, they seemed to gather into a denser group, but none of the towering summer thunderstorm clouds could be seen. Instead, a dense haze had spread far across the sky from the south and now cast itself across the entire sky like a high ceiling above the hot autumn afternoon. The sun above burned dimly through the haze.

Although Tahumpka could not understand the mechanisms at work, great forces were changing his world. Florida had lain under a warming sun while generations of human experience swept over her. The Younger Dryas Period of ice and snow had faded and as the ice melted, the rising seas had shrunk the broad peninsula to half its previous width, forcing both humans and wildlife into smaller ranges. The Gulf of Mexico had swallowed many thousands of square miles of land, drowning the sites of their tribe's ancient villages. Yet the new conditions would soon bring other, more dramatic changes to the lives of Floridians.

The warm sun that shone down upon Florida also heated the surface waters of the sea on a vast scale, and in response it expanded, pushing toward the north on the surface of the Atlantic, while denser cold water flowed south from the Arctic along the bottom.

As the sea had warmed over the millennia, the currents had gained strength until the most powerful river on earth flowed northward along the eastern seaboard of Florida. Florida's climate was shaped by the warm waters of the Gulf Stream. Fifty or more miles wide and hundreds of feet deep, the river helped to warm lands far to the north and cool the lands to the south. As the seas warmed, the rains had increased, a sign of the changing climate.

Yet despite that enormous release of tropical heat, the ocean contained far more, and that energy sought an outlet. The warm water readily evaporated, escaping into the sky to rise in thermal currents, condense, and release its heat in the colder upper atmosphere before falling back to the sea and land below as rain. It was a steady vertical conveyor belt that worked to cool the ocean.

Warmed through the long days of summer, even that process was now not enough to disperse all the excess heat energy. It began to build up, and the atmosphere became saturated with moisture, fuel for violent storms. Sometimes vast clusters of thunderstorms gathered, condensing millions of cubic feet of steam, dropping thousands of tons of water. In those cases, the process was enough to lower the pressure of the atmosphere, drawing in yet more warm air to fuel the process. As air flowed in to fill the gap, the very turning of the earth below bent those winds to the left, so they spiraled into the deepening vacuum.

On this day, out across the open waters of the warm gulf, a whirling mass of clouds had gathered and deepened, drawn ceaselessly by the falling atmospheric pressure of the growing storm. Faster and faster the winds swept into the center of the growing cyclone, carrying the abundant supply of warm, moist air that was the fuel of this enormous engine of nature. Soon the wind had accelerated to a mighty gale.

Drawn up by the lessened weight of the atmosphere upon it, the surface of the sea rose in a vast dome. Ten, fifteen, twenty feet higher it rose, a massive swelling of the ocean more than a hundred miles across. As the storm moved and strengthened, the gigantic dome of water, the storm surge, was drawn along below. Many creatures of the sea and the air felt the expanding ripples of lowered pressure and fled while the storm was yet hundreds of miles away. But for the tribe, there was no comprehension of the danger they faced, and no safe-haven.

Leaving his rough canoe and his tools, the young chief walked back toward the camp, following the still-visible footprints of his father through the sugary sand. He thought of the new life that Ahyoka would soon bring to the world. He felt a great responsibility upon his shoulders, yet he knew that he would be proud to be a father, as he was proud of his own.

Arriving in camp, Tahumpka noticed that things were astir. Dozens of the pesky sand crabs, large and small, scurried out of his path. Never had he seen them this far from the beach, as far as four stone's throw. Small children tried to flip them onto their backs with sticks, to see them try to right themselves. Their mothers eyed them curiously, wondering what the men would do about this strange invasion. Tahumpka stopped to greet his mother and could hear the voices of the other men raised in discussion of the strange signs.

"Are you well?" he asked, touching her hand gently as she nodded. He could detect uncertainty, a hint of worry in her eyes and she glanced toward the council circle and then searched his eyes in return.

"The council of chiefs will know what to do," he said firmly, but he himself wondered at the strangeness of the evening.

The sun had not yet set, but the forest around them seemed strangely silent. No birds were singing, and nothing moved but a fitful breeze that started and stopped without reason. To the west the sun had been sinking into a dense bank of haze that covered most of the sky and now swept away to the east in long plumes, like the ragged edge of a great cloak that had been thrown across the heavens.

Moving toward the circle of men, Tahumpka sat upon a branch of a huge fallen oak. He could detect the fear of the unknown that pervaded the discussion. These men lived and breathed the world around them and slept at night under the stars. They knew the changes of the seasons and the phases of the moon. Now they felt unsure, and the reasons were deeper than the armies of crabs, or the sudden departure of the birds. Even as they sat, they could hear the surf breaking with greater strength on the beach nearby.

"We should leave this place. It is cursed. Even the animals flee," one of the men was insisting, and murmurs of agreement followed. Tahumpka sat back with his arms folded across his chest, letting others take the lead.

Old Yaholo looked at the circle of worried faces and slowly stood, stretching himself to his full height. He looked very important, Tahumpka thought, as a chief should.

"Then it is settled. With the new sun we will leave this place and look for new hunting grounds," he said, gesturing toward the south. There was no word of dissension and the grim-faced group slowly dispersed.

Tahumpka wandered once around the camp, searching for Ahyoka. She had gone with the other young women, who were not yet back from gathering fruit, so he walked slowly toward the water and began to follow the beach to the south, past his new canoe, toward the mouth of a small stream just beyond.

Standing knee-deep in the water, he felt the gentle tug of the current and watched as the waves broke ever higher on the beach with the rising tide. The sun was already sinking into the thick gray mass of clouds, a blood-red ball that he could stare at without hurting his eyes. He watched as it sank into the heart of the clouds and its warming light was slowly extinguished.

Tahumpka lingered on the beach for a long time as the light faded and the grey smudge of cloud over the sea blended into the deeper grey of the dusk. Turning from the sea, he felt a fresh breeze on his face and his long, dark hair fanned briefly in the wind and settled on his back. Steadily he made his way through the dunes back toward the camp, his stride quickened by a sudden sense of urgency.

For long hours of darkness Tahumpka lay awake in his bed, while Ahyoka slept restlessly beside him. He listened as the wind sighed through the trees and the sound of the surf grew steadily stronger.

Long before dawn, Tahumpka awoke to feel cool drops of water splatter on his face and sat up to hear a gust of wind make a dull groan through the trees. Peering into the dim light of a full moon behind thick clouds, he could see a sentry standing near the edge of the thicker woods a short distance away.

Stepping over the sleeping form of his wife, he tugged the heavy tiger skin over her to shield her from the rain and stepped to meet him. Standing huddled in the darkness under heavy robes, the man clutched his spear and glanced warily at the sky. Stronger gusts pushed through the forest and the trees moaned as they grated against each other, complaining.

"What have you seen?" Tahumpka asked after a quiet pause.

"The wind grows and grows, yet no storm breaks," he replied, keeping one hand against the tree to steady himself. "I think we should ask the crabs what they know of these things."

Still another gust of wind swept through the forest and the men could hear its approach, like a wave breaking up a long beach. It grew louder and then suddenly swept over them. A small branch torn from the trees nearby fell before them.

Looking over the camp nearby, Tahumpka could see movement, as a few people sat up, and others stirred uneasily under their sleeping robes.

Walking back toward camp, Tahumpka staggered slightly as another strong blast of wind swept through the forest and their small clearing. Moving quickly now, he sought out the other chiefs in the darkness and they began to gather.

Throughout the camp, women and children were awake now, huddling in small groups for protection from the wind, crouched behind the boles of the largest trees. Rain began in fitful bursts, stinging against faces with each new gust of wind.

"We must leave this place," Tahumpka shouted above the howl of the storm as the men began to gather. They stared at him dumbly, as if surprised that the youngest should be the first to speak.

"Where will we go now, in the storm?" a voice shouted back. It was Yaholo, huddled under his old bearskin. Several voices joined in, arguing the point, and adding suggestions of their own.

Slowly old Yaholo raised his hand and the group fell silent, waiting expectantly in the wind and rain.

"We cannot move in the night, with nowhere to go. We must wait for the sun," he said flatly, and no one could dispute him.

But the dawn didn't come, at least not the dawn they knew. The hours passed, the moon set, and the sun rose, but only a dim light spread slowly through the wind driven clouds scudding overhead.

By the time the light was strong enough for the tribe to find their way, the wind was much too strong for walking. Now the entire group clustered together for protection, as the wind plucked at them, tearing at the cloaks they clutched in their hands. They clung to each other, afraid that they would be next carried away.

The storm grew in ferocity, until the shriek of the wind was a howling of a thousand voices on every side and the rain pelted them like stones. A steady thumping and crashing in the forest around them told of limbs and whole trees being battered to the ground. The air was thick with green leaves and branches, twigs and falling limbs flew like bats and struck at the huddled groups of frightened humanity. The wind had become the ruler of their world.

Yaholo clung to his old bear skin, souvenir of the day he had become a chief. When the wind tried to pluck it from his grasp, he refused to release it and it dragged him behind, flapping and snapping like a great whip amid the flying debris until it tore from his hands. Still, he refused to let it go and half ran, half tumbled after it, racing it toward the sea.

Ma'coura watched him go, fear in her eyes but powerless to stop him. She clung ever tighter to Ahyoka. Tahumpka, too, watched as his father tumbled out of sight, wondering if he would ever see him again, but determined to protect the family around him.

The wind mounted still higher and with each new blast it tore at the trees surrounding the small clearing, lifting them from the ground or snapping them like twigs. One towering Torreya pine snapped and spun crazily toward them, crashing over the huddled group. Few had raised their eyes to see it coming and there was nowhere to run if they had. The moans of those crushed beneath it were swept away like straws in the shrieking of the wind.

Already half drowned by the driven rain, Tahumpka was suddenly aware of still more water, warmer water, rising around him as he hunched, nearly prone, on the ground. Lowering his hand, he brought it to his lips and was as amazed as his legendary ancestor. It was salt water. Now the great sea, too, fought against them, even though they were above the highest dunes along the beach. For the first time in his life, Tahumpka knew real fear as his ordered world crashed around him.

Lying there clinging to the ones he loved with all his youthful strength, Tahumpka suddenly noticed that the wind didn't scream as loudly as before. Opening his eyes, he could see that it was brighter, and the wind was dying rapidly. Still, he could hear it, far away, howling like dire wolves through the trees, but here it was nearly calm.

Rising quickly in the ankle-deep water, Tahumpka pulled Ahyoka to her feet. Both stared at the tangle of fallen trees around them and Ahyoka only returned a blank look when he told her to move inland to higher ground. Giving her shoulders a gentle shake, he looked into her eyes and called to her, trying to bring her back from her shocked condition.

"You've got to move quickly! Please don't give up on me now..." he said.

Frightened, Ahyoka responded. "You must come, too," she said

"I will follow. Go quickly to the place of the blackberries. I will join you there," he said. Ahyoka immediately began to pick a trail through the fallen trees, scrambling over the boughs and between the branches. Others were moving away too and soon a slender column began to form.

Turning quickly, Tahumpka began to pull others from the tangle of fallen trees. Many who lay beneath the heavy branches would not rise again. Tahumpka felt a sense of rising despair when he saw his friend Shamata, pinned to the ground by a huge limb, already white with death. Others had been driven through with broken limbs and crimson stains spread across the water.

There was no time to mourn, for already the sea mounted toward them, released by the raging, offshore winds which had held it back. The huge dome of water rushed into the land, waves upon waves crashing above the dunes.

Hurrying to help the injured, Tahumpka turned when he heard the anguished cry of his mother, as she clutched the lifeless form of her youngest son.

"My brother, too," thought Tahumpka, adding his name to the list that already included seven others.

Moving quickly, Tahumpka helped the other men organize to carry the injured and followed the women and children away from the campsite, sloshing through a foot of rising water. They were forced to leave the dead behind.

A short walk brought them above the reach of the water, but Tahumpka was not satisfied. He watched as the water pressed inland, spreading along the ground almost as fast as they could move through the tangle of fallen trees. He drove the party onward, gathering the women at the place of blackberries and heading farther from the sea, toward the higher ground. "Would it be high enough?" Tahumpka asked himself, mentally considering the low, nearly flat landscape within miles of the camp. Stopping to let the others pass, the young chief scanned the sky. Dark clouds were all around, but above, a patch of blue sky could be seen through high, milky clouds. A pair of birds circled slowly far above, like themselves survivors and refugees of the storm.

From the low rise on which he stood, he could see the tumbling, raging sea through the denuded branches of the trees. It seethed with fury, white foam above black water. Even as he watched, Tahumpka saw a dark wall of clouds drawing steadily nearer across the water. Turning, he ran swiftly after his small band, leaping over the fallen trunks and branches of the once-lush forest.

Overtaking the tribe, he quickly looked about for shelter, for time was precious. Selecting a place between the fallen trunks of two huge oak trees that sprawled across the landscape, he ordered them to seek shelter under the tangle of massive limbs.

Looking over the small band that had readily accepted his orders, he noticed that several more of the men were not among them. Questioning wives and daughters, he was told that they had run to retrieve the canoes when the wind had ceased.

Tahumpka turned and ran back down the path they had just followed, dodging the obstacles and ducking under the branches that blocked his way. As he ran, he glanced at the sky and could see the ominous form of racing clouds, towering into the sky, drawing ever nearer to the exposed beach. Shouting over the roar of the sea, he called the names of the missing men and was answered from ahead. He soon found four of the men struggling with one of the canoes, pulling it through waist-deep water. They had found it tangled in the branches of a tree bobbing in the surf, near where the camp had been. The others were nowhere to be found.

"We must hurry! The storm returns!" Tahumpka shouted, panting from his sprint down the trail. Quickly grasping the canoe, he helped lift the heavy weight of solid cypress and together they hurried inland.

They worked as an efficient team, lifting the canoe over the larger logs, lowering it beneath the fallen branches, moving steadily through the shallow water toward higher ground where their families waited. Then, glancing over his shoulder toward the rising sound of the wind, Tahumpka saw that their time had run out. "We must leave it here and run," he shouted, as a strong gust of wind swept over them.

Already the rising wind made an audible howl from the beach and the others knew that he was right. Dropping their only canoe, they sprinted up the path behind Tahumpka, struggling against the rising wind at their backs. By the time they were back among the huddled group of women and children, the wind had mounted to a deafening shriek.

For several more hours, as the afternoon slipped away and darkness crept about them, they held in a tight group between the fallen boles. With most of the trees stripped bare or uprooted, Tahumpka could see the mountainous waves that pounded their former campsite and watched as the water was driven far inland. Waves came surging through the forest and several times pushed water through the huddled group. Mercifully, it stopped short of flooding the small rise where the group huddled and Tahumpka was glad that he had sought the highest ground.

At last, as night fell, the winds slowly abated. and the small group began to count themselves as survivors. Somber faces shared the pain as eyes met, full of the anguish of loss. Tahumpka took a count of those present and made a mental note of those who were missing, his own father among them. In all, seventeen of their small band were lost to the storm, nine of them skilled hunters who had helped to feed the tribe.

Tahumpka knew, too, that their precious food stores had been lost and that by morning, feeding the children would become a pressing need. He pondered the problems they would face far into the night, as most of the group slipped into the deep sleep of exhaustion.

Finally, his mind overwhelmed by the tasks at hand, he slipped into a fitful slumber, dreaming again of the fury of the storm. There was no peace for him that night, even in sleep.

•

The days of mourning which followed the storm were the darkest the tribe could remember, and despair at times threatened the rule of reason. Although they were fortunate to find sustenance in the form of a deer killed by the storm, there were no herds to hunt, and hunger would soon press upon the survivors with an urgent demand.

Within ten days after the storm, two of the injured died of infections in their open wounds, leaving the tribe reduced to only twenty-eight. Of these, only eight were adult males and their ability to hunt in the traditional ways were hampered by their lack of numbers.

Despite their searching, no trace had been found of Yaholo, or six other men and boys who had gone to find the canoes during the height of the storm. Of the other men, none were looked upon as leaders, and young Tahumpka was sought more and more for guidance. Tough decisions had to be made and his wisdom was sorely tested. He thought of Yaholo and the great chiefs of the past and wondered if they would make the same choices when no path seemed favorable. Three days of hunting and foraging for food produced little and the tribe was forced to subsist on whatever could be found. The armies of crabs, returning to the sea after the tides subsided, became easy pickings for the women, though. the scanty edible parts were foul tasting. The lack of cooking fires made a tastier broth impossible.

The men pursued a fruitless hunt for larger game, until finally Tahumpka suggested they return to the beach. Digging in the sea bottom, now scoured of sand, they soon found a large bed of shellfish deposited in a pile by the surf. They quickly pried open hundreds of the sharp-shelled creatures, enough to satisfy the most urgent pangs of hunger and keep the children out of danger of starvation.

Drinking water was a problem, too, as for several days the streams ran brackish with salty water driven far inland. The tribe made do with the water and had barely begun to get used to the taste when it began to improve as the rivers purified themselves with the help of the rains.

After five days Tahumpka knew that they must decide. The hunting ranges near their camp were empty, yet to leave the sea was to abandon their only known food source. After checking on the condition of the injured and being reassured that they could travel, he called the remaining men together on a fallen tree for council.

"The time has come for us to go from this place. When the new day comes, we must move toward the sun, where Yaholo would have us go. There we may hope to find new hunting ranges," Tahumpka said plainly.

None of the men cared to differ with Tahumpka but accepted his suggestion with simple resignation. They knew that the move would not be easy, for the tribe had only one canoe, heroically salvaged during the storm. It would be used for the worst injured, who could not walk the long miles on the beach.

The next morning, they made their preparations, filling several skins with fresh water and wrapping extra oysters in damp leaves to provide some assurance of sustenance. Before the sun rose high into the sky, the small party was heading south down the margin between sea and land, finding their way blocked frequently by tangles of driftwood on a shore stripped of sand.

The forlorn party had traveled only a short distance when Tahumpka thought he saw something familiar in the tangle of broken trees on the beach. Running ahead, he was soon pulling at something lodged there and called for help from the other men. A minute's effort uncovered a large cypress log with the unmistakable signs of his work upon it.

The rough tree trunk was far from a finished canoe, but it had potential and could serve in the meantime as a floating litter, helping to transport the injured and the children. Only grunts of approval from the other men showed their appreciation of the find, but during the next few days the extra canoe proved its worth.

For the women of the tribe, travel was a welcome diversion from their grief. Several had lost husbands or children in the storm and feared that they would be considered a burden by the rest of the group. Ma'coura was among those left without a husband. She mourned for Yaholo but was thankful for the life of her eldest son, whom she now looked upon as her protector, even her justification for the food she ate.

Tahumpka knew that he had much added responsibility but drove himself to be strong. Along with his mother, young sister, wife and stepdaughter, he felt an obligation to all the group.

Ten days of travel were wearying for the tribe, but the journey was eased when two of the men, scouting ahead, managed to kill a deer that was wandering near the beach. With plenty of food, spirits rose, and the mourning of the dead left behind began to ease.

Gradually as they traveled, they began to leave the area of destruction behind. Along the shore they began to find many trees left standing, though the damage of the wind and tide was still apparent. Low islands nearby showed only the ragged fringe of the forests that once crowned them.

The band trudged silently along the ravaged beach, the sand here mounded high, there swept away and sometimes cut by a new inlet, the work of the raging waves. The men took turns wading through the shallow water pulling the canoes through the gentle surf.

Finally, at noon of the fifteenth day of traveling, the scouts returned to tell of a wide bay ahead and a broad sweep of water cutting them off from further progress southward. Tahumpka, now respected by all the men as the chief decision maker, ordered them to draw the canoes ashore and the group set up camp on a dune. Tahumpka then went ahead with the scouts and together they sought the top of the highest dune on the rolling, sandy beach.

Scanning the horizon, they could see that they were on a long point of land, with open water to the west and south and many islands all around. In the distance they could make out the dark line of the far shore that enclosed the calm waters of the bay. They had made their way down a long neck of land, not knowing of the large lagoon just inland.

"We will stay here tonight and tomorrow we will seek fresh water," Tahumpka told the others, who readily accepted his word.

The new campsite proved hospitable. Water was found in plenty, flowing from dozens of springs into small streams that fed into the shallow bay and the sea. Fish they found, too; large schools they could trap with ease in the shallows. Game was plentiful as well and soon the small parties had great success with the many animals that lived on the peninsula and the islands which surrounded it.

After a week of hunting and feasting, Tahumpka led the small band back to the north and then east around the curve of the bay, seeking protected waters and higher ground. They crossed a river and moved into an area of low hills to the east, but still only a short walk from the bay. Here the hunting was good and there was little evidence of the storm. Slowly, as the weeks passed, the people of the tribe began to feel safe once again and put the tragedy of the past behind. Tahumpka knew that he had passed his first true test as a chief. He hoped it would be his sternest.

•

The small band spent the winter near a spring, where the sweet waters burst forth crystal clear. There the manatees gathered, seeking the constant temperature of the spring as a refuge against the chill. One manatee easily taken in the shallows was enough to feed them all for a week.

With the plentiful food, the family began to feel prosperous once again, though the accidental deaths had created new social problems. The most significant was the surplus of women. With only eight adult males, there were five extra women of child-bearing age without available husbands.

Tahumpka, though still a young man himself, was the unchallenged leader of the group. Ahyoka had become the principal confidant and adviser to her young husband and the two spoke long hours of the needs of the tribe and her wisdom surprised him. He became a vessel in her hands and she a fountain of insight and guidance that filled him. It was through her words that he came to understand that there was far more to the dreams of his people than plentiful food and safe campsites. He knew that some at least among them longed for a better future for the children of children yet unborn. Both Ahyoka and Ma'coura spoke of their hopes and dreams for the future.

It was Ahyoka, thinking of young women without hope of a husband, who had first broached the delicate subject to Tahumpka as they lay in bed one night.

"Husband, Aiyana is now a woman, and she will need a man. Yet there is no man without a wife. Four other women are also without husbands, though they would like children. What should be done?" she asked him.

"I do not know the answers to these questions," he replied after a long pause. "There are no others here and no boy who approaches manhood."

"In the past, when chiefs were great, they often had more than one wife. Even the great chieftain W'piapito had four wives, though he lived longer than each," she replied.

Tahumpka looked at her steadily, understanding what she was suggesting, yet waiting for her to finish.

"In these days, every man is valuable to the tribe. Each is a great chief," she continued, in reasoned tones. "Let those men who will, take a second wife, so that the women may again have babies and our people should grow in numbers. Without this, we will soon be too few to keep alight the cook fire and hunt the game, and the children will go hungry, and the people will be no more."

Tahumpka contemplated what she said and knew that it was true. Most of the men were older than twenty-five winters and life was hard. A man might not be expected to live more than thirty-five or forty years and death lurked in unknown places. Yet there was no male child older than six. Already he could see a day when there would be too few hunters. It was almost too late, he thought. The tribe may perish. He had not thought of these things, but it was obvious that Ahyoka had pondered them long and hard and found the answers she was proposing as the only hope of survival for her people.

"What shall I do, woman, to change this?" he asked finally.

"You should take Aiyana as your wife also and tell the other men that they should speak to the women and take new wives," she told him flatly.

So, he thought, she had seen the thing through to its logical conclusion and found a path which would lead to their survival. It was a simple choice and Ahyoka made it plain to all that it would be done. The men, in the end, demurred and the women negotiated with each other for their own choices. All understood the need.

For his part, Tahumpka had little time to prepare himself for his new responsibility, for Ahyoka invited Aiyana to their bed one night and lovingly kissed Tahumpka, before slipping away from them into the night. It was obvious to the young husband that Aiyana, for her part, had been long prepared for this moment and their tender loving was a new joy in his life.

Then, one bright summer morning, as Gokosasso and the other men walked toward the canoes, he found a pair of sand crabs walking up their trail before him. A dark look passed over his face and he turned to face those who followed. They stopped awkwardly, looking past Gokosasso at the two crabs marching fearlessly up the path. Even as they watched in stunned silence, another crab appeared.

Gokosasso scanned the sky. There was no trace of the milky clouds he remembered from that fateful day in the past. Yet he could not be content to wait.

"Let us go far from the sea and seek shelter in the high lands," he said without preface. The men only looked at him in silence. There was no word of disagreement. Turning swiftly, they rushed back to camp and spread the news.

While the women packed the stores of food and their few belongings, Gokosasso ran back down the trail to the bay, leaping over the land crabs which were beginning to fill the path. Standing on the shore, Gokosasso could see the exodus beginning, though the waters were calm. "It is the sign," he thought. "We must not ignore it."

Within the day, the small group had pulled their canoes far inland before making their way far into the interior, following the lead of the hunting parties which had explored the region. The day's march brought them to the banks of a peaceful river, where they camped on a bluff far from the alligators which filled the stream below. Here they stayed as two days of stormy, windy weather passed over. Though much rain fell, the tribe was safe, and relief replaced fear.

Each year thereafter the tribe made it their habit to move from the shore during the hot months and seek the inland hills. Their wanderings gave them ever-greater knowledge of the land about them, and the habits of the animals.

They explored a region of lakes and low hills four days walk from the bay and camped at the base of the highest of these. Here the men climbed to look out over many miles of green land and blue lakes, with the clear dome of the sky arching over all. They saw the red clay soil of the hill, which recalled the stories of their ancestral home far to the north, and they called the hill sacred. In future years, as their children grew, they would bring each there to see the world and tell tales of the world they had left behind and the great deeds done by the fathers of fathers, so they would not be forgotten.

•

In the winter of the second year after the storm, two of the women of the tribe gave birth and the one new son was especially welcome to the tribe, so short of men. All the women now had a husband, and it was hoped that soon more of the women would bring new life into the world. Ahyoka, too, began to show that she would soon become a mother again.

Tahumpka had become accepted as the undisputed leader of the group and the other men sought his word to settle any type of disagreement. That authority had been received by the tribe with an easy acceptance and he looked forward to new challenges requiring his instinctive knowledge. He was secure, too, in knowing that Ahyoka would be there as his confidant during their late-night discussions.

The young chief, now well-muscled, lean and tanned, spent his days hunting and fishing with the other men and his early evenings with the whole tribe, gathered by the cook fire for the families' social period. The long nights were spent huddled under warm robes with Ahyoka and Aiyana.

•

All during the prosperous spring, Ahyoka grew bigger with life, until one day in mid-summer, when her time to give birth arrived. Tahumpka had been sitting near the shore of the bay, patiently shaping a new spear, when Aiyana came running up the beach, calling his name.

"Come quickly," she panted. "Ahyoka calls for you." In a flash he leapt to his feet and began to run back toward the camp, still clutching the sharpened end of the spear in his hand, the butt dragging in the sand behind him. He overtook and passed the lithe shape of Aiyana, who followed in his trail.

When he arrived at the camp, it was strangely quiet. The women were clustered in a group as Tahumpka approached. Quickly they backed away to let him enter their circle. There, on her crude bed, lay Ahyoka. Kneeling by her side, he took her hand firmly and her eyes fluttered open to see him. A faint smile crossed her lips, but Tahumpka could see the strain that showed plainly on her features.

"It is my time, husband," she said with an effort. Tahumpka placed his finger on her lips.

"Save your energy, for you must be strong. I know what you would say, my wife. I will be at your side."

As he spoke, he could see that she was in pain. Her breathing came in gasps and her face was pale. He had seen the birth of children before and each one was celebrated by the entire tribe as a miracle of new life. He had seen, too, the face of death that sometimes came in place of new life and he knew a sudden fear.

Turning to the women gathered about them, he scanned their faces, hoping that one would know what should be done. One by one they turned from his gaze, helpless in the face of their own nature. Only his mother looked him in the eye.

"We will do what we can, my son," Ma'coura said and quickly took charge of the other women. Aiyana sat beside Ma'coura to lend what comfort she could.

Tahumpka stayed with Ahyoka through the long hours as she struggled to give birth to the son she had hoped for. The women of the tribe had witnessed breach birth before and knew that it would be difficult. Still, they struggled to help as they could, holding Ahyoka while Ma'coura attempted to correct the delivery position.

All through the long night they struggled, wearying with the effort and the lack of sleep. Still Ahyoka labored on, unconscious for brief periods between the wracking efforts at delivery.

Tahumpka sat quietly a short distance away, watching for some sign that help was needed and offering any assistance.

Finally, when the sun had climbed high into the sky and the day had warmed, there was the welcome cry of new life and Ma'coura held a new grandson and a son of the tribe.

Tahumpka gazed at the tiny red face wrapped in his bundle, then smiled down at Ahyoka. "You have done well. We have a son," he said. She smiled weakly in return.

"Keep him well. I love you, my husband," she answered slowly and closed her eyes to rest.

"You are a father now," Ma'coura said to her son as they walked, hand in hand, from the birthing place.

"I am proud," he answered.

"And I am proud of you," she answered. "You must remain strong to face great challenges ahead. Your son will need you, too."

He looked at her closely, trying to fathom her meaning. She looked away toward the water, where the sun shone brightly.

"Go and rest now," she said. "You will need your strength."

•

Hours later, Tahumpka was awakened from his exhausted slumber by Aiyana's soft voice.

"Wake, my husband. You are needed by your people," she said.

Opening his eyes, Tahumpka looked up at the young woman standing before him, who hung her head, tears streaming down her face. Suddenly awakened by fear, he bolted out of his bed and rushed to where Ahyoka lay upon her mat. The women in the circle about her quickly withdrew.

Kneeling beside her body, he took her lifeless hand in his own and kissed it gently, stroking it against his cheek. She was gone, this woman who had taught him so much of life. For the first time in his life, Tahumpka hung his own head in grief and let loose the tears, unafraid of what the others might think of him.

•

For thousands of years after Tahumpka had helped to save the people of Florida, they prospered in their new home. As their numbers grew, the people of the Forked Tree grew to populate a network of villages only a half-day's walk apart.

Over the centuries many changes had also come to their lands. Warming temperatures and shrinking ranges had been punishing for some species. Gone were many of the large animals that had once been present. No more did the camel or giant sloth wander the forests of Florida. Gone were the mastodon and the glyptodonts, the tiny horses, and the giant cats.

Hunters, ever better-equipped, used beautiful, fluted stone arrow-heads carried by traders from the distant south-west of the continent. They had also taken advantage of a new ally, the domesticated dog. Spread by traveling traders, these short, pack-oriented animals, their tails curled tightly over their backs, thrived in the shadows of the villages, and participated in the hunts by driving prey into the open. They were loyal, and well-rewarded, companions.

Generations of life on coastal dunes had allowed the construction of solid homes atop earthen mounds, above the reach of rising tides. The sea swept through canals to clear them of debris and usher schools of fish into shallow basins where they could be netted. Salt pans allowed the evaporating waters to concentrate the valuable preservative. After drying over a fire, the fine crystals made for a valuable commodity that could be exchanged for goods from distant lands. People prospered beneath the steady sun and withstood the changes wrought by the steadily-warming climate.

The long peninsula had proven a sustaining land for the first tribes and the many new groups that had arrived over the millennia. Each new family had found space within the embracing waters of the Atlantic and the Gulf, and conflicts had been few. Each, too, contributed to the growth of trade and culture and shared in the exchange of human genes fostered by inter-marriage between their groups. Florida had become home of a people unique among those of the world.

1,200 Years Ago

ADAHI HAD KNOWN THAT THERE WERE OTHERS who hunted along the river. His people were very aware of the town that had grown at the large bay to the north of his Calusa homeland, yet he hadn't expected to find himself in such a dangerous position. His small hunting party had found itself surrounded and confronted. They sat motionless in their two canoes, while four other canoes carried their clearly hostile occupants ever closer. There was no escape route. On the riverbank nearby two more men stood with notched arrows. They had been ambushed. Would they be forced to fight, four against ten?

"These hunting grounds belong to my people!" the wild-eyed leader of the strangers shouted as the distance closed. "The Tocobega have hunted these lands for a hundred moons, and we have seen no one else."

Adahi calmly mulled over his reply, mindful of the power of his own tribe with its large villages strung along the lower Gulf Coast, and their cousins the Mayaimi, who had moved inland to settle around the Big Lake where fish and game were plentiful. He knew that he could speak from strength, even though his life, and those of his companions, were in grave danger.

"I am glad that you have hunted here and seen no one," he began. "There is good game here because my people use this land wisely and take only what we need. We have hunted these grounds, not for a hundred moons, but for years numbered like the leaves of the trees."

His counterpart of the Tocobega paused, seeming a bit surprised. Adahi took the opportunity to press his case.

"I am a chieftain of the Calusa people," he said and cast his woven shirt back to expose the large copper breast-plate he wore as a symbol of rank. It was a gamble that might make his death more certain for purposes of robbery, but he knew that it would lend weight to his words. "The numbers of our people are like the stars. For twenty days you can paddle your canoes from here," he said, pointing to the south, "and still you will be in the land of the Calusa." He knew it was a gamble and might be taken as a threat and further antagonize their opponents, but he saw little choice. He paused for effect, waiting for the first sign of a response, before cutting him off.

"We do not wish you ill and find no purpose in war. My name is Adahi. You may hunt these grounds without threat from us. If you meet my people, tell them that I have granted you this right. In return we ask that you take only what you need and remember that we also share the bounty of these lands. Let this be the river of our peace."

The Tocobega warrior, almost flustered by the sudden shifts of the conversation, paused a moment, and whispered to his companion. At length he turned back to Adahi.

"You speak words of wisdom, Adahi. The people of Tocobega do not wish for war. If it is as you say, there is game enough to feed your children and ours. I am called Kanuna. I will mark this day and we will meet again."

"We go in peace and peace to you," Adahi replied as he raised his open palm.

There followed an awkward moment when the Tocobega warriors looked from one to another, as if uncertain what they should do. They had surrounded the intruders and now sat an easy spear-throw away. They had come to fight and were now expected to simply paddle away.

"We go!" shouted the warrior called Kanuna, and he and his companion began to turn their canoe. Reluctantly the others began to follow suit, backing their tapered craft through the tall stands of grass that had concealed them. Adahi and his fellows remained still, watching the departing war party.

"They must have seen us earlier and planned this trap for us," one of the men said quietly.

"That is certain," Adahi replied. "We must be more careful in our movements and alert to strangers. We must hunt, but not be hunted."

After a minute or two of silence, the four hunters slowly picked up their paddles and turned their canoes downstream, away from the others. It was a diplomatic move as well as a practical one. This hunt could be conducted farther from potential danger. They would follow a tributary creek from the east.

As they paddled, Adahi thought about the growing numbers of people who seemed to depend upon the land. He knew from the old stories that once there had been few people in this land and much game. Now they knew different times. Gone long ago were the elk and bison. No more were the mammoth, the horse, the camel and other great animals of legend.

The Calusa had grown in numbers, but others had come to their borders. To the east on the distant shore where sandy dunes were sculpted by wind and tide, the people of Tequesta made their homes, hunting the great turtles and sea fish. Their related tribes of the Jeaga, Jobe, and Ais populated the coastal lands to their north.

In the island chain that stretched south of the mainland, the Matacumbe peoples made their homes. Across the interior, beyond the bay of the Tocobega, lay the lands of Jororo, Ocale, Mayaca and Surruque peoples. The Timucua nations dominated those places, and their villages were encircled by round palisades of timbers for defense. Beyond them were the lands of poor Guale, who lived on the ocean shores north of the mouths of the great rivers and to their west, the powerful and wealthy Apalachee, who farmed the rich land in a way the Calusa could not.

All these tribes had shared in the new technologies, the improved spear and arrow tips from distant lands, the durable, fiber-strengthened pottery, the several new agricultural crops of squash and beans, and techniques that helped them grow corn amid the forests. Yet the land had become much more crowded.

Perhaps a hundred thousand humans now lived in the villages scattered along the length of the peninsula.

Now the Tocobega had begun to hunt in the lands of the Calusa. It was a thing that set much worry in his mind. "Today," he thought, "there may be peace, but what of tomorrow? What if the Tocobega take too much from us?" It was to be a growing concern for all Florida's people.

The Feather
900 Years Ago

THE TWO YOUNG MEN WERE BEST FRIENDS and often hunted together, but on this cool spring afternoon Wachita and Amagota had wandered far from their usual places and followed the tracks of deer deep into the forested wetlands and swamps. Their Ocale village offered safety, but the nourishment offered by a successful hunt would be worth the risk of encountering danger in the forests.

In their short lives they had already wandered far and seen both the bright and lively waters of the sunrise sea and the low, marshy islands of the sunset waters. They had visited many great springs where the seas were born and together canoed in many cool rivers. They had seen the boundaries of their world and believed they knew what it contained. The sight that confronted them now, however, was completely unexpected.

The two men stood in silence gazing at the giant before them. A great sense of awe had frozen them in their tracks. They glanced at each other wordlessly and then back at the mesmerizing sight. Flush with the bright green of spring leaves, a massive cypress tree towered high into the sky, far above those around it.

"It is the father of the forest," Wachita offered in a low, reverent voice.

"You may be right," replied Amagota. "It is like a god. The other trees stand around its knees like children listening to the wisdom of their elder!"

Cautiously they approached the gigantic tree and realized that a faint trail encircled it. At the foot of the tree, they discovered a small arrangement of objects, including thirteen white stones arranged in a circle. Other men had been there before. They walked a slow circle around the giant and measured their steps. "Thirty strides," Amagota said softly. "There has never been such a tree before."

"It is as tall as fifty men!" Wachita said, looking up at the tapering mass of the tree above him. The lowest limbs were far above the ground and the highest were out of sight in the distance. "They will not believe us when we tell them and will have to come to see it," Amagota observed.

"We will return with an offering and protection," replied Wachita.

Two days later, when they returned with a party of twenty men from the village, the group was moved to conduct a ceremony of blessing and made an offering of fragrant incense, feathers, and precious stones, which were placed at the foot of the giant tree.

They remained that night, completing a cycle of honor as light faded and returned, wakeful as the stars pin-wheeled above them. High above the tree the Chief of the Stars sat motionless as its bright followers moved slowly around it. They, too, seemed to honor the Father of the Forest.

Early the next morning the group heard movement, the sound of others approaching. They were barely concealed before a second group of people entered the small open space before the great tree. Poor Guale tribesmen, they came with their wives and children and were at first fearful when the Ocale rose from their concealment. Yet neither group made a threat and eventually the leader of the Guale turned from them to face the great tree, bowing his head before seating himself facing the giant. The Ocale leader did the same and both groups relaxed. Although hostilities had sometimes occurred between the two groups in the past, here it was clear to both groups that none should occur.

Amagota and Wachita watched as the Guale made their meal in the shade of the great tree and soon the two groups began to share a few words, building trust. The Guale, they learned, had known of the Father of the Forest for many years and believed it had powerful medicine. Here, they both agreed, peace would be honored and here they could meet free from fear of attack. The two bands completed their discussions with the exchange of a few trade items and token gifts in honor of the place of peace. It was afternoon when the Ocale band departed, leaving their neighbors to complete their own ceremonies.

For many years thereafter, the fame of the forest giant grew among the tribes of the region, and all came to recognize it as a place of peace and trade. It was to remain so for all the time that was left to them.

•

Each of the cultures which developed in Florida was unique, yet inter-linked by networks of trade and even religion. By the time of Columbus, there were many tens of thousands of people living in Florida, slowly advancing their societies. These First Nations peoples were descended from the early explorers who had wandered southward more than 15,000 years before.

Although the camels, mastodon and giant sloth had succumbed, Florida remained a land of plenty. Wild game was still to be found in the forests and the warmer waters burgeoned with fish and shellfish.

No American culture evolved in isolation, as the great civilizations of the Puebloans, Maya, Aztec and even distant Inca spread ripples of new ideas through the cultural fabric of Florida. Religious concepts advanced, too, and the entire Gulf coast from the Mississippi River to the Florida Keys became united in common ceremonies and deities. Their related cultures had evolved, as competing tribes evolved new relationships, dominating and subservient, cooperative or fiercely antagonistic. They loved, raised children, built cities, and dreamed. Seven hundred generations and more had been born, lived, and died on the narrowing peninsula. Many, although they were unaware, could claim direct descent from a man who had been known as Drink of Salt Water.

Florida was a land still unaffected by the events which had been taking place on another continent, far to the east...

The Gold Frog
June 1511

THE EARLY EVENING SKY began to take on deep shades of blue and indigo above the fiery orange and red clouds. The glowing colors were reflected in the restless waters of the sea, increasing the intensity of the scene. The young woman watching it fade felt her serenity renewed. All was at peace in her world.

Kamali loved to watch the sun set and rise again reborn in the mornings. A curious young woman, she often pondered why the sun and stars traveled ceaselessly and never rested. The priests of the tribe, she knew, marked the passing of the days on their stones and predicted the movement of the moon and stars and the wandering lights that moved across the heavens in their own patterns. It was a wisdom she longed to comprehend and although she had no one to teach her those mysteries, it was good to try.

She already knew well the phases of the moon and knew exactly when the tiny sliver of the new moon might be seen in the minutes after the sun set. She made a game each month of her efforts to see the new moon before any other and often succeeded. Tonight, though, was a special night, when the full moon would appear. It was then, when the departing sun and arriving moon shared the sky after a day of fasting, that the time of ceremony and festival would occur. All around were drums and drummers, arrayed to produce the maximum effect on the gathering.

Gradually the sun sank toward the horizon and Kamali yielded her concentration to the steady rhythm of drums and chanting voices coming from the meeting place before her. Without moving from her place near the water, she allowed herself to be lulled into an almost trance-like state, enjoying the slightly euphoric feeling the drumming produced.

The broad ceremonial island rose above the surrounding trees and served as the symbolic point where the natural forces of the universe met. Sky and earth, birth and death, past and future, each pair took its place in the beliefs and customs of her tribe. The vast mound was also the site of the tribal lodge, capable of containing more than a thousand citizens. There, around a square outlined with beautiful treasures of the tribe, the representations of that nature had gathered, arrayed according to their roles.

To the north were the old warriors, who represented the immovable pole around which the stars forever turned. The other cardinal points of the sky were the setting west, where the departing sun represented by the tribal leaders, chosen for their skills, knowledge, and wisdom. To the south sat a group of young men, solemnly recognized for their future leadership.

Kamali felt a sense of excitement as the moon rose, the drumming built to a crescendo and then stopped as abruptly as the snapping of a stick. "Now comes the face of the moon to smile on the people of Calusa," boomed the powerful voice of the high priest. He made a striking figure, looming over the broad meadow.

As the gathered crowds watched, a group of women entered the arena bearing gifts of food and herbs. Yet these gifts were not for the fasting people gathered around, but for the fire. Slowly they fed the flames with their gifts and offerings, gathered holding hands in a ring around the flames. After their chants of supplication to the spirits of nature and the universe, they slowly moved to their own shelter in the east, from which springs the new day, for it was the women who brought forth new life.

Silence reigned over the crowd for several long moments and then the priest spoke again. "Be glad, people of Calusa, for the spirits are pleased."

A great sound of thanks arose from the crowd as the flames burned brightly, a certain sign of favor from the spirit world. The gathered people showed their gratitude for this deliverance, which came partly at the pleasure of the moon and sun and partly, they believed, due to their great faithfulness to each other and their ceremonies.

After another pause, a few people on the outside of the crowd began to rise and gradually a muted murmur of voices rose into a loud chattering as the crowd of more than two thousand began to return to their stilt homes to break their fast before their cooking fires. Hundreds passed over the low-slung bridges that spanned the canals between the central island and the smaller surrounding ones. The rows of houses perched along the canals gave them each an ordered look and the canoes that lined the waterways showed the wealth of the sprawling town.

Using double-hulled dugout canoes they constructed vessels capable of trading with distant lands. Equipped with woven sails, adventurous traders traveled great distances along the coast and to distant shores.

The population of the town pursued a large variety of specialized trades. Fishermen harvested the sea, while farmers worked large fields of beans, squash, and corn. Women pursued their own trades as well, stripping plant fibers to weave soft cloth, or making fine fired pottery and beautiful shell jewelry and ornaments. Others built houses, produced fine dyes and paints from plants, carved canoes, or wooden utensils, traded with distant cultures, or simply hunted game. The Calusa people were content with the bounty of their world.

Kamali sat still for a long time as the crowd dispersed, happy to be anonymous in the midst of the multitude. People stepped carefully around her to leave, while a few others remained seated. Only after the crowd began to dwindle did Kamali rise and look about. The full moon peeking through the clouds gave an intermittent illumination to the scene as a few torches began to flare and the cooking fires became more visible, a long line of lights flickering into the middle distance. A steady, rhythmic beat of drums had resumed, though not as loud as before, as some of the younger men and boys began to amuse themselves with the instruments while the supper was prepared.

In the village she kept to the edge of a crowd and preferred to commune with the animals of the forest. She did love the festivals, though. and the summer festival of the moon was her favorite. It always fell on the first full moon after the longest day of the year and the night would be warm. Usually, the land breeze would take over after sunset, blowing out toward the warm Gulf nearby and the full moon would create a certain feeling of magic. Kamali loved magic. Stories of special deeds of long ago, or the powers of the priests and shamans, moved her. "I wish I could be a shaman," she thought, but knew that she would not be allowed to study under the men.

Her place, and her role in life, were largely preordained. Her name meant "Spirit Guide," and was a name from distant lands that her parents had learned from a trader. She was beautiful, although she did not know it. Her shy style made her more likely to take walks alone in the evening along the sandy beach, where dangers were few.

She had seen the giant sea turtles crying their salty tears as they cast their eggs into the depths of the sand and mourned when the men came to take some. She had watched, too, the emergence of the young, tiny bundles of energy that raced madly toward the safety of the water, guided by millions of years of instinct. She wondered how they knew, how the birds knew to fly before a storm and how manatees found their way back to the springs before the chill of winter could catch them.

Kamali knew that when the feasting was completed the crowd would again gather and the drums would sound long into the night as the moon coursed across the sky. People always took advantage of this annual holiday, and the celebrating was in order, for the year had been a good one. Many in the crowd were relatives from other villages and towns nearby and as far away as the big lake they called Mayaimi, who had traveled to join in the festivities. A warm feeling of reunion and celebration had filled the days. Many were reluctant to let that feeling go, even as the festival came to its conclusion.

Kamali rose and made her way toward the sound of the drums, since she had been relieved by her mother of the cooking chores this evening. Her mother knew that, since she was of marrying age, she should have an opportunity to meet young men from other villages during the festival night. Kamali was grateful, though she knew she was not really interested in boys. Still, their play with the drums drew her and she stood a short distance away to watch, surrounded by a group of other young people. The light of a small fire cast a ruddy glow upon their young faces.

Kamali watched as the young men took up a dance, tentative steps becoming bolder as the rhythm began to drive their feet. She watched their muscular young bodies moving, arms rising and falling in an intense beat that only grew louder as the dance became a reason unto itself, swallowing their inhibitions. Gradually others were drawn to the group and the sound began to dominate the entire festival site, drowning out the cries of mothers, calling their young children back to dinner.

"You like the sound they make?" came a soft question from behind Kamali's ear. Turning, she saw the smiling face of Holata. He was a young man about her age, whom she had known for several years. They were friends, although they saw each other only at festival times, when the villages would gather in an extended family reunion.

"It pleases me," Kamali smiled in return, her teeth unusually perfect and white in the moonlight. Holata caught his breath as he gazed into her dark, serious eyes, making their sharp contrast to her smile. The light of the fire glowed on her cheek, and he thought her the most beautiful girl he had ever seen.

"It is good to see you again, Kamali. I have missed you," he said happily, without taking his eyes from hers.

"It is good to see you again, too," Kamali responded, suddenly blushing as she realized he was staring rapturously at her. Turning away shyly, she looked again at the growing circle of young dancers. "How is your family?" she asked.

"Everyone is well," he responded. "We have had plenty."

A silence followed as Holata followed Kamali's gaze back to the dancers. He wanted to speak, but some mysterious force had frozen his tongue and he felt himself trembling slightly. "I am just nervous, that is all," he thought. "She is just a girl. I should not be afraid."

After a long pause, Holata spoke in a low voice, without turning his head from the action of the dancers. "I have brought you something."

Kamali turned to look at him, eyes smiling and inquisitive. "Why have you done that?" she asked him.

Holata shrugged. "Because I like you, I guess," he said, taken aback by the question. He himself had never wondered why; it had just seemed like the thing to do. Now he hoped he hadn't done the wrong thing.

"Can I see it now?" Kamali asked eagerly. She loved surprises and wondered what this young man had thought to bring her. She looked at him curiously, trying to probe his thoughts.

"Here it is. I hope you like it. I got it from a trader who traveled across the big water to the land of Maya."

Carefully Kamali opened the small leather pouch which Holata had taken from his belt. Inside, she found a small gold frog, its legs drawn up as if ready to jump. Its eyes were tiny golden dots. She thought it was beautiful.

"This is truly from Maya?" she asked eagerly, for she had heard many stories of the people and their stone villages across the sea.

"Yes," he replied. "I think it is important to the people of that place to make these frogs, for I saw some before, when other traders came. But those were made of stone, not metal like this one."

"It is very beautiful," she said seriously, looking into his dark eyes.

"I heard stories from the traders who went to the sunset land. They say there are villages with temples that rise to the moon and houses numbered like the leaves on the trees. One day I shall go there. I wanted this frog to remind me of that place."

"Why did you give it to me?" she asked.

"Because," he said, looking away from her intense gaze, "I think you are special and I want to make you happy," he said finally, looking back at her.

Kamali quickly looked away from his deep eyes, which had locked firmly onto hers. "Thank you," she said. She felt a tingle deep within and knew that this young man was himself something special. She knew without asking that more would pass between them and made sure that she was never far from him that night. The next day he joined her family at their cooking fire and her mother smiled at them.

The festival time flew by for the young couple and soon they were back in their home villages, separated by what seemed like an enormous distance. It was only a two-day walk, or a long day of strenuous canoeing along sheltered bays. Still, they thought of one another constantly and sent greetings and small gifts by friends who traveled between the several villages. Kamali's mother was pleased at their interest and knew that soon a wedding would be planned, for such was the way of the world. She smiled a bittersweet smile and kept her thoughts to herself.

The ways of the people of Calusa had remained largely unchanged for years unknown, numbering like the stars in the sky, she thought. Every young person knew the stories of the past and the great deeds and legends which had been passed down, father to son, by the shaman priests in the ancient rhymes. They told of the enemies conquered, the great leaders, the finding of the sacred places and the stories of the spirits who protected them and blessed the hunting. They even knew about how their people came from a world where all was cold and ice, far to the north.

Other tales told of the lands about them and the others who lived there, about the great sea upon which they lived and those who traveled along its shore to trade. They knew of the great rivers and the tribes who lived in faraway places like Apalachee, Coosa, Alibamu, and points beyond. With them they traded for copper and stone, jewelry and arrowheads, which came from much farther away, in the land of the Apache across the great deserts and plains where the great herds of bison thundered in their millions. In Florida, the only great animals she knew were the bear and the deer, the panther, manatee, and alligator.

Kamali's village, like dozens of others, was built on the shore of the sea, where an extensive system of canals brought the tides each day to play between their houses. The shallow bay had been terraformed into a land of high islands by the generations of excavation. With the bounty of the sea at their feet, the Calusa had no need to wander to hunt.

Sea walls of conch and oyster shells, the by-product of their rich diet, protected them from the surf and formed the low mounds upon which their houses stood. Before each home were wooden tablets, carved with totems of the various animals which represented each of the clans: eagle and bear, kingfisher and crocodile.

Next to each stout structure lay their transportation for hunting, fishing, and pleasure: ornamented log canoes designed to navigate the shallow bays and flats. Near the village, a large burial mound sheltered the bones of ancestors far more numerous than those alive and gave a sense of self-recognition and mortality to the Calusa people.

The technology of their lives was largely that of their parents and grandparents. In the village, much time was devoted to art and craft work. Skilled artisans made delicate tools from bone or shell, or powerful tools from the teeth and jaws of animals. Cups, bowls, and spoons of fired pottery, reinforced with palm fibers for strength and colorfully decorated, were most useful. Items of shell and conch were used in every home, while tubs, trays, mortars, and pestles of wood made the household work easier.

Most importantly, textiles were central to their lives. Colorful fabrics covered their bodies. Nets woven of the stout fibers of palm and reed were strung across bayous, reaping the bounty of the natural nurseries of the mangroves, where fish spawned by the millions. Clams, mussels, crabs, and wading birds were all part of their diets.

Beautifully carved and painted ceremonial masks were the pride of the craftsmen who made them for the priestly caste, which employed them in their ceremonies. Work in metal and glass was mysterious to them and the raw materials unavailable, but what they needed of these things they could acquire through trade. There was time, though, for the making of toys and generations of children clung to the dolls, toy canoes and carved animals patiently crafted by loving hands. The world of the Calusa was stable and ordered and little changed in five hundred, or even five thousand, years. The Calusa reigned over the western coastline of the long, watery peninsula.

That winter, after shy conversation led to serious, heart-to-heart talks of hopes and dreams, Kamali and Holata planned their wedding. They would be announced to the world as mated and their pairing would be blessed by the shaman, in the ancient rituals of fertility and shelter. Then, there would be feasting and dancing and celebration into the late night.

Then one day, the day before the festival at which Kamali and Holata were to marry, came traders from the south. They had traveled from the far seas beyond the coast, where they paddled their canoes among the islands. Along with trade, they brought stories of far-away places, but this time the stories were strange indeed.

Holata listened in wonder as the traders told of gigantic canoes with trees standing upon them, capable of making thunder on sunny days. He listened closely when the strangers told of entire villages which had been taken away by strange men, the peaceful people of Lucaya taken by the giant canoes.

Holata gleaned every bit of information and rumor he could about the strange men, the strange things they wore and the things they did. He had heard already of the strangers who had wandered through the lands of the Timucuans and Apalachee. They had heard, too, of the cursed illnesses which had gripped those people in the wake of the strangers' passing. Many had died and some of the shaman priests said that the strangers had repaid kindness with treachery

Holata knew little of the world beyond his shores. He had no way of knowing that in faraway Europe, men marked the beginning of the 16th century. He could not know of Spanish galleons, or cannons, or the slave raids that supplied labor to mine gold and silver. He could little understand how those precious metals would soon finance the spreading Spanish domination of the New World. None among the Calusa could understand the danger that approached them. It was a danger which their entire civilization would soon be forced to confront.

The gathered men of the Calusa sat late into the night debating the strange news and men from other villages claimed they had heard it, too, from other places, as rumors of rumors. Something strange was afoot in the world and they craved more news of it and worried about the danger it posed, even as they felt secure in their strength, with hundreds of warriors gathered about them.

Holata wondered at these stories. Strangers that had come to the lands of others. Would they come to Calusa also? Holata vowed that they would not carry his people away. Then, thinking of his precious Kamali, he raised his eyes and swore, upon the stars of his ancestors, that he would fight to defend his people against this monster that ate villages and the strange men who served it.

The wedding day dawned bright and clear and passed in hours of greetings and reunions as hundreds pour into the town to observe the festival day. Several other couples were to marry that day and when at last the hour arrived and the ceremony was held, there arose a great cheer and all the tribe blessed these few who represented the future of their people. A great wedding feast spoke of celebration and bright futures, but in the background a shadow was cast. Everyone seemed to share the fear that the story of the strangers had aroused.

Determined not to let worry spoil their new lives together, the young newlyweds confidently faced the new life they would build. Yet they could not know that the world they knew was in mortal danger. The people of Europe had learned of their hidden land and vowed to bend it to their will.

The Ring
February 1513

THE GENTLE ROLL OF THE SMALL CARAVEL had been a constant companion for weeks and on this fine day had not interfered with the rest of the brown, bearded man on the hammock strung between the bulkheads. Now he stirred and stretched, forcing the stiffness from back and limbs held too long in the curved confines.

He slowly opened his eyes, struggling to focus on the moving ceiling only inches above his head. Throwing his feet over the side of the hammock he stretched for the floor and stood, swaying slightly with the motion of the deck. Running his fingers through his beard and hair in turn he moved toward the steps and the pool of dazzling sunlight spilling in from above.

Diego Cortez de Gama was the third son of a successful merchant. His oldest brother would inherit the business and he had long known that he would have to find his own way in the world with only a small inheritance. He was a young man and the muscular build of his body showed plainly that he was used to physical endeavors. Despite his short stature he had gained the respect of his shipmates as a man to be reckoned with.

Diego, like most of the rest of the men-at-arms aboard the Spanish caravel, was an adventurer drawn by dreams of fame and fortune in the New World. Gold aplenty was flowing from the conquered lands of native cultures. Opportunity seemed to wait at every turn. Now he and his shipmates were bound for the rumored island of Bimini.

Stepping lightly onto the deck Diego paused for a moment as his eyes adjusted to the glare of full sun on the water. Several of the soldiers were gathered in a group on the aft deck while two or three others spent their time in solitary occupations, whittling or staring at the horizon. Two occupied themselves with a net hoping to snare a fish to add some variety to their limited diet.

Diego strode confidently up to the larger group who were idly discussing what they planned to do with their soon-to-be-won wealth. "I shall build a home in Valencia and have my choice of a wife from among the most beautiful girls in the city," one proclaimed, "and I shall take my time in the choosing!" he added, bringing a round of laughter from the men. The speaker was Francisco las Casas. He was a tall, handsome man, and he had carefully cultivated his reputation as a ladies' man during their entire voyage.

"We shall all win our fortunes and lose them ten times before you find one who pleases you enough to marry!" Diego interjected, bringing more laughter from the group. Francisco rose at this affront, but quickly broke into a grin of self-recognition.

"You perhaps know me better than I know myself, my friend, but I will keep up my search and the women of Spain will be glad to hear it!" he answered, and the small band of men grinned at one another. This was good entertainment for men weary of the confining twenty-meter length of their ship, but it began to remind them that they had not had liberty in weeks.

Sitting again, Francisco made room on his small crate for his younger friend. "Sit here, Diego and tell us of the woman who lures you below for sleep when the sun is high," he said with a wry smile.

Sitting with the group on the deck in the sunshine, Diego's thoughts were wandering among the islands of his imagination, riding in the shimmering blue water just beyond the horizon. "I dream not of women in the New World," he answered, "but of rich lands and islands of gold, where every man might be a king in his own right, under the King of Spain." This brought only a few grunts of agreement from the men. They had been *en route* to the New World for weeks and despite a brief stop at San Juan, had seen little but the deck of the ship and the rolling sea around them. They had already had their fill of boats and water and sailors. They longed for action.

"You are right, Diego, and I think the King knows this too. That is why he is sending Ponce on this new expedition," Francisco said.

Diego nodded, then lowered his voice to add "The King is sending him to find Bimini because the Indians tell of a fountain of miracles that can make a man young again. I heard that even El Papa in Rome would like to know more of this magic water."

At this, Francisco burst into gales of laughter and poked fun at his young friend, but others of the group came to his defense. "It is true, I heard it too," they said, but Francisco would not be silenced.

"I'll tell you what will keep a man young forever, my friends, and it cannot be put into a bottle!" he said, waving his hands in a fluid gesture, bringing more laughter from the men.

"You can say what you will, Francisco, but if I go to seek gold and find a fountain of youth in the bargain, I won't be disappointed with myself," Diego said to general agreement.

Across the deck from the soldiers, but still within earshot, a solitary figure dressed in the long brown cassock of a Franciscan friar listened to the conversation and made the sign of the cross. More important than gold, he thought, was the opportunity to save souls from perdition. He dreamed only of a chance to bring the word of Christ to the ignorant and superstitious savages that he was certain hungered for word of the savior of mankind. His, he knew, was the most important aspect of Spain's efforts. He smiled confidently, knowing that his cause and mission were just and that his rewards would come in the richness of the afterlife.

March 1513

DIEGO GRIPPED THE HIGH STARBOARD RAIL in the bright sunlight of a spring morning as his ship heeled, rippling the yards of white sail above him. Far behind and to the east he could see the retreating clouds which had carried the rain that had swept through during the night. The small caravel plowed forward into a brisk north wind and spray leapt before the bow of the boat, cascading upon the steel-blue water. White foam also marked their trail, mixing with the spray of the whitecaps all about them.

They had already been at sea for eleven days without sight of land. Diego was eager for a glimpse of their destination. Sniffing the air, the young Spaniard could detect the scent of winter. Different than the earthy fragrance of the mistral wind at home, he recognized a hint of evergreens, forests of pine far from the sea. Looking ahead at the rolling horizon, he could see distant banding colors, shades of lighter blues and greens. He sensed the excitement of impending adventure and new lands close at hand. Ahead, although he could not know it, the native cultures of Florida were unprepared for what would soon burst upon them.

Beneath his feet, the swaying decks of the caravel were bustling with preparation. His fellow men-at-arms were rechecking their weapons, mindful of the stories of the fierce Carib Indians that made war on San Juan. Besides the sailors who manned the rigging and kept the ships in repair, the small vessels were crowded with soldiers, weapons, stores of food and drink, and a dozen horses.

Along the gunwales were arranged ten small, breech-loaded cannons known as "bombarda," which were mounted to swivel. While they were ineffective against the hulls of ships, the bombarda were efficient at clearing the decks of hostile vessels. In the hold were lead shot, barrels of gunpowder, and dozens of long and short pikes, or lances.

The possibility of shipwrecks in uncharted waters was real, so each ship carried shipbuilding and repairing tools, including saws, axes, and a caulking iron for pounding caulking material into the gaps which sometimes formed between the planking.

The ship carried human resources as well, including the expedition's surgeon and the priest. Each soldier knew that the work of the surgeon, with his limited training and crude instruments, often required a priest at the conclusion.

The routine of the morning was suddenly split by an excited cry from a sailor on watch.

"Land! Land on the port bow!" came the cry from high in the rigging, as a first dark line began to take form on the far horizon. Instantly there came a scramble of men rushing from below decks, joining those already at the rail, straining for a glimpse of what could be seen from the crow's nest.

April 2nd was the Easter feast of "Pascua Florida," and Juan Ponce de Leon stood on the deck of his ship looking ahead at the long sweep of sandy shoreline crowned by a forest of brilliant green. A large cape jutted eastward and receded beyond into a faint line only visible from the top-most rigging. Assuming that this was yet another island, he ordered the ships to follow the coastline north in search of a bay that might provide good anchorage.

Throughout the day the ship made slow progress along the coastline. As evening drew near, Ponce ordered the ships to anchor in eight fathoms of water. The shore was so near the men aboard the ships could hear the waves breaking on the sandy beach as a full moon turned the land into a line of darkness, bounded by a glowing sky and the endless flickering of the moonlight reflected on the water.

During the night the wind shifted to a land-breeze and Ponce became convinced that this was much more than a small island. "Captain, order a company of your soldiers to protect a landing party," Juan Ponce told Francisco as they stood in the first rays of dawn upon the forecastle. Francisco immediately turned to Diego.

"I hope you are wearing your best armor today, my friend," he said, before shouting the names of sixteen soldiers who would go ashore with them. Diego only grunted, but half drew his sword in reply. He was glad to be chosen, despite the danger, if only to get his feet on solid ground for a few hours.

The spring sun blazed down on the three longboats as they approached the beach under the guarding guns of the ships. The sandy expanse featured a tangle of flowering vines and tall stands of grass. The sailors quickly beached the boats, low on the sand for a quick escape if necessary, and Francisco ordered the men to fan out into two skirmish lines to defend their small beachhead. Juan Ponce paid little heed to their precautions and sprang from the boat as soon as it was steady, drawing his sword to stride confidently up the steep, sandy slope. Francisco, Diego, the priest, and the party of soldiers were close behind.

Standing on top of the high dune, thirty feet above the sea, Juan Ponce scanned the green horizon and smiled to himself.

Then, calling up the priest, he ordered Francisco to assemble the men. Planting the banner of Spain carried by one of the sailors, he proclaimed, "I claim this island in the name of Charles the fifth, Emperor of Spain and the western seas, and her majesty, Isabella. I proclaim it *La Florida*." Then, kneeling in the sand, he prayed with the priest and the captain of his guard that this new land would prove fruitful for the works of both soldier and priest.

•

The company did not stay long on the isolated beach, for Juan Ponce was eager to press on with the search for the riches of Bimini. For five more days the expedition sailed northward, charting the coast while sounding the depths of the water in search of passage around or through the island. Three times they explored breaks in the shoreline, but each inlet proved to be blocked by shoals. They came at last to a river, larger than the others. Anchoring at the mouth of the flow, Juan Ponce again sent three longboats to explore the waterway and replenish their fresh water supplies.

It was Saturday, April 9th, when the ships turned about, sailing back on their course along the coast. Soon, with favorable southward currents near shore, they had passed the point at which they had first sighted the land and followed the sandy sweep of the Atlantic shore farther south. Twice they stopped to explore a short distance inland, the second time sailing into broad and shallow Biscayne Bay. The soldiers aboard the ships were by now eager to explore further but had seen no sign of cities or a native civilization. They had completely missed signs of the Tequesta and Jeaga tribes, who lived inland of the long lagoons hidden just behind the dunes of the shore. Yet dozens of pairs of eyes watched their passage from the shelter of the trees, with a mixture of wonder and fear.

As they sailed, Ponce and his navigator, Anton de Alaminos, took careful notes on the natural features and water soundings and Ponce noted the deep Bahamas Channel, formed where the Gulf Stream cuts through the continental shelf, and learned of the powerful current which runs there. He had no way of knowing that his fabled Bimini was again only a short distance away, across that channel.

After exploring Biscayne Bay and its protecting barrier of small islands, the expedition again sailed southward, gradually turning to the west as they followed the safe water offshore from the shoals of the island chain of the Florida Keys. Ponce promptly and prophetically named the islands "Los Martires," the Martyrs. Here they safely passed the dangerous coral reefs which would one day be the doom of so many Spanish treasure ships.

By Tuesday, June 21st, the first day of summer, the ships had passed the end of the Florida Keys, finding no safe passage to the northwest until they had passed present-day Key West. Sailing into the open water beyond the island chain, Ponce was still frustrated by his failure to find Bimini, or anything resembling an advanced civilization like that of Mexico.

Diego and Francisco stood on the deck in the morning sun as the ships traversed the rolling, open water after so long remaining close to land. They too were eager for action and a chance to set foot on dry land again. Their wishes were soon granted.

"Land!" came the cry from high above. "Land off the port bow!" Both soldiers reflexively scanned the horizon, but the blue water filled their view.

"I hope this proves something worth exploring," Diego said at last. "I would almost be glad for the sight of a cannibal in a war canoe, after all this sailing in circles."

"I hope you do get to see a cannibal," Francisco shot back, "before he sees you!"

A few hours later they dropped anchor near yet another of the low coral islands and this time Juan Ponce immediately ordered a shore party organized, for they needed to replenish their supplies of water. Again, the three longboats were prepared, and Francisco quickly selected his men, careful to choose the best fighters among them.

After landing, Francisco deployed the men to defend the beach, then organized a search of the island. An hour of marching revealed no inhabitants and no drinking water. The sun was low on the horizon by the time they had explored the interior of the island and the night was settling in when they again approached the landing place.

Walking along the sandy beach between the coral outcroppings, the waxing moon cast a beautiful light over the beach and the men were relaxed, when Diego suddenly froze in his tracks.

He had seen movement not far ahead. Francisco, at his side, caught the reaction and the whole company pulled up short, crouching in the sand.

"What do you see?" Francisco whispered, peering into the darkness ahead

"I'm not sure. Look there. Do you see anything move?"

Francisco stared in the direction indicated for a long moment. "I see only more rocks ahead on the beach."

"Watch closely and you may see it, too," Diego replied.

Gazing steadily at the dim shapes outlined faintly against the brown sand, Francisco watched as they seemed to shift their position. His concentration was interrupted by a firm tap on the shoulder. Turning, he found himself nearly face to face with a dark, leathery creature nearly his own size! With a yelp he jumped back, landing on his backside in the damp sand. Around him there grew an outburst of roaring laughter, for there before him was a giant sea turtle and a circle of his own men, who were having great fun at their captain's expense.

Without hesitation, Francisco looked the huge beast in the eye and spoke with a straight face. "Welcome, Madam turtle! I hope you remembered to invite your friends, for I have brought mine, and we sail for Bimini within the hour!"

On the northward journey from their islands, which their captain had named "Los Tortugas," or "the Turtles," the expedition wandered through the open Gulf of Mexico. Within the hold of the ship were more than a dozen of the turtles taken as a future source of fresh meat, a constant need on board ship.

Convinced at last that there were no further islands to the northwest, Juan Ponce ordered a course back to the east and so came again upon the "island" of La Florida.

The western shore was a pleasant surprise for some, but a nightmare for the navigator after the long straight beaches of the Atlantic coast. Here were large bays, broad rivers, and thousands of tiny islands to confound the sailors. Here, though, they soon found several likely harbors, which they would need for future explorations inland.

"This would make a fine site for a port city," Juan Ponce remarked to Francisco as they stood on the deck surveying a surrounding sweep of coast and the wide river which flowed into a broad bay. A chain of low, green islands encircled the dazzling blue water, and a thin green line formed the landward shore. There was no sign of any hills, but they could make out a series of peculiar mounds. The sharp-eyed lookout claimed he could see small houses there. Juan Ponce was convinced. "Here we will put ashore and seek information of gold, and perhaps other things," he added with a wry grin.

•

From the shore other eyes returned their gaze, as fear and awe spread through the people of Calusa. Among the watchers was Holata, and he thought of his beloved bride, now being ushered into hiding with the rest of the women, children, and old men. The long line of hunters, now to become warriors, lay prone upon the sand, ready to drive these feared enemies from their lands.

•

Aboard the Spanish ships, all was in readiness. "If you wish, my captain, I will take a party of men to explore the river and search for Indians," Francisco offered. "There are some low dunes there to the north which would make a good base of operations."

"Si, we should know more of this place," he answered. "We must ask the Indians here what they know of Bimini. For all we know, we may gaze upon it now."

Early the following morning, Juan Ponce de Leon accompanied a landing party of ninety-five men, in eight boats, who quickly established a camp and perimeter near the mouth of the wide river. The quiet, protected waters of the broad bay lapped gently at the line of boats on the sand as Francisco assigned two small scouting parties to follow the shoreline and river and search for Indians. It wasn't long before results were met.

Exploring south of the river mouth, a party of six men was met by a force of more than sixty armed Calusa, determined that their people would not become victims like the Lucayans. With a display of weaponry and threatening gestures, they waved the explorers back to the sea. Wisely, the Spaniards made no threatening moves and fell back in an orderly retreat.

Within thirty minutes, Ponce led a party of fifty soldiers back to the point of the first meeting, where they soon found the natives as before.

"Offer them gifts," Ponce instructed Francisco, who led four men carrying two small chests toward the Indians, leaving the body of soldiers behind. Glaring, brown-skinned Calusa quickly pointed long wooden darts at the Spaniards, resting them in notched atlatls. Francisco ordered the men to a halt.

Opening a chest, Francisco chose a few glass beads, paper, and a small wooden toy, and slowly walked alone across the last ninety feet separating the men. Stopping a few feet short, Francisco held his breath as he reached out toward the apparent leader of the men. The tall chieftain looked at him dubiously for a long moment, then finally stepped forward and took the objects.

Francisco tried to hide his delayed intake of breath and stood as motionless as possible while the man examined the small gifts. The long rank of Calusa Indians stood watching the exchange closely and a few pointed their spears at Francisco, obviously unhappy about his presence. After a long moment the chieftain looked again at Francisco and spoke harshly in a language he couldn't understand. Francisco looked at the man, trying to read the meaning of the words from the tone of voice. Slowly he turned and walked cautiously back to the open chest and grabbed double handfuls of trinkets.

Francisco again approached the long line of Calusa and held out his hands to offer the objects to others in the group. None moved forward to accept them, as Francisco stood awkwardly for a long moment. The chieftain repeated his earlier phrase, in an even more demanding tone and threw the gifts he held into the sand at Francisco's feet. Although the words were still a mystery, this time there was no mistaking the meaning. Several of the Calusa repeated their sharp jabbing motions with their spears, adding emphasis to their leader's demonstration.

Slowly Francisco began to withdraw, backing away from the Calusa, lowering his head in deference, but keeping his eyes upon the men, watching for any aggressive move, which would cause him to break into a full run. The Calusa merely stood and glowered at the sight of the retreating Spaniard, who soon made his way back to the body of troops.

"Sir," he said to Juan Ponce de Leon, the intrepid discoverer of Florida, "It would appear that the natives are not in a mood to shop for gifts today."

Juan Ponce looked at his captain and a hint of a smile passed across his face despite the seriousness of the situation. "You are a brave man, Francisco. I have chosen well, I think. I only hope that you will do as well with a sword, as with a word, if trouble follows us."

"I am impressed, as well, my friend," Diego confided when Juan Ponce had moved away, "but I fear that this is not to be the place where we will fill our purses with gold while the Indians bring us food and wine."

That night the company camped on the beach, their ships anchored in the bay nearby.

The night was still, but the Calusa were determined not to give the foreigners the rest they wanted. During the early evening, before the moon rose, war canoes approached the anchored ships and showered them with arrows. The shouts of the sailors echoing across the water quickly roused the soldiers, even before the few cannon blasts which followed. These seemed to have the desired effect and the canoes quickly fled.

Since the night was young, Francisco redoubled the guard, which soon had the help of a nearly-full moon to watch for attackers. The rest of the night passed uneventfully, though restlessly.

The next morning Juan Ponce de Leon ordered the men to break camp and march south along the shore in the apparent direction of the Indian settlement. The sailors were also armed and were ordered to follow the marchers in the long boats.

A few minutes progress along the sand, with scouts moving through the tall grasses and mangrove thickets, brought no further sign of the Calusa, but plenty of evidence of their regular habitation of the area. The trails of the Indians were much in evidence, but Francisco ordered his men to move in wide sweeps around the obvious trails, fearing an ambush on the narrow pathways. The intense heat of the tropical sun was baking the troops under the light armor they wore.

As the group moved into a broad expanse of open salt marsh, they spotted a plume of smoke ahead beyond the next tree line. Juan Ponce ordered the troops to move toward what he supposed was a village. It was a critical mistake, for moments later a shower of darts rained upon the troops, still too tightly bunched for unexpected guerrilla warfare. War whoops filled the air as several Spanish soldiers fired their crossbows blindly at the surrounding trees.

"Hold your fire! Reload!" Francisco shouted above the din and quickly ordered his men to disperse and form a perimeter. He had only seconds, for a second volley, this time of arrows, rained upon the troops. The cries of wounded men, calling for help, spurred Francisco's decision. He ran quickly back to where Juan Ponce stood, sword drawn, near the center of the troops.

"We must retreat. The smoke was a lure. They have chosen this spot to fight, and it offers them the cover they want, while we have none," he said.

"Will they not come out and fight us as men?" asked Juan Ponce, still standing erect, scanning the trees for signs of movement.

"They are not Europeans, Governor," Francisco said earnestly. "They will fight as they are accustomed. They know nothing of our rules of warfare. We must pick the time and place if we are to be successful against them."

Seeing the wisdom of the argument, Ponce nodded his assent and Francisco shouted at the men to withdraw. They fought both frontal and rear-guard action against the Indians all the way back to the beach, as the natives knew the ground and the trails and continued to circle ahead of the Spanish troops, moving slowly in armor, carrying their wounded. Two more men fell to the almost incessant showers of arrows and Francisco was wondering if they would never run out, when it occurred to him that they were being reused. Arrows which had fallen about them at the first skirmish were probably collected and passed ahead to be fired again! He quickly ordered a group of the soldiers to be alert and collect the feathered shafts and leave none behind. The order apparently worked, for the numbers of arrows being launched against the troops began to diminish slightly and the Indians sought to be more selective in their targets.

Finally regaining the beach, the troops had a stronger position, with the water behind and the Indians confined to the trees and brush before them. Soon two of the long boats were on their way to the flagship, evacuating the wounded men. Francisco took advantage of the improved terrain and had his crossbow men arranged prone on the dunes, watching for targets in the trees.

"Hold your fire until I give the command," Francisco called to his troops and continued to watch for movement from the trees. Then, seeing that another volley of arrows had been launched toward his men, he ordered them to fire at their suspected sources. A barrage rattled into the undergrowth and silence followed as the Spaniards reloaded. The silence stretched into long minutes, until Francisco began to suspect that his ploy had worked, finally handing the natives a taste of their own medicine.

"We have driven them off for the moment, but they will return, your excellency," Francisco reported to Juan Ponce. "We can hold this beach for a long time, but it will avail us of nothing. Do you have further orders?"

After a long pause, Juan Ponce de Leon, royal appointee as Governor of Bimini, surveyed the long strand of beach, the blue water, and the hot sun above. Sweat ran down his face as he watched the wounded being helped from the longboats onto the ships waiting on the bay.

"Let us go from here. We shall continue our search along the coast. Somewhere we shall find evidence of Bimini and the cities we seek."

Francisco moved his troops in orderly fashion along the beach to an easily-defended point from where they could be loaded onto the longboats and returned to the ships in two waves. The last of his men was climbing aboard the third of the longboats before Francisco turned his back to the shore and waded into the water to the boats. The waiting sailors quickly shoved off and soon regained the ships, where they tended the wounded and took stock of the situation.

"It has been quite a day, my friend," Diego said softly when he finally located Francisco looking over the treatment of one of his men, who had taken an arrow in his shoulder.

"You are lucky that it struck the muscle of the shoulder and missed cutting a blood vessel," Francisco told the suffering soldier, who grunted his agreement. Francisco then turned to Diego, with a look that Diego did not know.

"We were lucky that they did not kill us all," he said soberly. "We fought on their ground and our swords were useless. Our shot fell wasted in the trees and we had no cannon. May the heavens preserve us from more such encounters," he said and made a sign of the cross.

Diego looked closely at Francisco, wondering if this was some dark humor. His usual happy-go-lucky attitude had vanished and in its place was this sudden seriousness.

"Are you afraid of the Indians, Francisco?" he asked, half in jest.

Francisco suddenly grabbed his smaller friend and pushed his face into his. In a whisper, he said, "If we are forced to fight these Indians again, they will have no fear of the sound of our guns, or us. They see that we bleed, like they do, and this is their ground. They will fight to the death. We should be prepared."

Diego pulled himself back and shrugged his tunic back into place, looking strangely at Francisco. He could not understand the change which had come over his friend.

"You are a changed man, Francisco. I do not believe you can fear these primitives, with the good men of España around you!" he said.

The fiery look in Francisco's eyes faded slowly as he stared back at the smaller man, and at last he looked away, over a bombarda at the green line of the Florida coast, fading in the light of dusk.

"You know I have no fear, but I feel a sense of dread just the same," he said at last. "We should be alert. We face a great danger."

•

The night passed without incident and the moon drew near the western sea even as the first light of dawn began to blush across the east. The night watch had at last begun to relax as below decks the soldiers and crew slumbered, when suddenly a distant shout echoed across the water from one of the other vessels. It was answered immediately by the watch and followed by the sound of running feet.

"Que...?" Diego started, sitting up and rubbing the sleep from his eyes. He turned toward where Francisco bunked, but the space was empty. Instantly he heard his strong voice from above deck.

"Arise, men of Spain! To your stations! To arms!" he shouted, and Diego could not mistake the meaning.

Grabbing his sword, he scrambled up the companionway and was stunned by what he saw. Across the bay came speeding the warriors of Calusa, in not one canoe, or a dozen, or twenty, but fifty, seventy, more... Already the nearer of the caravels was surrounded at anchor and arrows flew at its decks as the first musket was fired in response. Sailors were scrambling into the rigging to let loose the sails as others lined the gunwales to fend off the attempts at boarding.

Looking up, Diego saw his own ship's crew high above his head and the sails beginning to fall and spread, but he knew the early morning calm would make them nearly useless. Looking to aft, he spotted Francisco, perched above the deck, waving his sword and screaming toward the oncoming war canoes. Already the first canoes drew into range and arrows began to fall among the men on deck.

"Come on, wind!" Diego heard himself say and then suddenly realized that they were still at anchor! Running forward, he ordered several crewmen to raise the anchor and put his own back into the effort. Slowly the capstan began to reel in the thick hemp leader, which was bound to the yards of chain and steel on the sandy bay bottom. The ship moved slowly toward the weight of the iron as the cable tightened. As he worked, he saw the ship's captain and Juan Ponce ordering the sailors in the trimming of the sails and hoped there was some movement to be gleaned from the bare breath of wind.

At last, the anchor was aweigh, and Diego turned his thoughts to defending the ship against the attackers once again. Running amidships, he saw at once that three canoes had pulled alongside the ship and their occupants were delivering a withering fire of arrows at any man who showed his head from the deck. Several were scrambling to find a way to board the ship. A sudden blast of bombardas echoed across the water, but the canoes were too close for the effective use of the big guns, the shot sailing over the heads of the attackers without effect.

"Bring out the pikes," Diego heard himself shouting. "We can hole their canoes when they draw alongside." In the confusion, no one paid any attention, for it seemed each man was already involved in some other life-or-death task. "What will happen if we cannot fight with our heads?" Diego asked himself with a rising sense of panic. Then, running aft to where Francisco held forth on the deck, ordering a small band of soldiers, he repeated his suggestion.

"Diego, at least one man has time to think in the midst of battle," Francisco shouted with a smile that denied, Diego thought, any shred of fear. "Take two men and retrieve the pikes from the hold and bring them here. "

Diego grabbed two who seemed least critical to the defense of the deck and headed for the hold. When he returned, the situation had only worsened and one of the soldiers had fallen, an arrow piercing his jaw. Blood flowing on the deck made the situation seem even more critical as they brought up the long pikes with their heavy iron tips. The soldiers had successfully beaten off the first attack by three canoes, but it was obvious the Calusa were massing for a larger attack, circling more than thirty canoes around the ship.

"You are back in time to help, I see," Francisco called as Diego arrived.

"And I see that we are beginning to get under way. I wish we had more wind!" Diego replied in a shout, above the noise of the battle.

It was at that moment that a loud salvo was fired from below decks, but they could see immediately that it fell not among the canoes massing for attack, but upon another group that was closing fast upon one of the smaller ships. The shot from the light guns had the desired effect, striking at least two canoes and throwing the wounded into the water. Moments later, the other vessel returned the favor, firing upon the massed canoes that were preparing to attack the port side of the slow-moving flagship.

"At least the gunners are learning how to fight against these canoes!" Diego shouted, but Francisco had already grabbed one of the wicked-looking pikes and was preparing to climb upon the gunwales to meet the charging war canoes, which were now too close to risk further bombarda fire from other ships for danger of striking their friends.

"Francisco, be careful!" Diego shouted above the din, as he moved to meet the attack in a new shower of arrows.

"Vaya con Dios, my friend!" came the grinning reply and Francisco turned with a shout toward the canoes which were now alongside the ship and with a quick thrust knocked a Calusa warrior into the water.

Seeing the success of the gunners, the pilots of the three ships were attempting to sail their vessels into favorable positions for further bombarda work, but the light winds made the maneuver difficult. The shallow waters and the fact that the bay narrowed to the north, where they inexorably headed, made the situation even worse. It was clear that the few soldiers and sailors on each ship would have to bear the brunt of the attack in hand-to-hand fighting.

Drawing his sword, Diego stood close to where Francisco towered above him, perched atop the gunwale, the long lance raised to strike. Francisco took careful aim, ignoring the feathered shafts which flew past his exposed position. With a graceful thrust, he hurled the shaft downward and as the occupants jumped out of the way, it plunged itself into the wood of the canoe. Immediately the weight and momentum of the long, heavy pike provided leverage that neatly capsized the canoe, leaving its four occupants floundering in the water.

"Quick, you men, run to the hold and bring more pikes!" Diego shouted immediately to several sailors who stood nearby clutching oars, the only weapons they had at hand. Turning with the smile of a man who has just found the keys to his salvation, Diego leapt to lift a lance and join his friend. The canoes massing at the side of the ship, within reach of the pikes, made them easy targets and three more heavy thrusts made an end of two more of the attackers.

A sudden shout from behind and a pounding of feet was all the warning the men had that the Calusa had boarded the ship. Even as he turned, Diego saw more Calusa warriors scrambling over the port gunwale and two more running toward them with knives. He barely had time to draw his sword before they were upon him and he fell backwards as he slashed, opening a deep wound across one man's arm and chest. The second was at his side, his knife raised to strike when, with a shout, Francisco brought his blade down upon the man's neck, killing him instantly. The first wounded man bounded over the gunwale and into the water and Francisco quickly helped his friend to his feet.

"Take care that you do not fall again, the decks are slippery!" Francisco shouted, running across to where other Calusa were threatening to overwhelm a group of sailors, fighting with improvised weapons.

Seeing that Francisco's charge effectively scattered the rest of the attackers, Diego hefted another lance and hurled it toward still another canoe approaching his starboard side. Then, as suddenly as it began, the attack was over, the retreating canoes scattering across the water. But even as they fled from the flagship, they were threatening to overrun one of the other two ships.

"Governor, we must take the risk and use the bombardas against our sister ship, or she will be lost," Diego shouted, running aft toward the poop deck, where Juan Ponce had regained a view over the battle.

"Si. Let it be so!" came the shouted reply from the Governor, even as Anton de Alaminos slowly brought the ship about to give the guns a better shot.

Aiming carefully, the gunners on the ship's crew began to fire the bombardas in sequence and the crew began to reload the guns as rapidly as possible, swabbing the hot steel to cool it before tamping in another charge of powder and shot. Each operation took about two minutes, but by the time each of the five port-side guns had fired twice, the Calusa were in full flight. Several were visible in the water, swimming toward the shore of the shallow bay.

Now a new danger was emerging, as the light winds had finally carried the ships toward shallow water, where linesmen were warning that they may run aground. Looking around, Diego could see that their third ship, which had successfully escaped the canoes, had indeed struck bottom, a mile or more to the west, where it was listing slightly.

Quickly Juan Ponce ordered the ships about, and they gradually began to put more distance between themselves and the mainland, where the Indians could be seen regrouping. Closing rapidly on the stranded vessel before a freshening wind, the men were relieved to see that the rising tide and the work of the sailors had served to lift the ship free from the sand. Shouts from the deck indicated that she was still sound, though the captain no doubt would soon wish to send swimmers to inspect her bottom.

"There is no time," Ponce signaled and ordered all three ships back to the mouth of the bay and out to sea. Looking across the water, Diego could see still-large numbers of canoes moving in the same direction, as if to cut them off.

"We may still have further fighting before us, it seems," Diego said aloud and among the group of weary men, several crossed themselves. Two of their number were lying on the deck, having received their last rites from the friar.

The run back to the south, which required them to approach the masses of war canoes, was a period of nervous preparation that needed no encouragement from Francisco or the officers. When at last the distance was closed, they found that the Calusa had learned quickly and approached the ships from straight ahead, rendering the bombarda nearly useless. Only by turning the ships could they be brought to bear, and that would carry the ships out of the narrow channel of deep water.

It was only the forward momentum of the ships toward the oncoming war canoes that prevented complete disaster, for Diego could see that the Indians had brought fire with them, flaming on turtle shells, and meant to fling the embers upon the ships. As a shower of arrows fell again upon the decks, it became apparent that the speed of the ships, modest though it was, would make it difficult for the Indians to bring their canoes alongside. Only a few who were most favorably placed managed the maneuver and continued the onslaught of arrows while they tried to deliver their fiery attack.

It was then, as Francisco again arose to strike with his lance, that Diego felt his greatest pain. As he watched, an arrow struck Francisco squarely in the neck. He turned slightly, eyes wide, as blood spurted from his throat. Before Diego could spring to his aid, the dashing Spaniard who had so inspired his men fell, still grasping his heavy weapon, and landed squarely upon the canoe below.

With a cry Diego rushed to the gunwale, prepared to leap over, but already he could see that Francisco was beyond help, motionless and slowly sinking under the weight of his gear, a crimson stain spreading between the swimming Calusa warriors. For a long moment he stood watching as his best friend disappeared into the turquoise waters. He was still standing there looking back when the ships drew away from the coast and into the relative safety of the deeper waters of the Gulf of Mexico.

"Vaya con Dios, amigo," Diego repeated aloud as he felt tears well in his eyes. His staunch adherence to the machismo of his culture was cracked, yet others gave him brotherly pats of comfort. They too shared his pain. In a few short months together, they had grown to love and respect this one man above all others.

Diego spent the next several days in a deep gloom, feeling lost without his friend at his side. Gone forever were the dreams of gold and great riches, power, and position. For him, the great adventure to explore the New World was over and he was poorer for it. Florida had already defeated them, Diego thought.

•

"I am proud of your actions during the fighting. You have served well, Diego," Ponce said the next evening, approaching the young man who sat staring at the water.

"I only did what was needed," he replied, rising to face his superior.

"I would like you to assume the captaincy and command the troops," Ponce said, smiling.

"I am honored, sir, and would do so at your wish, though I fear I cannot replace Francisco, who was respected by all the men."

"They respect you, too, Diego," Ponce replied. "You will do well."

Emboldened by the trust placed in him by Juan Ponce, Diego resolved to answer a doubt in his mind and understand how he had been selected as a part of the expedition.

"Sir, if I may be so bold, I have a question," he said. "You had told me in Española that you had heard of my coming and would have sought me out to serve, had I not presented myself. I am at a loss how you could have known..."

"It is no great mystery, Diego. In Spain, family must help family. That is how we survive and prosper. I received a letter from my brother, who had received one from your mother. You and I are cousins, though distantly. You, however, have earned your rank and success, as much as any man who has sailed with me. Together we will succeed in this new world."

Diego was silent for a moment, contemplating how his life had been changed by events, both happy and tragic. He chose his next words thoughtfully. "I hope you are right, sir. I know that my friend Francisco would have wanted nothing less. La Florida somehow holds our destiny. Perhaps it is best to try to make a future in this land. I hope though that I won't have to fight every Indian I meet."

•

For several more weeks the company traveled along the challenging Gulf coast of Florida, probing into the bays and estuaries, looking for deep-water ports and signs of an advanced civilization. They found no great temples, no elephants, no port cities or spice traders, and no gold. Instead, they discovered villages of round wood-and-thatch homes, large and mysterious earthen mounds, and inhabitants who were either hostile or hiding. Few would come forth to speak to them.

In his mind, Diego tried to imagine the shape of the long coastline they had sailed. The ship's mapmaker had shown the officers the rough, partial map he had been keeping, but blank space dominated the page.

Diego remained determined. It was a map that deserved to be completed. Francisco's death would not be in vain. There was a purpose to this strange new land, he believed, for each place on earth was created for a reason. Yet the unknown was all around them. A city of gold, or a fountain of youth could still be awaiting him. Somewhere out there, perhaps, lay his fortune, or his sudden end.

•

When the expedition finally returned to San Juan in September, they had been lucky enough to avoid hurricanes and most of them survived. Although they had created rough charts of much of the Florida coast and earned a place in history, Ponce de Leon was never to achieve the success and wealth he dreamed of. Yet through his efforts and those of his crew and thousands of others, a new land became known to the monarchs of Europe. The stage was set for continuing Spanish efforts to conquer this most-forbidding part of the "New World."

•

For Diego, the lure of Florida remained strong. In 1527, after returning from a long visit to Spain, he joined an expedition led by Pánfilo de Narváez. They landed on the west coast, pursued natives, discovered Tampa Bay, and eventually set out with six hundred men to explore the inland areas in a search for gold.

Each tribe they encountered seemed to live in the simplest conditions, and no trace of gold or silver mines could be found in the sandy countryside.

Assured of the wealth of the Apalachee tribe they marched north and crossed the Suwanee River. In each new meeting, they asked of wealth, but learned little. Few in this new land, it seemed, welcomed the presence of an invading army, but all seemed to be in awe of the horses the Spanish brought. Yet talk of gold brought only blank stares. Only by allying themselves with one local tribe against another could the Spanish win the privilege of sharing the stores of grains that the Apalachee had amassed. They wandered far to the north and then westward. Ultimately, starvation, disease and warfare took their tolls.

The survivors built crude rafts to attempt to sail back to Mexico, but they were separated by storms. After almost eight years spent as slaves, only four survivors managed to reach Mexico by land. They had been the first Europeans to see the North American interior and cross the mighty Mississippi River. Diego was no longer among them.

The Bone
June 1540

THE STEAMING CLAY POT offered an aromatic brew of steeped herbs and honey and Na-valah tipped it slowly toward the lips of her mother, who lay upon her bed. Kamali sipped the liquid gratefully, but after only a few seconds seemed to gag and turned her face to a basin as her body rejected even this tiny taste of nourishment. As she fell back, exhausted from even this small effort, Na-valah dabbed her fevered face lightly with a damp cloth. She was frightened and could not think of what else she could do to help her mother.

Taking a short break from her duties, she stepped outside to where Kalakamo waited, tending a small cooking fire, and keeping a watchful eye upon her younger brother. She sat close beside him, and he slipped his hand around hers, offering what comfort he could.

"She is very weak, my love, and I am very afraid," she said. "Is there nothing more that we can do to give her strength?"

Kalakamo sat silently for a moment, pondering his next words. Since the death of her father, Holata, only a week before, he had not found words that would give her comfort. At last, he turned to her, looking directly into her worried eyes. "The shaman has admitted that his medicine has no power over the fever. We use all our knowledge of healing herbs and still our people die. If I had the power, I would save them all, but I too am fearful. Every day more of our people fall to this curse." There was a long pause before he uttered the next words. "My thoughts now are not so much with your mother and those who are sick, but about how to save the healthy, so that they do not join the dead. I must go to speak with the shaman and the elders and will return shortly."

"Please hurry," she replied, looking at the man who was her only strength in her misery. "Please do not leave me long."

Kalakamo moved quickly across the town toward the longhouse, where he knew he would find at least some of the elders, who decided most of the affairs of the clans. There, he hoped, some answers to their dilemma could be found. He walked past the small chapel to which the friars called the people to hear the word of their god, but the friars were not there and would not return until the moon was again full, as they made their rounds of the scattered missions.

At length he stood before the longhouse, pausing a moment before entering the darkened interior. A small fire burned in the center and a thin column of smoke rose toward the small hole in the center of the roof. As his eyes adjusted to the dim light, he could see only a single elder, who alone had been tending the flames.

"Our chiefs Lachuata and Motariba have fallen," the sad-faced old man in the longhouse told him. "Even among the elders there is much death and confusion. Our council of twenty-nine is reduced to seven. All the others of the council are dead, with their families, or ill themselves. Only I sit here because I have no family left to tend. My wife died two days ago. My son is dead and his children. We do not know what can be done to fight this illness that stalks our people. It seems to visit new families every day and there are too many sick to tend. I cannot give you false hope."

The two men looked at each other helplessly. They both wondered if the scourge was not a curse. It had been only weeks since they had begun to see illness in their village, but it had spread rapidly to many.

"Bochaba, all I see here is sickness and death," Kalakamo replied at length. "Perhaps it is bad water, as some say, or perhaps the gods are angered. I cannot say why, but I see that, when the first hunters fell ill, others around them soon fell too. It started with their families and now has spread to three of five families in the village. If it is true, as I have also heard said, that it spreads among us, then we must leave this place, go on separate paths and hope that not all of us carry the illness with us. It is our only hope."

"You have my blessing, Kalakamo," Bochaba replied slowly. "Take your family, if they can travel, and go far away. Stay away from all others and have hope that you may hide from this curse. Tell any who wish to go that they should try to save themselves. This is a cursed place."

"Thank you, Bochaba," Kalakamo replied. "I think this is best. We do not flee our people because we abandon them. We flee to protect them."

He returned immediately to his home, his mind turning over his plan of how to transport Na-valah's mother, much too weak to walk. His effort was unnecessary. He spent the remainder of the day and evening comforting the grief-stricken Na-valah and arranging for the burial of her mother. She was added to a long list of respected members of the tribe who would be buried the next morning. Influenza was an almost unstoppable force among the Tequesta, who had no natural or genetic immunity with which to cope with the infection.

When the hurried ceremony was completed, Kalakamo led his wife along the pathway that led to the northern settlements. They were soon followed by others as more than a thousand attempted to escape the plague of death, dispersing themselves by hundreds of pathways into the surrounding countryside. Some fortunate groups left the disease behind them, but fear drove them onward, ever farther from their homes. Too often, the fugitives carried the seeds of destruction with them and fell ill in remote areas beyond the reach of even the basic comfort of friends in their dying. The village of the Tequesta was soon reduced to a shell. The only people remaining were those too sick to travel, or too involved in the care of the sick and dying.

Kalakamo traveled with Na-valah to a small clearing near a creek where he had camped before during a hunt. There he hastily arranged a simple shelter using a few animal skins, fallen branches and the ever-present palmetto fronds. "Tomorrow," he thought, "I will improve it." But the morning found Na-valah suffering from severe cramps and soon the familiar fever came over her. Kalakamo tended her closely, brewing strong herbal infusions and keeping her warm through the alternate fevers and chills that wracked her.

For four days Na-valah lingered in a delirious fever unable to eat or drink and Kalakamo feared that each hour might bring her final breath. Clutched in her hand, she held a tiny golden frog and called upon her mother's spirit for strength. At last, on the fifth day, the fever slackened, and she drank deeply of his warm brew. By the following day, he was sure that she would live, and she was able to eat a small amount of food.

"My husband, are you well?" Na-valah asked when she began to regain a bit of her strength. "If you fall ill, I will die with you!"

"I am fine, my love. Please rest and we will talk in the morning."

•

For several days Kalakamo stayed close to his wife's side and was pleased when she gradually regained her strength. He avoided falling ill himself but did not know why. As Na-valah returned to health, he resumed his hunting and built them a new home near the sweet flowing waters of the stream. He saw no others but feared a return to the village they had left behind.

The spring and summer passed and only with autumn did Kalakamo feel the urge to attempt to contact others. They followed the twisting pathways of the forest to return to the village. His fear of the unknown killer was only increased when he arrived, for it was as if a giant hand had wiped it from the earth. Only a dozen survivors remained where there had once been a town.

"Have all fled here, never to return?" Kalakamo asked a young man who sat alone before a cooking fire. "Where have all our people gone?"

"They have gone and will not return," he was told. "Many have gone to meet their fathers. For two moons our people fell to the curse. We buried them as best we could, until there were few to do the work. Always, it seemed, those who served to honor the dead would be the next to die. Even their children died with them."

"Did many other flee to escape the death?" he asked.

"Yes, but few have returned from the forests and those told us that the curse was there, too. Only we remain now," came the reply, with a wave of an arm at the half-dozen occupied homes. "This place is accursed and if we had another place to go, we would leave as well. At least the death has ceased, but only because it had no more victims to choose from among our people. Our nation is dead now, only we few remain."

Kalakamo did not linger long in the ruins of the village but spoke to most of those who remained. They had seen no new sickness in three moons but seemed to remain in the grip of a dark spirit, with little love for the life they still held. He did what he could to revive their hope and smiled at the handful of children who played among the empty chickee huts. He could not bring himself to fall into despair and carry that new form of illness back to Na-valah.

He led Na-valah swiftly along the faint trails to find all well in their home and soon the smell of roasting meat wafted in the air. Na-valah had caught a rabbit in her snare.

Their evening discussion was a great comfort to his troubled heart. "Come let us speak of our future," Kalakamo said. "We must find others, in a safe place, where we can resume the ways .of our people. Let us leave this place."

"You know best, my husband," she replied, "and it would be good to be with the women, for I will bring new life to the world. You will be a father. We will have need of new blankets," Na-valah told him as she leaned comfortably against his chest. She smiled at him in her mysterious way and he was suddenly filled with a great joy that wiped away all the fear and pain of the previous year.

Kalakamo smiled at her and marveled at the happiness she could bring so easily to his life and their world. Her hands still worked at her weaving after their meal of game and herbs. She had long ago mastered the technique of stripping and shredding the leaves of the palmetto to dry the fibers into a tough material that could be spun into workable cloth. Her nimble fingers pulled thin strips of twine through her simple loom, working to create the new wrap she would need for her child. Life would continue, he thought, and this was the great confirmation of his dreams.

•

In the years that followed, Spanish efforts to extract the wealth of gold and silver elsewhere in the Americas led to the forced labor of tens of thousands of native people from the shores of North and South America and the Caribbean. Florida was not safe from the menace. Slave raiders would strike again and again until they believed the last of the Calusa were captured to die in the mines of Cuba or Hispaniola. In little more than a generation, the ancient tradition of Calusa life in Florida was wiped away, leaving only a handful of survivors to remember what had been.

The Blue Cloth
April 1562

AMICHUA SAT ON THE DUNES near his home and stared out at the broad blue sea. Day after day he sat and day after day the world seemed little changed, but his fascination never flagged. For most of his nine years of life, it seemed, he had spent watching the changing face of the endless waters, wondering at the waves that never seemed to cease, at the changing light on the ocean, at the strange creatures that lived there. He wondered where it might end, whether there was truly another side. If there was it was too far to swim, he knew. The elders who spoke of such things told stories of men who had traveled far to the south to trade with other tribes, and of lands far away across the water. Maybe, he thought, that was true, but in his mind, he sat at the edge of the whole world and beyond there was nothing but water.

His Timucuan village of Saturiwa sat in an ideal, but perhaps unfortunate, location, aside a broad harbor carved from the dunes by the tides and the river. Before it lay the protected bay, and beyond, the river mouth which admitted the salty tides. Both were filled with fish and shellfish, turtles and manatees, and always the sea gave up its bounty.

On this day, however, the sea would reveal something the youngster had never seen before. Out on the face of the ocean appeared a series of white smudges which slowly grew. He shouted and ran toward the village calling, but others had already seen the strange shapes. In a moment all the village was abuzz, a fact that amused Amichua immensely. Today would not be an ordinary day, and today he would learn something new about the world. Were they animals, he wondered? Even the elders seemed unsure.

Like the rest of the town, Amichua had heard the rumors that had made the long trip from Caribbean islands by word of mouth. Relayed by traders, news of other places was always welcome and fascinating, and human curiosity demanded detailed accounts from those who had seen them. Among those stories last year had been the unsettling news of strangers in enormous boats, wearing strange clothes and speaking strange tongues.

The next day changed his life forever. At high tide ships had begun to enter the bay. The people of Saturiwa could see the blue banners and the fleur-de-lis symbol of the French king atop the masts but had no inkling of what they might represent. One by one the ships crossed into the river and dropped their anchors in the protected waters. Then long boats filled with men had been rowed to their shore. Their silvery armor gleamed in the summer sun, and as they stood upon the sands, they made clear to their cautious Timucuan observers that they meant no harm. They brought a colorful blanket and laid it upon the top of the dune and placed a variety of gifts and trinkets upon it before retreating a short distance away.

Amichua watched from hiding as two of the men of the tribe approached the offerings and began to examine them. Then they took a few objects and returned to the gathered men of the tribe, where they had a brief and animated discussion. Within minutes two of the men returned to the beach and cautiously approached the strangers, then sat upon the sands in a clear offer of peace. Two of the strange men came forward and sat with them and the four began to communicate, using their hands to make signs and indicate meanings.

Amichua marveled at the changes that came over the village during the following days. The newcomers spoke a language at once strange and delightful to his ears, and soon erected a wonderful stone pillar near the mouth of the river. To the chief of the tribe they presented a beautiful coat the color of the sky in a token of their friendship. They also gave small gifts to many of the men of the tribe, beautiful tokens of colored glass that many marveled to see. Yet all too soon the men returned to their ships and sailed away, leaving Amichua and his Timucuan tribe eager for further contact.

The Nail
October 1565

JACQUES DEVEREAUX WAS A PATIENT MAN. Now, he knew, he would need all he could muster. Sitting on the sandy shore of the Atlantic Ocean, Jacques was once again on Florida soil, and once again stranded. Behind him, a low ridge of sand dunes was covered by stumpy palmetto bushes, sea oats and vines. They had chopped their way inland in search of fresh water, encountering a variety of snakes in the process, only to find a long lagoon filled with brackish water, scarcely drinkable. Still, it was better than nothing. As he sat facing the sea, watching the surf pound against the hull and exposed bottom of his ship, he pondered again the reckless and impatient leadership which had brought him to this unhappy state of affairs.

Jacques was familiar, by now, with the experience of being stranded. He had arrived in Florida only months earlier with Jean Ribault to join the French settlement of Fort Caroline on the River of May. Rene Goulaine de Laudonnière had convinced him and his fellow Huguenots that they would be free to practice the religion that had led to years of bloody fighting in France. The thought of a vast New World, full of free land, exotic peoples, and exotic foods, had been enough to tempt him to joining the expedition.

His arrival in the New World was a shock. Not only was Fort Caroline not the thriving settlement he had imagined, but their arrival had also been just in time to prevent the flight of the original colonists. Led by Laudonnière, they had been there two years and were nearly starving. Luckily, Ribault had arrived with seventy women and five hundred soldiers before the settlers could carry out their plans.

Jacques had been pleased to see the column Ribault had erected marking France's claim. The settlers had made friends with the nearby Timucuan village and the natives' gifts of fish, corn, beans, and squash had helped them survive. Ribault had won great favor by giving their chieftain, Saturiba, a blue cape with gold fleur-de-lis as a symbol of their friendship.

Jacques had quickly befriended several of the young natives, who were both helpful and interested in all things French. One young man named Amichua had made a strong impression on him with his perception and curiosity, and they became fast friends.

Devereaux had soon learned, however, that many of his fellows were not really interested in settling the new world, but rather in plundering Spanish gold and returning to France as wealthy men. The scarce food supplies and primitive conditions were difficult, and some of the original settlers had stolen two small ships and taken to attempting raids upon Spanish shipping. One French ship had been captured, the crew probably hanged, he thought, before the second fled back to the colony to face the music. Now they had provoked the Spanish and made them aware of their presence. Impatience, Jacques thought. It was all because of impatience.

The new arrivals had only a few days to unload stores and begin to settle into their new home, hoping that they could soon set things in order and develop farms and social structures. Then the Spanish had come.

As soon as the Spanish ships had appeared, sailors manning their four largest ships had cut their anchors and fled. All that then remained for the defense and transport of the settlers had been the small vessels able to cross the sand bar, which were sheltered safely within the river. The Spanish had soon sailed away again, but Ribault had then decided that they should attack the Spanish, who were no doubt based nearby.

"More impatience," thought Jacques. 'They are always in a rush.'

Soon after, Jacques and the bulk of the colony's fighting men were aboard their remaining ships and approaching the Spanish camp at the River of Dolphins. Waiting at the river's mouth for favorable tides, they had been caught unawares by one of the legendary September storms. Their ships were soon driven south by massive waves and eighty-knot winds and now lay broken on the beaches, scattered along miles of this wilderness coast.

After that disaster, Jacques knew, patience would be a commodity in very short supply, indeed. Soon the sailors and soldiers on the beach were confronting Ribault, demanding they return to their Fort Caroline, at the River of May. Never mind that it was more than one hundred fifty miles to the north, and that the Spanish were now between them and their fort.

Jacques had watched as more stranded Frenchmen marched up the beach from the south where, no doubt, the rest of the French vessels also lay stranded. Eventually more than three hundred were gathered, and they had only a small amount of food or stores salvaged from any of the wrecks. With patience, he thought, perhaps they could deal with the Indians, as they had so successfully at Fort Caroline.

Jacques Devereaux was, unfortunately he thought, not in charge of the expedition. He followed along dutifully when Ribault gave into the demands and ordered the men to march north toward Fort Caroline. Some three hundred twenty men were accounted for on the march. Hundreds more from other vessels were missing and probably shipwrecked elsewhere along the coast. As they moved northward, they soon found evidence that some of the others had marched ahead of them.

Weeks of struggling through soft sand or the undergrowth of the dunes had brought the men at last to a large inlet, where swift tidal currents blocked their way. Inland, a large lagoon stretched for miles to the north and south. They were effectively cut off from the mainland and were quickly running out of food.

Finally, on October 10, who should appear across the water but a body of armed Spanish soldiers, equipped with longboats. Spanish ships approached offshore. "Now we've got real trouble," Jacques thought, "and we've marched all this way to find it."

The Spanish leader was Pedro Menéndez de Avilés. Menéndez, whose mission was to destroy the French intrusion upon the Spanish claim to Florida, planned to eliminate the threat to Spanish gold shipments. Ribault negotiated with Menéndez and agreed that the French would surrender and be ferried across the inlet in the Spanish vessels.

"I would sooner place my head in the mouth of a lion," thought Jacques. "It's better to take our chances swimming than to trust the Spanish," he said aloud and many around him agreed. After a parley, it was finally accepted that the party would divide. Those who accepted the Spanish offer would travel by boat. Those who would not accept would take their chances with whatever they could find.

Of the three hundred twenty Frenchmen, one hundred seventy turned south, marching with Jacques back the direction they had come. Desperation they could face. Surrender to Spanish soldiers they could not.

Behind them, the remaining French soldiers and sailors were bound and ferried across the inlet by the Spanish. After questioning, sixteen men, either Catholics or musicians, were separated from the group. The rest, including Ribault, were bound together in small groups and led away through the dunes to the north. There the Spanish soldiers followed the orders of Menéndez, drew their swords, and began to murder their captives. It took hours, but in the end, every man died.

The bloody slaughter of the one hundred thirty-four men by Menéndez was only a repeat of a scene two weeks earlier, at which the earlier party of one hundred ninety-eight shipwrecked men were slaughtered after surrendering. The inlet at which the terrible events occurred was known forever after as Matanzas, the "Place of Slaughter."

Jacques Devereaux, however, was a patient man and determined to find his own way to safety.

The one-hundred and seventy remaining Frenchmen marched back to the south, scouring the beach for anything of use which had washed ashore from their ships. At length they came upon the wreck of the *Trinity* at Cape Canaveral. Salvaging timbers and planks, they set about building a fort and a smaller vessel with which they could sail themselves back to Europe.

It was already November when a Spanish vessel dropped anchor near their improvised defenses and a group of Spanish soldiers came ashore. The French were mostly unarmed, but instead of attacking, the Spanish offered safe passage to Europe as prisoners of war. Made desperate by hunger, deprivation, and clouds of mosquitoes, another hundred and fifty of the French survivors accepted the offer. They were more fortunate than their fellows because they were ultimately transported to Spain as ransom hostages.

For Jacques Devereaux, however, the choice was simple. He would be patient and take his chances with what he knew and trusted. He and the remaining twenty Frenchmen worked with the timbers and nails they had salvaged and eventually completed a small vessel. Sailing at night, they slipped unnoticed past the new Spanish base at San Augustin and headed for the River of May. It was their good fortune to miss the mouth of the river and sail by mistake into a neighboring bayou, where they beached their boat. After completing their trip on foot, the group was prepared to run the last several hundred yards to Fort Caroline when they were halted by a question.

"Wait a moment, have patience, my friends. Is that not a Spanish vessel which lies in the river?" Jacques asked.

It was, indeed, and part of a fleet which brought the three hundred Spanish troops who now held the fort they had known as Caroline.

During the very storm that had wrecked the French fleet, before he had slaughtered the prisoners on the beach, Menéndez had marched his troops northward and fallen upon Laudonnière and his settlers from the undefended land side. They had attacked the fort and settlement in force, killing hundreds of the settlers. Fifty women and children were taken prisoner, as were half a dozen musicians.

Laudonnière and sixty colonists had escaped in a small vessel and fled to France and with them they took the last shred of French control in Florida. Menéndez then hanged thirty prisoners marked, as he said, "Not as Frenchmen, but as Huguenots."

Now the last twenty survivors of Florida's French colony were stranded. The Spaniards had taken their last hope of refuge and renamed it San Mateo and were reinforcing its defenses. Jacques alone avoided the despair that overcame the group and thought of the kindness of the curious youth, Amichua. "What of the

Timucuans, who have been so good to us in the past. Shall we not seek them out?" he asked.

In desperation the small group turned to their neighbors and shared their story of woe. It was there that they found comfort, food and shelter, and it was there that the French survivors would leave their indelible mark upon Florida. Yet no one would know of their survival, and no stories would find their way back to France. They were lost to the world.

Two years later, a private French fleet was raised by Dominic de Gourgues, bent upon revenge for the slaughter. When his fleet suddenly appeared at Fort San Mateo it meted out a harsh revenge upon the Spanish occupiers, killing them as the Spanish had their countrymen. Thirty survivors of the fighting were hanged upon the trees nearby and de Gourgues mounted a plaque which stated that they were hung, "Not as Spaniards, but as traitors, thieves and murderers."

When these terrible events occurred, Jacques and his surviving companions were many miles away, living happily unaware among the civilized and peaceful Timucuan natives of the north Florida hills.

Although few of the Frenchmen ever gave up their hope of returning to France, Jacques Devereaux adapted himself patiently to the ways of the Timucuans and eventually took a wife from the tribe and raised his children in the forests. There he taught them stories of far-away France and warned them of the brutality of the Spanish, who had destroyed their dreams.

With patience as his ally, Jacques and his companions made a decent life among the Timucuan people and carefully avoided contact with the Spanish at San Augustin, who continued to believe that they and they alone influenced and controlled La Florida.

May 1668

IT WAS A SHORT SAIL FROM NEW PROVIDENCE in the English-controlled Bahamas to the coast of Florida, and Captain Robert Searle was confident that the trip would be worth the effort. Like many others, Searle was a pirate. In the minds of Searle and his compatriots it was an honest living, and Spain's possessions in the New World were ripe for picking. The Spanish fleets, after all, couldn't be everywhere at once, and now he had his motivation. Revenge for a Spanish raid on the Bahamas would shield him from the punishment of British authorities. and the lure of riches made the prospects sweet for his men.

Like many of the privateers, Searle found the habit hard to break. Searle could smell the money and awaited only an informal nod from the English authorities to resume his preferred trade. The moment had come as his ship lay at anchor at New Providence, in the English Bahamas, a favored port for the buccaneers. Two Spanish warships, bent upon revenge for the earlier attacks, had raided the town, but did little real damage. It was all the excuse Searle and his compatriots needed to resume their ways. Now he would return the rude greetings. Searle's plans were developing nicely and his would soon be the name that would strike terror into residents of Spanish Florida.

Efforts to build new towns and fortified harbors in Florida were Spain's biggest failure. Only two settlements had ever survived more than a few months, though efforts were made at several points along her fourteen-hundred-mile coastline. Florida was an isolated outpost, surrounded by unfriendly forces, and little more than a port of refuge for the treasure fleets.

Spain still had a purpose for the settlement of San Augutin. A short distance from the coast her great river of plundered gold and silver plate passed aboard the treasure ships. That trove of riches was boosted by the addition of precious gems, pearls, spices, and other goods brought from distant Asia and carried across Mexico or Nicaragua to be re-boarded on ships bound for Spain. San Augustin wasn't a treasure port, only a refuge for ships fleeing storms or English attack.

Over almost 150 years a small town had grown near the crude fort while Spanish missionaries had worked to develop a chain of mission churches across the inland areas of Florida's peninsula. They had linked them with crude wagon trails to bring supplies and Christianity to the natives.

On the entire North American mainland, only San Augustin flew the Spanish standards above their wooden stockade. The English privateer Sir Francis Drake had sacked and burned the nascent settlement eighty years earlier. Now re-built, it was a tempting target for Searle's ruthless men.

•

Hector Ynes didn't care much for Pancho. The man was constantly driving him, shouting at him, demanding that he stand straighter, hold his musket just so, march this way and that. It was all more than he cared to bother with. Hector could tolerate it only for so long and that was just long enough to collect the tiny cash stipend he was awarded for being part of the militia defending the town of San Agustin.

What should he care about San Agustin anyway? Hector didn't get much respect on the streets. People called him "mestizo" because his mother was a native and his father a Spaniard. He was one of hundreds of mestizos and mulattoes in the town. Hector's father had been sent back to Mexico and his Timucuan mother had long since returned to her tribal village to the north, but Hector preferred the rustic town to the primitive Indian village. His main reason for staying, though, and the only person he truly cared about, was Elena.

Elena was the daughter of the doctor, Señor Suarez. His potions, Hector thought, were no match for the intoxicating sight of Elena. Hector daily detoured from his route to pass by the doctor's home, hoping for even a glimpse of his desire. Elena was a recent arrival from Spain and enough to inspire him to carry the musket correctly and stand a bit straighter. Pancho was pleased, but it was all because Elena lived in San Agustin, and for that, Hector would do his best.

Medicine was a primitive art in San Agustin, but that ability was boosted by the skill of Dr. Henry Woodward of South Carolina, who had been brought to the town as a prisoner years earlier. He resided with Dr. Suarez and was now practically part of the family. His crime had been to attempt to settle in lands claimed by both England and Spain, known as Carolina. Unlike the Suarez family, though, Woodward's fervent hopes were about to come true.

Standing by the wall of the rough wooden presidio that defended the village, Hector saw himself as the keeper of the peace and the defender of honor. After years of living in the town, Hector had become used to the comings and goings of the shipping that used the harbor of Matanzas Bay. He knew the cut of Spanish sail and the profile of the colony's own frigate which patrolled the nearby coast, often escorting arriving vessels. As it returned this day, he saw that it was accompanied by a larger galleon, by looks a merchant ship from New Spain to the south. It was no doubt laden with wheat flour and other essentials that couldn't be coaxed from the sandy soils of the Florida coast. "A good sign," Hector thought. "We shall have plenty of bread in the coming weeks."

At the sight of the arriving Spanish vessels, Governor Don Francisco de la Guerra y de la Vega had relaxed. Both ships were approaching the bar and would be crossing on the evening tide to anchor in Matanzas Bay. Tomorrow would be a day of transferring cargo.

Francisco was responsible for her defense and the military officers answered to him. "Have the men stand down, sergeant major, and return the weapons to the armory," he told his aide. Sergeant Major Nicolas Ponce de Leon the Younger was the senior officer of the presidio and eager to show his worth. Promotion, he knew, only came by extraordinary performance. He felt certain he would have his chance.

With the other militiamen, Hector dutifully added his matchlock musket to the long rack within the stout armory. Nearby, barrels of gunpowder and skins filled with shot lined the walls. From the wooden stockade walls of the presidio, stout cannons were aimed toward Matanzas Bay and the waterfront. Hector had never seen such a collection of arms before and thought that, if nothing else, the town was well defended. This day his idea would be sorely tested.

Leaving the defenses, Hector strolled casually, moving up the dusty street toward the small cantina that was a favorite respite from the summer heat or winter chill. Already the May weather had turned warm, and the near cloudless skies had generated only a modest breeze. The dark interior of the cantina would be cooler, and a glass of excellent Spanish Tempranillo wine a welcome reward for his tolerance of the endless orders of Pancho. Grilled meat sliced from the freshly-killed hog turning on the spit behind the building satisfied his only remaining desire, aside for the pining in his heart for Elena. Would she never notice him in his smart uniform, and see how he worshiped her?

Dreams of her filled his head later that evening. Safe within the walls of the doctor's residence, Elena, too, slept peacefully as the evening wore into midnight. Like Pancho and Don Francisco himself, the people of Spanish San Agustin had never heard the name of Robert Searle, or John Davis, for that matter. None would dream that the clever Searle had captured the Spanish merchant galleon with the guns of his own ship, used it to lure the frigate close, and captured it as well. Most of the people of San Agustin knew only restful slumbers.

One man in the town, however, had noticed something unusual. From his small fishing boat, the sleepless Corporal Miguel de Monzon heard a sound. Was it muffled oarlocks? What could that mean, he wondered? Now from across the dark waters the sound was multiplied. Not one, but several boats were rowing toward the town.

Immediately suspicious, Monzon pulled in his lines and put his own oars to work drawing him back toward the wharf a short distance away. Hearing the distinct sounds of the following boats, he called out a challenge. The answer came in a volley of shot that struck him as he stepped upon the wharf. Twice wounded, Monzon raised the alarm. "To arms! Defend the town!" he screamed, as he scrambled for the safety of the presidio.

Alerted by the shouts and the sound of muskets, people began to stir and rush to see what was happening. Hector also heard the commotion and knew that trouble was afoot. But what of Elena? Would this be his chance to prove his worth and perhaps save her from attackers? His next thought was of his weapon and those of the rest of his small company, carefully stacked and locked within the armory. He dashed from his rough cabin and turned toward the presidio, joining a rush of startled residents running chaotically in the streets. The attackers were already among them.

Sergeant Major Ponce emerged from his quarters only to see a dozen of the invaders running across the plaza toward Government House, cutting him off from the Presidio. The town was already over-run. Powerless to stop the attackers, Ponce turned back toward the residential neighborhood and began directing people away from the attackers. Within minutes he led almost one hundred forty, including seventy unarmed militiamen, to the relative safety of the woods south of the town.

The governor also heard the tumult and saw the buccaneers advancing across the plaza, some shooting unarmed men as others seized women and children and led them back toward the waterfront as hostages. Realizing that he was a prime target, he quickly slipped out a rear door and ran through the darkness toward the stronghold of the presidio. The officers there had heard the fighting, and quickly opened the gates to allow him to join the wounded Monzon and a few dozen citizens and militiamen inside the walls.

"Load the cannons!" the governor shouted, but already Searle was leading his men in a frontal attack upon the wooden stockade. "Too late, every man to the walls!" came the countermanding order of the sergeant major as the militia struggled to load their muskets. Quickly they raised a sharp fire and repulsed the first assault, but the pirates were being rapidly reinforced as Searle's men responded to the rattle of muskets.

Hiding in the shadow of a house, Hector could see several bodies lying in the streets around the open square and a house on fire opposite. He dodged between buildings, attempting to make his way toward the presidio, where he would at least have arms and companions. At last, avoiding detection, he made his way to the edge of the plaza, from where he could see that the attackers had now concentrated on the presidio and had turned their backs to the town. He was effectively cut off from his weapon and behind enemy lines. His knife was his only defense against the swords, pistols, and muskets wielded by the pirates.

Reversing his path, Hector moved quickly through the deserted streets, thinking now only of Elena. Was she safe? Silently he sneaked down alleyways and through gardens as the sounds of the battle boomed behind him. At last, he reached the doctor's home and found the door barricaded. "Hello, are you there?" he called in Spanish, but got no answer. Putting his shoulder to the door he shoved, and barely missed being struck by the musket ball that splintered the wood near his shoulder. "Don't shoot, it's me, Hector, of the militia!" he shouted. "I've come to lead you to safety!"

A face appeared briefly at a window and then the door opened. "Why have you come for us?" the doctor demanded. "Why aren't you fighting the enemy?"

"I have no weapons, and the invaders are attacking the presidio. We must fly to the safety of the woods, for they will surely return and find you all here and burn you out."

"Then let us hurry," the doctor replied, returning to the house. Hector stood for a moment in the doorway, looking into the darkened interior. Suddenly the doctor was there before him, carrying a heavy sack, and leading his wife and daughter. It was the closest Hector had ever been to Elena, and for a moment he froze, his heart in his throat. Then, with a quick smile at the girl, he turned.

"This way!" he said softly, dashing down the street away from the sounds of battle. At the edge of the town, he followed a familiar trail into the woods, moving swiftly. Suddenly he found himself with a sword at his throat and a demand for his name. "I'm Hector Ynes!" he almost shouted. "Of the militia!" he added. The sword was withdrawn, and he was told to enter a small clearing beyond. There, huddled in the darkness, was a large group of others who had fled. Hector was pleased to see about seventy militiamen, including many of his friends, but they seemed to have virtually no weapons among them. He turned back to accept the expected thanks of Elena and her family, but they had already hurried to join the other civilians.

"Hector, fall in with the others," the sergeant-major ordered, and he did as he was told.

"What can we do without our muskets or swords?" he whispered to his friend in the darkness.

"We can only await orders," came the reply.

The refugees huddled in the woods, killing only the ferocious mosquitoes, as the far more fearsome sounds of battle raged only a league away.

After more than ninety minutes of repeated assaults against the presidio, Searle's attackers had made no progress, but had taken thirty casualties. Eleven of those lay dead. Inside the stronghold five of the defenders had also died and five more were seriously wounded. Only twenty-one men were still fit to defend the wooden stockade. Enthusiasm for the fight was finally flagging on both sides.

At Searle's orders, the Englishmen withdrew to sack the town and search for additional hostages. Their wounded were loaded into boats and returned to the ships as the pirates conducted a thorough search for the town's doctor. They stripped the town of silver and gold, raiding the treasury and the cathedral. They pillaged the tiny hospital, taking the bandages and meager medicines stored there.

The governor saw the opportunity presented by the English withdrawal and sent messengers to attempt to round up more of his fugitive troops. At first light, Hector and his seventy companions were led by Sergeant Major Ponce, first sneaking around the town's stockade walls, followed by a mad dash into the presidio. There they were finally armed with swords and muskets. Things were looking up, he thought.

"Governor, we have more company!"

The unwelcome call from the watch alerted them to the arrival of yet a third ship into Matanzas Bay. It was the *Cagway*, Searle's flagship, and no doubt the source of the pirates who had used their own vessels against them. Aboard the *Cagway*, yet more English raiders were ready to join the fight for San Agustin. The Spanish governor knew that he had only minutes to attack the enemy ashore before they would be reinforced and could renew their attacks against the presidio. Quickly he ordered a sortie, and sent out two squads of twenty-five men. Hector, like the rest of the Spanish forces, had never been in a firefight and moved reluctantly toward the enemy.

Afraid to spread out from the perceived safety of numbers, the Spanish militia advanced in a huddle, ready to fire their clumsy muzzle-loaders at the first sign of movement. Hector, determined to prove his worth, crept at the head of the pack. It wasn't long before their approach was noticed, and the shouts of the English rang along the streets. The small English force still ransacking the homes and shops in search of valuables organized a resistance in short order and began a sharp fire from their places of concealment. At the first volley, Hector felt a sharp sting and looked down to see a dark hole in his leather jerkin. Reaching his hand to his lower chest, he could feel a wetness that confirmed his fears. He slumped to his knees in the street. Within minutes two of the leaders of the sorties were also wounded and the governor ordered them to retreat to safety. They fled in a disorganized rush, dragging their wounded along.

All through the day the raiders continued their sacking and looting, searching houses for hidden safe places and carrying hostages back to their ships in the bay. The Spanish militia watched helplessly, and the cannons of the fort were of no use against ships that now held hostage their wives, children, and friends. Hector lay in pain, but his fear was not of death, but of his precious Elena. Was she still safely concealed, or had the English found them?

At last, long after dark, the English pirates withdrew from the town, but kept their anchors fixed in the bay. Cautious probing by the Spanish soon convinced them that the raiders had retreated from the town, and they began the disheartening work of collecting the casualties from the streets and houses. More than sixty were dead and many injured. Another seventy were missing, apparently being held for ransom on the ships at anchor.

Early the next morning a small boat left the *Cagway* under a flag of truce. Negotiations were soon conducted and as a sign of honorable negotiations, Searle ordered that the captive women were to be released, unmolested by their captors. With that sign of faith, over the next six days the governor of San Agustin provided the wood, meat and barrels of water demanded by the raiders in exchange for their remaining hostages.

Low on provisions, the governor also managed to convince Searle to release some of the food stores on the captured Spanish galleon. Soon the crews of the two Spanish ships, and a ration of flour, were safely ashore. On the final day the royal treasurer was released, and the English sailed from the bay with their ships and booty.

Of the good English doctor, there could be found no trace, for he had fled with the attackers and was no doubt caring for the wounded Englishmen on the ships. Hector opened his eyes two days later to find himself in the town's rustic hospital under the care of Doctor Suarez. He was relieved to see the concerned face of the doctor's lovely daughter, Elena, looking back at him. He smiled through his pain.

The Dried Corn
May 1669

THE AFTERNOON'S WARMTH HAD SLOWED the speed of his wooden hoe, but Tecofalo had a goal of tilling around the entire patch of half-grown corn plants before dinner, and the weeds were suffering as a result. Corn was an important staple for the young man's family and provided steady nourishment in times of lean hunting. Even so, Tecofalo's efforts were brought to a sudden halt by the sight before him. A pair of riders in polished armor and helmets, mounted upon large brown horses, had suddenly appeared on the narrow trace of a road that led from San Agustin through his village of San Luis de Apalachee.

As Tecofalo watched, an ox-cart appeared from behind the trees. A moment later a second cart came into view. From his position in the corn field, he was well concealed from the Spanish, but watched their approach without fear. The Spanish Road was the best way to travel by land, and his village astride the route remained a trading point for the two cultures and many surrounding villages. The Spanish had been a part of his community for many years.

San Luis was the largest and most prosperous of the eight dozen missions the Spanish had established across Florida. It had been built upon the site of the original hill-top village of Anhaica. Like most of the missions, it was served by traveling Franciscan friars, but some others had been abandoned after attacks by hostile tribes. San Luis had persevered.

Spain needed the Apalachee for their rich agriculture. Skilled farmers, they produced an abundance which they readily traded to the Spanish, as well as some neighboring tribes. The alliance had brought a sort of stability and prosperity to San Luis, but tensions had flared from time to time.

The Apalachee had long been regarded as the richest and most-powerful native culture in La Florida and the Spanish had been eager to employ these resourceful farmers to help supply their town of San Agustin, as well as the network of missions, with the produce of their fields. To secure their alliance, the Spanish had participated in subduing certain hostile neighboring tribes.

Following Spanish overtures, they had been invited by tribal elders to bring their friars and their soldiers and the two cultures had cooperated in building the town. Following the lead of the tribal chieftains, most of the population had accepted the Spanish religion and now incorporated many Spanish words in their language. The children attended a school run by the friars and learned about the far-away world of Spain.

Although most of his family worked closely with the Spanish, Tecofalo had no trust for them. He shook his head as he watched the lengthening procession with mild contempt before returning to his work. He remembered the stories of the terrible deeds they had done in the name of their mysterious god. He had heard them all from his father and grandfather, who had learned them at the knee of the father of his fathers, the bearded one they called "Chaka." Chaka had come from a land far away called "Fran-cha," but the Spanish had killed his people and taken their town. That knowledge was legendary among his people, who had risen against the first Spanish friars and soldiers. Tecofalo was sure that there were no more people in Fran-cha because the Spanish had killed them all. He wished them gone from his lands forever.

The colonists in San Agustin raised cattle and had some success in the cultivation of citrus fruits, principally oranges from Valencia in Spain, but most of the other crops from the Mediterranean region failed in Florida's hot, damp summer climate. Most Spanish colonies required constant subsidies of both cash and food. It was only natural that they should begin to depend upon the successful agriculture of the natives. Beans, corn, and squash were augmented with several leafy greens, as well as gathered nuts and fruits from the surrounding forests.

The Apalachee, in turn, had benefited from the technology that had been brought by the Spanish settlers in their midst. Refined metal for axes, plows and adzes helped farmers and builders. Spanish mules helped do the work, while their cattle, pigs, and chickens helped feed the growing population. Many young native women hoped to marry a Spanish soldier, because it was a guarantee of higher social status and a somewhat more comfortable life. Their Mestizo children now made up almost a quarter of the community of two thousand.

From the original small chapel and log house, the town had risen around the broad, round central plaza. Now a large church stood on its western side and many of the Apalachee people followed the words of the two friars that lived there. Nearby was the rectangular European-style home of the friars, along with their barns and chicken coops. The workshops of the blacksmith and carpenter, the potter and the harness-maker stood nearby.

Surrounding the plaza stood other Spanish log-and-plank houses, the homes of the Spanish deputy-governor and his family and those of his clerks and administrators. A garrison house sheltered the small group of soldiers who sometimes drilled and marched in the plaza, or practiced with their muskets, swords, and pikes.

The eastern side of the plaza was dominated by the round lodge of the Apalachee people. Like the church, it was constructed using the boles of tall trees. The chieftains had decreed its design using important numbers representing the order of things. It would be as tall as ten men and as wide as forty paces.

The Sachem blessed the chosen spot, broad and level with long views to the lower lands, and placed a sacred totem on the ground. Corn, fish, fruit, feathers, and water were included in the sacrifice. Then eight men stood in the center and turned their backs to the ceremonial marker, facing the directions of the earth and sky. Each strode slowly forward twenty steps, counting one pace for each finger of their hands and one for each toe of their feet. When they stopped, the gathered people could see the size of the new tribal lodge and they were pleased. The watching Spanish friars, who warned against such heretical beliefs, were not. Yet here the walls would rise.

The resulting building was a hundred and twenty feet in diameter. The enormous timbers leaned inward to form a dome, supported by short vertical columns standing in a ring just inside the walls. These also supported a ring of raised platforms, a sort of low balcony which allowed those in the back of the gatherings to see over the heads of the crowd and observe ceremonies in the center. The center of the roof was open to the sky, allowing the smoke of the ritual fires to rise. When the tribe gathered for ceremonial purposes, a thousand people might be contained within, seated on the ground or on one of the elevated platforms. Whole hogs, deer, or other game could be roasted over the central fires. It was a remarkable testament to the future of the town.

Dozens of children, both Spanish and Mestizos, filled the homes and slept on rough pallets laid upon the dirt floors. They played games in the plaza and spent most days in the Spanish schoolhouse learning to read about the Spanish homeland and the religion they kept there.

Patiently the tribe sat through the sermons delivered by the brown-robed friar. Knowing only a few words of their Muskogee language, the priest struggled to describe their strange god, who had been tortured to death. "If a man is a god, how can he be killed by other men?" Tecofalo wondered. He puzzled over the story of his return to life. For his part he was happy trusting in the spirits of the winds and waters, the forest trees, and the animals with whom they shared their world. Always when he killed an animal, he would thank it for its sacrifice, taking a moment to bless it with his meditation upon its life. That, he thought, was enough.

•

As the Spanish caravan passed, Tecofalo resumed his work. It had been a dry spring. Rain was needed, or the corn crop would be small. For two days prior he had worked carrying skins full of water from the well to his corn plot, carefully rationing out the liquid to the roots of each plant, hoping to nurse them to growth. The stunted stalks were not encouraging, but at least the game was still plentiful.

Three days later, two hours of storms preceded a spate of cooler weather, and he knew the crops would flourish. There would be plenty of food for his wife, Tlacata, daughter Sara, and all the children of the tribe. Life was good, but Tecofalo dreamed of better things: his own horses, a musket, and black powder for hunting. These things could only come from the

Spanish, and they would not trade them, but a young man who could dream could also plan.

When evening drew near and Tecofalo could smell the aromas of the evening meal, he left his work among his garden of corn and carried his stout hoe back to camp, placing it carefully among his possessions next to his home. There he knew it would be safe, for no one in the Apalachee village would touch the property of another without permission.

After washing himself he walked to the central kitchen of his small clan. There the women had prepared the communal dinner and were ladling generous portions of a thick stew onto shallow wooden platters. Greens, corn-meal bread, and roasted rabbit were offered as well. He was soon satisfied, and relaxed to share a pipe of tobacco with his closest friends.

"What can we do to earn horses and weapons?" one man asked the others when they had withdrawn to talk. "These things will make us stronger, but the Spanish do not wish us to be strong. They demand only obedience."

"I refuse to obey these men," Tecofalo told the others. "They are the sons of the men who killed the people of the village of Fran-cha. My fathers knew of their treachery. The Tocobago obeyed the Spanish and now there are few Tocobago people remaining. The Mocama people, too, are mostly gone. They died of sickness, the sickness that comes from the Spanish. If you allow me, I will take what we need from them, for they have a debt to me and my fathers. I will take their horses and we will keep them in the forests."

At this suggestion there was a division of opinion. "We do not wish to war against the Spanish. Their weapons are strong," said one, "and only they have the horse, which can outrun the swiftest warrior."

"We cannot live forever without the things they have, but here it is too difficult to take them. We should wait and take them from those who travel through our lands," said another.

After several minutes of discussion, Tecofalo stopped the argument by explaining what he would do. "We need their horses. If we have a few, soon we will have many. Then we will no longer need the Spanish. There are only two men who watch the horses, and they sit to eat their meal. It is then that I will strike and ride the fastest horse and lead the others that I can take. The Spanish will not know that it was me. We will say that they have escaped."

It took much insistence and cajoling, but at length the group grudgingly agreed to the plan. It was perhaps their best hope of improving the lives of the tribe, and worth the risk involved.

The plan came off almost without a hitch. Four nights later, Tecofalo had quietly slipped the latch on the gate of the Spaniards' corral and led four horses into the darkness without being detected. At first light he had mounted one to hurry on his way. It was then that a chance encounter disrupted his plan. As he crossed the quiet trail that led south of the town, sitting silently on a log aside the road was a robed friar, enjoying his simple breakfast. He looked up, surprised to see the young man astride the horse. Tecofalo turned his head quickly, but was fearful that the man had recognized him.

He took a circuitous route to the south, passed through marshes and sedge-grass prairies, and then turned west, knowing that the Spanish troops would be searching the area carefully. He had to spear an alligator that attempted to take a horse during a river crossing but had no other problems. He hid the horses in the wilderness before turning north toward his destination.

That evening found him safely back in Tallahassee and the welcome of his friends. For several days they kept the horses far from the village, and the watchful eyes of the friars and the small garrison. The troops searched for the horses but could not explain where they had gone. The governor, after making demands of the surprised tribal leaders, assumed an ominous silence.

Each day the young men would take their hoes to their gardens before quietly slipping away to visit and care for their new charges. A few weeks of practice with the horses brought a new sense of confidence to several of the young braves, who rode the animals bareback. The horses, used to the heavy Spanish saddles and gear, seemed to revel in the style as well. Using the horses had allowed the hunters to outflank a herd of deer and carry their prize close to the village in relative ease. They considered the animals a godsend.

All seemed well until late June. Early one morning a reinforcing party of four dozen mounted Spanish soldiers from San Augustin appeared at Tallahassee. Mounted native scouts had encircled the village from the west and quickly located the horses. A tense stand-off ensued.

"We will not leave without our horses and the thieves who stole them," the angry major in charge of the troops demanded from the elders. "If we don't have the thief in our custody within the hour, we shall take ten men of our choosing to be punished for this crime," came the next threat.

A hubbub of voices rose in the tribal council as some of the younger men quietly took positions of defense at the edge of the village, facing the mounted Spanish troops. Quickly the women and children were evacuated from the main camp and led to the relative safety of palmetto thickets, where they were hidden and guarded by a group of warriors. War had arrived on their doorstep.

A few voices said it would be better to fight than to give in. "We can kill many Spanish and take many horses!" one suggested.

"We have more warriors, it is true, but the fire-sticks of the Spanish are too strong, we do not wish to sacrifice so many lives!" proclaimed an elder, to murmurs of agreement.

"I will go with them," Tecofalo told his brothers. "It is my fault that this trouble has come to our people, and I alone will pay with my life. It is only I who can keep peace for our people, I will go now," Tecofalo said and rose and walked from the longhouse. The others stood as well, but none moved to stop him, watching in a reverent silence. They knew that it was very likely that he walked to his death.

Facing the Spanish major and his guard, Tecofalo stood with chin held high. "I am the one you seek. It is my deed. Take me and leave my innocent people in peace, without bloodshed. Do with me as you will," he said, as the native scout translated his words.

The major waved a hand and from behind the troops emerged the robed friar on a pony.

"Is this the man you saw?" asked the major.

"It is he," replied the monk sadly, knowing that he was condemning a man to a terrible fate.

"Take him and bind him," said the major. Then, turning back to the assembled elders of the Apalachee who stood silently a short distance away, he gave them a warning. "Do not think that you may take what belongs to Spain," he shouted. "Follow the wise words of the friars, or death will follow you!"

With that he turned away and the Spanish troops began to slowly withdraw. Tecofalo was seated on a horse and tied to the animal, his own wrists tightly bound behind him. It was a long and uncomfortable journey to San Agustin.

•

"Normally I would just have him hanged," observed the governor when he was told the details of what had happened, "but we are certainly in need of more labor, and he looks strong and healthy. Put him to work with the other slaves on the Castillo, but keep him under close guard. If he attempts to escape, go ahead and hang him." It was a practical solution. The new fortress would be the solution to many problems, and Tecofalo would help to build it.

The Castillo de San Marco would be a stout structure of thick stone, unlike the simple wooden stockade that had fallen easily to English cannons. With the use of the coquina-stone concrete they had devised, the Spanish also were able to begin construction of many other substantial buildings in the town, which soon began to take on the appearance of traditional Mediterranean villages. It was to lead to the brightest period in Florida's Spanish colonial years.

•

Spain's repeated attempts to find gold or silver in the interior of what had proved to be a large continent had resulted in repeated failures. Despite the setbacks, the Spanish continued their efforts to colonize Florida. It was a Spanish discovery and a strategic base that helped to defend the treasure fleets against the repeated raids of English privateers, and they were determined to hold it against their European enemies.

Tecofalo's fate and that of dozens of other Spanish prisoners, was soon clear. From early morning until evening, they dug. Using only crude tools, they heaped large piles of the tiny coquina shells from the deep sands of the coastal dunes near the town. Rinsed of excess sand, the slurry was mixed with lime, then shoveled into kilns to be fired.

It was back-breaking labor without rest and the slaves suffered mightily. Some were overcome by their efforts and weakened by heat, malnutrition, cold and disease. They died at work or in the camp. Replacements were obtained, some brought in the holds of Spanish ships from remote islands.

Slowly the walls of the great fortress began to rise from the trenches the slaves had dug, using only the roughest tools. Soon San Agustin would be an unassailable strong-point, Spanish shipping would be secured on its northern flank, and the English pirates would be driven from the coasts.

June 1680

The authoritative voice sounded across the barnyard, disturbing the early-morning reverie.

"Hector, I've got a job for you."

His crude spade halted its work mucking the manure from the rude barn that housed the horses of the Spanish officers as Hector Ynez took quick advantage of the excuse to catch a few deep breaths and wipe the sweat from his brow even as he turned to face the man who had addressed him. He was used to taking orders from multiple bosses, so he wasn't surprised that the quartermaster had now pinned him down.

"Si, Señor?" Hector replied, hoping that it wouldn't take him all night to finish.

"We need you to go with the detail to get cattle from the finca at Potano, in the land of La Chua"

Hector paused for only a moment before nodding his head obediently. "Sí, Señor. When will we leave?"

"In the morning. Meet them at first light in front of the gate. Don't be late. You should bring a change of clothes, some good stout shoes, too."

"I will wear the best I have, Señor," he replied, knowing that what was on his feet would have to do. Hector, like many of the laboring population of San Agustin, had only one pair of rough sandals, which served in every kind of weather, from freezing winter cold to the storms of summer rains. Potano, though, was enough to get his curiosity up. Despite having carried himself well in battle, he remained constantly under the thumb of others, and in his entire life in the small Spanish colony of San Agustin had never ventured farther than a half-day walk from his home.

The big inland ranches had been established by the Spanish following in the path of the brave Franciscan friars who had established missions across the inland areas. It was almost a week's walk away, and a source of a significant portion of the beef for the stew that was a local staple, augmenting the plentiful fish brought in at the salty riverfront.

Hector knew that that hike ahead of him would be difficult, but he was excited at the chance to see a bit more of Florida at last, even if it meant time away from his beautiful wife, Elena, who had defied her father to marry him, and been disowned as a result. His young son, Miguel, was his pride and joy.

Wrapping his small personal supply of fruit and tortillas in his thin blanket made his kit complete, and the starry morning seemed perfect for the start of an adventure as he made his way to the tall columns that marked the city gate. He waited in the dark, tapping his feet excitedly, until at last he heard approaching voices and made out the forms of two mounted officers and a low cart pulled by a pair of oxen. He quickly recognized the others he would be traveling with and knew that he should have no difficulty getting along with the group. San Agustin was a small town, and among all its citizens there was only one man who seemed to do everything possible to make his life difficult. Pancho would not be among their expedition.

Other than his lovely wife and son, the frontier held little more for Hector than hard work, military drills, and primitive life in a rustic home little better than a shed. Yet his die had been cast, and now he was to travel to an even more primitive ranch deep in the wilds, far from even the simple comforts of the town. He shrugged to himself. Life was little more than such challenges, he thought.

With a minimum of discussion, the group was soon on the road, Hector happily perched on the back of the wagon with the supplies, where he had been invited to ride while the road was relatively good. Once in the thick of the woods, however, the oxen struggled harder to pull the narrow-wheeled cart through the deep sand. Hector was often called upon to chop fronds from the plentiful palmetto shrubs to throw into the sandy path of the cart, and from time to time was forced to push the wheels to help get through softer patches.

That evening the group made camp under spreading oaks, their long beards of moss swaying gently in the breeze that fanned the glowing embers of the cook fire. Hector's eyelids fluttered as he watched the dancing shadows, holding off needed sleep to savor the moments of freedom.

The second day they followed the road westward, although Hector thought it little more than a trail. At times it was difficult to see where it might turn next as it threaded through prairies of tall cabbage palms and tangles of low palmettos. They were deep in the lands of the native people, but he saw no sign of their presence.

The next day brought the group to the banks of the broad Rio de San Juan. They paused to rest near the sluggish expanse and could see the water crowded with what at first appeared to be driftwood. "Alligators are thick here," the group's leader commented, and nervous nods seemed to be the uniform response.

As they followed the stream toward the ford that would allow them to cross, Hector nervously eyed the banks of the river which could occasionally be seen through the undergrowth. At each glance he could make out more of the dark lines upon the waters, the dark knobs of watching eyes visible above the water that hid the long line of their powerful jaws. They kept their bodies submerged, but Hector knew from experience that they were often gigantic. Hunters had dragged one into the city only a few months before and its massive jaws were half as long as he was tall. He had a very healthy desire to avoid getting near one of the monsters.

Happily, the party soon came to a perfect camp site only a few hundred feet from the bayous of the River of San Juan and their leader called a halt for the night. Here, Hector believed, safe from the threat of attack, they could sleep in peace. Tomorrow, and no sooner, he might be forced to face his fears. He slept the sleep of the honestly weary.

•

The hunter lay quietly concealed among the branches of the spreading Live Oak tree. It was an ideal hiding place. Branches held thick festoons of grey Spanish moss, their filaments disguising him from his unsuspecting prey. The massive trunk of the tree, more than six feet thick, held a sprawling network of solid limbs. Some touched the ground like massive outriggers, creating an oaken pathway that spanned more than one hundred thirty feet.

The thick masses of dark-green, two-inch long leaves were a permanent fixture, for the oak, one of hundreds in the sprawling natural grove, was never without them. Unlike its northern cousins this tree had no need to shed its leaves in winter. There was no fear of heavy snow that might burden its limbs to the breaking point. Instead, it waited until spring when the growth of new leaves would push the old from its limbs. The ground was carpeted with the fallen leaves, and little grew beneath them. The clearing made an ideal place to camp for unsuspecting travelers.

The hunter watched carefully as the small party pitched their simple lean-to shelter to repel the morning dew or unexpected rain. He watched with interest as the strangers tethered their horses and oxen and fed them hay from a small cart. His interest was piqued at the intense scent of meat roasting on a small fire.

Just who were these strange creatures? The hunter could not know. He had expected perhaps an unsuspecting deer that might wander beneath his perch, or perhaps a turkey or even a careless raccoon. Now, with the arrival of this group, his hunt was certainly spoiled for the night, yet he lingered, watching the activities in the camp. Silently he flexed his toes, his sharp claws gripping tightly into the gnarled bark of the tree. An involuntary shudder passed through his body and his sleek coat of tawny fur rippled in response, but his dark eyes and sharp ears remained fixed upon the scene nearby.

The panther was one of many thousands roaming the Florida Peninsula and surrounding lands stretching west toward the Mississippi River. He was a large male, stretching seven feet in length and weighing over one hundred twenty pounds. His lithe, muscular body was able to travel many miles in a single night, or scale the vertical tower of a Longleaf pine if necessary. The wild territory provided a bounty of prey for his kind. Males of the species roamed great distances in search of mates, while the females stayed within smaller ranges where they could raise their young in safety. The long millennia of human habitation had done little to affect their numbers. They were one of the few climax predators who roamed these forests. Although he could not know it, these mysterious humans provided an existential threat to the survival of his kind.

Curiosity had the better of him. For three long hours the hunter remained on the broad oak limb scarcely a hundred feet from the unsuspecting travelers. Only when the waxing moon began to draw low in the west and the evening began to offer a suggestion of the chill that would greet the dawn did the big cat stir from the limb. There was no chance of suitable game venturing so near the strange scents of the humans with their horses and oxen. It was time to move. Then, with a long backward stare at the sleeping camp, he strode to the far side of the big tree before dropping to the ground and winding his way eastward. The night was yet young, and other challenges awaited.

•

Hector stared at the broad expanse of the river ford in trepidation, but knew he had no choice but to cross on foot at the side of the wagon, the plodding oxen breaking the waves ahead and the mounted soldiers following behind watching for danger. "It's safe, I have crossed here a dozen times," their commander told them, but then told them to keep a close watch on the waters and to keep their lances ready. "We might actually take a prize," he told them, adding that the thick tails of the alligators provided tough but tasty meat. Hector's thoughts ran much more to avoiding becoming a meal than enjoying one. The smell of lake and marsh mingled their essences in the morning air.

As they strode through the waist-high waters at the ford, the sluggish stream tugged gently at their legs. The oxen made good progress, and the small cart, built with a water-tight bottom, now seemed to float as it was dragged through the waters. All was going well until one of the horses stumbled. It may have stepped into a hole, or tripped upon some unseen waterlogged tree bole, but it mattered little to the rider, who was flung free as the horse suddenly lunged and flopped in the tea-colored water. Hector ran to help the man regain his feet and then grasped the reins of the horse, which was still struggling to regain its footing.

"I hope she didn't break her leg!" the unhorsed soldier said as he adjusted his clothing and recovered his lance. He turned back toward Hector and gave a shout, even as the struggling horse let go a sudden scream. "There is an alligator right there!" shouted the soldier and Hector turned to see the very giant he most feared in the water scarcely a dozen feet from him. He could see the long, reptilian tail and much of its broad black back as it suddenly slashed across the water.

In a split-second move, the monster suddenly lunged forward and then presented a creamy underbelly as it rolled over in the water. The horse on Hector's rein suddenly lurched backward and flopped on its side, eyes wide with fear. Hoofs flew as it seemed to try to run across the water, but the only result was a cascade of water that flew into the faces of the stunned witnesses. The other mounted soldier tried to spur his mount toward the battle, but the animal merely reared as if to throw its rider. Only with difficulty was he able to gain a measure of control of the horse.

By this time the driver of the ox-cart had whipped his beasts into flight and together they were putting good distance between themselves and the danger, growing closer to the far shore at an impressive pace. Hector stood in the water, still more than waist-deep, at the side of the gasping soldier. Neither was able to do anything to help the unfortunate horse, which was slowly being dragged backwards along the muddy river bottom toward deeper water. Hector felt that everything was still moving in a sort of slow-motion.

"Behind you, there's another!" the horseman shouted and the two of them turned to see the dark shape slide past, barely visible as it submerged. Without even turning, the two wet Spaniards leapt forward as one, the western bank of the river the one thought in both their minds. It took only a moment for the panicked horse of the mounted soldier to realize the wisdom of their strategy before it, too, began to bound in the same direction, carrying its rider still desperately clinging to its back. Behind them, not one but several alligators were rushing toward the lost horse, ready to contend for their own piece of the meal.

The panting party caught up with the resting team of oxen and their small cart almost a half-mile beyond the riverbank. There they paused for an hour, still talking excitedly of the events, and mourning the loss of the good horse. Hector had found his first real Florida adventure to be more than he had hoped.

Three days later the bedraggled party arrived at Potano, and Hector marveled at the sight of some two hundred head of cattle as he looked from the rim of a shallow basin upon the herd below. The ranch was a rich pastureland filled with small ponds and a stream, tall grass promising good grazing for their remaining horse and oxen.

"Here we have the best pasture in the state!" the foreman told the group. "We have selected two dozen head of cattle for you to take to San Agustin. But while you are here, you will eat like kings."

The foreman's boasting was not in vain, for Hector ate the richest meal of his life, with a huge slab of beefsteak that covered his plate and fresh roasted sweet corn to accompany it. Small white potatoes had been boiled as well, along with a sour green vegetable that he had never tasted before. He ate like it was his last meal alongside the soldiers and ranchers, for once in his life treated as an equal at this frontier outpost.

"How do you keep the alligators from your cattle?" Hector asked one of the ranch hands as they were tucking the last morsels into their over-stuffed bellies.

"We have to kill them," he was told. "Each month we conduct a hunt. We cannot catch all the little ones, but the big ones we must track down. They come especially in the springtime. We use a big iron hook and a chain with fresh meat and then drag them to the shore. It takes ten men and horses to pull the biggest ones ashore. Then we must use our lances because they are very dangerous and can run very fast."

"The one that killed our horse in the Rio San Juan was as long as three men," Hector told him.

"Come, and I will show you what big is," his new friend replied. Hector followed him into a barn nearby and there gaped at a skull hanging on a wall. The jaws alone were almost as long, and wider, than his body. "That, my friend, is what the big lizard can become. Truly, in this strange land, dragons do exist."

November 1694

TECOFALO STOOD FOR A MOMENT, stretching his muscular back as he gazed out upon the thick walls of the fortress, now almost complete. He had learned much from his captors. The Castillo de San Marcos was an engineering marvel, with thick walls of porous coquina stone. After firing in a kiln, the material took on a stone-like consistency which could absorb the force of the heaviest cannon. The stone had stood before a Spanish cannon that was fired to test them from a short distance. The solid shot of a lead ball made a dent, but that was all, as it fell heavily and harmlessly to the ground.

The design of the fortress, with protruding battlements that allowed defenders to fire down at attackers, even at the base of the walls themselves, would make the fortress virtually impregnable.

Despite his labor as a slave, living in squalid conditions on tortillas and left-over meat, he had retained his health, unlike many other slaves. Outside the walls, many graves had been scattered among the older parts of the quarry, bodies tossed into pits and covered with the sands of the dunes.

Tecofalo credited his survival to his hard work and willingness to tolerate what others would not. Despite the very few messages that had been passed to him through Apalachee visitors to San Augustin, he had tried to focus on his love for his wife and daughter to give him strength.

His youth and high spirit had served him well. To retain a positive mind-set, he had also managed to develop a sense of pride in what had emerged from the sandy tract of land at the entrance to Matanzas Bay. Yet throughout his labors, he had kept to his ways and watched for the opportunity to escape. Yet the solid iron band around his ankle was never removed and the chains that held him at night were too strong to allow his plans to flower. He would wait for the right moment.

He was surprised to be among a group of natives separated from the other slaves one morning as the construction neared completion. For an hour the group waited in a cell within the structure, fearful that they would be executed. At last, they were led, still in chains, to a room above, where the governor soon appeared. He cast his eyes over the group, assessing each one in turn. Then he spoke to his attendants. Tecofalo could scarcely believe his ears. The Spanish language he had learned made him among the first of the group to relax. Minutes later they were led to the city gates and their chains were removed. It was a rare act of charity.

"Go, now and never return. Your debt has been paid," they were told. Tecofalo would at last see his beloved wife, Tlacata. and daughter Sara.

His arrival at Tallahassee was greeted with surprise. He was a man returned from the dead, for all who knew him were convinced that he would die in chains at San Augustin.

The twenty-five years had been unkind to many, not least of whom was his wife, Tlacata. He fell to the ground upon learning that she had died two years earlier. His daughter, Sara, had been only two years old when he had been taken away, and now she did not know him, but was assured by the elders that this was, indeed, her long-lost father.

When he had regained his composure, she introduced her own husband and presented her two children. The sight of the young faces brought him to his feet, and he introduced himself to them. Minutes later he was sitting quietly with the group, trading stories of twenty-five years of their lives.

June 1763

While Florida's Spanish settlers continued to struggle in their attempts to wrest a living from the land, larger troubles were looming in Europe. The great powers there allied themselves into two opposing camps. Britain, the constant enemy of Spain, allied itself with Prussia and the German kingdoms.

Spain set aside old rivalries with France and joined them in facing the British. It was a risky undertaking for the fading power. The dwindling flow of wealth from the New World had reduced Spain's military might.

Throughout the fighting, Florida remained a pawn in the global movement of forces. In the end, Britain and her allies had triumphed. The Treaty of Paris had brought a temporary end, not only to seven years of war, but to a hundred years of open hostility between England, France, and Spain. England's domain extended from Canada in the north to Florida in the south, making her ruler of the continent.

England acquired Florida from Spain as ransom for the city of Havana. Spain was left with her West Indian possessions and all the Americas south from Mexico, except British Honduras. France retained control of only a few Caribbean islands.

Two hundred forty-seven years after establishing their claim to Florida, and one hundred and ninety-eight years after the first settlement was established, the Spanish had little to show for their investments. Florida had been a disaster for them, never producing a profit in over two hundred years. They were less than heartbroken to trade the peninsula to England for the return of their precious city of Havana, Cuba, captured by the English during the war.

Spanish dreams of gold, silver, and fountains of healing waters had come to nothing. As the Spanish left departed there were less than four thousand loyal subjects to be evacuated from the territory, including faithful Indians, convicts, and slaves. Spain's long experiment had ended in an abject failure.

The Half-penny
April 1764

"COME NOW, CHARLES, DON'T BE THAT WAY," said the well-dressed man who strode briskly back and forth across the polished hardwood floor of the second-story office. The heels of his boots made a hollow clunking sound as they struck those boards, which reflected the brilliant sunshine that poured through the open windows. A gust of cool wind stirred the white curtains, causing the man to turn his gaze outward over the rooftops toward the broad river beyond.

After a brief pause, he returned to his friendly prodding. "I simply must hear you say that you'll accept, for I won't take no for an answer. You may retain all your interests here, if you like, and still make your fortune in Florida. Take my word, you won't regret it, I promise." He stopped, smiling, before the broad desk where his friend was still seated, his legs firmly planted as if prepared for a counter-charge.

Charles was 28 years old and well on his way to becoming very wealthy. Like the city he lived in he was named after the former king and was loyal to the British Imperialism that had given him such opportunity and shaped so much of the modern world. He looked keenly at his friend, hesitating, as he slowly accepted the decision he had already made. After two weeks of listening to stories of the opportunities before them, he could resist no longer. "Well, then, Stanley, I shall give you my decision and it shall be final and then I don't want to hear another word about it."

Stanley looked at him, somewhat grimly and shook his head very slightly, knowing that Charles's involvement and investment in the venture would be insurance for his own, and convinced that he had failed to persuade him. It was a great deal of effort wasted, he thought ruefully.

"Your tales and assurances are vaguely convincing, I must admit," Stanley continued. "Our fathers would naturally advise caution. "Don't take too many chances in business" they would tell us, but then...aren't they the ones who came running off from England to the colonies? And haven't they done well enough for themselves? I certainly say a voyage across the wide Atlantic for a land they had never seen and knew little about was a risk that has paid them quite handsomely. Perhaps this venture is just what I need. The truth is, I am eager for some. I shall accept your offer, and I expect that it will be all you say, and more."

"That's wonderful, Charles! I will be most happy to share this news with the others of our group!" he said, grasping Charles's hand and enthusiastically pumping his arm. "I have no qualms about inviting you, and I'm sure you will thank me ten-fold in the future."

"Then we have a deal, and it's worth celebrating. In fact, I would like to propose a toast to our future."

Rising, Charles slowly retrieved a dark bottle from behind a row of books in his chamber and poured two small drinks of sherry, passing one to Stanley. Holding his own aloft, he said "To the health of His Majesty, King George, and the success of our new venture in East Florida."

"To both, and rightly!" the other responded. "I shall be seeing Governor Grant on the morrow, and I can hardly wait to tell him that you have accepted his kind offer." With that, he downed his drink and gathered his hat and cane. "I take leave of you now, until Thursday. And I shall look forward to seeing you in Saint Augustine in the spring!"

Charles stood at the window for a long moment, watching Stanley Wilson disappear down the bustling main street of Charles Town, in the English colony of South Carolina. As he watched him disappear into the crowd, he pondered long on his prospects. Florida was the new frontier, a fourteenth addition to the thirteen English colonies already settled on the Atlantic coast of North America. Recently acquired from Spain, the territory was a land of opportunity that the Spanish had failed to exploit in nearly two hundred fifty years.

Charles Westbury still thought of himself as a young man at 30 and was proud to think he had retained his sense of adventure. Although he knew that his wife would not be especially pleased at the prospect of relocating, he turned over in his mind the design of a fine new home he would build her, which would soon quiet her protests, he thought. Yes, peace had set the stage for the exploitation of Florida, and for once he would be at the vanguard and share in the profits.

Now, English citizens and gentlemen farmers were eager to settle Florida and believed they were in position to attract the influx of capital necessary to make the effort a financial success. Charles had just agreed to risk most of what he owned and cast his lot with the settlers. Standing at his window, watching the passing traffic of Charles Town, he hoped that he had done the right thing.

•

On the following Thursday, Charles waited at Government House in Charles Town for the arrival of the new governor, General James Grant of Ballindallach. As a prominent citizen of South Carolina, Grant was just the sort to attract the help he needed, Charles thought. The new governor had quickly set about recruiting some of the most successful citizens to join him in Florida, offering them grants of land and public offices, including positions on the Royal Council.

Charles quickly rose to his feet as he saw Governor Grant enter the parlor room, followed by an impressive entourage, which included their mutual friend, Stanley Wilson. Several other gentlemen also rose from their seats, awaiting the attention of the governor to their special cases.

"Your Excellency, I believe you are familiar with the name of Charles Westbury whom I present to you now," Stanley Wilson said, directing Grant's attention to Charles with commendable speed. "He is a special friend of mine and I beg you to receive him with favor."

"Yes, Mr. Westbury, I am pleased indeed to meet you, for I have heard a great deal of your success in business here in Charles Town and elsewhere. Please join me in my office."

Charles's doubts faded as they left the rest of the party to wait. Obviously, the governor considered his contract a most pressing business. That must bode well, he thought, for the future attention of government to the needs of the colony.

Passing through a short hall, they entered a door into a well-appointed salon. Broad bookshelves lined the walls, filled with hundreds of tomes. A row of tall windows was open to the gloomy morning and the sounds of voices could be heard as people greeted each other on the street below.

Ignoring his writing desk, Grant seated himself with some aplomb on a comfortably upholstered sofa, inviting the others to seat themselves on the facing chairs. A servant quickly appeared with tea and sweet biscuits.

Turning at length to the business at hand, the governor turned to look at Charles. "I am pleased to be given considerable authority by the crown as to the disposition of lands and resources in the new colony of Florida. I have only the highest expectations of success in our ventures there. I want you to know that I am seeking only those of the...shall we say, "best cloth," to receive the benefits of the empire."

Charles looked him straight in the eye. "I am pleased that this is the case. I much prefer to deal with such as these myself, Your Excellency."

"I trust Stanley has communicated sufficient details of my offer of a land grant to you, dependent upon your agreeing to meet certain conditions?" he asked, raising his brow slightly.

"He has, Your Excellency, and I have agreed."

"So that there shall be no misunderstanding of the terms, I have had a document prepared which will be offered for your signing and the seals. Of course, beyond the agreement to provide the necessary resources to farm a portion of the land grant, and reside upon it for a portion of each year, there is nothing more I would ask of you." He paused a moment, glanced down and then returned his gaze at Charles. "I am pleased to tell you, though, in great confidence, that I am considering you for nomination to the Royal Council. Of course, I am under great pressure to name several others, but your name is among them."

"I am honored to hear you say so, Your Excellency. I would be most pleased to serve, if you and King George see fit," Charles responded, admittedly feeling very pleased.

•

Within months, Charles Westbury stood on the deck of an English merchantman, one of several under the watchful guns of two men-at-war of the Royal Navy. From their place at anchor, Charles scanned the shoreline, hoping for his first glimpse of Saint Augustine.

"Stanley, where's the town?" he asked, puzzled. "I can see that great stone fort, there, but I don't see any other sign of the town."

"Of course not, for it's not here, but inland, on the bay, well protected."

"But why have we stopped here, then? Why don't we sail up to the wharf?"

"Well, that is one small problem we will have to correct. You see, the tide here has caused the inlet to the harbor to fill with sand. Large ships can't cross the bar, so we'll have to put off in smaller boats to reach the city."

"But that means that all our goods, in both directions, will have to be handled the same way!" Charles exclaimed. "That would be expensive, Stanley and a beastly trouble!"

"Don't panic, Charles, it's only temporary. The governor has already proposed to clear the channel and the Royal Navy supports the request. Funding should be approved very shortly. We'll surely have it opened before the first crops come in on our new farms."

Four hours later they found themselves walking down the streets of the town admiring the stone construction of many buildings. The Spanish had made much use of the same coquina concrete used in the Castillo to create churches, a school, public buildings, and some of the houses.

It was the second day when they arrived at the plantation house some distance from the city. Broad fields, mostly grown up in weeds, surrounded a comfortable but relatively modest house. "It will have to do for now, but I will expand it soon," Charles thought to himself. His trunks quickly stowed, he toured the property to assess the few small barns and outbuildings that had been left behind by the former owners. The property had potential, he thought, feeling a momentary pang of sympathy for those who had first cut the farm out of the rough country. "Well, no sense in wasting time, now, is there?" he thought. He threw himself immediately into the work, hiring a staff and organizing the new business.

By the following spring, land was being actively cleared and planted and substantial new buildings were being erected throughout the area of Saint Augustine. Work was nearing completion, too, on the new King's Highway, which stretched south from Georgia, crossed the broad Saint Johns River at Cows' Ford, entered Saint Augustine, and then extended south to Mosquito Inlet. It was a crude road, rutted by wagon wheels, but it was the first overland connection with the northern colonies, and soon a few settlers began to arrive in the area by horse and oxcart.

Enthusiastic about the prospects of the land, Charles had a new house ordered, and soon it began to rise among the endless ranks of palmettos a short distance west of the town.

Stanley Wilson also set about his own new grant lands with a similar sense of industry. Both of their plantations, like those of their neighbors, were situated along waterways, for other than the King's Highway there were few decent roads to speak of. Both people and goods were transported by boat virtually everywhere outside of the town itself.

Governor Grant had proven to be a wise administrator, and quickly set out to build alliances with the local native Indians. He called for a council at Picolata, on the Saint Johns River, where he treated with their great chief, Secoffee. Grant was liberal in his trading policies, offering many goods the Spanish had withheld, including liquor and firearms. It was quickly agreed that all the land east of the big river would be left to the whites, while the lands to the west remained to the Indians. Soon a thriving trade developed and manufactured products such as farm equipment, cloth, saddles, mirrors, axes, and ammunition flowed to the Indians. They reciprocated by visiting Saint Augustine and their new friend, Governor Grant, frequently, so that it seemed there was a constant population of fifty or more natives, come to celebrate the new peace with the settlers.

If peace had brought economic benefit to the English, it brought it also for the Indians. The distribution of new technologies brought a higher standard of living than they had ever experienced and their numbers, once depleted, slowly began to increase once again. A few bands of Miccosukee Creek Indians had migrated southward from Georgia and Alabama, mostly to escape bloody internecine fighting between the Upper, or Miccosukee and Lower, Muskogee, tribes of the Creek nation.

After the construction of his house and the successful planting of over one hundred acres, Charles could see that his decision had been a good one. Already he had turned the proceeds of his few holdings in Charles Town into a plantation worth several times as much, using only a small portion of his cash. He persisted in employing his small army of workers, both hired and slave, to clear and plant new lands, and had grants totaling over nine thousand acres. In addition to his own food crops, his farm already produced cotton, sugarcane, and indigo, while neighboring plantations produced rice and corn as well. A steady stream of oaken barrel staves, pine boards and ship masts and spars flowed from a sawmill which he had erected.

Stanley Wilson's success was as great as that of Charles and so, a year after his plantation was settled, he returned to East Florida from Charles Town with his wife and son. The addition of women brought new life to the far-flung plantation society. Soon, the Wilson home was surrounded by formal gardens, ponds and outbuildings, assuming the look of a traditional English farm. Proud of his accomplishment, Wilson named the place Stillwater.

With a solid peace at hand between the settlers and natives, small communities soon began to spring up all along the coast, from Fernandina at the Georgia border to Mosquito Inlet north of Cape Canaveral. At the latter site, Dr. Andrew Turnbull, a highly-placed London physician, had formed a syndicate and agreed to establish a large new settlement. The successes were still limited, as after four years both East and West Florida remained dependent on annual subsidies from England, with the crown providing about six thousand pounds sterling each year. The money went to pay for the salaries of government officials, Indian trade, operations of the Church of England and education.

Stanley and Charles soon became partners in a block of buildings in town and operated a store of merchandise brought from England and the trades. Other buildings were rented, so that a good flow of income was soon produced. On their grant lands they began large cattle operations, providing beef to a ready market. The Florida investment was proving to be a wise one.

The Chain
September 1767

THE DREAM ENDED THE SAME WAY every time. The pleasant images of his father hoeing in the garden, his mother sitting before the fire and its steaming cauldron, his brother and sister, neighbors and friends, gradually devolved into the nightmare: the terror of his abduction, the tight bonds on his wrists, the rope around his neck binding him to other captives on the long march to...where were they going? As consciousness slowly returned, he remembered being paraded in front of the foreigners, the white men who barked orders at their black captors and the rumors that ran among the captives. Yet no one really knew.

The young man in the shackles had long since become accustomed to the pitching of the ship, and the nausea that had overcome him during the first days in darkness had largely passed. It was, he had discovered, a contagious condition, made much worse when those around him were sharing their own. Now, after more than two weeks at sea, it was instead the smell of death that brought the taste of bile to his throat.

His name was Sekou. He remembered the long process of loading the ship after the horror of his first glimpse. Long rows of chains stretched along the length of the hold and every two feet there were another pair of shackles. It had taken five days to fill it with men, women, and children. Mostly children, he remembered, led aboard in groups of twenty or thirty. Many were from powerful and hostile tribes, now reduced to the same shared misery.

Sekou sat up to the best of his ability, dragging the heavy chain forward to relieve himself of its weight on his wrists. His ankles, clamped in their own irons, could move only slightly. The arrangement had made it difficult for the prisoners to accomplish basic bodily functions efficiently and the odors added to the general hellishness of the low-slung deck. Casting a cautious eye about him he checked to see if his immediate neighbors were still alive. Relieved to see that they were, he was still distressed to see that the boy to his right, no more than eight years old, looked even sicker than he had the day before. Who knew how many more days he would be able to tolerate the conditions, or even how long they might remain in the ship? Would their trip never end?

The prisoner looked down at his own emaciated body. The thin gruel that composed most of their diet was disgusting, but he had never turned away a mouthful, even though it was obvious that the tiny scraps of meat it contained were too often the rats sometimes killed by the crew of the ship. Despite this, he could see that he was much thinner. His legs, so used to bearing him miles each day, wasted from lack of use. His bones ached, his back was stiff, his joints moved only with pain and difficulty.

Above his head the low deck of heavy beams carried the tread of the sailors. By the thin light from above he knew that morning was breaking and that soon they would come down to the hold and count the prisoners, looking for those who had died during the night, unlocking their bodies, and carrying them away. He made a mental note each morning of the number of splashes as they were cast overboard. The early evening would repeat the process.

Every day since the third day he had seen them with the dead. Now nearly half of those who had been loaded on the ship were gone. He almost wished to join them, yet he lingered, determined to endure. What would his mother do if he died, he wondered, then realized that she would never know, for who would tell her?

To keep his spirits up, Sekou thought of his family, his aunts and uncles and the extended group that had shared their rambling collection of rough huts. He thought of the children of his village, the games they played, the joy of the feasts they had shared. The passing thought of food, though, renewed his hunger and he lay himself back down, resuming his habit of staring at the wood above him, picking out the fine details in the grain, the whorls that resembled animals and faces, anything that his imagination could coax from his coffin-like surroundings. He didn't know where he was bound, but he knew that it could be no worse than where he was.

The Crucifix
June 1768

"CHARLES, HAVE YOU HEARD THE LATEST NEWS?" Stanley asked one afternoon after rushing in, dismissing with his customary pleasantries. "About the new settlement, that is?"

"Of course, I haven't, Stanley. I haven't been able to leave the plantation in a week and neither have my foremen. But now I suppose it's important, for that must be why you've come calling on a Tuesday." He paused and tried to read the emotions playing over his friend's face. "Well, are you going to share this news with me?"

"I certainly shall, and you won't like it," he said, and the words fairly tumbled from his mouth. "It seems that Dr. Turnbull's colonists, for whom the governor has been preparing for months, have arrived at the appointed place in good order. They are more than fifteen hundred in all, man, woman, and child." He paused briefly for effect. "The blow is, they are not English at all! They are Greeks and Italians and the most from Spanish Menorca! They don't even speak English! And they are Catholic!"

"But Stanley, that's impossible!" Charles retorted. "It's against the king's law to bring Catholics into an English colony!"

"I know, and some of the other planters plan to send a protest to the crown immediately. But they say that the backers of the venture are so highly placed in London that they have received a special permission, at least secretly. I personally doubt anything will be done about it."

"At least they are at Mosquito Inlet and not near Saint Augustine," Charles observed.

"That's another thing! They've gone and named the place New Smyrna, after that place in Greece! And this, an English colony! It's outrageous!"

"Well, you may know, Stanley, that Dr. Turnbull's wife was born in Smyrna," Charles observed. "If this is permitted to stand, we shall have to trust Dr. Turnbull to keep his people in close order. I only hope he speaks their language. Mine is called business."

Stanley's insight proved to be true, for the new farmers were to remain, but under the agreement, would not be allowed to openly follow their Catholic faith.

•

Despite the hostile reception by the English "gentlemen farmers," the settlers at New Smyrna were soon set to work clearing and planting vast acreage. By the following spring, more than seven miles of shoreline along the great saltwater marsh called Mosquito Lagoon were cleared and set in new crops. To those in Saint Augustine, the settlement of New Smyrna seemed to be a qualified success. The array of English plantations around Saint Augustine also continued to expand, with a slow but steady stream of new settlers arriving each year. The great majority were British subjects, including many from the colonies to the north, but a handful were other Europeans, including a few Swiss and German settlers.

East Florida began to take its place as a part of the success of English colonization in the New World. From the new colony of West Florida at distant Pensacola, the news was not as good. The isolation of Pensacola provided an added hardship. The nearest neighboring settlements were French and Spanish, both claiming colonies to the West along the Gulf of Mexico. Difficulties arose, too, in dealing with the native populations. Conferences with the Choctaw and Chickasaw tribes were generally successful, but the hostile Muskogee Creeks controlled large areas to the north, and the settlements of West Florida were constantly threatened. Charles counted his blessings.

March 1774

"BLESS ME, FATHER, FOR I HAVE SINNED," intoned Juan Martin, kneeling in the darkness of the secret chapel at New Smyrna to bare his soul to God. A dozen flickering votive candles added their faint illumination to the light from the small windows, reflecting upon the crucifix above the altar.

The chapel was carefully concealed inside a communal house, and the few overseers who had become aware of it were wise enough to say nothing. Within the tiny confessional, a priest sat behind a cloth drape, listening to the modest infractions Señor Martin named, preparing to assign him a litany of prayers that would serve as penance for them. Juan had come to confess his sins and ask for mercy from God so that he and his family might be blessed. He was a humble farmer who had found little mercy in his former home in the faraway Balearic Isles.

Juan, like many of his neighbors in Menorca, had known little of world politics. They were unsure why British masters had controlled their little island in the Mediterranean, or why God had sent three years of hard drought upon them, bringing them to the point of starvation. But he was certain, when he had heard of Florida, that he must go. What farmer could resist the tales of rich earth and daily rains? Dr. Turnbull's terms had seemed reasonable in faraway Menorca when starvation seemed the alternative. Promises of religious freedom and the presence of a priest and a monk on the expedition had given him and his brothers faith that this was a move ordained by God.

The voyage to this new world was a horrifying experience. Juan's older brother had died, along with more than a hundred others, aboard the creaking wooden ships. They arrived at the settlement only to find a mosquito-ridden marsh surrounded by palmetto thickets. No land had been cleared, and food was scarce because a supply ship had sunk. Malaria had soon begun to decimate the settlers, but Turnbull and his English foremen treated them as slaves. Forced to work through their illnesses, they had cleared hundreds of acres of land by hand. Hundreds more died in the process.

Farming in the new land was also not as expected. He and his kinfolk had been disappointed in the failure of their carefully-packed grapevines, for wine-making was an old tradition for their families, and necessary for the sacrament of the Mass. Other crops flourished, however, and food was eventually plentiful. Yet, although every member of the family worked, including the children, it required six years of hard labor in the steaming heat of east Florida summers before he had finally arrived at the point of paying off the indenture on himself and his family. The cost of feeding and clothing his growing family had delayed their liberation.

When at last the day came that he had earned his freedom and the promised fifty acres of land he would receive, Juan was told that the terms on his letter were worthless. He would work, or he would be imprisoned. It was a betrayal that made him a virtual slave. What was he to do?

Some who refused to work were locked away, or chained to logs in the fields. While their Greek and Italian neighbors became ever more rebellious against the harsh conditions and the cruelty of the overseers, the Menorcan community had mostly remained quiet, peacefully seeking their way.

Now, Juan was more disturbed than ever, and he prayed for understanding. His friends, leaders of the indentured Menorcan settlers, had been arrested and charged with treason. Their crime, and that of the priest, was communicating with the bishop of Havana. A rebellion among the Menorcans was put down with brutal force and many were killed. Now he had no hope of liberty. Turnbull had proven to be a wicked man. Yet now, it was the name of Lieutenant Governor John Moultrie that rang fear in the hearts of his people.

"Please, dear God, I am an honest man and seek only to do your bidding," he prayed. "Help me find release for my people, so that my children may grow strong and free in this new land."

Many miles to the north in Saint Augustine, events were unfolding that Juan Martin could not understand, but which would play a significant role in his future.

July 1776

THE SWELTERING SUMMER OF 1776 brought ever more ominous news to the loyal citizens of East Florida. Meeting in Philadelphia, delegates representing the thirteen colonies to the north had signed what they called a "declaration of independence," stating plainly, once and for all, their intent to break away from the mother country. Even neighboring Georgia and South Carolina had sent representatives.

"They'll all hang like traitors and it's really a shame," Stanley told those who would listen, and most agreed.

The scattered fighting in the other American colonies soon became open rebellion, splitting colonial society wide open. Only in Florida were the loyal Tory elite in clear supremacy, and by the following summer the trickle of loyalist refugees from the north became a steady stream.

•

"I don't know if the king has made the right move with the appointment of Colonel Patrick Tonyn as governor of East Florida," Stanley said to Charles one day over brandy. "Things have gone from bad to worse ever since Governor Grant left."

Charles turned to glance at his friend, weighing his words, hoping he chose them wisely.

"John Moultrie's attitude as acting governor only stirred up those who demand an elected council," he replied. "And Tonyn, from what I can see, is no diplomat, either. He's only been here a short time and he's already widened the feud with Dr. Turnbull. There's some sense in the argument that we be given an elected assembly, so that we might have a voice in our own governance, Stanley. What harm could there be in that? After all, how could King George know what we need here in Florida?"

Stanley Wilson was shocked, but sat for a long moment, gazing out his window at the peaceful waters of the Halifax River. Smoke curled from a well-seasoned pipe which he cradled in his hand. Carefully he considered his friend's words and measured them against the broader background of revolt which had fomented in the colonies to the north. Even in his own South Carolina, where he still returned each year to maintain his business contacts, whispered rumors of intrigue told of the deeper rifts that had formed in public opinion.

"Careful, Charles. What you are saying borders on sympathy for the rebels in Boston. I know you can't possibly support that rabble."

"Of course not, but if they had been given a larger voice in their own affairs years ago, they might have been content to quarrel among themselves, rather than directing their anger at the crown."

"Perhaps you're right, Charles, but I certainly think it much too late to attempt such a course now. It would only be perceived as a sign of weakness on the part of the King and add fuel to the fire. These rebels demand nothing short of anarchy, for that is what we would have if each colony were allowed to make its own laws. What might we do, let each of us decide what we will pay in taxes?"

"Of course not, Stanley," Charles replied slowly.

The sun gradually drew lower in the west, its slanting rays entering the front windows of the house, casting the interior in a golden glow. Outside in the well-tilled fields, young cotton plants, promise of another year's prosperity, stretched to reach the slanting rays. Rank upon rank they filled the horizon. Already his young orange trees were filled with fruit from the spring bloom, and a time of plenty seemed inevitable. Revolution, thought Stanley, seems a very unlikely prospect.

"Gentlemen, the dinner is served," said a well-dressed servant who appeared from the dining room, breaking the slight tension which had arisen between the long-time friends. With reluctance, Stanley rose from his place at the window and gestured for his guest to lead the way. Within the well-appointed dining room, Stanley's wife, Elizabeth, stood at her chair, while his strapping son George, born on the plantation and now sixteen, stood at another.

"Please, take your seats," Stanley said as he helped his wife with her chair.

As soon as everyone had been seated and the wine had been poured, Stanley raised his glass. "To the health of the King," he said.

"To the King," all replied mechanically. Before another word could be said, a sumptuous Sunday repast began to flow in courses from the kitchen and Elizabeth smiled, proud that the staff under her supervision had done so well. Yet her active interests extended far beyond the kitchen and home, as she frequently reminded her husband. This time she waited until the meal was well under way to bring up her burning topic.

"Stanley, you know that I rarely take an interest in politics, but as I was in the town this morning, I happened to hear something of interest. It seems that our new Governor Tonyn has placed Mr. Turnbull under arrest."

"Really! That is a surprise to me! Despite all the grumbling from the investors, I never thought it would come to that." Stanley set down his fork and Charles did the same.

"It seems, or so I understand, that the good governor has accused Mr. Turnbull of plotting to defraud his partners in the venture at New Smyrna," Elizabeth continued. "Furthermore, he has released the Menorcans from their indenture, saying that they had long ago satisfied their terms. He has invited them to settle in Saint Augustine."

"What!" Stanley burst out, rising to his feet, unable to contain himself. "That is outrageous! What is the governor trying to do?"

"He feels that their presence strengthens the town against the possibility of trouble from the rebels in Georgia and Carolina."

"Well, we won't stand for it, not for one minute! The planters will protest this with every means available..." A moment of silence passed as Stanley's face grew increasingly red.

Charles saw his opportunity to make his point. "Now how do you feel about the idea of an elected council, Stanley?" he asked levelly. Stanley looked at his friend, unable to respond for the moment, so great was his frustration.

"I think it's a splendid idea, myself," young George suddenly volunteered. "After all, the king hasn't a whit of an idea what's what, here. And to tell the truth, I've never seen England, or the king. What good is a king in England when we're here in America, anyway?"

Stanley looked at his son and all color drained from his face. There was a moment's awkward silence, before he found his voice. "That will be quite enough out of you, son. Now, leave this table and wait for me in your room and I will see to you after dinner!"

"Now, Stanley," Elizabeth interjected as George closed the door behind him, "don't be too hard on the boy, he doesn't understand all this political business, you know."

Charles quietly resumed eating but listened intently, curious to see how this interesting challenge would be resolved.

"I don't care what he does or doesn't understand about his namesake, or politics. So long as he eats at my board, he'll speak well of King George, or go without," Stanley said firmly, and the matter was settled.

•

The battles being fought far to the north had little effect on Florida, and St. Augustine did a brisk business supplying foodstuffs to the British armies, but in 1778, disconcerting news arrived.

"Have you heard the latest, Charles?" Stanley said one day as he stormed into his friend's small office, quite beside himself.

"I don't believe I have, Stanley. I haven't left the plantation in several days."

"These Continental rebels have signed a treaty with France! A Catholic country, no less! It has already been ratified by their so-called "Continental Congress," and I suppose the French will soon be sending armies to attack us," he shouted, pacing briskly.

"Now don't get too excited, Stanley," Charles said to him, "or you'll have an attack yourself. Are you quite sure?"

"Oh yes. I have seen the Charles Town papers, brought in this very morning on the ship. They toast the treaty as if it were a marriage made in heaven!"

"The last I heard, the Continental Army was freezing, without food or ammunition, and on its last legs," Charles offered.

"That's still the word," Stanley told him. "The rebels haven't been able to field an army yet this year. I am surprised that anyone, even the French, would be so foolish as to ally themselves with a revolt that has already gone to seed. What can they possibly gain by it, besides a good thrashing, which they sorely deserve? I'm sure that even some of those sympathetic to the rebels' cause will agree that, with this alliance, they've gone much too far."

"Only time will tell, Stanley. Meanwhile, we must take the opportunity to produce as many foodstuffs and naval stores as we possibly can, whilst the market lasts. I dare say that, once the fighting ends, the demand for our products will be reduced."

"By the way, I heard some other news. It seems the governor has convinced Chief Secoffee to take his warriors north to raid the settlers in Georgia and South Carolina. He's paying them in silver crowns."

"That should keep them busy for a while. Maybe they'll think twice before raiding at Fernandina again with their damned Patriot's Army."

•

The two entrepreneur farmers needn't have worried that the fighting would too soon be decided in favor of England. The Continental armies were shortly on the move again, with the added help of the French navy.

In June 1779, Spain joined in fighting her traditional English enemies, perceiving an opportunity to even old scores. In the spring of 1780, Bernardo Galvez, Spanish colonial governor of Louisiana, attacked English West Florida and captured the small English settlement at Mobile Bay with a force of thirteen hundred men.

In East Florida, however, English sympathies were still strong, and the towns better defended. Outside of a few raids on commerce, no serious fighting took place. The huge Castillo de San Marcos was converted into a prison, which soon held scores of captured seamen of the French, Spanish and rebel Continental navies. To them were added a few significant prisoners from the rebellious colonies, including Arthur Middleton, Thomas Heyward, Jr. and Edward Rutledge, signers of the Declaration of Independence. There they waited until they could be exchanged for loyalist prisoners of the American rebels.

Problems and complications came for Charles and Stanley in the changing loyalties and control of Charles Town, through which most of the trade still passed. American Patriots there soon had an influence on the flow of commerce and began to direct their goods, not to England, but to fill the needs of the

Continental armies, presenting certain "complications" in business negotiations.

For Juan Martin and his family, however, things were looking up. The English community in Saint Augustine had embraced their skills as farmers and virtually every shred of food they could produce was consumed locally, or quickly sold to the traders. Juan smiled as he worked his own small plot in the evening, after returning from his work on the plantation. "Surely my prayers have been answered," he said aloud, palms turned toward the heavens.

December 1780

STANLEY WILSON PLANNED TO CELEBRATE the holidays in fine style, hosting a new year dinner party for much of the Saint Augustine society at his home on the Halifax. His short wharf was filled with the boats of the leading citizens, even as more arrived. People were in a mood to enjoy themselves. The mood of the colony had been cheered when, in May, the happy word arrived in Saint Augustine that General Sir Henry Clinton had captured Charles Town for the British. The success greatly strengthened the hand of the British in the southern colonies, after a series of defeats in the north.

"I see that you have had a great many acceptances for your entertainments, Stanley," Charles observed, as he was greeted by the host. "Do let me thank you for including me, despite my lack of escort."

"Fear not, Charles, that you might ever be excluded from my home for such a reason. However, I understand that Colonel Pruitt and his wife are reported to be aboard the ship from Charleston that arrived on the tide yesterday afternoon and of course they're invited. Therefor I might point out that Colonel Pruitt's sister will be here, unaccompanied as well."

"I shall take the time to visit with her, as a courtesy, of course."

"Then I hope you shan't mind that my wife has taken the liberty of seating you at her right during the dinner."

"I'm sure that I will survive, somehow," he answered dryly, with a sideways glance at his old friend.

"Good day, gentlemen," came a voice before them and the two men looked up to see none other than Colonel William Pruitt himself, of His Majesty's grenadiers.

"Hello, Colonel, welcome to Stillwater," Stanley immediately greeted him. "I'm so glad you could come today. We've been blessed by glorious cool weather and the company of our fondest friends."

"I am pleased, too, Stanley and I'm sure you will be further cheered to know that I've a bit of news from London, which you may have my leave to impart to your guests in making the toasts this evening. I'm sure they won't have learned it already, for I've only days ago heard it myself, when my vessel crossed paths with a frigate outward bound, just before arriving here at Saint Augustine from Charles Town. I dare say that even in Charles Town they did not know and likely still do not."

"And what news might this be, Colonel?" Stanley asked. "Pray tell, for you have certainly piqued my curiosity."

"That the parliament has opened a state of war upon the Dutch."

"Ye gads," Charles muttered, forgetting the setting. Stanley glanced at his friend, who quickly apologized, but added, "Are we, then, to make war with everyone, all a result of this insurrection? The Dutch have been no great friend of the Continentals, refusing to recognize their government."

"Yet the parliament was angered by their continuing trade with the rebels and even the supplying of armaments," Colonel Pruitt replied coolly. "They could not accept such effrontery without response, could they now?"

"I suppose not," Charles replied, "yet it seems that we've all we can do to control the ambitions of France and Spain. A French army stands unchallenged in Rhode Island colony and already, that Galvez chap has taken Baton Rouge and Mobile for Spain. I dare say he may well have his eyes on more of Florida, yet little has been done to stop him."

"And I say to you, sir," Pruitt replied stiffly, "that you should not question the determination, nor the ability, of the British forces, who will soon complete their work against the insurrection and turn their attention with great success upon our foreign enemies."

At this Charles simply bowed his head, not wanting to provoke further debate on an issue he knew he could not carry, but his doubts remained beneath his polite smile.

Despite Charles's slight embarrassment at the beginning, the rest of the afternoon and evening proceeded smoothly. The sixty guests dined at tables arranged upon the broad lawn and followed the dinner with dancing on the patio, while a small but serviceable orchestra played the popular tunes of the day. Cheers and laughter greeted the playing of "Yankee Doodle," which made fun of the "bumpkin" Continentals and their attempts to imitate the "macaroni" fashions which had become popular in London and across the empire.

Toasting and brief speeches interrupted the dancing, while frequent best wishes for the New Year's success were most often heard. A bright, waxing moon lit the cool evening as the guests returned home, their voices ringing across the shimmering water from the clustered boats as they disappeared down the still river.

"A complete success, I would call it, Stanley," Charles said to his host as the servants began the job of gathering the remaining glasses and tableware, folding tables, and rolling the carpets.

"Oh, Charles. I didn't realize you were still here."

"I made myself a bit scarce, for fear of being forced to accompany Lady Pruitt to her door. She seemed fond of me, despite the unfavorable impression I made upon her older brother, the colonel."

"Indeed, he did seem just a bit put out at your concerns over the ability of our forces."

"I only hope his confidence is not ill founded, Stanley, for our sake."

•

It was to be only five months before Charles's fears began to come true. In late spring word arrived that General Bernardo de Galvez had moved his victorious Spanish forces eastward from Mobile. With more than four thousand reinforcements arriving from Cuba, he then laid siege to and captured Fort George at

Pensacola. Although badly outnumbered, the English had intended to make a fight of it, but a lucky Spanish cannon shot hit a powder magazine. The resulting explosion killed eighty-five defenders and breached the walls. The Pensacola defenses were shattered, and the British rule of West Florida was over.

Although they were still hundreds of miles to the west, the Spanish army began to be a serious worry for Stanley, Charles and several thousand other loyal British subjects along Florida's east coast. The world seemed to be crumbling around them.

Waves of loyalists from the north soon became a problem, then a crisis, after the British Parliament gave up trying to control the colonies and ordered the evacuation of many of the port cities. The refugees soon outnumbered the permanent populace of Saint Augustine by almost three to one. Demand for housing, goods and real estate made both Charles and Stanley very wealthy but worried men.

Then came the piece of news that stunned them and all the loyalist gentry of Florida: The British armies had surrendered to Continental and French forces at Yorktown, Virginia, in October. The English band captured the thinking of the loyalists when they played a popular tune called "The World Turned Upside Down" at the surrender. Far away in London, British Prime Minister Lord North, upon hearing the news from Yorktown, gasped, "My God! It is all over." They were words repeated around the world. The American colonies were granted at least a temporary exercise in independence.

English initiatives moved quickly from the battlefield to the peace table and Charles and Stanley knew that they, too, might be pawns in a great game of international chess. English armies still controlled Charles Town and New York, but no further significant fighting took place for two years.

"The War of Revolt" officially ended with the signing of a treaty between Britain and the thirteen colonies in November of 1782, and English armies were withdrawn from the new American states. Yet the troubles for the English settlers in Florida didn't reach a climax until September 1783, when the English government signed the Treaty of Paris, which brought a conclusion to eight years of war between the European powers. As a result of the agreement, signed by representatives of Britain, France, Spain, The Netherlands, and the new American Confederation, the British agreed to cede Florida back to Spain. The authorities ordered the population to prepare to evacuate. The world was, indeed, turned upside-down.

For Charles, Stanley, and many loyalists, this was the ultimate betrayal by England. Yet, like most citizens, they packed their bags once again, left their rich plantations, and moved to the British-controlled Bahamas, Canada, or the West Indies islands. Very few chose to remain.

A Spanish governor returned to find that Florida was now home to a variety of diverse interests, and more difficult to rule or settle than ever. Pioneers, hunters, and fugitives of every race were arriving from the independent states to the north, and many were less than friendly to Spain and each other. The Spanish authorities had little use for the Americans who wandered into Florida, for many were slave-hunters or troublemakers.

The Spanish referred to the fugitive natives as "Seminoles" because they called themselves the yat'siminoli, or "free men." The Spanish Catholics, little used to Protestants of any stripe, called the North American settlers Quakers, or "Cuacaros." The Americans, like the Indians, proudly adopted the Spanish name as their own. "Crackers," they pronounced it, and it stuck.

Amid the cultural turmoil, among one group of former British subjects, there was joy.

"Now, all my prayers have been answered," Juan Martin told his family as they gathered for their Sunday evening meal. "For years I prayed for rain, yet the Lord gave us another way, delivering us to this land of plenty. Then I prayed that we would be delivered from our harsh servitude, and the Lord saw that we were freed. Now, I have prayed that we may worship in freedom, and he has delivered our new land to Spain. Men who speak our language and practice our faith will soon be here to defend our rights. It is a miracle."

Yet Spain's attention was focused primarily on retaining other, more productive colonies, while Florida became a neglected land full of renegades, intrigue, and piracy.

Among the few remaining English-speaking neighbors of the Menorcans of San Agustin was a young man named George Wilson. He soon employed many of them on the fields of a rather substantial plantation called Stillwater, which he had agreed to oversee for his English-loyalist father, with whom he had reportedly had some slight political differences.

The Army Cap
March 1818

A DENSE FOG LAY HEAVILY over the low hills all around, and Lieutenant August Booker's blanket was damp with moisture as he peered at the increasing light of morning through sleepy eyes. Sitting up slowly, he stretched to relieve the stiffness of another night spent huddled in a thin blanket on a meager mattress of grass and leaves. Around him the sounds of a military camp coming to life echoed in the stillness of the forest. The clank and clatter of metal cups and pots competed with the muffled voices of those already huddled around the flames they had managed to coax from the remains of last night's cooking fires.

His morning belonged to the Army and the troops to the Seventh Military District of the United States. They were only a day's march from Fort Scott but, unbeknownst to the President of the United States, had already crossed the border into Spanish Florida.

Knowing that free time was not a luxury to be wasted in camp, August quickly pulled on his marching uniform and stowed his bedroll. His uniform, like everything else in his world, already seemed to smell of smoke and sweat. How long would it be, he wondered, before he'd have a chance to take a proper bath and dress in fresh clothes?

He knew that he should be proud to be a lieutenant, proud of the job, but his thoughts strayed home and the letter he had written to his mother and his beautiful promised, Ellen. He could almost see her, long dark hair tumbling down in the evening's last light, sitting beside a lamp reading the letters aloud to his mother. Since his mother's eyes were weak and she couldn't read, he had written the long letter to Ellen, so she could share the news. He sighed deeply, thinking about all the miles between North Carolina and northern Florida. Then he stopped and stood for a moment next to a huge oak tree looking over the encampment.

Ellen had become more and more important to him since his last leave, and now he knew he was ready to put the army behind and settle down. He missed her so much, yet now he was going farther south, to chase Indians in the godforsaken swamps of Florida.

Making his way to a small group huddled around a steaming pot hung above a fire; August greeted the men with a subdued "g'morning."

"Good morning, Sir!" came the response from the group, as they made room for him at the fire. Pouring himself a steaming cup of coffee, he began to feel a bit more the officer as the scalding liquid helped to lift the fog of sleep from his brain. There was business to be conducted, he remembered.

"Sergeant, call the men together. I got a few things to tell them this morning," Lt. Booker told the rather grizzled-looking, bearded man who was standing nearby. The sergeant quickly shouted to the men to gather around, and August told them to remain at ease. Some thirty-five men formed a loose circle around their leader, eager for news or orders. They were invading Spanish territory under the command of Major General Andrew Jackson of Tennessee and August had some grave reservations.

"We were informed last night at the officers' meeting that we are heading on south to the mouth of the Apalachicola River," Booker told them. "General Jackson says he normally takes orders from the President and General Gaines, but that this is something that he can judge best, from the field. He plans to do whatever it takes to stop the Red Stick marauders. He says the Spanish can't control the Indians or the pirates and believes he can claim Florida for the United States, so I don't guess we'll be doing the job halfway."

Several of the experienced soldiers exchanged glances, knowing they may be in for a rough time. They were conducting an invasion of foreign territory, which could easily start a full-blown war. August kept his doubts to himself. He suspected that the president had no idea what General Jackson was doing on his own initiative, while suggesting that he was following orders. It wasn't the first time. Jackson was a well-known saloon brawler and self-promoter. He had made a name for himself in New Orleans against the British and didn't like to "take orders from politicians."

"I wish I could tell you more, but they don't tell us any more than we need to know," he continued. "I just want you to do your jobs, earn your pay, and be a credit to this unit and the United States Army. We'll be moving out in about half an hour and a mail rider will be leaving this morning, so if you got any letters to go, turn 'em in."

Most of the men stood talking in a group as the young lieutenant moved away. and the voices carried across the camp. Several of the new recruits were eager to take on the threat of the "In'juns" and laughed boastfully about what they would do when they met them.

The older veteran troops were more cautious in their discussions. Many of them had fought under General Jackson in 1814, against the Muskóki in Alabama Territory and West Florida. They had battled the British at Pensacola and at New Orleans in January of 1815. They knew that war was no game, especially on the enemies' home ground.

Jackson had already succeeded in driving most of the First Nations people south into Spanish Florida with relentless attacks. Though it had all seemed heroic and romantic when he enlisted, August was beginning to feel that he didn't really understand the need for the continuous fighting he had witnessed. He had fought Red Stick Muskóki before, too, but had learned to trust the Lower Creeks who served alongside the army. They were farmers who called themselves Oconee, and he had even picked up a fair amount of their Hitchiti language.

Many of the Oconee and their enemies, the Muskóki, had been driven into Florida, where they were all known as Seminoles. Among the groups were fugitive itálwa, or bands, of natives. They were Yuchi and Yamachi, Choctaw, Chickasaw and Muscogee.

Yet Jackson would give them no peace. The Muskóki had fought violent battles against settlers, defending their ancestral home to the north, and now allied themselves with the Spanish, who hadn't tried to drive them away.

Also migrating south were the Upper Creek, or Red Stick tribes, who had long been allied with the English. They were generally hostile to the Spanish, and often to the other tribes.

Since the Spanish also recognized the freedom of the African slaves, many escaped and headed south from plantations in Georgia and Alabama. In Florida they were violently resistant to capture and re-enslavement.

The Spanish, often with the assistance of English settlers, began to arm and train the former slaves and eventually built them a fort. The natives also protected the blacks and gave them their own lands in exchange for annual tribute to the chiefs. Intermarriage had blurred the lines between them, so that in many ways, they were as much Seminole as the Creeks. The Spanish called these people "Morenos," or browns. To Jackson they were Maroons, and fair game.

Florida had become an intense melting-pot of cultures, and the focus of the most intense ethnogenesis that had yet occurred in the New World.

•

August walked slowly toward the command post, lost in his thoughts. His army life hadn't been easy. He was only 23 years old and had already served with the General Jackson's army since war against the British began anew in 1812. He had earned his commission in battle when his own commanding officer was killed before his eyes, blown apart by an exploding bombarda shell at the battle of New Orleans. That bloody American victory had occurred weeks after the war had ended in 1814, only because the news hadn't arrived from Europe. Now Jackson was ready to start a new war.

Jackson wouldn't hesitate to invade foreign territory if he could kill a few enemies in the process. To Jackson they were all obstacles to be killed or removed. He intended to kill all he could. Two years earlier he had violated international law by leading an army into Spanish Florida to lay siege to the Morenos' fort near the Gulf coast. A heated cannonball had ended the battle by igniting the fort's powder magazine, causing an explosion that killed two hundred seventy-four defenders, Morenos and Seminoles alike. Only sixty were left alive to be returned to slavery. Two were singled out as leaders and executed as an example.

August pondered all this as he prepared to move out with the troops. His melancholy reverie was brought to an abrupt halt by the sound of footsteps behind him.

"Good morning, August."

August turned to see Major Drake approaching up the slight slope. "Good morning, Sir," August replied.

"Lost in thought, son, or just watching?" Drake asked in his deep, booming voice. Somehow listening to those tones inspired confidence, and it seemed natural to August to be called "son" by the man, even though he was only ten years his senior. August suspected that Major William Drake's voice had as much to do with his rise through the ranks as his competence as an officer.

"I was just thinking, sir. I guess I shouldn't be concerned about folks back home, while we got our own problems to face."

"It's perfectly natural to think about things back home when you are off in the wilderness. Everybody gets a touch of homesick on a long march," Drake said, standing beside August, joining him in his gaze over the camp.

"You know, I got a wife and three children back home. I've been in this army almost fifteen years and I haven't spent a year with my family in all that time. My kids are growing up without me." After a long pause, Drake turned to look at August. "You got a girl back home, son?"

"She's just a kid, really, or she was when I saw her last. Her father was killed fighting the British and her mother died of the fever. She's staying with my Ma while I'm gone, just helping out. Now that I'm down here, I figured out I should have married her when I had a chance," he said aloud and added, "If I get through this alive, I'm gonn'a marry that girl and settle down. I think I've seen enough of adventure and this man's army to last me a lifetime."

"I can't say as I blame you, son," Major Drake said at last, looking back toward the encampment. "Sometimes I think I haven't been very fair to my wife. Maybe I should have let her marry the banker's son and have a decent life, instead of waiting for me all the time."

Both men continued to stare out toward the bustle of the camp, where preparations for moving out were almost complete, and towards the green southern horizon beyond.

"What do you know about Florida, August?" asked the older man after a long pause.

"Not much except there's Indians, swamps, and alligators, and the Spanish don't really control it."

"Not only don't they control it, they never got a good hold on her in three hundred years," Drake observed. "They have allowed the Indians to make war on us and the British to use it as a base during the war. Hardly anyone lives down the peninsula, most of the original Indians down there died of fever a couple hundred years ago. There're more pirates in Florida than Spanish troops. About five years ago, I was a lieutenant, and my brigade was sent down here with orders to destroy the Indians, because they were allied with the British. We burned their villages, destroyed their crops, stole all their horses and cattle..." his voice trailed off. "I've never felt quite right about it. Never looked forward to coming back. It's an outlaw place. It'll be tough going and it'll be plenty dangerous. I want you to take good care of yourself, son. Don't take too many chances. Bring yourself back home and marry that girl," Drake said. Then he walked away back down the slope toward the camp, leaving August to wonder.

Five days later the troops arrived at the Gulf of Mexico. US Navy supply ships were waiting for them. They quickly began construction of a fort that would command the Apalachicola River, at a place called Prospect Bluff. Jackson's command numbered 800 regulars, 900 Georgia militiamen, and some 300 allied Indians. It seemed strange to August that they were building an American fort on Spanish territory. It didn't take two thousand men very long to build a respectable fort, with substantial earth works and a wooden palisade. General Jackson named the place Fort Gadsden.

The march through Florida was hard, but August was impressed with the beauty and serenity of the land they traversed.

It was ironic, he thought, that he was part of an armed company moving through paradise. It was April, and the rolling hills were covered with stately pines and scattered giant live-oak trees which held their leaves all winter. The deep green of the forest was decorated with the familiar grey-beards the men called Spanish moss, presumably because of the similar beards worn by the Spanish rulers.

Some areas they passed held vast tracts of longleaf pines, standing tall and straight, far above the palmetto-covered ground. The strange palmetto trees took many hundreds of years to grow thirty or forty feet long, but remained only four feet from the ground, their long trunks lying prone, safe from hurricanes. August could see the mark of past fires on both the pines and palmettos, but somehow, both had survived.

A man could make a good home in that wilderness, he thought to himself, with wild turkey and deer, plenty of straight lumber for building, and good soil for farming. The only real problem was the hostile Indians and a weak Spanish government. But, deep inside, he really ached for North Carolina and Ellen, far away.

•

After only ten days in Fort Gadsden, Jackson left a garrison behind and advanced with August's unit and the bulk of the force toward San Marco, at the mouth of the river by the same name. An American supply ship had arrived early and anchored off St. Marks, flying a British Union Jack to confuse the Spanish defenders. When Jackson's army arrived the small Spanish garrison had no desire to oppose a force that numbered twenty times theirs and surrendered without a fight.

The ruse had borne other bitter fruit when an Indian named Homathlemico and his companion, Josiah Francis, a Red Stick Creek leader, were captured when they had rowed out to the ship to parley with the British. As soon as Jackson arrived at San Marco, he ordered the two captives brought ashore and hanged without a trial. August was privately disgusted by Jackson's actions but could do nothing to change the situation.

•

The American occupation of San Marco was profitable for General Jackson's purposes. From there he led raids deep into Spanish Florida, attacking settlements, and capturing or killing the natives. Hundreds were rounded up and shipped in chains to Oklahoma Territory.

Hearing that two Englishmen suspected of inciting the Indians were expected to show up in the area, Jackson had British flags flown at the American encampments. Days later, one of the two, Alexander Arbothnot, walked into the camp with a group of Seminole chiefs. Jackson knew that he had once owned several trading posts in the area and had been an ally of the Indians and British during the War of 1812.

Encouraged by the capture of one enemy, Jackson took a force eastward toward the Suwanee River, where he had heard that other plotters were camped. Although the troops killed a few Indians in a skirmish, Jackson found no sign of his real target, a former British officer named Robert Chrystie Ambrister. August's company captured several small bands of Indians, and they were ordered off under armed guard. His discomfort at his situation grew.

Then, after making camp near the Suwanee, Jackson's windfall came when Ambrister and his men, mostly Indians, simply wandered into camp one night. The shock he felt at finding American troops deep in Spanish Florida did nothing to help him in his predicament. He and Arbothnot were reunited at San Marco as captives.

Arbothnot threw himself on the mercy of the court, but after a tribunal sentenced him to a year of hard labor and fifty lashes, Jackson overruled the court and ordered Arbothnot hanged. Because Ambrister was a military officer, Jackson ordered that he be executed by firing squad. August witnessed the executions and grew to hate his job more with each passing day.

Having rid the area of what he considered to be two of the worst troublemakers, Jackson left a body of occupying troops in San Marco and returned to Fort Gadsden. August was relieved to be back at the Apalachicola River, a step toward home.

At the end of the week, one of the supply ships brought his long-awaited mail. August found a quiet place to himself in the shade of an oak before opening the plain envelope from home.

"*Dear August,*" it began, in Ellen's spidery script. "*I am sorry to have to write this letter, because I would rather tell you about these things in person, but you have taken yourself so far away...*"

August put the letter down, not wanting to continue and stared away into the woods. It was true, he thought. He had made the choices which had led him to this place, and now he felt regrets emerge that had hidden just below the surface for a long time. At last, he steeled himself and began to read again.

"*Your mother, who was doing well until recently, took ill last month. Although I sent for the doctor right away, there was little he could do. She got very sick and couldn't breathe. She passed away on the 23rd. Her last words were of you. I am so sorry, August. I feel very bad for you, and I hope you don't blame me, for I did all I could.*

"*The house was just too empty to stay in alone, so I have decided to go north. A friend of mine who came to call has a brother who is a doctor in New York. I have never been there, and he has promised to take me along when he goes to visit. I may be able to get work in his office there.*"

August blinked back a deepening mist in his eyes as he felt the impact of this double loss.

"*I am taking nothing from the house,*" the letter continued, "*Mr. Fulsome at the bank says he will hold it, along with your mother's savings, until you decide what to do. I'm sorry things didn't go as we planned, August. I do care for you and wish you well in whatever life you make for yourself. God bless you and keep you well... Ellen.*"

August folded the letter and placed it back in the envelope, his face a mask without expression. Raising his eyes, he stared up through the branches of the trees into the deep blue of the afternoon sky. Tears welled within him, but he fought them back. "No sense in crying. It won't help now," he told himself.

Feeling a deep loneliness within, August slept fitfully. He was almost relieved when Major Drake approached him the next morning.

"Time to get your men together, August. We're going on another hike," he said, while looking with feigned interest at the defensive works.

"Yes, Sir," August answered, waiting expectantly for more details.

After a long pause, Drake spoke again. "Make sure that they've got full packs, especially ammunition. We're heading for Pensacola. It seems the Spanish have been interfering with our ships moving supplies back up the Escambia River to Fort Crawford, which is a violation of the treaty. And it seems that they've got another Indian uprising stirred up. They're gathering at Pensacola. The General's decided that the Spanish have to be taught a lesson." August remained silent and Drake turned to face him.

"From the look on your face, I guess you got some bad news from home, August. I'm sorry."

"Thank you, Sir. I am too, but I guess it's my fault. It seems I have nothing left to go home for."

"There's always a reason to want to go home, even if you're not sure where it is," Drake answered.

•

On May 22nd General Jackson arrived at Pensacola with twelve hundred soldiers after a march of two hundred seventy-five miles. Two days later they had captured the city and August walked through the streets of a humble settlement that had never really prospered in two hundred years of existence. It was not what he had expected, and his impression was one of lost opportunity.

The Spanish garrison had retreated into Fort Barrancas, and Jackson laid siege. After three days they had surrendered without a serious battle. August was one of the officers present for the signing of the truce, and had a sense of the turning point in history that he was witnessing.

General Jackson took personal responsibility for everything he had captured from the Spanish and offered his ships to transport them wherever they might wish to go. August watched as the Spanish troops boarded US vessels for the trip to Havana, never to return to West Florida.

Jackson's invasion of Florida brought storms of protest from both Spain and Great Britain, and the administration of President James Monroe was deeply embarrassed by the military action, which it learned of as a fait accompli. Jackson had claimed that he had received tacit authorization in the form of a letter from one of Tennessee's US senators. The president denied authorizing the letter and the issue was never resolved.

Less than a year later, on February 22, 1819, representatives of the Spanish government signed a treaty of cession in Washington, D.C., giving Florida to the United States for a sum equal to the claims that American settlers had filed against the Spanish government. Spain also relinquished its claim to Oregon territory. In exchange, the US gave up its claims to lands west of the Perdido River, leaving Texas to Spain. Florida had again become a pawn in a game of powers. The United States was still expanding. and Jackson, like many others, was intent on reaching its "manifest destiny" of controlling North America. To thousands of settlers who began drifting south into the new territory, he had assumed a heroic stature.

On January 24, 1821, President Monroe, who had earlier been enraged by Jackson's unauthorized invasion of Spanish territory, gave in to popular acclaim and offered to Jackson the territorial governorship of Florida. This time, to the surprise of many, Jackson accepted. While it may have been, as some suspected, Monroe's best hope at revenge, Jackson came determined to make a success of governing the territory, despite the repeated Spanish failures.

That July Governor Jackson stood in Pensacola watching the ceremonial lowering of the Spanish standard and the triumphant raising of the Stars and Stripes, while the USS Hornet thundered a 21-gun salute from the harbor. In the civilian audience that day, freshly bathed and in a new suit of clothes, stood August Booker, late of the United States Army.

December 1819

AUGUST BOOKER WAS A MAN OF FEW DREAMS and those had been destroyed when Ellen had written to tell him of his losses back home. Since he had completed his enlistment in the army, he had requested the bank to liquidate his mother's few assets and forward what amounted to the humblest of family fortunes to him in Pensacola. He had no family left in North Carolina and no desire to return. Now he would seek his future, whatever it may be, in the new Florida Territory he had helped to open.

Pensacola was a rather pitiful town of about 700 inhabitants, but they were mostly Spanish citizens and soldiers who soon departed for Havana. Only three dozen Spanish officers remained behind to conclude the affairs of the Spanish government. On the nearby Escambia River, however, was a community of more than 300 American "Crackers," and about seventy slaves, who had moved into Florida in earlier years. They had grown a variety of food crops and raised the cattle and pigs which had helped to feed the Spanish troops. Although they were technically illegal immigrants, the Spanish governor had tolerated their presence.

Within a few months, however, thousands of Americans began pouring south into Florida, coming mostly from Georgia and Alabama, but many from the Carolinas, Tennessee, and points beyond. All were eager for a chance to claim land by homesteading and make their fortunes.

August was not particularly impressed with the area, though, and uninterested in farming. He found himself doing very little, trying to disperse his gloom with shots of rum, hunting trips into the woods, or just sitting to stare out at the calm Gulf of Mexico. The blue waters with their clouds of fishing birds and vast shoals of fish were a sharp contrast to the settlement. Sanitary conditions in the town were poor and the mosquitoes were fierce. The few brick sidewalks and handful of decent buildings left by the Spanish were far outnumbered by the sandy ruts of washed-out streets and crumbling buildings and barracks that made up most of the town. August thought of leaving but had no idea where to go.

At Christmas time he was living alone in a small Spanish-built house he had taken over. With no family, no love, and no idea what to do next, he hated to even think of the happy Christmases of the past. Out of boredom he took the day to head down the road for a real meal at the rustic inn. While there he encountered a few of the new American arrivals, mostly rough sorts that had drifted into town in the past months. He knew a couple of them by face, if not by name. They settled in at a long table laughing, leaning a collection of shotguns against the wall. "Well, Bud's done won, best shot around these parts, I reckon," one of them announced loudly.

"I'm not surprised at all," the innkeeper replied.

"Won what?" August inquired quietly of one of the men when the opportunity arose.

"Why, he's won the side shoot. We been doing this every year at Christmas back home, figured we'd just do it here too," the man replied. "All's you do is go out on Christmas day and shoot as many birds as you can. Whoever gets the most, wins."

"What kind of birds?" August asked.

"Oh, any old kind, it don't matter," the man told him. "We ain't gon'ta' eat 'em, it's just for fun. Bud racked up two hun'erd twenty-one, beat me by more'n two dozen birds."

August shook his head but kept his peace, finished his meal, and left.

•

August lingered in Pensacola all year, until the outbreak of a yellow fever epidemic. Real estate speculators, who had begun to buy up land, gave up. August joined most of the four thousand persons who had arrived by packing up and departing just as quickly. Unlike most of the others, though, he had no desire to leave the state. He bought passage on a coastal freighter, the first steam-powered side-wheeler he had ever seen.

"This is quite a boat," he told the captain as he passed him on deck, an hour out of port.

"Aye," the man replied with a clipped Yankee accent. He stuck out his hand. "Captain Billy Baker, out o' Gloucester," he said. "And ye might be?"

"August Booker, North Carolina. I came down here with the Army, but had enough of the fighting," he replied.

"Well, you should enjoy our little cruise, we're going ta' be delivering some supplies to Fort Brooke," Baker said. "It'll be fair weather, so just relax and enjoy her."

"I think I've been doing too much relaxing lately," August replied.

"What do you do ta' keep body and soul t'getha?" Baker asked him.

"Not so much lately, I guess I've been wasting too much time now. It's good to be out of there."

"You evah' worked aboard a ship?" Baker asked.

"Never been on one before."

"Well, you look like a healthy sort. If you don't over-do the liq'ah, I might have a job for you."

"What sort of job?" August asked.

"Nothing fancy. It's stoking a boila'. That's what it takes to make this ship go. The sails help, of course, but the engine is what gets us there and back fast."

"Well, I haven't been doing anything useful for a long time," August told him. "I think I'll take you up on the offer."

"It pays four dolla's a week and of course, your bunk and board are included."

A handshake sealed the deal, and that evening August found himself serving a scorching fire. He learned to watch the gauges to judge the steam pressure that turned the cam and piston, driving the noisy, splashing wheel. He soon developed a technique: open the furnace door, shovel in three scoops of coal and slam it shut to avoid the heat.

August had begun an unexpected working tour of every town on the Gulf coast east of New Orleans, where most of the goods arrived from the north. The ship hauled freight back to familiar ground at Saint Marks, formerly the Spanish settlement of San Marco. Most of the cargo they landed there was bound for the new territorial capitol of Tallahassee, midway on the old Spanish Road between Pensacola and St. Augustine. Gradually he got used to filling his lungs with salt air and began to forget the darkness of war and lost love.

Although it was a rough, frontier land with few comforts, August was satisfied. Florida offered a man a chance to make his own life. He soon re-gained self-discipline and confidence aboard the boat.

August eventually visited every new settlement along the Gulf coast of Florida, including Apalachicola, near the Fort Gadsden he had helped to build, as well as Saint Joseph and a village called Tampa, next to the new army post of Fort Brooke. Within a year he had learned their bays and harbors and eventually gave up the boiler work to crew on a small, but much quieter, coastal schooner, where he grew to love the names of the sails, the points of the wind, and the grace of the sea.

During his visits to many of the coastal communities, August saw the tremendous fear and destruction generated by the repeated outbreaks of yellow fever. An outbreak at Saint Marks caused such panic that the ship's crew refused to unload cargo and beat the tide out of port. The town was simply abandoned.

August eventually called at the new US Navy base at Port Rodgers, on an island the Navy commander referred to as Thompson's Island. While the ship's captain and owner negotiated the sale and purchase of cargo, August visited the tiny village that had sprung up nearby.

August found the island a fascinating and beautiful place, as unique as the inhabitants, most of whom spoke Spanish or various native languages. They were hardy people, a mixture of Caribbean Islanders, Americans, Bahamians, and Cubans.

Sitting in a rough tavern he struck up a conversation with a man named Carlos Alvarado. He told August that he was from Cuba and had moved his fishing boat there. He explained that only the Navy called it Thompson's Island. All the Spanish locals called it "Cayo Huevo." A cayo was a small island, and "Cayo Huevo" meant Egg Key, so named because hungry sailors had often raided the nests of the seabirds there. The American immigrants didn't understand the name, so they had taken to calling it Key West.

The handful of locals called themselves "Conchs" after the giant snails that lived among the coral reefs, and Carlos bought August a bowl of conch chowder to accompany his warm beer. August hesitated at the idea of eating any sort of snail, but agreed that it was tasty, if a bit chewy.

He was surprised when Carlos told him that most of the Conchs made their living salvaging, or "wrecking" the many ships which came to disaster on the reefs of the long island chain.

When not wrecking, fishing, or sponging, the Conchs spent their time in leisurely pursuits, waiting for the storms and reefs to do their work. They were a curious mixture, and he respected their fierce independence. August was impressed, too, with the simple, barefoot lifestyle of these island people, who had survived the Yellow Fever epidemic two years before. Now the island was again prospering, and he considered putting down roots there.

The US Navy ships patrolled the islands and coastlines principally to prevent escaped slaves from fleeing to the freedom of the British colony of The Bahamas. Many found assistance from sympathetic Seminoles. Britain had banned the slave trade in 1807 and was actively seizing slaves from ships and re-settling them in their islands.

August and his ship, however, were soon off to Savannah, Georgia, completing the trade loop before sailing back south the new town of Jacksonville, a short distance upstream on the Saint Johns River. There he found it nothing more than a village, strategically placed at the site of Cow's Ford, where the old King's Road to St. Augustine crossed the wide St. Johns River. An ambitious civil engineer named Abram Bellamy had laid out a city a few years earlier, providing for broad boulevards and streets to serve a large population. Although less than a hundred people were living within the new town site, more than a thousand had begun farming in the surrounding area.

August was impressed with the sense of industry, and lingered in the new town long enough to meet John Brady, who operated a ferry at Cow's Ford, making the site most attractive. His neighbor Sarah Waterman exerted considerable influence among the few settlers since she, with the help of her four daughters and two sons, operated the town's inn. There, August was pleased to enjoy real home-cooked greens and vegetables on a table that didn't move. It was a welcome relief after the monotony of shipboard meals.

August followed the crowds to get a glimpse of the *George Washington,* a new two-deck steamboat which had just begun carrying passengers and freight down to the scattered settlements along the St. Johns River. It was the pride of the region and the talk of every settler as it brought news of the wild interior of the territory. August was impressed by the relative comforts it offered compared to the steam freighter he had served on but wondered how it would find enough passengers to make it pay.

While enjoying a drink in the tavern, a local promoter was talking up the idea of digging a canal clear across Florida. "It would be great, and open up the whole territory," he exclaimed loudly. "Andrew Jackson is all for it. It would make the St. Johns the route all the way to New Orleans. Jacksonville would be a boomtown." The idea seemed far-fetched, and August took him for a real-estate promoter. He knew that, since the end of Jackson's war on the natives, several permanent Seminole towns had sprung up around the hundreds of major springs scattered across Florida. They sure weren't going to be paying passengers, he thought.

The only known attraction for visitors in the un-mapped inland areas were the Silver Springs, up the tributary called the Ocklawaha River. They were a popular camp site for a handful of adventurous sight-seers, but even more popular with the Seminoles, who were unhappy at the stream of tourists invading their territory. Already a defended trading post had recently been built nearby at some old Spanish cross-roads.

All too soon, August found himself back on his own ship, the captain carefully timing their departure to high tide so that, with the help of a brisk wind, they could escape over the dangerous sandbars that plagued the mouth of the St. Johns River. Fate, though, was about to put an end to August's restless days on the sea.

It was during a return visit to the broad west-coast Tampa Bay that events occurred to change August's life. Given a chance to spend a brief time ashore, August wandered about Fort Brooke, where two hundred and fifty-six square miles along the Hillsborough River had been designated as a military reservation. More than two hundred soldiers drilled on the grounds and carpenters were busy erecting new barracks for more. The small civilian community of Tampa was just a collection of wooden structures in the shadow of the outpost.

Wandering the dusty main street of the village, August saw a party of Seminoles, accompanied by a platoon of soldiers, move up the street toward the commander's quarters. A small crowd of local people were watching with curiosity and August soon joined them.

"What's going on with the Seminoles?" August asked the nearest man, who had begun to turn away from the scene as the party disappeared into the building.

"They come in here from time to time, mostly to trade," he told him. "The army always has to talk to 'em, try to find out more about what's going on in the interior, before they let 'em buy anything."

It was hours later, when August was ready to head back to his boat, that he walked out of a trading post and straight into the party of Seminoles. Beside five men, there were two women. One of these, who came face to face with August, stared at him with open eyes and he found himself staring back. She was, he thought, the most beautiful young woman he had ever seen.

"Don't worry, they're peaceable," called one of the half dozen soldiers still escorting the party around as they did their trading.

"Oh, I'm not afraid of Indians," August replied as he collected himself. "I served with hundreds of them under General Jackson, and fought against them, too. I respect them, but I'm not afraid of them."

The soldiers, mostly new recruits, seemed impressed at August's experience, but one of the Indians stepped forward, until he stood shoulder to shoulder with the young woman who glanced shyly at August's gaze.

"I am Blackwater. You know our people?" he said in English.

"Yes, I do," August answered, using the Hitchiti language he had picked up from the Lower Creeks who had served as allies to the army. Blackwater's eyes showed a tiny hint of approval.

"I am August Booker," he continued in the native tongue. "Where do you live?"

"Four days walk toward the rising sun," Blackwater responded in Hitchiti. Then, glancing at the woman at his side, he said, "This is my sister, Nighthawk. The man who would marry her must prove his worth."

"Oh!" August flustered, realizing that he had been staring. "I just... I mean, well, I didn't mean..." August found himself repressing a blush, at a loss for words for perhaps the first time in his life. "I am sorry," he said at length. "I didn't mean to stare. Nighthawk is a beautiful woman."

Now it was Blackwater's turn to smile, as some of the soldiers within earshot strained to understand the conversation. He looked at Nighthawk, who now smiled as well and asked her something softly that August couldn't understand. Then he turned again to August. "If you are here when the full moon returns the second time, you may meet Nighthawk." he said, then began to walk away.

With only a brief coy glance back over her shoulder, Nighthawk followed, and the group walked away. The soldiers caught the meaning of the exchange of looks and offered a few catcalls, making their fun of August's embarrassment.

During the weeks that followed, August found himself dwelling on the chance meeting, daydreaming about Nighthawk's dark, doe-like eyes, lustrous hair and brown skin and the offer of a meeting. He had known the Indians only as helpers and scouts, or the toughest of enemies. Now, he thought about one constantly. In those moments when there was no work to keep him busy, he stared out at the blue gulf waters racing by the ship and watched the dolphins at play before the bow. He stared at the sunsets and pined. Everything he saw seemed to remind him of the woman he had seen for only a moment.

Five weeks after their first meeting, August found himself on another boat arriving in Tampa, this time as a paying passenger. He wasn't sure what it was he wanted to say to Nighthawk, but he knew that he wanted to see her again, for longer than two minutes, and without the catcalls of the soldiers.

After helping unload the freight, he barely had time to get back to the local canteen when he was approached by a sergeant and two rifle-bearing solders. As soon as they entered the shady bar room, August knew that they were there to complicate his life.

Minutes later, he was led before a serious-looking colonel sitting behind a large wooden table, who inquired of his interests in Tampa. August's stumbling excuses were enough to confirm the colonel's expectations.

"I've heard all about your last visit here, Mr. Booker and I've been waiting for you to show up again," the colonel began. "Trouble like you always comes back around. Let me explain something to you, Mister," he continued. "These Seminoles are my charges. They have been on this reservation less than a year, and it took all the power of the United States to get them to agree to live there. My job is to see that they stay, at least until the government decides what to do with them next."

"They aren't likely to cause trouble," August answered. "They're from several tribes, Yuchi and Yamassee from South Carolina, some of the Lower Creeks...I served alongside lots of them in Alabama, fighting against the Upper Creeks, the Red Sticks."

"Well, they're all Seminoles now, upper, lower, or sideways, it don't matter to the government and it don't matter to me," the colonel replied. "The treaty of Moultrie Creek they signed says they're gonna' live on this reservation. They got just about all the land south of Ft. King and north of Charlotte Harbor, that's not within 20 miles of the coast. That gives them some four million acres, by most accounts. That ought to be enough to keep them happy for a while. I don't need you coming in here stirring things up."

August gritted his teeth and struggled to keep his cool in the face of the arrogance of the officer, who represented the worst of the army in August's mind. "Sir, I'm not here to cause any trouble. I respect these people," August said, standing straight and looking the colonel square in the eye, but without a hint of defiance in his voice.

"Just know this, mister..." the colonel said in a cold, flat tone. "I'm not going to lock you up to protect you from yourself, even though I could. But if you go running off into the swamps and get yourself in trouble, don't expect me and my men to come shooting our way in to rescue you. Do you understand me?" he said.

"Yes, sir," August responded, suddenly feeling very much like a junior officer again.

"Don't go starting any Indian troubles. I got all I need now. Dismissed!" he concluded.

August had barely gotten out the door onto the porch to put his hat on when one of the guards outside leaned into his face with a sneer. "Indian lover!" he said in a threatening tone. The second guard just glared at August, his rifle in his hands, as if eager to smash the butt of the weapon into him at the slightest sign of provocation. August simply backed up a step, put his hat calmly on his head, stared at the two a moment, turned and walked away.

The third day following found August waiting at his campsite at the opposite end of the main street from the stockade. It was the appointed day, and he was confident that Blackwater would keep his word. As the afternoon sun slowly retreated behind the tops of the few trees left standing to provide a bit of shade, August saw Blackwater approaching, his regal form distinguishable even from a distance. Like a conqueror he passed along the dusty road, his eyes never glancing toward the tents and shelters of the settlement. As before, he was accompanied by an armed escort, for the Seminoles were always watched within the boundaries of the military reservation. Blackwater's demeanor was as if they were his bodyguards. August watched the unlikely parade approach and contemplated his options.

Blackwater never hesitated but walked directly up to August and stood looking at him. August motioned for him to sit, and Blackwater eased himself onto an adjacent stump. The half dozen soldiers looked around uncomfortably, unsure what to do.

"You men hungry?" August asked the sergeant in command. Although the military provided decent rations, August knew they would rarely pass a chance to eat.

"Sure, if you got some grub, I'm sure the boys could use a bite," he answered, adding "thanks," almost as an afterthought, when August pulled half a ham from his pack.

When the soldiers chose a spot about forty feet away to divide their bounty, August turned again to Blackwater and spoke softly in the Hitchiti tongue. "I have returned as you told me. I would like to see Nighthawk again."

Blackwater looked August in the eye for a long moment. August looked back, unflinching.

"You are a strange man, August Booker," Blackwater said at length. "We must talk. You may come with me."

The two men got up and August swiftly broke camp, put his few things into his pack and slung the parcel over his shoulder with a sense of determination. Together they began to walk quietly down the street.

"Hey!" called the sergeant, looking up from the half-eaten ham. Reluctantly, the soldiers got to their feet and followed the two men down the road, which soon tapered into a rough, sandy trail. When they came to the guard post and watch tower marking the edge of the military reservation, the soldiers' responsibilities ended. They stopped and stared after the departing pair.

"You better watch out, mister, or we'll be finding you with no hair!" the sergeant called after him. August ignored the remark, knowing that deep within he had no fear of the man he followed. Together they quickly disappeared into the fragrant pine woods.

•

For three days the pair traveled on foot into the inland wilderness and August had opportunity to wonder if he had made a wise decision. The landscape consisted of miles of flat land, with only a couple of low sandy ridges separated by small creeks. Blackwater led August skillfully through the country, following the barest of trails, too scant for less than an experienced tracker to find. They camped at places that seemed to have been used before, always near water. Occasionally they would talk, mostly about the land through which they traveled, but only once of

Nighthawk. The conversation gave him very little new information and August reflected on the ludicrous position he had placed himself in, wondering what had come over him. He was taking his life in his hands to see a woman he had never spoken to.

"Our mother's people came here from Oconee," Blackwater said at length as they walked. August recognized it as the name of a river in Georgia. "My father was one of the ancient ones."

"Ancient ones?" August asked.

"The people who have lived in these lands since the beginning of time," Blackwater replied. "There are very few of those people now. Others here are Yamassee, Yuchi, Choctaw and Hitchiti Miccosukee. "This is my itálwa," he said, using the Seminole word for a tribal band. "Now all our people are called Miccosukee."

"My people lived in North Carolina," August replied. "Now I am the only one left."

Blackwater stopped and turned to look at the man who followed in his footsteps. For a long moment the two men stood, face to face, while Blackwater studied August's eyes. After a long pause he spoke again. "I will take you to Nighthawk now."

A short time later the two men walked into a rough village on the bank of a large spring-fed pool. The camp was large and seemed to August to house more than two hundred people. It consisted of a scattering of small hide-covered shelters and several "chickees," shelters built of poles and thatched with the plentiful fronds of the palmettos on roof and walls. Most had only partial floors elevated above the ground, to provide space for sleeping and storage.

The appearance of a white man in the village caused a sensation and August felt the eyes upon him as he strode toward one of the larger shelters. Telling him to sit, Blackwater soon had women provide a hearty meal, which consisted of flat, somewhat bitter, meal-like cakes made of coontie flour, along with some stewed rabbit. He was also given a basket of small, sweet berries. Another piece of roasted meat, which August could not identify, was accompanied by a second kind of flat bread and some sweet green sprouts.

After he had eaten and been given a chance to bathe himself in the pool, August was invited back to the campfire, where several dozen of the men had gathered in a kind of council. After a few introductions, August was questioned at length and given a chance to speak in his rather limited Hitchiti. Blackwater served as a translator when August's knowledge failed him. Although the conversation was muted, August could not help but sense hostility coming from a few of the assembly.

"We were happy in Apalachee, but the soldiers said we must go," Blackwater explained to August. "Our chiefs signed papers that say we can stay in these lands for all times to come. Will the soldiers keep their word?"

August hung his head for a moment, looking at the earth at his feet, which had been given to these Miccosukee and thousands of other Seminoles. "I don't know what they will do," he replied. "Today there is peace, and it is good. If leaders remain strong and faithful, peace will last."

"You speak truthfully, August Booker," Blackwater said in reply, "for you do not know the future, but the past is a story of lies and death. We do not wish to fight, but only to give our children good land and game and good water. Learn our ways and perhaps you can teach us to respect each other."

At this, many of the assembly grunted their agreement, unspoken fears and beliefs suspended for the moment. With a wave of his hand, the senior chief dismissed the group.

"Wait here," said Blackwater, only to return a moment later, leading the one called Nighthawk by the hand. As before, August stared in a sudden fit of speechlessness, as if his very ability to talk had been taken from him.

"I am Nighthawk," she said at last in English, as if to break the silence. "Let us speak to each other." She turned to walk away, and August fell in beside her, his heart racing.

•

The following days passed swiftly for August, and Nighthawk came to trust his gentleness as she showed him her home. The tribe gradually came to accept his presence, though not without resentment by a few. After two weeks, Blackwater invited

August to hunt with them and he participated in stalking a deer, which provided a great feast.

August and Nighthawk sat together during the dinner, laughing, talking, and teaching each other new words in their own languages. Her first glimpse of this man had intrigued her. Now, she felt warm in his presence and enjoyed sharing with him the small commonplace things she knew well, but which to him were strange and new. Already August was learning the ways of the wildlife, the edible plants, and the names of the birds.

Nighthawk explained how they made coontie starch, a staple of their diet, by cooking, mashing, and drying the roots of the primitive palm-like plant. She showed him how they built small snares to catch rabbits and squirrels, bending a sapling over a leather loop and staking it loosely. It was a life of subsistence he had never known, but the band seemed to be completely satisfied with it.

They began to take long walks and August was fascinated when Nighthawk showed him the white sand hills of the scrub country, like the dunes of ancient beaches. She told him tales of the floods which had swept the land and built the dunes high, according to the shaman story-weavers. He sat amazed when she made a strange noise like a bird and half a dozen scrub jays approached them to sit and eat bits of berry from her hand, small blue birds without a natural fear of man. She showed him the strange "strangler" fig, which grew from high in the branches of other trees, or even the crowns of palms. Seeds dropped by birds took root and eventually formed multiple trunks that seemed to slowly strangle the host plant. She told him about the gopher tortoise, living deep in his burrow for a hundred years, a welcoming host to dozens of other animals and insects. He was fascinated by the strange new world.

Nighthawk loved to listen to August's stories of the places he had been and the towns and cities he had seen, and she took every chance to expand her own knowledge of English. He told her of the ancient civilizations he had learned about in school and the railroads, which she had never seen. She laughed when he imitated the speech of the English and the French, thinking them strange and wonderful. She looked up to this special man and respected his bravery. She could not imagine that he would give up his wonderful world to live in their land, even though he sat with her hand in his.

Throughout the days, Blackwater watched from a distance. When the tribe ate together, the pair were always side-by-side. One evening when the meal was finished and the tribe broke into groups of men and women, he lingered and approached the pair.

"Our father is dead," he said to August, as Nighthawk watched and listened. "I am the guardian of my sister. I believe you would wish to marry her, as white men do, and live with her and have children. Our laws are much the same. Is this what you desire?"

Though August had wondered where their relationship would lead, the question from her brother cemented the answer already forming in his mind. August looked at the man for a moment, then turned his gaze upon Nighthawk.

"I cannot think of leaving this woman, whom I love. If she will have me, I will marry her." Nighthawk lowered her eyes for a moment, then returned his gaze. "I would be your wife," she said simply.

The two were married in a traditional ceremony, though August promised himself that one day they would marry before a minister, in a real church service. With the marriage, August became one of the tribe, though he knew that the prejudice against his pale skin would never be completely gone. He would pay that price to be with the woman he loved. They built a simple chickee hut a short distance from the main camp, but always participated in tribal gatherings.

•

August and Nighthawk spent the following months in the bliss known only to lovers. Time seemed to fly as he learned the ways of the Seminole band and became ever more proficient at their language. He listened closely in the evenings as storytellers shared memories of events long ago and the heroes of their people. He marveled as they drew artifacts from their basket, now filled with items drawn from several tribes, and told the tale associated with each object.

One day August walked with a group on a pilgrimage to a high hill considered sacred by the Calusa and Timucua peoples, and still honored by the itálwa. There he sat with Nighthawk to watch the sunset color the western sky and saw a glint of sunlight upon distant waters. They spent the night on beds of pine "straw" under tall, sighing trees that swayed gently in the breeze.

August was gradually accepted by the rest of the band and worked hard to earn their trust and respect. Slowly accepted into the council, his opinion began to be sought on any question regarding the whites and what they might do next. He did his best to give honest answers and found himself often embarrassed trying to explain the endless greed of the settlers and the dishonest dealings of the government, who found treaties to be temporary conveniences.

August's trusty Army-issued sidearm was rarely used and he carefully conserved his dwindling supply of percussion caps. Few of the Seminoles owned the flintlock rifles that had proven to be an effective hunting tool, and most relied upon their long bows, many brought from northern climes through trade.

Later that winter, a party of well-armed white men came upon the camp, searching for black slaves they said had run away. Although many bands of Seminoles took in escaped slaves, none were in hiding with their itálwa. August concealed himself, unwilling to provoke possible trouble, but watched in case any broke out. The slavers were hostile and arrogant, but eventually satisfied themselves that there was nothing of value they could take and turned back toward the north.

The men of the itálwa were angry about the invasion of their lands, but August succeeded in calming them, pointing out that they had sometimes left the reservation. The white men, he told them, were only searching, as they themselves had done.

The following year the summer rains were sparse and by the fall of the year drought had set in, and streams began to run low or dry up completely. The Miccosukee's few crops of maize, collard greens, squash, and peas, watered by the few pots of water that could be carried by hand, failed to produce much, and soon the shortage of food became serious. In small parties, the group sent forays out beyond the reservation lands, seeking food along the coasts, or in areas already settled by whites. August knew that it was a formula for disaster, but also knew that they had no other options, for the local game alone could never support the entire group.

Several times the leaders of the band called upon the federal Indian agent at Fort Brooke who served as a liaison to the government. They succeeded in getting small amounts of food, but it was not enough to satisfy their needs and they were often hungry.

The rains returned in the spring of 1827 and the crops were successful. August scarcely missed the outside world he had known but continued to worry about the future of the tribe.

In December of that year August chose a new home site and built a solid cabin of timbers near the big lake called We-oh-ya-kapka. It was a big change for Nighthawk, who had always lived as part of the itálwa, but she was devoted to August. She explained the change to her family, and they grudgingly accepted. As a compromise, she and August often traveled the day's walk to visit her friends and family, as well as receiving reciprocal visits from them.

Their life was simple and rugged. An open-air kitchen at the rear of the cabin provided their meals, while a "wash-up" along the wall, with a basin, bucket, and dipper, along with a comb and mirror, provided most of their grooming needs.

To obtain clear water far from a muddy bank August built a "sweep," consisting of a long wooden pole which he rested in a notch upon a tall stump. A bucket attached to the end raised water from the lake for drinking, bathing, and cooking. Frequent excursions to a clear stretch of a creek gave them an opportunity to bathe in cool waters during the hot summer. Nighthawk admired the way the water rippled the sandy bottom and the light played upon it. August explained that the stripes were like that of a tiger much larger than the panthers that stalked the forest around them.

Summer passed and the nights grew cooler, and August was comfortably snuggled under their robes with his wife when Nighthawk gave him one of the most pleasant surprises of his life.

"My husband," she whispered, "before the summer I will bring a new life to the light. You will be a father."

August lay speechless for a moment, before giving her a gentle squeeze. "You make me very happy, my love," he told her. His most fervent wishes were coming true and his love for her redoubled with the news. But it also brought him to a quandary. Babies, he believed, should be born with an experienced midwife, or even a doctor, nearby. He could scarcely trust the women of the tribe to be able to perform the task, discounting the fact that they had done so for hundreds of generations. This time, it was his own wife and child at stake, and they deserved a real doctor, he thought.

"I need to go to Ft. Brooke," he told Nighthawk as the days began to grow longer. "I want to see about a doctor if we need one." Although she tried to dissuade him, August was adamant, and left for the bay the next day.

Walking into the military reservation of Fort Brooke, August found that the community had grown slightly. While more civilians had arrived and begun to build, there was still only a single small general store, and no private doctor. He would have to depend, as did everyone, on the military. His first inquiries into the services of a doctor brought him a real surprise.

"Mister, not only can't a doctor go onto the reservation to deliver a baby, neither can you," a captain told him at the headquarters. "The territorial council has passed a law that says whites can't go on the reservation and the Indians can't leave."

"But that's ridiculous! I live there!" August cried, but the captain was unmoved.

"I'm going to have to lock you up for violating the territorial law and the federal treaty with the Indians," he said. Without an opportunity for a trial, he was quickly escorted to the stockade.

Almost a month went by as August was forced to suffer the repeated abuse of the soldiers, who had recognized him as the man who had left with the Seminole. "Indian lover," they called him, and several times contrived to lose his meals, leaving him hungry and alone. In the confines of his cell, August lost weight as he paced and worried. Nighthawk, he knew, would be worried as well, and that weighed on his mind worse than any physical abuse he could be subjected to.

Finally, a hearing was arranged before a territorial judge, who agreed that August could be released for the time he had served if he would abide by the law of the territory and stay out of the Seminole reservation. August had no choice but jail or accepting the terms. He knew if he agreed and walked away a free man, he would soon find a way to evade the preposterous edict and find his way back to Nighthawk. That was the only thing on his mind as he walked out of the hearing room.

August was stopped immediately by an army detail. "Not so fast, mister," the sergeant in charge told him. "We've got a little surprise here for you."

The soldiers quickly led him down the street towards the wharf, where he was shoved up a gangway onto a sloop and put in the charge of the captain. August was handed an envelope and told that the soldiers had orders to shoot him if he left the ship.

Two hours later, with the detail encamped on the dock, the ship cast off and August was bound for Key West. His life was shattered as he sat on the deck contemplating how to regain control and reunite with the woman he loved. How would his expected daughter or son be raised in the wilds of Florida, never knowing their father? Would they be fully accepted, or live a life as a pariah in the itálwa?

August Booker mourned the tragic circumstances that had led to this moment, and the blunder he had made in going to Fort Brook. Most of all, he mourned the loss of his beloved Nighthawk.

BOOK TWO
AND STILL THEY CAME

The Trail Map
March 1829

AUGUST BOOKER SAT ON THE DECK watching the Gulf coast retreat slowly behind. His ordered world had become a nightmare. He had left his home on the Seminole lands only to run afoul of the Army and arcane rules, finding himself arrested and now Shanghaied. His desire to protect his beloved Nighthawk from the assumed danger of childbirth had resulted in his absence just as he was needed most, and he drew farther away from her by the minute.

His years of service under the renegade General Andrew Jackson had brought him to Florida, but the army had become his biggest problem. It was his years as a civilian, spent sailing on the coastal schooners, that had led to his chance encounter with the woman he had married in the face of social stigma.

He had sworn to love and protect Nighthawk. Accepting life in the wilds of central Florida among the refugees of several tribes that made up his itálwa was but a small thing to trade for the love of his life. Now it had all backfired on him.

August could only fret as he contemplated how he would get back to his beloved wife while evading the troops that had forced him aboard the ship. He struggled to contain his emotions and considered jumping from the ship to attempt to swim to the shore, but his familiarity with the threat of tidal currents, not to mention sharks, stifled the thought. He would find a surer way.

Assessing his situation, he realized he had only two dollars, which he had found in the envelope issued him by the commander at Fort Brooke at Tampa Bay. It was only enough to prevent his vagrancy. All during the trip he was consumed with plotting how he would return to his beloved Nighthawk as soon as humanly possible.

The weather had turned warm when the sloop arrived at Key West. He was surprised to see the changes since he had called at the port only a few years earlier. The Navy base had been removed to Pensacola that year, but the island town was now a bustling civilian community of about two hundred, plus many more from the ships visiting to trade and take on provisions. Gone was the name of Port Rodgers and the designation of Thompson's Island. The town had a bustling feel and would soon become Florida's largest town.

It took August only a day after his arrival to find work on a large clipper sailing to Savannah. Two weeks later he had worked his way back south to Jacksonville, on the St. John's River. His boat docked a few miles from the town at a large plantation near the river's mouth to take on a load of indigo and cotton.

August wiped the sweat from his own brow but stood aside as two dozen slaves loaded bales and barrels in the heat, stacking them tightly into place under the supervision of the captain. Invited ashore by a plantation foreman, he walked to the sprawling home of the owners, where he stood on the high porch to gaze out over many acres of indigo and the huge vats that produced the valued dye. A warm, thin breeze wafted a sharp, poisonous stench to his nostrils. He walked along the upwind side of the broad cement-walled tanks to see how the indigo plants were steeped for hours to soften before being beaten to release their color. The liquid then flowed into a settling vat, where the concentrated mud-like indigo product slowly dried in the sun. The sludge seemed to stain everything.

"We got almost a hun'erd slaves workin' here," the foreman volunteered to August by way of explanation. "We got to watch 'em real close to get any work out'a them. Now's the gov'ament won't let them bring over anymore, we try to keep 'em breeding, too. Most of 'em's only good for fifteen or twenty years a' work and you got to raise 'em up for seven, eight years first, and that costs a lot. They grow their own food and most'a ours too, though, so it's not too bad."

August looked with pity at the bent backs and bobbing heads that were evidence of the hard work being done under the sweltering spring sun. With the weather already so warm, what would it be like in mid-summer, he wondered? He had never gotten used to the idea of slavery but kept his peace while on the plantation. "It will take a war to stop it," he thought, "and that will be another tragedy."

As his small ship headed back toward Savannah, August was invited aboard the plantation's own small jack-boat and made the crossing to Jacksonville only a few miles away. The town had grown only a little since his earlier visits, but several new buildings lined the waterfront. Orchards of peach and citrus trees were blooming, and the warm spring air was perfumed. It was a lazy and idyllic setting, but August was on a mission and couldn't linger. He needed to get home.

Using his new earnings, he quickly bought passage on the *George Washington* to the settlement of Enterprise, which was to be found where the St. John's River met Lake Monroe, the southern-most stop on the river.

Aboard the boat August had the good fortune to meet a man named George Wilson. He was a rare Englishman who still owned a plantation in Florida.

"Tell me, Mr. Wilson, how is it that you came to be here?" August asked him.

"My father moved to Florida after Spain turned it over to Britain back in '63," George told him. "He started a great plantation, and we grew bananas and corn and sugar cane and vegetables. He was a Loyalist during the Revolution, like most of his friends. I…disagreed with him. When Spain got the territory back, he moved to the Bahamas and left me in charge. I sold our crops to the Spanish and worked with the Menorcans that Governor Turnbull brought to New Smyrna. My wife is a delightful Menorcan woman, and we have two sons."

"My wife," August said quietly, "is a Seminole. Now I am on my way back to her."

"You are a remarkable man!" George said. "Like me, you reject the fabric of convention and make a life as you see fit."

"Your plantation is near St. Augustine?" August asked.

"Yes, just a short way up the San Sebastian River," George replied. "Come see me there if you can. You shall be my guest!"

The two men spent their afternoons on the top deck and shared a few nips from a bottle of Scotch whiskey that George had brought along. They became fast friends.

The broad river flowed from the south for another hundred and forty miles from that point, keeping twenty or thirty miles inland from the coast. It was, by far, the best highway to the interior. Cruising down the river on the paddle-wheeler took him through some beautiful regions of the state, unlike anything August had seen elsewhere and different too from the sandy scrub he had come to know in central Florida.

The river exhibited only the slightest evidence of flow, and thick forests of live oak draped with the beards of Spanish moss gave the shores a mysterious and haunted look. The trees took their name because they held their leaves all year and were only now dropping them as the spring flush replaced the older growth. Along with cypress trees, they lined most of the banks, which widened to a few miles in places. The boat stopped at the village of Green Cove Springs, where a few northern visitors departed the boat to bathe in the famed warm mineral waters.

After the second day the boat tied up each night, letting out line to move away from the shore and its teeming mosquitoes. They were several days out and halfway down the river when a series of storms slowed their progress, soon followed by wintry blasts that put an end to the buzzing of insects. The temperature dropped enough that the entire complement huddled together for warmth in the main cabin for three nights and frost formed on the deck as the river produced skittering clouds of steam. August wondered about those blooming fruit trees in Jacksonville and the vagaries of nature.

Stopping again at a rickety wharf, the steamer let off passengers who would meet wagons to connect with St. Augustine on the coast. August's new friend, George, went with them. "I'll take a fork that heads straight to my plantation," he told August. "When you come to visit, just remember to turn right after about six miles on this road. There's a sign with my name on it."

"I hope to see you again, George," August called as the boat cast off.

Along the rest of the trip the boat stopped and left crates and barrels on apparently nondescript sand banks, where they would eventually be retrieved by settlers homesteading in the woods. August marveled at the various streams that joined the main flow along the way, most fed by the gushing springs of the interior.

Overall, though, the voyage was a discouraging one for August. During the entire trip a small group of men sat on the fore-deck of the steamer, aiming their weapons at anything that moved. They blasted away at the wading birds, the eagles and ospreys, the alligators, even the turtles that sunned themselves on the floating logs along the river. A rookery full of nesting storks was an entertaining target for the killers and they left it decimated. They shot the manatees, the gentle, lumbering "sea cows" that swam in the river grazing on the water grasses, leaving them trailing blood through the clear waters. They killed indiscriminately and quickly, seeming to derive a twisted pleasure from their ability to do so, never thinking of the value of what they destroyed.

After the boat left the village they called Pilatka, the river narrowed to a tight channel and the armed party on the foredeck occasionally spotted and shot game like turkey and deer as well. Yet the boat plunged ever onward, and the dying bounty was left to rot in their wake. They also passed fields of half-submerged stumps, evidence of where loggers had cleared stands of cypress trees, which were being floated downriver to supply the building needs of Jacksonville.

The boat chugged across the broad waters of Lake George, named by English settlers in honor of the king, before threading its way into a narrow channel on the far side. To August the river seemed a braided morass, enough to lose oneself in, but the pilot kept his course.

After several days the boat reached its terminus at the village of Enterprise, where the river broadened to the large Lake Monroe, named after the president The town was a small collection of clapboard buildings and rough log cabins perched on the north-west corner of the lake, and the setting sun left the waters ablaze with an orange glow as they tied to the wharf. The shooters who had spoiled so much of the trip for August quickly disappeared into the woods.

August explored the tiny settlement and was surprised to see a wealth of bird life apparently undisturbed along the lake. Shoals of ducks floated on the broad river as they passed through on their migration and there were large rookeries full of egrets and herons building nests for the spring hatching. Warmer weather had returned, and August was glad to see the birds were making up for lost time.

The next phase of his trip now confronted him. He was determined to find his way home. August knew it was going to be rough. He hadn't been able to earn enough money in his weeks working aboard the ship to afford a horse. He would have to do it on foot. Worst of all, there were no known trails where he was going.

The merchant who ran the lone store seemed to be about the only person in the area who had taken the name of the place to heart. His was a rustic enterprise with meager supplies, but August bought some good boots for the hike ahead, along with a supply of hardtack and some beans. Anything else he might need to eat he would have to find on the way. The only maps he offered had only sketchy details of most of the interior, which had never been surveyed.

"What you want to go down there for?" was the response August heard when he asked about directions down toward the ridge area.

"I have to meet someone," he replied, concealing unnecessary details.

"It's your skin, mister." he was told. "That's the middle of Seminole lands and sometimes they can be less than friendly to strangers, I've heard."

"I'll take my chances."

"If you really want to go, you should catch the next boat back north, but get off on the west bank just as soon as they turn onto the river. There's a good landing the captain knows. From there just go around the west side of the lake, follow that main trail. When you see the big tree, take the fork going south. After that, just see where it leads, I never been down that a'ways."

"Big tree?" August asked. "There's lots of big trees around here."

"Not like this one," the merchant replied. "You'll know it when you see it."

August followed the advice and hopped off a boat two days later. Too impatient to wait for the steamer, he had gone aboard a small fishing boat powered by a pair of oars and a lateen sail. The skipper said he knew the place and brought him right to it, for a small fee.

He camped at the landing, covering himself against the hordes of mosquitoes despite the warm night and the next morning set off on foot into the interior. A narrow path, perhaps started by wild cattle, had been fairly ridden by the few pioneers who had risked settling in the isolated place. The waters of Lake George shimmered, reflecting the morning sun, but soon the heat became oppressive. He stopped at every opportunity to refill his empty water bottle and take a rest. By late afternoon he was exhausted and knew he would have to stop.

His camp the second night was as miserable as the first. He swatted and rested, but couldn't sleep, staring at the big moon in the sky. "This is useless," he thought to himself. "I'll never get to sleep. I might as well be walking." He pondered the thought a moment, looking around at the pale light that illuminated the surrounding trees. Quickly he rose, packed and set off on the trail. By the time fatigue overtook him, he had covered ten more miles and laid out his bedroll in the pre-dawn chill. He was surprised to find that not a single mosquito showed up to torment him.

He slept until late morning in the shade of a pair of large live oaks, then made a light meal, keeping out of the sun. He slept though most of the afternoon as well. When evening approached, he was suddenly awakened by the buzzing of insects in his ears. It was time to move again. He quickly wrapped his kit and stepped off, still following the thin line worn in the grass. He had gone only a short distance when a strange sight drew him up. There in the middle distance a tree towered above the forest like the castle he had seen in a book.

August approached the big tree and gawked. He had never seen one so large and he tried to calculate its height, coming up with about two hundred feet. The surrounding trees were tall, too, but at most barely over half its height. "It must be thousands of years old," he thought to himself. Now he understood why it was such a landmark. There could be no other like it.

The sun's light had faded, and the moon was just rising as he struck out on the southward, left-most fork. That night, refreshed, he covered almost twenty miles.

After that August traveled every evening, stopping after midnight to sleep. He came across game and had no trouble with food or water, passing many beautiful lakes while avoiding the swamps and marshes.

A week later he was well around the west side of the big lake they called Kissimmee and back in familiar country. He kept the hills of the Ridge to his right, passing by the high sacred hill of red clay with a sense of urgency, his tired legs driving him steadily onward. It was well after dark when he stumbled back into the Miccosukee camp exhausted. Nighthawk had been in mourning since his disappearance and feared to believe he would not return to her. She had moved back to her family's village when he departed and was in the care of the tribal women. She wept with relief as he related the story of his misadventures.

Two days later, a much-renewed Nighthawk bore him a son, whom they named John Eastwind Booker. August swore to himself that he would never again try to leave the reservation without his beloved Nighthawk at his side.

March 1831

ANDREW JACKSON, THE INDIAN FIGHTER and former Governor of the Florida Territory, became President of the United States in 1929 and wasted little time in pursuing his personal agenda. He was as racist a man as had ever stalked the halls of government and moved quickly to advance his plans to eradicate the native populations from the growing United States.

Jackson was never a man to let lesser men get in his way, and his hatred of the Indians dominated his thinking. He soon cajoled Congress into the passage of the Indian Removal Act, ordering the relocation of all native people to a tribal area west of the Mississippi River. It was to mean trouble for August, Nighthawk and all the yat'siminoli people of Florida.

August Booker had managed to live contentedly on the reservation with no inkling of what his former superior was up to, but he was aware that many of the Seminole people were living in terrible conditions, often without adequate food. The meager supplies they could obtain from federal Indian agents, often used as inducements or bribes, were insufficient to feed the population. Entire tribes traveled many miles to set up camp near growths of the low coontie plants to cook the starchy flour. Although August often spoke with the village chiefs about the government offers, he never visited the trading posts for fear of revealing his presence on the reservation.

Only nine years earlier, the Treaty of Moultrie Creek had given the tribes the permanent control of a section of the interior of Florida, while white settlers controlled the coasts and major rivers. Now the chiefs were being told that they had no remaining choices and that they had to accept the president's plan to move them to Arkansas country, west of the distant Mississippi. It was yet another in a long string of broken promises.

The following year Indian agent James Gadsden called a meeting of the tribes at Payne's Landing on the Ocklawaha River and hundreds had taken part in the discussions. The government made promises, but no written record was made of the meetings. Several chiefs volunteered to take part in a committee to investigate the new lands and advise the rest.

While traveling in distant Arkansas they were presented a treaty committing the parties to the move. It was a bit of treachery. Seven chiefs, unable to read English, signed after being misled as to the contents of the document. Citing the treaty, the Indian agents informed the Seminoles that they would be expected to move within three years. The frontier was full of tension, yet there remained an uneasy truce between the Seminoles and the ever-increasing numbers of settlers encroaching upon their hunting grounds.

For two years, negotiations continued between leaders of the various Seminole bands, led by their principal chief Micanopy and the territorial government determined to move them west. August tried to follow the arguments and often discussed the deteriorating conditions on the Florida reservation with the leaders of the yat'siminoli. Starvation gave the Seminoles good reason to consider the offer. For August, however, moving to Oklahoma was not an option. He would likely be imprisoned.

The Apalachee tribes from the Florida panhandle, also under constant pressure from the government, packed their belongings and headed west, but evaded their monitors and reached Louisiana. There they would survive the coming storm.

That same year the Army built a new fort on the site of a trading post in the heart of the lands granted to the Seminoles by the Moultrie Creek treaty. Fort King was intended to be a collection point for tribes that would be sent to Fort Brooke, shipped by boat across the Gulf of Mexico and then up the Mississippi River to the new Indian Territory of Oklahoma. Several small bands, coerced by troops, made the march to the coast to be packed aboard ships. Transported to Arkansas, they were forced to walk to Oklahoma. Many died on that "trail of tears."

In the early winter of 1834-35, several chiefs informed the government agents that they would not leave. The government responded by halting all sales of gunpowder and lead to the tribes. It also stopped the food allotments agreed to under the Treaty of Moultrie Creek. A young firebrand named Osceola was angered and his words were like wind to a smoldering fire. Soon the flames would begin to spread.

December 1831

"Halloo, George! George Wilson! Are ye home, mon?"

"Yes, I'm here. Stop banging on the door or you'll break it down. Now what's the bother?" The demanded personage opened the door to his sprawling plantation house, to find his old friend James MacLeod standing on his porch, soaking wet.

"What has happened to you, now, Mac? Have you gone and fallen in the river?"

"No, lad, ye see, I jumped. I din'na have a boot, ye see and I couldna' wait."

"Mac, you old fool," George scolded the elderly caller, as he ushered him into the foyer of the house and ran to find a towel to dry him. "Don't you know there's alligators in that river?" he said when he returned with a bundle of dry cloth. "You could have been eaten! And you, in your good clothes now!"

"No alligator would waste his time wi' a' poor morsel such as me," the Scot responded, grinning broadly despite the chill. "And, as ye know, I've got nae use fer things like fancy clothing."

"Well, where's your boat?"

"The parson needed her to carry some children back to his school, so he took her for the week."

"Well, what on earth brought you to Stillwater in such a hurry?"

"Well, I know how ye always complain o' so few visitors..."

"Not you, my man! I see you every week, or one might say every day, of late!"

"It's not me I'll be speakin' of, George, if ye'd only le' me finish wha' I'm tryin' to tell ye…"

"All right then, I'll be quiet, and you can tell your tale, Mac. And I'm sure it must be a good one, to bring you here with half the Halifax River in your pockets on Christmas Day."

George surveyed his red-haired friend, half-a-head shorter than himself and now several inches broader in the beam. James MacLeod had come to Florida shortly after Britain had taken control of the territory from Spain, having spent a career with the Royal Navy. The wanderlust he had suffered as a lad had brought him to the service and he had seen much of the world. Yet now he was one of only a handful of British subjects who had remained behind.

George had been the proprietor of the peaceful plantation on the Halifax since his parents had departed with most of the English settlers fifty years before. Now seventy years old, he still treasured his lovely wife, Maria and his two strapping sons, George Jr. and Martin, named for his wife's family. He had thoroughly enjoyed life on his plantation, which still turned a thin profit on crops of sugar cane, corn, potatoes, and vegetables.

True to his word, George sat quietly while the colorful Mr. MacLeod told his tale of the visitors who had arrived at Bulow Plantation, a short distance away. One was a painter of some note, apparently, recently published in Europe to great acclaim. To George, hungry for distinguished visitors of any kind on his isolated plantation, Mac's news was welcome, indeed. Most of the new settlers who had filtered into the territory had been illiterate "dirt farmers" who shared little with the former "gentlemen" of the plantation culture the English had sustained.

As the disheveled Scotsman dried himself before the fire, George warmed at the thought of a new and interesting visitor from civilized parts. He thought of his lonely existence on the Halifax and his struggles to make a living on the land. His house had fallen somewhat into disrepair and the fabric of the curtains framing the great windows was in distress. It was not really suitable for entertaining and there were few neighbors anyway, none of what one would call high society. Most of the great plantations in the area had gradually been broken down into smaller farms and his was no exception. A scarcity of slaves, or available labor of any kind, had forced him into fearful reductions in the lands he held. Although his father had been dead for many years, he still felt he had let him down somehow.

"He's only gon' to be here a short time, now, so I knew ye'd want to know right off," Mac finished.

"Well, I am ever so grateful to you, Mac. I hope you would take a bit of supper with me, now and plan to stay the night. In the morning, we'll take a skiff to Bulow Ville and pay a visit."

"Sounds like a capital idee ta' me, lad," the old widower answered with a nod, his eyes crinkling into a smile at the thought of a warm plate of Christmas dinner from the kitchen of Stillwater. Though he was only fifteen years his senior, Mac treated George like the son he had never had. George in return looked to Mac as a sort of father figure, though just a bit on the daft side, he thought with a grin.

The early morning mists had barely risen from the water before they were of, the work of their oars moving them steadily along in the still waters. They passed quickly through two miles of twisting passages and reached their destination. The Bulow Plantation of Colonel Orlando Rees was a prosperous place and the two were greeted warmly as old friends, despite being unannounced. George and Mac feigned surprise when told that other visitors had arrived and extended their Christmas greetings to Lucy Audubon, her husband John, and Henry Ward, a taxidermist who was traveling with them.

Audubon was fuming about being left "almost castaway" after a sharp argument with the captain of a US Navy river patrol boat Spark. Audubon's friendship with the Secretary of the Navy had led to orders to patrol craft to take him where he wished to go, but the friendship hadn't extended to the captain of the Spark, who had refused his request to take the boat into what he considered unsafe waters to allow Audubon's party to shoot specimens for mounting and painting.

George was a bit crestfallen when he learned that James Audubon was not a painter of portraits, for he had half fantasized that he would be invited to sit for a study. Instead, he learned, the younger man painted birds, an occupation which particularly puzzled Mac.

"Ye say ye paint only birds?" Mac questioned Audubon. "Well, then, who pays ye? Surely not the birds?"

The mystery was cleared up when Audubon displayed some of his newest works, featuring bird life which they both knew well. They marveled at the fine details captured in the delicate lines made by the tools of the artist. John Audubon, it seemed, was a very good shot and was able to bring down specimens of the birds he wished to paint, which his companion quickly prepared and mounted into the poses Audubon preferred, often with wings and tail feathers spread to display them. These images he quickly transferred to canvas, which could be replicated to the delight of Europeans curious about the exotic bird life of the Americas. Among his works they noted large egrets and herons, a Carolina parakeet and large woodpeckers, as well as songbirds and several species of ducks.

Audubon was outspoken about many topics and was highly critical of St. Augustine, where he had earlier arrived from Charleston, calling it the poorest town he had seen in America. Wilson could easily see how the opinionated and strong-willed Audubon could have come into conflict with the captain of a US Navy vessel.

"I am exploring Florida in search of new and unusual birds," Audubon told them. "I will go, eventually, to Key West, where I understand there exists a great number and variety of magnificent birds. I hope to include them in my next volume of work."

"Well, if these works are any example, I'm sure it will be a welcome addition to the world's knowledge of its inhabitants," George said with sincerity, gesturing toward the stack of drawings they had seen.

"Audubon. Now that's a curious name," Mac observed. "What manner of name is it? Surely not Scottish..."

"No, sir, it's French," Audubon replied with a patient smile at his elderly questioner. "My father was a sea captain."

"Well, we'll fergive ye fer that," Mac replied, seriously, as George only shook his head in amusement. Audubon, too, grinned at the sentiments of the old gentleman.

Despite Mac's direct style, the hospitality of the house was extended to the two surprise guests, who were invited to join the party on a hunting trip down the Halifax aboard the colonel's fine boat to Live Oak Landing. Regretfully they were forced to decline, for they were ill-prepared for hunting. "We'll be taking our leave after tea, I'm afraid," George said. "But I am so glad to have met you, Mr. Audubon and of course you, madam, and you, Mr. Ward. I do wish you well in your journeys," he added, before they boarded their own small boat to depart.

"You know, Mac," George observed as they glided slowly home in the evening, "the world is a curious place and I have seen all too little of it, spending most of it here on the plantation. I have only seen London in the woodblock prints. It's hard to imagine the big cities of Europe that my father knew."

"Well, I have seen 'em, lad. They're a wonder such as I canna' describe, but I dare say that half the people in 'em would trade their right arms for a chance to live a life of peace and quiet such as ye have right here."

George pondered the odd circumstances that had led him to spend his life on the shores of the Halifax River under successive English, Spanish and American regimes and thought about what might have been. In a wordless conspiracy, they both stopped their paddles to drift, taking in the quiet of the day. For a long moment the boat drifted slowly on the lazy current. Herons and egrets watched them from the safety of the cypress trees that stood hip-deep in the tea-colored water and turtles called cooters and red-ears slid from fallen logs with a plop. In the distance they could hear the hammer-like blows of an Ivory-billed woodpecker working on an ancient oak in search of termites or beetles. They watched as turkey vultures descended toward evening roosts from high above, their broad wings leaving the thermal currents that had carried them thousands of feet into the air and scores of miles a day in search of carrion. In the far distance they thought they heard the faint call of a wolf. Much closer, a great horned owl began its rhythmic two-note hooting and was answered by its mate. George sat silently, a far-away expression upon his face.

Mac pretended to stare up at the darkening sky, while watching his companion closely from the corner of his eye. Finally, with a deep sigh, George dipped the oars and pulled strongly for home.

"Yes sir, peace and quiet..." Mac said again softly.

July 1834

Jimmie tried not to gag as he poked the stinking purplish stew that filled the low-walled open tank with a long rake, dragging a solid mass of vegetation back from the drain to allow the thick liquid to flow into a lower tank. The plantation on the St. Johns River was never particularly pleasant, but on a windless day like today it was particularly miserable.

Of course, it wasn't that the plantation hadn't been successful. Crops of cotton, sorghum, corn, and indigo flowed from the land to enrich the coffers of the wealthy owners, but it was the later crop that had Jimmie feeling so poorly. While just across the broad expanse of the St. Johns River he could see the white houses of Jacksonville and the sails of the ships that called there, between him and that vision of freedom were steaming vats of simmering, stinking indigo. In a matter of a week, each tank would be filled three times by new batches of boiling indigo plants, and he would be employed moving the resulting sludge from tank to tank in a repeating progression that would last most of the year.

Born into slavery, Jimmie was used to hard work since he was six years old, but since he had been sold to this new estate on the St. John's River, his life had taken a turn for the worst. Jimmie once had a wife and often thought lovingly of her and his two sons, sold to another plantation a year before. He doubted that he would ever see them again but kept their love in his heart to steel him through each day.

Far from the dangers of the Seminole War to the south, the plantation culture of the south was thriving across northern Florida and the thousands of slaves who powered it made up half the 50,000 who populated the frontier state. Most, like Jimmie, worked on the sprawling commercial operations that produced most of the products being shipped to northern and foreign markets. Only a few were the property of the migrants who found their way into the state in search of homesteading land.

March 1835

The sun set ablaze a careless band of clouds which had lingered too long on the western horizon, throwing the evening landscape into a riot of false colors. Gold trees and red water sparkled, dazzling the senses of the lovers who sat gazing at the spectacle. August Booker slipped his hand around Nighthawk's slim waist and drew her closer. Her smile captured the light as she glanced up at him, before turning back to watch the slow fading of the light. The growing Booker family had found a world of repose deep within the wilds of central Florida. Here, some distance from the main campsites of the tribe, they raised their two sons and a daughter.

The large, shallow lake was filled with fish and game was plentiful. They tended a small garden and gathered many of the native edible plants. August traded for hens and a rooster and built a sturdy shed to lock them in at night, to keep them safe from the prowling raccoons, bobcats and panthers. The children often accompanied their father on hunting and fishing trips and quickly learned the ways of living in the wild. The Booker family had no way of knowing that in far-away Washington, D.C. the Florida territory had just been granted statehood, but the new government was no less hostile to the Seminoles than the territorial officers.

One evening in the late summer of 1835, Blackwater appeared at the cabin in the company of another man and his mood was somber. "This is Osceola, a friend. I have been to Ocala. There is trouble," he said, speaking in the Hitchiti tongue of the Miccosukee

August invited the pair into the cabin, to share the meal. Blackwater greeted his sister warmly and spent time with his nephews and niece and he was pleased to see that they wore the traditional garb of the tribe and spoke Hitchiti well. Young Eastwind was now already growing tall at seven and was a handsome, strapping boy who could move through the woods in total silence. Blackwater looked upon the young man with special pride although to each of the children he gave a small present and many smiles, showing no favoritism.

As the men ate, sitting cross-legged on piles of skins, Blackwater told him of a skirmish which had taken place between a band of Indians and some militiamen near Gainesville, well to the north. August frowned at the news and exchanged worried glances with Nighthawk.

"There is more," he continued. "An army courier was murdered riding from Fort Brooke. Soldiers are blaming it on Seminoles. I do not know the truth."

"This is bad news," August said after a pause. "What will the chiefs do?"

"They are lost and afraid," said Osceola. "They are afraid to defend themselves. The white man has broken every treaty."

August looked closely at the man called Osceola. He noted his unusual appearance, which seemed to him a mark of European blood. Dark eyes, a fine, aquiline nose and a regal bearing added to his unusual appearance. August had a sudden realization that he had seen this man before. Was he the same child, then a boy of about fourteen years, that August's company had captured in north Florida during Jackson's second raid? He had been with his mother then, a woman he had guessed was of mixed French and Indian blood. Osceola returned August's gaze steadily and August realized that he had changed much less than the child and it was very likely that Osceola also remembered him.

August glanced at his own children, playing quietly at the opposite end of the one-room cabin under the supervision of Nighthawk, who listened intently while supervising the youngsters.

"No more can our people be forced to move, again and again. We have run enough. It is time to fight for our lands," Osceola said firmly, looking closely at August, watching for a reaction. It was slow to come, and he chose his words carefully.

"I know there has been much injustice which has passed between our people," August said at last. "I have seen it with my own eyes, but I do not believe that war is the way to peace. We must learn to understand each other."

"The time for peace is passed," Osceola answered bluntly, and August was surprised to hear that he used the language of Maskókî, of the Upper Creeks. It was a more direct answer than the words themselves and showed his disdain for the Lower Creeks and other itálwa who had often allied themselves with the whites.

August's heart sank and he confirmed and understood the origin of the man before him and the course he had chosen. He looked at him with a feeling of ebbing hope.

After their dinner was concluded, " August and Blackwater stepped outside the cabin door and August took the opportunity to pose a new question of his old friend.

"Will the chiefs join in a new war?" August asked.

"They listen to a new leader, to Osceola," Blackwater said slowly, nodding toward the brooding figure sitting with Eastwind by the fire. "He is not a chief, but he speaks with wisdom and power. The chiefs are weak and divided. They will follow him, for they do not know what to do for themselves. Osceola and Micanopy say their people will give no more land. They will stand and fight against the whites."

"You bring me news of dark days ahead and I am saddened," August said to Blackwater. "Always I hope for peace."

"You have the protection of the tribes, for you are family of Blackwater," Osceola said, rising and stepping toward them. "If you remain with your family, you have nothing to fear from us."

"My only fear is not for me," August said, turning to look the man in the eye. He had no way of knowing how much of their conversation he had heard. "It is for the children, who are Seminole, white, Negro, Mulatto, Miccosukee, Maskókî... It is they who will suffer, when we, who are men, do not try enough to learn from one another."

Osceola stared at August for a moment, then nodded, acknowledging the unhappy truth, but then shrugged. "The choice has been made by them," he said. "We fight only because we have no choice."

The following morning August and his fragile family watched silently as the two men mounted their horses and disappeared into the morning mist with a silent, final wave from Blackwater. Trouble hung thick in the air and in August's heart.

Although they were far from the frontiers, travelers passed through several times a year, bringing news from the outside world. August and his family were always eager to welcome friendly travelers and the exchange of hospitality for information was a welcome trade. Soon the news began to grow very bad. General Wiley Thompson had informed the Seminoles that he had orders from President Jackson to remove them to Oklahoma Territory, but Osceola was forcing the tribes to bow to his will for war and would not tolerate those who wanted peace.

"He will fight and force others to fight, or die," an elderly man told them over a dinner of venison and fish with yams. "The army offered to buy our cattle if we would agree to go to Oklahoma. Charley Emathla brought his herd to Fort Brooke. On his way home, he was ambushed and killed. They threw his money on the ground around his body."

August and Nighthawk both knew that Charley Emathla was known as an influential chief and a reasonable and moderate man. Osceola was immediately suspected of the murder, for he had warned the chiefs not to sell out or prepare to leave. After the killing, fear spread through many peaceful tribal bands. Fourteen chiefs brought five hundred of their people to Fort Brooke for protection, ready to depart for the west, afraid of war.

The Army was preparing for much more trouble and was steadily reinforcing a network of military outposts. Fort Harrison rose on the shores of Clear Water Harbor and Fort Drane was established to the north of Fort King. Yet there were only five hundred fifty regular Army troops in the entire territory. Osceola could rally two thousand Seminole warriors. After two skirmishes on December 17, the entire state was on guard, nervously awaiting the worst from the marauding Seminoles. It soon came.

On December 28, Seminoles in the region of Ocala acted. Snipers attacked Fort King, killing General Thompson and several others in a surprise attack. The single company of troops based there would be insufficient if a real attack was mounted, but reinforcements had already been ordered. Two additional companies, one hundred and ten soldiers, under the command of Major Francis Dade, were en route to reinforce Fort King.

Marching from Fort Brooke, they traveled the Fort King Road afoot, with wagons filled with supplies. It was a fateful expedition. Near Chassowitzka, about fifty miles north of Fort Brooke, a party of Seminoles had gathered and lay concealed in wait.

The extended column of troops was moving down the narrow road through a forest of pines with thick palmettos of head-height when the warriors attacked by surprise from the flanks. Major Dade was killed instantly, and command was left in the hands of an artillery officer who had no experience with the Seminoles' tactics. Hours of withering fire under poor defensive conditions decimated the troops. Of the one hundred and eleven men in the command, only two survived. The battle would be forever after known as the Dade Massacre.

Three days later, unaware of the earlier battle, one hundred fifty regulars and volunteers were marching to attack the Seminoles in their gathering place at the Withlacoochee Cove, only a short distance to the north. The Seminoles again struck first, attacking the troops as they crossed the river.

With troops split between the two banks the Army was not prepared for an intense fight. The soldiers accounted well for themselves but suffered four dead and fifty-nine wounded. The Second Seminole War was on, and bloody days had come to Florida.

Upon hearing the news from a Seminole family passing through in late January, August loaded his weapons and considered his options. It was Nighthawk who convinced him that they should remain where they were unless the danger drew closer. "We should not flee the safety of our home and fly into more dangerous places," she told August. After thinking of his limited options, he agreed.

The uprising spread rapidly, as the Seminoles made a concerted effort to drive the white settlers out of the peninsula. From Key Biscayne to New Smyrna and at the Matanzas and Tomoka Rivers, Osceola's forces struck at the plantations, the property and the people who had threatened them. Seminoles ranged far to the north, attacking and burning the village of Pilatka on the St. John's River. The Army responded by building Camp Monroe, an Army garrison upstream on the river at Lake Monroe, to protect the settlements to the north. They began construction of a road across the interior to link with Fort Brooke.

Despite the Army's efforts, the Seminoles were winning the battle for control of the interior. The settlers of Florida lived in fear of attacks which seemed certain to come. For many, it was time to seek safer places. At a lonely plantation on the Halifax River, an elderly planter named George Wilson packed his most valued possessions and turned to the safety of St. Augustine. He knew he was forever leaving behind the simple comfort of his beloved Stillwater. His plantation, like many others in the area, would soon begin to fall into ruin. The Seminoles were succeeding in driving the settlers from rural Florida.

For August, Nighthawk and their growing young family, the days of the war passed peacefully in their isolation. News still came only occasionally when a wandering group of Seminoles passed through. It was always bad. Nighthawk had not seen her brother since his visit a year and a half earlier. She had learned that he had joined in the fighting alongside Osceola and had been present at the fighting with Major Dade's troops. Nighthawk passed along the news she gathered from her family in long, late night conversations with August, as they lay huddled together during the chill nights in their small cabin. Always they would drift to sleep clinging to one another, fearing the dreams of a war that would tear them from each other's arms.

In distant Washington, President Jackson demanded progress. In the fall of 1836, after a series of changes of command of the troops, his administration sent General Thomas S. Jesup to Florida. He took the war to the Seminoles, building a force of more than nine thousand troops and including eight revenue cutters which patrolled coasts and rivers. He pursued reports of Seminoles gathering north of Fort Brooke with a force of four thousand soldiers.

After a parley with Micanopy, he agreed to allow the Seminoles to keep their Black and Mulatto allies, mostly escaped slaves, if they would leave Florida, calling them the "bona-fide property" of the tribes. With the consent of Abraham, the leader of the black Seminoles, Micanopy accepted the terms. More than seven hundred Seminoles gathered at Fort Brooke for transport by ship and the Army began transporting them to islands at the mouth of the bay, where they could be isolated and controlled.

Jesup immediately betrayed them, and slavers were allowed into the camps to seize the blacks, many of whom were second and third generation free Seminoles. Those unfortunates were marched away in chains to begin new lives of manual labor on plantations as far away as Alabama.

Micanopy was furious but unsure how to react, as seven hundred of his people had been disarmed and remained camped within the reserve of Fort Brooke. Word traveled quickly through the wild lands of Florida, however and Osceola learned of the situation. He rallied his fighters and contacted Micanopy with promises of food and weapons to those who would join the fight. To the chagrin of General Jesup, Osceola and two hundred warriors entered the encampment at Ft. Brooke bringing food and arms and the entire group of Seminoles simply walked away during the night, disappearing back into the wilderness.

In February, after the start of the new year of 1837, Seminoles attacked the new military garrison at Camp Monroe, which was defended only by a simple breast-works arrangement. Their goal was to continue to drive the Army and the settlers along the St. John's River out of the interior and back to the coasts. The Army responded by building Fort Mellon, a stronger position and part of the Army's strategy of reinforcing all the critical points in the territory.

August Booker kept his family isolated at Lake We-oh-ya-kapka, but got news through Nighthawk's family connections and marveled at the stories of incompetence and betrayal he heard. "The Army has no leadership to settle this war," he told her.

"Will the soldiers leave the Seminole lands?" she asked, looking at his with hope in her eyes as she brushed her daughter's gleaming black hair. The children were growing strong and tall, but August and Nighthawk feared for their future every day and hung on every shred of news.

"There will be no peace until Washington acts," he said. "Not until we have a President who will stop the fighting and treat in good faith."

•

By the end of the summer of 1837, many in the government were voicing August's opinion. General Jesup was frustrated and ready to try anything. His feeble attempts at a summer campaign were a failure and he was under increasing pressure to bring a stop to the actions of the renegades. Then Jesup's first break came, through the actions of General Joseph Hernandez.

Hernandez commanded a body of territorial militia east of the St. Johns. He learned at the beginning of September that a group of Seminoles had set up camp near Mosquito Inlet to the south, where they were harvesting coontie to make flour. On September 9th, Hernandez's troops surrounded and captured the band, led by a chief known as King Phillip. The next day, he captured a second band led by Yuchi Billy. In the two encounters, only one Seminole and one soldier were killed. The prisoners were put under lock and key at the old Castillo de San Marcos in St. Augustine, which had been renamed Fort Marion. Among the prisoners were Blackwater and most of Nighthawk's extended family.

The Seminole captives proved peaceful and cooperative, to the extent that General Hernandez allowed two of their number to leave to contact Osceola to parley. One of these was a young chief known as Coacoochee, or Wild Cat. He soon communicated the willingness of Osceola and some of the leaders of the uprising to negotiate with General Jesup, who had by then arrived at Fort Marion. It appeared that an end to the bloodshed might be at hand at last.

Jessop, however, feared for his own safety. He took a hard stand during negotiations, which might otherwise have had great success. He ordered General Hernandez to attend the parley and then sent other forces with orders that the assembled bands be captured and held.

When General Hernandez found Osceola and his band standing as agreed under a flag of truce they were quickly surrounded and arrested. Within hours, the entire group was locked in the dungeons of Fort Marion. The best chance at bringing the war to an early end had been destroyed by the treachery of the American government.

During his short incarceration in St. Augustine's Castillo de San Marco, Osceola resumed preaching to his fellow prisoners of the treachery of General Jesup and the Army. The old Spanish fort had been built to defend the approaches to the bay and the city. While the walls could turn away cannon balls, it was not designed as a prison. The two hundred Seminoles within the walls felt angry and betrayed. They looked for a chance to renew the struggle. The chance for some came in November, when Coacoochee led a band of twenty warriors in an escape. The young leader, who had walked willingly into the city of his enemies to help bring about peace, would soon begin to rally Seminole fighters for a renewal of war.

•

In January, General Jesup erected a coastal defense he called Fort Jupiter, along the lower east coast. There, Brigadier General Abram Eustis, with the support of other senior officers, prevailed upon General Jesup to allow new negotiations to end the war, offering the remaining Seminoles a small reservation at the southern end of Florida. A messenger was sent to Washington for approval of the plan and other messengers went to the Seminoles to offer the settlement.

Weary of the fighting, more than five hundred Seminoles encamped near the fort, under a flag of truce, for the negotiations. At last, the response came from the administration: no deal was possible. The Seminoles must leave Florida. Jesup, as he had at Fort Marion, immediately ordered them surrounded and captured. The entire group was shipped off to Oklahoma Territory.

It was the third major violation of the flag of truce by forces of the United States Army in two years. Jesup spent the remainder of his career and his retirement defending his actions against the unfavorable public reaction.

December 1837

Although Nighthawk and August hoped for an early end to the fighting and peace in their place of isolation, it was not to be. To the west, soldiers were building a corduroy road at a place called Cow Ford on the Peace

Creek, felling trees and lying them on the ground in order to carry the wagons and cannon across the marshes west of the long sandy ridge. Between the troops and their small cabin lay little but the big hill of red clay and sand which had looked down upon hundreds of generations of inhabitants.

In early December, while August was out hunting, he heard the commotion of a body of troops and quickly dropped into cover. Since he did not own a horse, he was hunting on foot and quickly crawled into a deep thicket of palmettos to observe.

Within a few minutes, he saw riders passing to the east. Well-spaced but keeping a watch on each other, it was plain they were familiar with Indian fighting tactics. A short distance behind the riders came a large body of troops, moving in several columns through the undergrowth. August recognized the uniforms of the regular troops. He could also make out a group of Florida Volunteers and some uniforms he didn't recognize. Within a few minutes he calculated there were nearly one thousand troops.

August remained hidden for a few minutes after the men passed, taking care not to be seen. He was still technically an outlaw trespassing on the reservation. He would have difficulty explaining his presence if spotted and a tougher time concealing his family.

As soon as the way was clear, August burst from his hiding place on the run. As quickly as he could move, he sprinted north up the narrow cow path he had followed, to warn his family of the danger. It was then that he regretted having brought a rooster to his cabin, because that noisy bird might attract attention even from a distance. As he ran, he whispered a prayer that they had heard the approach of the troops.

Arriving at the cabin, August dashed inside. It was empty. Quickly he searched the room, looking for clues as to what had happened. His pistol was gone, along with the ammunition. So were most of the food stores. He ran back outside and looked around the cabin. Fresh tracks of horses could be seen, along with the footprints of several men in moccasins and two in army-issue boots. Gone were the chickens, as well as the sow and piglets he had been raising. "They have beaten me here," August thought and his mind filled with fear for his wife and children.

"Hold it right there, mister," said a voice suddenly. August froze before the door of the cabin.

"Drop the rifle and the knife. Slowly."

August's greatest fears were coming to pass. He could only do as told and sensed several rifles now trained upon him from concealment. Men were moving toward him from the trees around the small clearing.

Slowly August dropped his weapons and held his hands up, indicating he was unarmed. "What can I do for you men?" he said.

"First of all, who are you and what are you doing here?" said a gruff sergeant, stepping into the clearing followed by an army private and four Indians. A quick glance told August the latter were probably professional trackers, not Seminoles, but perhaps Delaware.

"I'm Lieutenant August Booker, US Army, retired. I live here," he answered without moving.

"You live here, in Indian territory? How come you're not dead?" the sergeant asked gruffly, stepping in front of August with a sour expression on his face. "And who else lives here? Somebody cleared out fast."

August almost let out an audible sigh of relief. Nighthawk had escaped with the children and was probably not far away. "I had some visitors this morning before I left to go hunting. An Indian woman and some children were walking through here, alone. Probably trying to stay ahead of your troops. I gave 'em some food and they left," August lied, while admitting the presence of those whom the soldiers would have to be blind not to notice for themselves. He hoped they hadn't searched the cabin closely and noticed the children's clothing.

"If that's true, it still don't explain what you're doin' here," the sergeant said, giving August a doubtful look. "I think I ought to bring you 'round to the Colonel. He may want to ask you a few questions."

At the sergeant's orders, August found himself tied and seated on a horse, which was led by one of the scouts as the group moved back toward the main body of troops, now only a short distance away.

By this time the sun was getting low in the west, and they found the main body of troops as they were beginning to set up a camp, with pickets just assuming their positions. The group rode into the perimeter and August was taken from the horse. "Tie his feet so he don't go walking away and I'll go report what we've got to Captain Morse."

Within a few minutes, August found himself lying on the ground, bound hand and foot while the patrol that had captured him prepared their own campsite. The Indians left to a separate bivouac. Looking around, August could see a string of horses a short distance away, guarded by a couple of privates with bayonets fixed on their rifles. Two others worked hauling feed and water to the animals from a wagon nearby. The clearing was mostly covered with saw palmettos, but it was more open than some of the surrounding land. It was rough country to fight Indians in, August thought to himself.

August knew his predicament was serious and it was possible he might never see his family again. He prayed that Nighthawk had led the children to safety, as he knew she would try to do, back to their hidden island refuge. His spirits sank lower as he thought of them trying to carry on alone without him and he knew that they would eventually be forced to surrender and probably imprisoned and shipped to Oklahoma territory. A deep gloom crept into his soul.

August was still lying on the ground when the sky darkened to night. Maybe the Captain hadn't been impressed at the news that the troops had caught a former soldier, he thought. August was almost afraid he had been forgotten and hoped for release from the ropes so he could stretch his aching arms and legs and maybe get a drink and a bite to eat, but he stifled the urge to call out to the guards, choosing to see what might develop.

Suddenly, as he pondered his predicament, he heard a familiar sound. A soft clicking noise came from the bushes a short distance away. August slowly turned his head and looked around. He could barely make out the two soldiers still guarding the horses, some forty feet away. The others were busy with the last of the evening meal. Softly he made an answering cluck with his tongue. Peering closely into the deeper darkness, he suddenly saw a small form creep slowly toward him. When the shape was six feet away, August's heart stopped. It was John Eastwind, his son. August felt like shouting at the boy for the chance he was taking, or telling him to run, but he knew he would only increase the danger. He held his breath in silence.

Quickly, Eastwind drew a knife and slashed through the lashings which bound his father. Together they lay still for a moment, while August slowly stretched his arms and legs to get the blood flowing. When he could linger no more, Eastwind whispered softly. "Follow me," he said.

Creeping slowly into the underbrush, they followed a thin line of saw palmetto toward the picket line beyond. Creeping on their bellies, they slithered quietly past the guards, passing less than thirty feet from the nearest, making no sound. The covering sounds of the camp and the moonless night was all the concealment they needed.

An hour later, they were reunited with Nighthawk and the two younger children, hiding on a small hammock surrounded by wet prairie. After a lingering embrace of Nighthawk and hugs for the children, August turned at last to Eastwind.

"Son, you did a foolish thing tonight. You could have been killed if they had seen you."

"I knew that, father, but I could not leave you. We watched from hiding when you were taken to the camp. I followed and watched and waited for a chance to strike. I do not fear the soldiers," Eastwind said, with a note of defiance in his voice that August had never heard before.

"Do not be hard on your son, August," Nighthawk interrupted. "I told him he should follow and see where they took you. I risked one I love very much, to save another I love as much. I would have thought to do it myself, but your son is smaller and quieter and without fear. You owe him your life."

August looked at his wife, who he still clung to with one arm and then looked again at his brave son, who clasped his arm. He looked down at his daughter and second son, who clung to his waist.

Tears suddenly filled his eyes, and he pulled them each close. He had his family, and they were safe. That was all that mattered that night.

Within minutes of their joyous reunion, the family was on the move again, August carrying little Katrina on his back, the rest followed in his footsteps. They walked through the night and by dawn had put several more miles of woods and swamps between themselves and the army. Since the army was moving east, August led the way west, as far from harm's way as possible.

At noon, after an hour's rest, they turned northward, crossing open savanna lands with only scattered pines and the ever-present palmettos. They camped that night at the edge of a range of low, steep sand dunes. By evening on the second day, they reached their shelter, wading through a marsh to the safety of a small island on the edge of a large lake. A long crescent-shaped burial mound occupied much of the dry land and spoke of the long habitation of the place by earlier generations of First Nations peoples, perhaps Ocale or Tocobega, now long since passed from the earth.

Far behind them to the east, the troops had moved farther east and crossed the river below the big Lake Kissimmee. There they were beginning to build new fortifications, soon named Fort Gardiner after a soldier killed by the Seminoles. The men worked under the command of an experienced Indian fighter, who would soon be known to his troops as "Old Rough and Ready." By his escape, August had missed his chance to come face-to-face with yet another future president of the United States, the new commanding officer, Colonel Zachary Taylor.

Two days after arriving on the island, August and his family were surprised when a band of a dozen warriors arrived, among them one Black and one Mulatto Seminole. After an awkward meeting with the group, the warriors accepted the white man, whom they had heard of before. "This is the one known to us. He is not our enemy," they told Nighthawk. "You have our protection," the leader told August. They listened quietly when told of August's rescue from the troops by his young son, smiling at the boy with approval.

A sharing of the meal and a description of the war situation filled the evening. August was surprised to hear that Osceola had been taken captive by General Jesup while under a flag of truce. Now he lay imprisoned in the fortress at St. Augustine.

"It is true," the warrior chief assured him. "We go to join Coacoochee at Okeechobee, to avenge Osceola."

"Then you will have much work. There are many soldiers. And if they die, more will come, like the leaves of the trees," August told him.

"Our people have no fear of the soldiers;" the young chief said. "It is better that we should die as fighters for our land, than be swallowed up as a people and no more walk this earth."

"It is only through your death that your people will disappear from this world," August responded. "If I could, I would turn away the armies, so that all could live in peace. There is land enough."

"We have given our lands before and always the whites want more," the chief said. "This time, at least, when the white man walks upon our land, our bones will lie within, and it will still be ours."

In the morning the small band was gone, melting into the woods to join the forces of Coacoochee. A few days later, on Christmas day, they lay in wait, four hundred strong, while Colonel Taylor led eight hundred troops upon their position in the watery stronghold they had chosen. When the smoke had cleared, eleven Seminoles lay dead and fourteen seriously wounded. They had killed twenty-six soldiers and wounded one hundred fourteen, but in the end, they had been driven back. Forced to flee, they were hunted through the swamps of Florida. A month later, the Seminoles made another stand at the Battle of Loxahatchee, where combined fire from cannons and rockets drove their bands across the river, but still they gave worse than they got.

Even as they continued to resist, the Seminoles' hope was fading. Osceola was transferred to a prison at Fort Moultrie, South Carolina. Three months later he died for unknown reasons, without a trial. His body was decapitated, and his head preserved in a jar.

May 1839

The Second Seminole War was proving a long grind for US forces and public support for the effort was steadily eroding. Most Americans considered the cost far beyond the worth of the swampy peninsula and preferred to leave it to the Seminoles, but the War Department and the administration pressed on with the efforts, sending gunboats up rivers, burning Seminole crops, and rounding up hundreds under flags of truce to be shipped across the Gulf up the Mississippi, then to be marched overland to their new reservations on the plains of Oklahoma. Many died on the way, and the survivors found themselves in isolated settlements without hunting territories, dependent on the largess of government "Indian Agents" for sustenance.

The army continued its methodical efforts to fortify strong points around the state and develop better inland routes and communications, gradually dividing the Seminole lands into smaller and smaller sections. Forts named Pierce, Lauderdale and Harvie defended coastal areas and served as bases for forays into the interior. Forts Denaud, Thompson, and Center flanked the Caloosahatchee River. Fort Bassinger guarded the lower Kissimmee and Forts Frazier and Meade stood watch over the Peace River.

Reduced to less than a thousand, the remaining Seminole bands hid deep within the interior marshes, or in the watery stronghold of the Everglades. Yet the resentment of their treatment still boiled over among the youth of the Seminole nation.

Violence flared again in the summer of 1840 when a Seminole band attacked the settlement of Indian Key. The small key was a wrecking port which was the seat of the newly-created Dade County, housing a medical clinic. It was also the home of the botanist and former United States Consul in Campeche, Mexico, Dr. Henry Perrine. He planned to introduce tropical plants from around the world to test many crops new to south Florida.

When Perrine heard the fighting, he quickly sent his wife and children through a trap door to a space under the house, concealed the door, and prepared to defend the house. Ann Perrine led the children to an enclosed turtle crawl under the wharf in front of the house as the fighting continued over their heads. As the house began to burn, she placed her children into a small boat, which had been half-filled with goods already looted by Seminoles tramping the boards overhead. She cast off and began rowing quickly away from the scene, her hopes for her husband's safety gone. Two Seminoles spotted the departing boat and jumped into a canoe to give chase but arriving sailors from the Navy base on Tea Table Key a short distance away had heard the shooting and came to her rescue.

Since the entire settlement boasted a population of only fifty, including patients, the war party intended to wipe it out. In the end a half-dozen sailors managed to hold off the attackers long enough for 40 residents to escape. Dr. Perrine's bones were found among the ashes of his home and buried on Lower Matecumbe Key. Army troops soon tracked the attackers into the swamps and killed many, hanging some of the leaders.

The fighting slowly ended when the US government wearied of the cost in lives. Bribery became the most effective option and succeeded in convincing numerous groups to migrate to Oklahoma. More than $40 million had been spent on the military efforts. No more than five hundred Seminoles remained in Florida, having been driven deep into the southern swamps open marshes and islands of the Everglades. An unsteady truce developed. Pioneers again began to pour across the borders and arrive in the scattered sea-ports. Yet bigger problems were brewing across the young nation.

February 1864

The predawn darkness had an otherworldly feel, with dozens of flickering lights glowing through a ghostly pall before the arrival of the broader light of the approaching day.

Slowly, the rim of the sun rose blood-red above the horizon, fulfilling the promise of the pre-dawn glow. Its stabbing rays attacked but could not pierce the great banks of smoke that drifted above the landscape. As the entire sphere cleared the horizon, it began to illuminate the hellish world below, a smoking vista of scorched trees and bare limbs.

Deep banks of fog mixed with the smoke to make a choking soup of the air as Willie Lewis struggled to his feet. Using his small patch of swept sand, he quickly folded his thin bedroll, tying it around his waist. With his bit of johnny cake, it was the only possession he had managed to take along when he had fled the plantation.

It would be tough to get his bearings, but Willie knew that he couldn't just wait where he was. There was always the chance that the fighting could come back this way and a black man, alone in the woods, would have serious explaining to do. Without hesitating, he struck out through the woods, hoping to make his way to the south prong of the St. Mary's River, where he could cross the stream into unburned forests beyond.

An hour of steady marching brought him at last out of the burned area and he reveled in the sweet smell of the clean air that filled his lungs. The smoke had been a punishment of its own, beyond any other he might experience if caught. Willie's relief tempered only slightly the fear he felt at his situation. Never in his thirty years had he experienced anything like this week.

The Civil War had raged on for three years and had brought hard times to the small plantation where he lived. Now, in the winter of 1864, the arrival of fighting had brought new difficulties. As slaves he, his wife and three children had borne a good part of the hardships, although he knew that his mistress Sara Lewis and her family had suffered, too. Her husband had been killed in Virginia, far away and she had lost much of her once buoyant optimism. Willie was grateful that although Sara required much of her servants, she had treated them well and allowed the family to stay together. He knew well that many times children were sold to other plantations and sometimes even husbands and wives were separated for the economic gain of the business.

Brought to the plantation as a small child, like many slaves Willie had been given his owner's family name, partly as a mark of his ownership.

Although he understood little of politics, Willie knew a great deal about the controversy around slavery and had listened through the walls as local whites discussed what they called "The Northern Aggression." Like millions of black slaves across the southern states, he knew that in the north slavery was forbidden and he quietly hoped for any outcome which would lead to freedom for his family. But most of all today he wished for peace.

After a brief rest, Willie's thoughts turned to more immediate needs and foremost was finding his family. They had fled their shanty near the plantation house when they had heard the crack of musketry fire near the edge of the fields. Although Willie had no idea what had happened, a small body of Confederate cavalry had attacked a column of federal troops, trying to delay the advance of invading Union armies under the command of General Truman Seymour. With about five thousand soldiers, artillery and cavalry, Seymour was determined to press inland to the area of Lake City and on to Tallahassee, following the route of the railroad line. The Lewis's small plantation lay directly in the path of the fighting.

When the sound of rifle fire disturbed the morning chores, Willie had run for the cabin, collected his family, and quickly led them into the deep woods, hiding in thickets near a small creek. By late afternoon, the children were very hungry and needed to eat. Willie gambled on the mercy of the soldiers of both sides and sent his wife, Clarice, back with the children to the plantation, where the fighting seemed to have ended. The thought of life without his children always filled him with dread. Sam, six, Mary, three and Myrtle, just eight months old, were his pride and joy. Soon, he resolved, he would be back with them.

Knowing that an adult male would be in greater danger, he had returned to the relative safety of the woods and avoided the fires by circling around and following the flames, where few men would be likely to travel.

As the new morning wore on, Willie's progress was slow but steady and he picked his way cautiously through the swampy, unburned lands along the creek. He kept alert for the sounds of guns or voices which would reveal the presence of troops of either army. He heard nothing and continued his slow progress toward home.

At last, he came to the bend of the creek which made the closest approach to his home. He knew it was there, across two fields and a row of trees, although he couldn't see it from his place of hiding. Late in the afternoon, he finally resolved himself to climb from concealment and make the final dash for home. He tried to look nonchalant as he strode across the first field, as if he had just finished his chores for the day. "Slow down," he told himself. "You wouldn't be running for home at the end of the day."

He had cleared the first field and was heading for the familiar trail through the woods to the home fields when he was suddenly interrupted.

"Where might you be going, mister?" a voice asked, seeming to come out of thin air. Willie froze in his tracks but had enough sense to respond.

"I'm jus' heading home," he said, turning slightly toward the voice and raising his hands above his waist to show he was unarmed. To his surprise, a black man stepped from the bushes, wearing a military uniform, and carrying a rifle with a fixed bayonet.

"Who are you?" the man demanded, with a determined expression clouding his young face.

"Willie Lewis, sir. I work on this here farm," the slave replied, staring at the younger man.

"You alone, mister?" the soldier asked, looking down the trail he had just used.

"Yes, sir," Willie responded, unable to contain his surprise. "Who are you?"

"Private James Adams, Eighth United States Colored Infantry Regiment," he responded with a proud smile, grinning at the obvious surprise on Willie's face. "What's the matter, mister, never seen a black man in a uniform before?"

"No sir, I cain't say as I have," Willie answered, hands still held aloft.

"It's OK, you can put your hands down. You don't look like any rebel spy I ever saw," Private Adams told him. "Have you seen any other soldiers in this area?"

"Not today, no sir, but yesterday I saw enough to hold me for a while. My family went back down to the farm, over there," he said, indicating the direction he had been heading. "I was jus' heading back to make sure they's OK."

Adams' face fell slightly. "I got to tell you, it don't look too good now. We come by there earlier and found the place on fire. We didn't see anyone around, though. I can't say what happened."

"I got a wife and children there, mister. Can I please go now?"

"I think we'd better let our officers ask you a few questions first, then we'll go check up on your family," Adams said, motioning with his rifle, before shepherding him back through the trees. There, hidden in the woods, was an encampment of several hundred soldiers, all, to Willie's surprise, black men like himself, with only three white officers present.

A brief interrogation convinced the commander of the troops that Willie had nothing new to add to their intelligence of enemy troop movements and he ordered him released, with an admonition to tell nothing of what he had seen. Private Adams' platoon, led by a young corporal, escorted Willie toward the plantation house, moving carefully along the edge of the open ground.

When the group arrived at the main house, they found it a heap of smoking ashes and blackened timbers. Willie nearly wept at the sight of the rubble of what had been a substantial house. The brick of the chimney presided over the charred remains. Looking about, Willie saw that the main barn had also burned in the fires but found the slave's quarters still standing. Running into the rough building, however, he found no sign of his family.

"They must'a been carried off by whoever set the fires!" Willie shouted to the federal troops. Across the wagon yard, Adams waved his hand.

"Over here, Willie," he shouted, and Willie broke into a sprint. At the sound of his name and voice, however, came a call from a thicket behind the fence.

"Willie! Oh, my God, Willie, you're alive!" It was his Clarice, running from the thicket to greet him, with his three children close behind. A round of grateful embraces gave him reassurance and relief. His family was safe, and they were together again.

"Willie, Sam was such a brave boy," Clarice said as they clutched one another. "He told us not to worry, that he would fight all the soldiers on earth to protect us."

"I am proud of you, son," Willie said at last, holding six-year-old Sam by the shoulders. "Thank you for taking good care of your mama and your sisters like I asked you to."

"Willie, get yourself over here," Adams called again, and Willie gratefully responded, his family trailing close upon his heels. There, where Adams pointed, was a white face, peering fearfully at them from among the bushes. It was Sara Lewis, the mistress of the plantation, reduced to a frightened figure clutching a pistol. Her face was smeared with soot and her dress was torn. The woman Willie had feared and respected all his life as his superior was reduced by the fortunes of war to a figure of pathos.

"It's al'right, Mizz Lewis," Willie said. "These men won't hurt you none," he said, looking to Private Adams for confirmation of his assurances. Adams nodded, but kept his rifle handy, mindful of the revealed pistol. "You can come out now," Willie called.

After a long hesitation, Mrs. Lewis finally arose, arranging her dress and composing herself as best she could under the circumstances. She emerged walking erect, the perfect figure of a proud southern woman, unbowed by the situation. Yet she looked fearfully at the band of armed black men who surrounded her.

"Please drop the gun, ma'am. We won't hurt you," the unit's corporal told her, and she complied, placing herself completely into the hands of the hated Union Army.

"These men are Negroes and they've given them guns!" she thought to herself, unable to comprehend that the world she had known was changed forever. In her darkest fears of invasion, she had never imagined herself captured like this.

"By the way, Willie," Private Adams announced, so that Mrs. Lewis could hear, "I guess I should tell you that you, and your family, are now legally free. President Lincoln has emancipated all the slaves in the rebel states."

Willie looked at the soldiers, who stood grinning at him and at Mrs. Lewis, who looked away. His own wife stood beaming and clutched her children to herself. Willie turned slowly back to Private Adams. Willie considered the world-shaking news for but a moment before turning his attention back to the more important immediate situation. "Thank you, sir, for giving me my family back," he said.

That evening, when the troops had returned to their encampment, Willie watched silently as Sara Lewis picked through the warm ashes of her home without apparent purpose. Her husband, dead in the war, had left her to manage a farm that struggled even in good times. Without Will and Clarice she would have been reduced to poverty long before this dark day. Now it had come to her in all its blunt ugliness. In three short years she had lost her husband and one white hired hand and now, in one day, her house, her barn and her slaves. She was completely ruined, without a home or barn, her horse and mule missing, her wagon burned in the fire, her slaves freed. She still had claim to two hundred acres of land, including seventy-five good acres. Alone, however, it was worthless to her, as she would be unable to farm it. If she could sell it, it would be worth no more than a few dollars, she expected, that might sustain her a month.

Willie was surprised by his own sympathy for this woman who had long pretended to own him body and soul. He finally made his decision. "Please, Miss Sara, won't you come and rest? Clarice has the bed-clothes from the wash yesterday and we can make you up a fresh bed."

She turned and stared numbly in her exhaustion. What was she to do? What option did she have on this isolated farm? So it was that a pitiful and beaten woman joined her former slaves in their poor hovel, the only real shelter remaining on the farm. There, they sat on the dirt floor, huddled around the cooking fire to ward off the February chill.

Sara looked at her former charges and wondered what would happen next. The pitiful pension she received from the government was too little to live comfortably on and it was paid in Confederate scrip, which was worth less every day. Her thoughts brought her to the verge of tears, but she stiffened her lip and held her head up, unwilling to show her vulnerability to Willie and his family.

"I suppose you'll all be running off to Jacksonville, now that Lincoln and the Yankees have said you're free to go," she said.

Willie looked at his wife, who cupped a tin of warm soup which she was feeding to her youngest, taking care not to spill a drop. Willie looked about the rough, windowless cabin, and at the few things which they used in their daily lives, but which legally remained the property of Sara Lewis. He was in the same situation that faced millions of other slaves being freed across the south.

On this small farm Willie Lewis's family had been more fortunate than most, who were part of vast plantations owned by wealthy aristocrats and employing hundreds of slaves. Here, at least, his family was intact, and their treatment had been reasonable. If he took his family from this farm, where would he go? Many would head north to uncertain futures. Others would hope to remain farmers working their own homesteads, but without resources to start, what were their chances? Most would face a future of hunger and desperation, lost in a strange world that shunned them and their kind. Their choices were as bleak as Sara's.

After thinking about the situation for a few moments, he turned his gaze upon the woman who made such a pitiful sight, even in her assumed pride. Despite her sometimes-harsh attitude, she was one of only a handful of people he knew in the whole world and the one he had become accustomed to depending upon. 'Better the devil you know than the devil you don't," he thought to himself.

"Mizz Lewis, I reckon we'll jus' be staying 'round here to do the spring plantin', if you think tha's all right now. Thay's no place else we needs to be right away, anyhow. Maybe you could jus' see your way to give us somethin' of the money if the crop comes in all right. I think that might work out jus' fine by us."

Sara Lewis stared at the man a long moment and wondered at how little she knew of him or appreciated him before this day. This time, her resolve finally broke. Tears welled in her eyes and soon she leaned sobbing against the wall while Clarice attempted to comfort her, speaking of the many assets they had which could still make the farm and their future, a success.

During the next two days, Willie and his family worked at salvaging what foodstuffs they could from the ruins of the farm, while a steady stream of federal military units passed. They saw cannons and wagons of supplies and long columns of soldiers marching to the west. Willie kept his eyes and ears open, ready to move his family to safety at the first sign of danger.

Ahead of the advancing Union forces the Confederates had massed five thousand troops at a natural defensive position near the town of Olustee. There, General Joseph Finegan shrewdly ordered the construction of battle fortifications and entrenchments along a line stretching from Ocean Pond to the cypress swamps to the south, directly astride the rail line. General Seymour was forced to spread his equal number of Union troops out along his path to guard his rear and supply lines. When the forward elements came upon the Confederate positions on Saturday, February twentieth, fighting quickly broke out.

Union forces soon found they were unable to outflank the Confederates. Commanding officers also failed to organize their assault, resulting in piecemeal attacks out along the one-and-a-half-mile front. From noon until five o'clock, the fighting raged along the line, federal units bravely advancing to test the rebel lines without waiting for the full force of available troops to be applied to the battle. Even as nightfall came over the battlefield, fresh Union troops were arriving, but the day had already been won by the dug-in Confederates.

About three hundred men died in the fighting that day, two-thirds on the Union side. Another two thousand of about ten thousand men engaged in the fighting were wounded, many severely, some suffering amputations of wounded limbs. It was the bloodiest encounter of the entire war for most of the men involved.

As the day ended the Union army began a retreat, falling back to the east toward Jacksonville, and Willie Lewis watched them pass as he worked in his field. At the end of the long column came the proud black infantrymen of the Eighth United States Colored Infantry Regiment, still in battle array and assigned to a rear-guard action. The Confederates hadn't pursued them. Many were engaged in murdering wounded or captured Union troops in the wake of the fighting.

As they marched along, the men of the Eighth were bone-tired and saddened by the loss of their comrades, but they maintained their spirits, for they were fighting for liberty. Yet it was to them that the Army itself looked to take on the most wearing tasks. Private Adams and his companions were halted in their march and ordered to march two miles north. There, they were told, they would find a military train loaded with wounded men and a broken-down locomotive. Save them from capture and get them back to the hospital in Jacksonville, they were told.

As before, the Eighth responded. Finding the locomotive useless, they used levers and ropes to topple it from the track, then tied themselves to the train full of wounded men. With guns still at the ready, they began the Herculean task of dragging the string of rail cars back along the tracks to Jacksonville.

The next few days were hard work for the Lewis family as they struggled to get their lives back into order. Into their small hovel they brought whatever cookware and metal could be salvaged from the main house and set up a crude partition in one corner of the small room to make a place for Sara. Willie was soon busy preparing for the spring planting.

On the third day after the fighting, a large group of Confederate horsemen rode up to the cabin where Willie was chopping firewood, even as Sara was scrubbing clothes in a large tub. Willie eyed the men with trepidation but stood holding his ax amid his handiwork.

"Evening, ma'am," Their captain said, an earnest-looking young man who dismounted a large black horse. "We're patrolling through this country hunting any loose Yankees or escaped slaves that might be hereabouts. Have y'all seen anyone suspicious?"

"A good evening to you, too, sir, but no, we haven't," Sara responded, pausing from her work. "I'd invite you for supper, but we've barely enough left to make a meal for ourselves, let alone your company. I thank you for askin' after us, though."

"Don't worry ma'am, I manage to keep my troops fed. I'm glad to see your slaves ain't among those who run off during the fightin'. We've caught up with quite a few. Had to hang one or two of 'em who tried to fight us off."

Sarah Lewis paused a long moment, then straightened herself and thrust out her chin.

"Captain," she said, "these people are not my slaves, and they are free to go whenever they like. And furthermore, I'd kindly ask you to leave them alone, if they choose to do so," Sara responded curtly.

The captain's mouth moved wordlessly, then simply went slack as he stared in stunned silence.

"Now good day to you," she added abruptly and turned back to her scrubbing.

Both Willie and the Confederate troops stared at the woman, before Willie took the cue from her and began once again to wield his ax on the woodpile. There was a long moment while the two worked and the soldiers sat still upon their horses. At last, the captain remounted and with a wordless wave of his hand, led the troops away from the humble cabin, the pounding of their horses' hooves slowly fading into the distance.

Willie worked wordlessly a few moments, then straightened to watch as the tiny grey forms were swallowed by a dusty cloud of the same color. He turned slowly toward Sara, who stood with tears in her eyes. "Thank you, ma'am," he said and wiped the back of his hand across his own cheek.

May 1865

The two Lewis families saw no more of the war but worked their farm while the rebellion crumbled around them. The Confederate currency they earned was virtually worthless and bought less each week, until finally they could accept payment for the crops only in trade. Willie used his own skills to add a room onto the little cabin they shared and slowly began to improve the quality of their lives.

Southern resistance had all but ended before the United States Army finally entered and subdued Florida's rebellious legislature in Tallahassee. Florida's Confederate governor chose suicide over surrender.

The following summer, Sara remarried, accepting the proposal of Wilton Johnston, a Confederate infantryman who had lost an arm at Gettysburg serving under General Robert E. Lee.

Wilton proved to have real skills for the farm and with Willie's able assistance, began the task of rebuilding the plantation house. It was work often delayed by the lack of time and money, but slowly, progress was made.

In payment for Willie's services, Sara and Wilton Johnston gave the Lewis's a ten-acre tract of land to call their own. There, anything they could grow in their free time would be theirs to sell or keep, as they saw fit. They also worked out a formal agreement to sharecrop the rest of the farm, giving both families a small part of the proceeds after the expenses had been paid. Life was hard but Willie thought it far better to be free and owe money than to be forever tied to land and master.

The Johnston family was soon expanded by one, as Sara gave birth to a healthy son, whom they named Hannibal. "He was a great general," Wilton explained, "and you never know when fighting might start up again. We'll always need smart generals."

The slow progress of the southern economy after the war took a turn for the worse in 1866. Florida, along with some of the other states of the former confederacy, passed strict laws regulating the actions and activities of former slaves. Known as the Black Codes, because they applied only to blacks, the laws provided for strict punishment for offenses as minor as loitering.

Willie took care to avoid giving any pretense for trouble and avoided going to town for any reason. Likewise, his children were under his strict orders not to leave the farm. Instead, they were tutored by Sara, using a few books she could borrow from the itinerant preacher, who used the opportunity to lecture her about her situation, which clearly did not make her popular with any of the distant neighbors.

Although many southerners expected much trouble from the newly freed slaves, little happened, and the laws were unneeded. Nevertheless, they raised the ire of radical Republicans in the Congress, who were determined to punish the southern states. Using the Black Codes as emotional justification, they overruled the lenient policies of "reconstruction" set in place by Presidents Abraham Lincoln and Andrew Johnson.

Congress came down hard on those they saw as unrepentant rebels and slavers and refused to seat southern senators and congressmen. Instead, they passed laws giving the vote to freed slaves and attempted to set up friendly state governments dominated by southern Republicans, placing most southern states under military rule. On the first of April 1867, a military government was set up in Tallahassee.

The two Lewis families were little-affected by the politics which raged about them, until the local economy began to sag under the weight of corruption. Unscrupulous persons soon began to take advantage of the situation and several factions sprang up to vie for control of the state government. Newly freed former slaves made up about half the population of Florida and continuous efforts were made by Republicans to register them to vote.

Politics were fractured between Conservatives, mostly former Confederates, and Union supporters, almost uniformly Republican but further split into several rival factions. Many former confederates refused to register to vote, which required an oath of allegiance to the federal government, giving the Republicans an edge in state politics.

As the only one of the Lewis's who could vote, Willie chose to exercise his right, but the corruption of the carpetbaggers and opportunists made it futile. Willie refused to be deterred, walking several miles to the polls for each ballot. Finally, in 1868, his vote helped to approve a new state constitution which recognized the freedman's right to vote and granted homesteaders a partial exemption from land taxes. A civil government was elected, which ratified the fourteenth amendment to the Constitution of the United States, outlawing slavery forever.

On July 4, full civil government was restored and on July 25, Florida was readmitted to the Union. Willie's freedom and that of his descendants, was at last guaranteed by the Constitution of the United States. Willie and his family, however, found little changed. They stayed with the farming life they knew well and kept to their own social circles among other former slaves. Willie made sure that his children had a chance to study enough to read and write, telling his wife "The day will come when a Negro child will have the same opportunity as any other, but it won't happen without learning."

Clarice smiled as he spoke. Her dark eyes made pools so luminous that Willie couldn't help but be drawn to her whenever she looked at him that way and he thought that this early morning, she was especially beautiful.

"I know you're right, dear," Clarice answered him, "and I thank you for keepin' these children safe and strong. Someday, one of your children's children will be on top of this world, 'cause of what you do here today. You're a good man, Willie Johnson. God is my witness."

Willie swept her into his arms and held her and for a long moment, the world outside was gone and only their love remained. "Clarice, don't you ever think for a moment I don't love each of my children, but God knows I love you more than I can ever say."

Clarice looked at him again for a long moment, then just burst into a big smile and picked up her baskets. "Come on, Willie," she said. "We got work to do."

The Lucky Horseshoe
April 1881

"GAINESVILLE! THIS STOP GAINESVILLE."

The shouts of the conductor passing from car to car swept away the dreamy reverie that had the young man wandering through faraway fields and sailing on a steamship. With a start, he reached for his bags, still safe at his feet and twisted his neck to get a glimpse out the window. No city was in sight, but a seemingly solid wall of leathery-looking oak leaves, interspersed with gray beard-like moss, filled his view.

With a decreasing rumble and a climatic gasp of escaping steam, the train came to a halt at the platform. Anthony Blake Crews picked up his bulging carpet-bag and joined a queue of passengers waiting to escape the train.

Bounding from the step-box the conductor had provided, Tony took a deep breath as he surveyed the scene. "Florida, at last!" he thought to himself, pleased that he had finally arrived. He was unfazed by the pitiful appearance of the dusty town before him. No gleaming city of promise, the town of Gainesville was rough-hewn and roughshod, but with a certain busy air that immediately appealed to the young man.

He was a lanky, good-looking youth, with a shock of unkempt brown hair and a smile that came easily when adventure was before him and the past behind. His dark eyes had seen their share of trouble and shone with a renewed fire as he faced this day. His immediate goals were now within reach, and he was excited to be breathing the air of this southern frontier.

Tony wandered down the sandy streets of a community of some three thousand souls, making it one of Florida's biggest towns. All of them were apparently busily engaged in building a future. The main street was busy with a broken stream of buckboards and wagons hauling lumber and freight from the train. The young town had quite a few stores, two railroad depots serving different lines, and boasted of the East Florida Seminary, one of few places of higher learning in the entire state.

Anthony had come to Florida to seek his fortune, convinced that here a man could still get in on the ground floor. Philadelphia was behind him now and his dreams of prosperity lay ahead. Florida, it was said, had work for every willing man and fortunes to be made. With almost twenty-five dollars in savings and a relative in Tampa, somewhere south of here, Tony was self-assured and ready for anything that this frontier could throw at him. His head was filled with such dreams as he wandered down the rutted street.

"Hey, boy! You got work?"

Tony hesitated, then realized that the question was directed at him and snapped his head around. The speaker, or rather shouter, was a bear-sized man with a thick brush of beard holding a sheaf of papers. The booming voice rang out again across the broad street, over the rattle of passing wagons.

"Can you talk, boy? I could use some help, if'n you can work."

"Yes, sir, I can talk," Tony replied, moving a step closer to the stranger. "I was about to get a room at the hotel."

"Don't bother tryin'," the man abruptly replied. "Hotel's full. Been that way for four months. You'll be needing a tent. We got room at the camp, if'n you can work."

Tony's jaw went slack at the revelation, and he slid the heavy carpetbag off his shoulder and slowly lowered it toward the ground, where it dropped with a dusty thud. "Are you saying there's no rooms at the hotel?"

"That's what I jus' said, son. Now, if'n you weren't so slow on the uptake, I'd give ya that job I mentioned, but maybe you'd best be getting along..."

"No, sir!" said Tony suddenly, snapping out of his dismay. "I mean, yes, sir, I'm interested in working, sir and I'm smart, really, sir. I can even read and write."

"Well, then, git yerself over here so's I can get a good look you," the big man responded, and Tony quickly closed the distance, stepping over the road-apples and the deep ruts the wagon wheels had carved into the sandy street.

"A mite puny, but you look healthy enough. How old are you, son?" the bearded stranger commented when he had drawn closer.

"Seventeen, sir. But I'll be eighteen in September."

"Where's your folks?"

"My father got killed at Gettysburg. He was a real hero, my uncle said. I never knew him, sir. My mama died last winter. She got consumption. Told me before she died to get out of Philadelphia and go someplace warm. So, I came here."

"You come to the right place, son. Be warm enough to last you a lifetime in another eight or ten weeks. You got a name?"

"Yes, sir. Tony's my name. Anthony, really."

"Well, Mr. Anthony Really, would you like to take a crack at fixing a stretch of railroad? I work three teams of men and I pay three dollars a day, paid every Saturday, green cash money."

"Yes, Sir, I hadn't really thought about... I'll take it, sir. Thank you, sir."

"My name's Trout. John Trout." He replied, sticking out a huge hand. "I'll charge you twenty-five cents a day for your bed and fifty cents for your food and there's plenty of it, a man can't work on an empty stomach, and neither can a boy. You just keep up with the "sir" stuff and you and me, we'll get along just great."

Back at the camp, Trout introduced Tony as "our newest hand. His name's Anthony Really. At least that's what he says," and the men shared a laugh at his expense. "You fellas make him feel at home."

The railroad work, it turned out, was mostly involved in repairing the crumbling lines that carried passengers and commerce in and out of the area. The confusing jumble of short-line railroads ended only a short distance south of Gainesville, but the east-west track from Fernandina Beach was being repaired or replaced beyond the village of Archer on the line to the west coast, linking up with the port at Cedar Key.

Most of the rail lines had been built before the start of the war and were older than Tony, with rotting ties and rails so soft they warped, so that the ends rose above grade. The railroad men called these rails "snakeheads," and watched carefully ahead of slow-moving trains so that they didn't end up thrown from the track. A heavy steam locomotive, once turned into the soft mud or sand along many lines, was almost impossible to recover. The crews spent many days righting derailed cars, which to Tony seemed to happen every time the train rattled down the track.

The weeks flew by and the boy everyone called "Rilly" worked hard. Trout's prediction about the weather quickly came true. April faded into memory and soon June filled the hot afternoon sky with thick clouds full of rain and lightning enough to make a man afraid to touch the rails.

The work crew was a team of eight men, three whites, plus five freedmen, former slaves who were looked down upon by the whites and often were assigned the most difficult tasks. Tony learned that the men, both black and white, called themselves "gandydancers," and were quite proud of the title, though none of them could tell him what the term meant.

The black men slept together in a separate tent and sang as they worked. They drove themselves with a steady rhythm and were always singing to set a pace. "Shove it over," the leader would sing as they set the rails and the crew would respond, "shaka-laka-laka...ommph!" as they all pushed with their heavy iron pry-bars. They seemed to never hurry but were always moving and the work flowed smoothly.

"You know, Rilly, they say his name ain't fo'sure Trout," Tony's young black co-worker, Sam Lewis, ventured one day as they were jacking rails to replace old ties. The two had quietly become friends and spoke when opportunity arose, despite the disapproving glances from some of the other men.

"It's not?" Tony replied, watching the boss depart to check on another crew.

"They say he kilt a man in Georgia. Changed his name and come down here to hide."

"I don't know... he seems all right to me."

"Oh, he's all right, sho' nuff, jus' like half the men in Flar'da. They's here to put their pas` behind. We all got a pas'," he shrugged.

"You're right, Sam. Even me," Tony replied, suddenly feeling a bit mysterious as the older man eyed him curiously. "Even me," he thought again to himself.

In conversations with Sam, Tony learned that he was married, but saw his wife no more than once a month. "I try to get a day off," Sam told him. "I got two beautiful little girls, and maybe another one on the way," he said. "Someday I'm going to have a nice farm where we can all live together. They might have babies of their own, too, someday, and they'll be needing a home."

Tony was surprised to learn that, although they worked at least as hard as the whites, the black laborers were paid only half-rates. When asked why, Sam just shrugged his shoulders and told him "That's jus' the way the bosses do it. They won't pay me the same as them, so there's nothing I can do." It struck Tony as unfair, but he knew that he wasn't in a position to change anything. He decided to keep his thoughts to himself, or risk being branded a trouble-maker.

Trouble had already found Tony once, while on a Sunday outing to town with a couple of the other gandydancers. A rough-looking man had accosted him in a bar, calling him a "carpet-bagger." The term had a rough edge in the former states of the Confederacy, where locals resented northerners coming south during "reconstruction," considering them profiteers and manipulators. Some loaned money at exorbitant rates or snatched up government contracts intended to aid in rebuilding the railroads and industries. Although some northerners were only well-intentioned new settlers, they were met with hatred and abuse.

Surrounded by the accuser and a few of his buddies, Tony had been backed into a corner. His two white workmates were cowed by the crowd and weren't sure whether they could stop the gang. They hung back. It was only a commanding and familiar voice carrying over the rabble that brought a halt to the impending beating.

"Hold it right there!" Trout's voice rang out in the dim barroom. "The first man that lays a hand on that boy will answer to me."

The mob paused, some turning to see just who was so bold, others taking a step back to make room for what they saw as an impending battle. Dozens of pairs of eyes scanned the well-built foreman, but none savored the idea of taking him on. Tony's co-workers quickly fell in behind their leader.

"He works for me and anyone who thinks he can't, should just step up now and tell me to my face. Otherwise, just shut up and sit down!" Trout said calmly but forcefully. The crowd shuffled their feet, turning back to their whiskeys and warm beers. Tony felt a wave of gratitude pass over him. Friends were good things to have.

The crews worked through the heat of summer, stripped to the waist to heft the heavy hammers driving spikes, or carrying the long rails in slings, four men to a rail, working from stacks dropped by the construction train that served their camp. Dinners sometimes came from town on the train, but more often the men browsed off the plentiful local game, bagging deer, turkeys, ducks, and cranes. If those seemed scarce, they would grab a lumbering gopher tortoise and cook it up like a chicken. A mix of wild greens and berries could usually be scrounged up and Tony learned how to identify the cabbage palm, which could be cut down and stripped of its tender heart at the growing tip. Cooked up in a pot, this "swamp cabbage" was a rare vegetable the men could procure themselves.

Moving around from camp to camp in pursuit of the next assignment, Tony and the crew had an opportunity to see a bit of the wide variety of the country. Broad swamps filled with cypress trees, each surrounded by mysterious protruding "knees," stood side by side with rolling sand hills covered with the enormous live oak trees and stately pines that provided their favorite camp sites. Just south of Gainesville was the broad expanse of Alachua Lake, and Tony used one of his days off to cruise the length of the lake in the *Chakala*, a steamboat that ran mail and freight to isolated settlements and returned with fresh game, eggs and produce. The lake filled a broad basin with a raised rim, much like a gigantic saucer. Thousands of ducks, alligators and wading birds crowded its surface and the long shoreline.

At nights the men stayed in their camp tents, mosquito netting drawn tight, and swapped stories and sometimes entertained each other with remembered songs. Although the black hands and white each had their own tents, on a few occasions Tony sneaked over to sit near the black's fire, where he would listen to the gospel tunes the men could harmonize. One evening they exchanged stories about their own past and Tony was surprised to realize that all of them had once been slaves. Somehow it hadn't occurred to him. Sam, he learned, had been a child when fighting had destroyed the farm he worked on. His parents had homesteaded some land, but both had died of yellow fever. Somehow, he had survived, found work, and still hoped to have his own farm someday. The money he managed to save would go toward that goal.

On the rare trips back to town, when Tony was prone to stick close to Trout, he noticed that several of the door-frames of the otherwise bare, clap-board houses were painted a distinct shade of bright blue. "What's that color for?" he asked his burly foreman.

"That's to keep the haints away," Trout told him.

"What's a haint?" Tony asked.

"You know, a ghost. They say that some of the old places can get to be hainted houses."

"Ohhh!" Tony grinned, "and ghosts don't like blue?"

"Not that shade, apparently, 'cause none of them houses is hainted. And see those bottles hanging in the trees?" Tony glanced at the empty bottles dangling in the branches. "They do the same thing. Haints can't stand 'em 'cause they get caught inside. If you blow across the mouth of the bottle, you can hear 'em in there, moaning. Some of 'em got two or three inside. Just don't break the bottle and you'll be safe and sound."

•

September came and Tony marked the days until his birthday, eager to pass another hurdle on the way to manhood. The work was doing what the calendar could not, however and he was several pounds heavier, with new muscles bulging on his once-lanky frame. He had saved his money and now had almost a hundred-and seventy-dollars cash, most of it in the bank back in Gainesville. He had been disappointed that the work was still in the same area and wished the crew would move to laying new track.

Cooler autumn weather and the steady growth of his savings convinced him to stay on, but by the late spring of '82, with the arrival of more hot weather, Tony made up his mind to go on to Tampa. "I've got an uncle there I haven't seen since I was a little kid, and I set out to look him up," Tony told Trout one day. "I think I ought to finish what I started."

"You're right, Rilly. But when you've had an eyeful o' that place, come on back. I'll have a job for ya, steady."

Since the railroads didn't go south, Tony chose to skip the four-horse stage that ran to Tampa or go to Cedar Key and sail south, preferring to ride his own horse. "I'll get to see more of the state that way," he told his friends. With a round of handshakes and a salute to Trout, Tony mounted his horse on a sunny Sunday afternoon.

"Take care, Rilly. Stay away from the alligators!" came the calls, as he made his way out of the railroad camp at Arredondo. He headed south along the shore of Alachua Lake and passed through the town of Micanopy, the oldest inland town in the state. It had arisen at the site of Chief Micanopy's town of Cuscowilla.

Farther along the trail brought Tony through rolling hills covered with black-jack and live oak, palmetto, and pine. He spent a night camped at the big Silver Springs near the village of Ocala and dreamed of the Indians who had once made their home there. The spring gushed out incredible amounts of water and Tony spent a few minutes staring at the clear, rapid river that poured past his campsite and tried to figure the amount of water that came from the ground. He soon realized that he was lacking at least a zero and maybe two, from his calculations. Peering down into the depths of the river, he could see enormous fish hanging close to the bottom. He had seen a giant channel catfish once in Gainesville, brought up on a train. Bigger than a man, it had fed more than fifty people. Yes, he thought, Florida was a land of some mighty strange sights.

The next morning, he surprised even himself by turning away from the well-worn Fort Brooke trail and instead rode on through the beautiful high-hill country of the ridge. Dense forests of longleaf pines towered atop the high, sandy hills, and blue lakes stood at the foot of almost every rise. A couple featured small homesteads, but he saw few other signs of habitation.

He left the ridge at last and rode into the deep cypress forests of the Green Swamp, following the barest hint of a trail. The water-table was high, and his horse waded through still marsh lands and small rivulets of flowing water seeking to equalize itself across the broad, flat basin of the swamp. Enormous "domes" of cypress trees were spaced across the landscape, appearing as islands on a marshy inland sea, though each gathered in a shallow depression in the wet ground. Between were open fields and slight rises featuring stands of pines and oaks, and Tony saw plenty of turkey, quail, deer, and a couple of incautious bobcats.

Two nights sleeping on the ground amid thousands of alligators was no way to rest, and his nervous horse began to show signs of fatigue. "Lack of sleep," Tony decided. It was with a sense of relief that he achieved higher ground at the community of Socrum, at the northwest corner of Polk County. For more than forty years a handful of white settlers had farmed the area, the earliest having braved the possibility of attack by renegade Seminoles. They had raised vegetables for themselves and had begun to plant a few orange trees. There they had also erected a fine church they called Bethel Baptist during the dark days of the Civil War. A local settler named Martin proudly pointed out his acres of corn, potatoes, melons, and row crops. It was a side of Florida Tony had never seen before. After a day spent resting and exploring the area, Tony headed back onto the trail to Tampa, another thirty-five miles to the west.

Tampa had grown up at the site of Fort Brooke, a major outpost in the Seminole wars. Now, it was a humble collection of buildings, less than eight hundred people living near both the broad bay and the Hillsborough River which flowed into it. It was an isolated frontier town, without so much as a telegraph line to bring news from the outside world. Each of the small collection of houses was fenced to keep out the free-range cattle and wild hogs, as was the custom all over Florida.

A few well-placed questions directed Tony to a modest saloon and boarding house of six rooms, where he was told that his uncle, James Crews, would show up around dark. A small room with a cot, warm food and a bit of rum made him forget the trail for a while and he watched the comings and goings of the locals. Mostly rough-dressed, they stood at a bar, boots on bare plank floors, quaffing drinks and exchanging news and gossip. Though eager for word from outside, they seemed to respect Tony's apparent desire to be alone.

As he sat, he reminisced on his faint memories of family and the uncle he hadn't seen in so many years. James Crews, he remembered, was his father's younger brother. Too young for the army, he had avoided the war.

He had come to Florida a few years later, when the economy went sour in the '70's. In a letter his mother had received, James had said that things weren't much better there, but he didn't have enough money to return to Philadelphia, anyway, so he was staying. "At least there's no snow," Tony recalled the letter had said. It never mentioned the mosquitoes, he thought with a grin. Or the alligators.

As he sat and nursed his rum, he tried to imagine what James might look like now. A cross, perhaps, between his father, looking young, bright, and professional in his military uniform in the lone daguerreotype picture, and his uncle John, a burly man who had moved away to work in the new steel mills at Pittsburgh. They seemed like night and day, those two, but perhaps, Tony thought, it was because his father had died so young.

As he sat lost in thought, he suddenly became aware of a tall, lanky man approaching him, with a hard, serious look on his face.

"They say you're looking for me. What do you want with Jimmy Crews?" the man said abruptly.

Tony stared at the man for moment, then struggled to find words. "Uh, Uncle James? I mean... I'm looking for my uncle from Philadelphia..." Tony stared at the improbable stranger before him, no northern gentleman, but a hard-looking man with a full beard, heavy boots, leather chaps and a broad-brimmed hat. A bandanna around his neck and a Smith and Wesson revolver on his hip completed the picture. He reminded Tony of one of the renegade cavalry officers, described in the northern newspapers, who kept raiding after the war had ended.

There was a long, puzzled silence as the lanky stranger stared at Tony, then he broke into a hint of a grin. "Anthony? Is that you?"

"Yes, sir, it's me all right. I hope I didn't cause you any trouble. I just thought I'd look you up."

"Well, I'll be battered and fried," he said, breaking into a broad smile that lit up his face. "I guess I was expecting a boy and here you come a full-grown man! John wrote me an' said you were coming south, but that was last year, and I didn't expect you would make it this far! Hey, welcome to Tampa!" he said, hauling his nephew to his feet and clapping his arms around him. "It's good to have some family around here!"

Two hours later the pair had eaten all they could hold, downed cool, strong beer from a barrel in the inn, and exchanged every detail they could recall about family and relations far away. They strolled to the door and paused briefly as the bright light of the westering sun struck them in the face and Tony flinched as he felt something brush his pant leg. Looking down, he saw a rangy-looking hound sniffing carefully before looking up at him.

"Down worry, he don't bite," Jimmy told him. "That's my buddy, Boomer. He knows he's not allowed inside, because he got in a bit of a fight there once. He just waits for me out here. He's been ranging with me for the past four years and he's pretty handy to have around."

Tony reached out tentatively, letting Boomer sniff his fingers before scratching the top of his head gently. He got a couple of quick licks of his fingers in return.

"You're friends now and if you ever need him, he'll come running," Jimmy told him.

The next few days were filled with a tour of the settlement and the pitiful port and an introduction to some of the leading citizens, all of whom seemed to know Jimmy on a first name basis.

Tony was impressed that the small town had a colorful group of inhabitants. James introduced him to Dr. John Wall, the town physician, who seemed to know a good bit more than Tony would expect from an isolated country doctor. Tony had read his astute political observations and satire in letters to the editors of the newspapers in Gainesville and Ocala. "I'm a follower of your writings, Dr. Wall," Tony told him. "I'm very honored to meet you."

"You'll be more pleased, then, to meet my wife. This is Matilda McKay Wall." Tony gave a slight bow to the woman the doctor presented and returned her pleasant smile.

"Have I perhaps met your father, James McKay, who owns the shipping company?" he asked her.

"I see that you have, indeed," she smiled again. "I welcome you to Tampa. This is a small town, still, but it's bound to grow and it's a healthy place to start a family. Have you a wife, Mr. Crews?"

"No, I haven't," Tony answered, slightly embarrassed by her boldness.

"Well, that is a situation that I'm sure time, and Tampa, will cure," she replied. "It is indeed a pleasure to meet you."

"Stay indoors at night and take care that you don't get bitten by the summer mosquitoes here," Dr. Wall told him. "They carry yellow fever."

"They told me in Gainesville that it comes from being around manure and filth," Tony replied.

"That's nonsense, Tony. I know. I've had the disease, and my first wife and daughter died of it. I've been working to keep yellow fever out of here for years since and it's worked. Take my word for it, Tony, and take my advice."

•

"You know, you were lucky to catch me here," Jimmy said, as they walked up the main street toward their boarding house. "I just got back to town two weeks ago from Punta Rassa. Captain McKay owns most of the shipping here, and all those cattle over on Ballast Point, but we can take our own cattle to Punta Rassa to meet the boats from Cuba and sell them direct. In a couple of months when the weather cools off, I'll head back out east to start rounding up another herd. The woods are full of them if you know where to look. They're wild, left over from some the Spanish brought in, two, three hundred years ago."

"Sounds like a lot of work, rounding up cattle out there. I rode through some of that country, and I never saw a one," Tony responded.

"You wouldn't, coming from Gainesville. You got to head east toward the Kissimmee River. You cross over the Ridge into the old Indian country and there's plenty of them."

"Indian country! Are you crazy! I heard that they'll kill you on sight!"

"That's city talk. There's not supposed to be any more Seminoles in that part of the state but come on along with me and I'll introduce you to a couple of them. I always bring them something I know they can use, and they let us round up the cattle. They're good people. Been lied to and misused something terrible, but good people. All that land was supposed to be theirs forever, but the government gives, and the government takes away again."

"Well," said Tony after a pause, "I really planned to go back to work for Trout on the railroad, but, really, it's too damn hot in the summer, anyway."

"Now you're talking like the Philadelphia kid I expected!" Jimmy grinned.

Tony was soon working with Jimmy's lasso, practicing his toss around stumps and fence posts. Jimmy critiqued his method and showed him just how to hold his thumb as he swung the stiff rope over his head. It would be an important skill.

The time in the Tampa settlement went by quickly and soon Tony was feeling like a local, on a first-name basis with dozens of the shopkeepers and fishermen. He began to feel at home in the dusty streets lined with picket fences.

"You know, this town is going to grow one day," Jimmy said over lunch at the boarding house, where they served generous portions of staples like black-eyed peas, corn grits, and fried fish, along with local game. "It's got to grow. It's got that great bay, aching for a real port. One day the boats will start coming here, instead of Punta Rassa. Then, watch out."

"You really think so?"

"Sure thing. I already bought a couple of pieces of property here. You know, you ought to do the same thing. It's so cheap, you could afford it. You got a couple'a bucks, don't you?"

"Sure. I already took some of it down and put it in the bank, if you can call it that."

"Don't worry, It's probably safe there. You ought to take the rest and buy yourself a chunk of land. You can't go wrong in Florida. A friend of mine has a nice place along the river, just a little way upstream. It's covered with big gnarly oak trees they never got around to cutting when they took the cypress and pines. You could get it for about fifty cents an acre, I'll bet, maybe less. He could use the money right now."

Before he knew what had happened, Tony had followed Jimmy to the bank and soon owned not only the land on the river, but four hundred more acres east of the town and a mortgage to the bank. He was already worried as he watched the smiling eyes of the seller and the banker when they shook hands on the deal.

"You know, Jimmy, that was all the money I had in the world, except the four dollars I got in my pocket, and that won't keep me a week at the hotel," Tony said as they walked away from the bank. "I must be crazy, letting you talk me into buying a piece of this bumpkin town."

"Don't panic, nephew," Jimmy answered. "You won't be needing any money where we're going, there's no payment due until next year, and your land will still be there when we get back."

"That's if we get back, you mean. I don't like all your talking about not needing any money where we're going. It makes me nervous."

In October Jimmy brought Tony down a dusty side-street to a large, roughly built barn, and as their eyes adjusted to the dim light, they could see a dozen stalls. Most contained horses, and a good-looking stallion caught Tony's eye immediately. "Out back there's more to choose from," Jimmy told him. "You need to sell your horse here and get one that knows how to work the cattle. That roan stallion you're looking at there was part of my string last year. He's a fine cutting-horse. Let's start with him." Jimmy reached into his pocket and took out a large gold coin. "Spanish gold," he said. "That's my seed money. I always put some back that I can't spend or invest. When we get back, you pay me back your half."

As Tony was nodding his agreement with a grateful grin, he noticed a man with a thick leather apron that reached his shoe tops. He had been watching them from one of the stalls, where he was now resting his chin on the neck of one of the horses. Tony immediately recognized him as a man he had seen Jimmy talk to before in the saloon at the hotel.

"Don't worry, gentlemen, we will soon have you outfitted with the best horses in the whole state," he told them.

"Tony, this here's John Straub. I should'a introduced you to him before, but he's a busy man, I can't get him to stay around long enough to buy him a drink."

"Sorry, Jimmy. You know I got to be back here to take care of my horses. Just you make sure to take good care of 'em too!"

"Don't worry, John, I haven't lost one the last two seasons, I'm not about to start now. And now I got my nephew here, all the way from Philadelphia, to help me keep an eye on 'em."

"Pleased to meet you," Tony said as John came forward to shake his hand. "Think I can arrange to ride that roan stallion?"

"I don't see why not, get your horse in here and swap her saddle."

While Tony busied himself with the horses, Jimmy and John went into deep conversation, with John taking plenty of notes. They walked around the barn and shop, choosing horses, packs, extra reins and a saddle. Jimmy pointed at a sack of oats. "I'll take one of those, too, just to keep your ponies happy."

"You're a good man, Tony!" he laughed.

"I still got about six hundred feet of good rope left from last season, but I do need a couple of extra canteens."

Within an hour, Tony had most of his gear arranged. Jimmy had Tony outfitted with much the same equipment he wore, along with a cow pony and a long bullwhip. "This is what you'll have to use to flush the stubborn ones out of the palmettos," Jimmy told him, stepping into the corral to demonstrate the swing and snap motion that created a loud "crack" from the leather as the whip snapped around. "There's not more than two dozen men in the state can really handle one a' these." While Tony's was not quite as long as the eighteen-foot model that Jimmy used, it still took him days of practice to develop a technique that didn't threaten to take off his own ear each time he used it.

Picking up the horses and gear three days later, they led a string of five extra horses, four of which were soon fully laden with gear and the food they stuffed into extra packs. The fifth horse, a cutter, carried a much lighter load. "No sense in risking the insurance policy," Jimmy said.

Soon they were headed east, following poor trails that gradually faded away. They passed through a varied landscape of low hills and shallow valleys, mostly wooded. On the second day they reached the Peace River.

"You call this the Peace River?" Tony asked. "The map I saw in Tampa said it was the Pease, with an 's'.

"Don't worry, the man can't spell, or can't hear," Jimmy told him. Tony shook his head and chuckled.

They forded the stream near Bartow. Still flush with late-summer rains, it was the biggest one they'd had to cross. "I'm glad my horse seems to know where to put his feet in this," Tony called to Jimmy as he was wading the sluggish stream.

"I'd'a brought us up north around the big lake at the source, but that's another day of riding to where we're going," Jimmy replied.

They had soon left the Peace River and its line of frontier villages behind and rode on into the barely explored interior of east Florida. Until only a few years earlier, it was strictly Seminole territory and they had raided near Fort Meade on two occasions during the fighting. Now the land was finally at peace, only because the government had finally given up on trying to relocate the last of them.

Tony was surprised at how rapidly the land changed as they headed east, and how many different forms it took. From the familiar moss-draped live oaks they passed quickly through broad swathes of pine and oak forests and vast expanses of prairie that featured little more than cabbage palmettos. After a few miles of maples, bays, and sweet gum, they were back on slightly higher ground and back in the pine woods. Tony reveled in the fragrance they lent to the air. The pines cast a soft shade as the sun was filtered through their foot-long "needles," and the tallest towered far above them, many reaching nearly a hundred feet into the air.

They passed at last onto a series of dunes of bleached-white sand with a scattering of stunted oak trees, no more than tallish bushes. Tony was especially surprised to find thick stands of prickly-pear cactus three feet high, sometimes barring their way and forcing them to wind about to find the path through. They guided their horses on foot to avoid the two-inch spines. The paddle-like flat leaves were crowed by yellow flowers and Jimmy explained that, once the small "pears" they left behind had swelled to maturity, they could be roasted over an open fire and made a passable vegetable.

They eventually wound their way around broad lakes and made their way to a higher hill of white sand that sported a canopy of towering longleaf pines. Some were nearly three feet thick. Looking out through the trees Tony could see a distant smudge of blue that he took for another large lake.

"Let's stop here," Jimmy said as he rested his mount.

"Suits me fine," Tony replied.

As they made their evening camp, Tony spotted a variety of strange birds and a foot-long gopher tortoise browsing on the purple flowers of a slender vine. He was especially surprised to see that the tiny leaves of the plant folded when touched. "That's a sensitive plant," Jimmy told him. "There's lots of strange stuff grows up here. Nothing like what we had up north. You see that lake out there?" he asked, nodding to the east. "That's We-Oh-Ya-Kapka. At least that's what the Seminoles called it. I think it means the place to walk in the water. It's maybe five, six miles across, but so shallow you could ride a horse across it just about anywhere you choose. They say that the Army once had some Seminoles cornered up against the lake there and they just walked across the water during the night. Army found their camp empty."

Tony found the wildlife interesting and even though he had seen plenty of animals working on the line, being seated on a horse was a much better vantage point. He was watching a pair of ospreys working hard to drive a bald eagle from their territory when he was startled by a loud, gurgling scream that sounded almost human.

"That right there is what we call a "Lord-god" bird," Jimmy told him nodding toward a huge woodpecker with a white bill. "Liked to scare me to death the first time I heard one. I was sleeping and it landed about six feet above me, gave out one of its calls, and I thought I was about to be scalped! I almost jumped out of my skin and yelled out "Lord god!" and my old partner Bill laughed 'til he cried."

The next morning, they rode over several low hills and looked down upon beautiful lakes from beneath stands of majestic longleaf pines that cast their filtered shade upon the yellow-white sands at their feet. At length they passed down the eastern side of the ridge, descending by a series of terraces into a desolate-looking world of tall grass, scattered pines and saw palmetto. This pancake-flat land was the home of the scrub cattle and had become a second home to Jimmy. Here he led them onto familiar trails, avoiding the wet areas he called "sloughs," rhyming them with clues.

"Those sloughs don't look like much," he told Tony, "but come summertime you'll be wanting to avoid them, 'cause they can be boggy for a horse and sometimes they'll be some danged big 'gators moving up them from the lakes looking for mates and food. Watch out for that saw palmetto, too. The edges of those stems will cut you to the bone if you're not careful. Your horse knows enough to avoid 'em. He also knows enough to warn you if there's a lion around too, or a bear, but they gen'rally avoid a man. Don't be afraid to get one if you can. Keep an out for the big rattlers, too. Horse won't smell them, but if they get stepped on, they bite. Speaking of biting, the mosquitoes will leave us alone once we get a good cold snap."

On another occasion, Jimmy warned Tony to keep an eye out for rustlers. "They can be damn sneaky, and they might just shoot you out of the saddle to get a few cows."

"They would really do that?" Tony asked.

"Let's put it this way," Jimmy replied. "A few years back, before I started out cow hunting, a man named of Mose Barber decided that Orange County couldn't tax his land or cattle. He had been in a dispute with the sheriff, a man by the name of David Mizell. He accused him of stealing his cattle. When Barber found Mizell on his land he killed him. Before that war was over, there was more'n forty men dead."

Tony reviewed the new list of hazards and came to the conclusion that he was in for some tough times. He wasn't mistaken. The next seven months were the most challenging and interesting in Tony's entire life. Sleeping on a hammock and fighting mosquitoes under the simple lean-to shelter they erected, the two men ranged through vast pine flat-woods. In many places the ground was almost covered by four-foot-high palmetto thickets. Soggy with rain in the summer, they were prone to burn at the drop of a hat in the spring.

They roamed onto low islands, called hammocks, surrounded by thousands of acres of marsh, that once provided shelter for Seminoles and now hid the stringy, long-horned "scrub cows." Boomer ranged ahead, his deep baying a sure sound that he had found some cattle, or maybe a bear or wildcat. They drove cattle from the deepest thickets of saw palmettos, where even the heavy leather chaps that protected them and their horses couldn't prevent them from occasionally drawing blood.

Once Boomer had flushed the cattle out, the easiest thing to do was to drive them to a lake and corner them in the water so they could get a rope on them. Jimmy was a pretty good toss, but Tony missed more than he liked. Eventually, though, between the two of them they got the job done, tying the cattle temporarily to any likely tree.

After they had rounded up the small groups of cattle, they drove them into a log-built corral under the biggest, shadiest oaks. Partly blocked by dense palmetto thickets which they had reinforced with cut timbers, they completed their crude enclosure with a stretch of real fence and a gate. It took them a full day of digging, sharing their one small spade, to dig enough of a hole to allow the cattle access to water. Hauling in extra forage was a job every third day.

One day when the pair were deep in the brush they flushed out a small horse, which Billy spent an hour trying to lasso before finally succeeding with the help of Boomer. He proudly displayed his catch. "That there's a Marshtackie," he told Tony. "It must'a gotten loose from somewhere, or maybe it was born out here, who knows. They are the best sort to have around here, though, as they can find their way through any kind of ground. They're tough, too, never seem to get tired."

Tony eyed the rough-looking horse, three hands shorter than his own and covered with a shaggy fur. "It doesn't look like much, but I'll take your word for it."

"Just wait 'til I get him broken in to take a saddle and I'll show you what he can do," Jimmy assured him. That project occupied many an evening over the following weeks, Tony watching with interest as Jimmy got the horse to calm down, accepting first a blanket and later a saddle upon its back. The sight of Jimmy being thrown off at his first attempt to mount the animal left Tony laughing, but Jimmy eventually persevered, and his new horse soon began to prove its worth.

Many afternoons the two were able to return with new additions to their herd and camped near the gate to keep the cattle in and hungry bears and wolves out. It proved a suitable place to gather them, and the numbers slowly grew.

Jimmy found plenty of adventure at the side of his worldly uncle. One day, when Tony assumed they were riding aimlessly well to the west side of the huge Lake Kissimmee, they came upon a lake shaped like a skillet, with its long, watery "handle" stretching to the north. The trail ended near the water and Jimmy forged ahead, wading his horse until they came upon a hidden hammock island, surrounded by the wooded swamps.

Before them was a simple thatched chickee, with a central dirt floor surrounded by elevated planks for sleeping and working. Palm fronds covered its roof and walls. Inside was an old man who had silently watched their approach. There, true to his word, Jimmy introduced Tony to the real Seminole, whom he called "the Old Chief," as well as a younger Seminole man who lived with him. They were the caretakers of the island, which had a long, crescent-shaped burial mound. It was a traditional gathering place, or so Tony determined from the little bits of explanation that Jimmy offered him.

Tony was surprised to hear his uncle carry on a conversation in an Indian tongue. Jimmy produced a gift of a box of ammunition for the rifle that leaned against the wall and a second, a box full of raisins he had purchased in Tampa.

The two visitors were treated well and feasted on venison, greens, swamp cabbage and a turkey that Jimmy had brought down. Boomer lay patiently nearby, eagerly snatching tossed scraps out of the air. They spoke until late in the evening and camped near the small chickee overnight.

They took their leave after a quick breakfast cooked over the smoky fire at first light, heading out as dew still dripped from the oaks overhead.

"Just west of here, on the ridge, is a hill that the Indians believe is sacred," Jimmy said as they rode away from the island. "If you look through the trees you can see it, there," he pointed. "They held gatherings of sacrifice and even their law courts, here on the island and then traveled to the hill for more ceremonies and thanksgiving. They tell me that the hill protected the first people who came here from the great flood, sort of like the story in the Bible. I don't know how the Seminoles would know much about the first Indians who were here, because in Tampa they say they were all killed off. Some other folks say that maybe they didn't really all die out and some of them were still here when the Seminoles started coming down."

"You seem to know a lot about the Indians here, Jimmy."

"I made it a point. I don't like to trust my life to people I know nothing about."

"So, what if all the original Indians weren't really killed? What if some survived, hidden away, like on that island?"

"That, Tony, is something we'll probably never know for sure."

By the time the coldest days of winter had passed, both men were craving greens to go with their diet of game. Tony showed Jimmy the fresh sprouts of poke weed growing lushly from their thick roots. "Cut 'em off and they'll grow more," he told Jimmy. "Then we got to boil 'em good and pour off the water twice, or they'll poison us."

"Really?" Jimmy asked in disbelief. "You expect me to eat something that's poison?"

"Once we boil it down, the poison's gone. Don't worry, everybody around here eats 'em. You just got to be careful how you cook 'em."

Jimmy later admitted that the boiled leaves made an acceptable vegetable but was much relieved a few weeks later when Tony showed him a thicket of green briar, hundreds of thick, juicy shoots that could be snapped off and eaten fresh and made a tasty salad. At Tony's coaching, Jimmy soon became a proficient forager, keeping an eye out for wild blackberries and tiny strawberries, along with ripe persimmons, cow peas and a variety of other plants. "Most of these I learned from the Seminoles," Jimmy told him. "They can cook up some pretty tasty dishes right out of the woods and they make a sort of flour from coontie roots that makes a decent flat-bread."

They wandered around the big basin of lakes called the Kissimmee chain, connected by the river. Lake Kissimmee was only the largest. Other lakes were also connected to them by broad sloughs, creating a maze that soon had Tony completely lost as they zig-zagged to follow a trail that only Jimmy could see.

At the northern end they passed around East Lake Tohopekaliga, "The name means the lake's a gathering place to the Indians," Jimmy told him. "I think it's where they used to get together for trade and ceremonies."

At last, they came into the village of Kissimmee, where they could stock up on supplies. The town had a row of new cypress-plank buildings, and a sawmill was busily cutting more of the material. They bought flour, corn meal and all the fresh greens and fruit they could carry and killed an hour in the small saloon, sampling the warm, yeasty beer.

Heading back south they followed the shore of a big Lake Jimmy called Hatchi-ne-ha. There they were more than a little surprised to come upon a large crew of men and a floating dredge that was churning the tea-colored water to a frothy, muddy brown. The machine was disgorging the mucky bottom mud into the bordering marshes and forest. Tony was amazed at the sight of the huge steam engine on the barge in the midst of the wilderness, for it had seemed that they were miles from any sign of civilization.

"What are you men up to with that contraption?" Jimmy called to a shoreman working lines for the huge machine.

"Mr. Disston owns this dredge and he's got a contract with the state to drain all these swamp-lands," came the shouted reply. "Disston's gone and bought four million acres of land from the State Trustees for twenty-five cents an acre. He's opening up the Kissimmee River all the way to Lake Okeechobee, and Okeechobee to the ocean. He's gonna' drain the whole thing! They're gonna' start running mail and freight all the way up to the top of Lake Tohopea-whatever..."

"Imagine that!" Jimmy said, as the two cow hunters rode off pondering what it might mean to their future. As they continued southward, Tony shook his head. "Twenty-five cents an acre, huh? You think that's a good price?"

"I guess if you can afford to buy that much of it, you get the good deal," Jimmy replied. "That works out to a million dollars! I didn't think there was that much money in this whole state!"

The two cow hunters could scarcely grasp the scale of Hamilton Disston's work. Although they didn't know it, Lake Okeechobee spanned nearly half the width of the state. The vast but shallow lake caught the flow of the Kissimmee River, which flowed south down the interior and fed its waters into the broad flow of the Everglades. Enormous monsoonal floods filled the basin to overflowing each summer and ebbed each winter. The lake's waters had spilled across its southern shore onto the ancient limestone and coral of former seabed in a sheet flow for more than a million years. Detritus from the floods settled from the water and added to a thick lens of rich, black muck soil. From there it flowed through low sloughs and bayous into Florida Bay at the southern tip of the state. Spreading out from the lake and the surrounding glades were hundreds of rivers and creeks connected by broad marshes, a world of cypress trees and saw-grass. This was the watery world the Seminoles called Pa-hay-okee. The Everglades were the liquid heart of South Florida, an ecosystem unique in the world.

Along the coasts, mangrove thickets stopped the eroding forces of the sea and sheltered billions of infant fish, shrimp, clams and other species among their roots. Those in turn fed a rich marine environment. Perhaps more than a billion birds at one time would feed and nest in this aqueous environment. Only a broken ring of slightly higher ground contained this incubator of life. That ring would soon be pierced by a thousand cuts.

What the politicians in Tallahassee viewed as a wasteland and a curse, Disston believed could be turned into a vast tract of rich farmland, if only he could lower the water table. That meant he had to drain the lake to make his holdings more valuable.

Armed with his contract from the state and a flow of tax dollars to support him, Disston had set out to recreate South Florida. He and the powers in Tallahassee agreed that, if only something could be made of all those submerged lands, Florida might become a prosperous place. The fact the Everglades were also sheltering the last of the Seminoles didn't hurt the bargain, either.

He had started by dredging a canal between the lake and the Caloosahatchee River, unleashing a torrent of fresh water heading for the Gulf of Mexico. The waterfalls that resulted from the rushing river were dynamited to speed the flow and allow boats to navigate inland. Disston soon opened drainage canals to the Atlantic Coast as well, and then began dredging up the Kissimmee River more than a hundred miles to Lake Tohopekaliga. As channels were deepened and widened, Florida's water began to bleed away. As the dredges moved on, steamboats followed, carrying freight and mail to inland towns and settlements. Florida was being changed forever.

December 1882

By Christmas, Jimmy and Anthony had gathered more than eighty head of the lean wild cattle, herding them together in a long neck of land along a lake and roping each one to cut a distinctive notch in its right ear while checking for diseases. On Christmas Eve, Jimmy led Tony through the woods on a fifteen-mile ride to another cow camp to the east. There, they shared a Christmas meal with three other cow hunters and agreed to share the chores of the long drive to Punta Rassa on the Gulf coast. There they would sell the herd to Cuban buyers in exchange for Spanish doubloons.

Three weeks later, on January 14, they met at a prearranged location in the wilderness. Tony could hear the approach of the second herd for miles as they came through the pines and palmettos. Combined, after more than six months of hunting, the five men had gathered almost one hundred sixty head of cattle. Each decent cow would fetch a Spanish gold doubloon, worth about sixteen American dollars. Allowing for some losses on the 120-mile drive, Jimmy calculated they should each earn about $450 if the price of cattle stayed up.

They moved the big herd slowly west, stopping at favorable pastures near the Ridge lakes, then crossing and following the course of the Peace River to Punta Rassa and a quick sale to eager buyers.

By March the Crews family's Florida branch was back in Tampa. As Jimmy had said, the land was still there, but Tony still had his regrets as well as the two headed into town to make the annual payment. A large part of his earnings would soon be gone again.

The regrets evaporated soon after they arrived at the bank.

"Ah, Mr. Crews!" the bank president gushed upon seeing them. "I am so glad you are back! There is a gentleman who has been waiting some weeks, hoping you would return. It seems that he is interested in your property!"

"My property? Why is he so interested in my property?" Tony asked

"Well actually, Sir, he is interested in several properties. He has already acquired some choice parcels. I dare say that the price of land hereabouts has risen accordingly."

Tony looked over at Jimmy. "Sounds like we need to know a lot more about this fella and why he wants the land," he said.

"I told you it was a good investment, Tony. You never should have worried," Jimmy told him when they were alone.

"We'll see. But, meanwhile, I think we should ask around some."

When they stopped at the saloon to reward themselves for their months of hard work, the local talk was full of rumors about the stranger, who was obviously a northern speculator.

"He's going to start raising cattle on a ranch and wants stockyards near the port," some said. "No, he's going to open a shipyard and haul naval stores and turpentine from the forests to refit ships," said others.

The next morning, bright and early, the two "Crews boys," as folks had taken to calling them, met with the mysterious buyer, who offered a price almost double what they had paid for several of their various holdings. After a long discussion, during which the offer was raised, they decided that they would rather hold on to the land for a little while longer and try to figure out why the stranger was suddenly so interested in buying land in Tampa.

"I think it's time you and I went for a little boat ride," Tony said to Jimmy as the two sauntered away from the bank one day, their senses of self-worth suddenly increased. "What say we sail on up to Cedar Key and catch a train back to civilization, see what news we can sniff out there and think this over."

"Sounds like a plan, nephew," came the response.

None of the stories rang true with the Crews boys, so they pondered their situation on the ship, a small coastal steamer half filled with livestock returning to the rail head in exchange for an earlier southbound load of window glass, bolts of fabric, dishes, and other manufactured goods.

Cedar Key was a busy place, with several ships tied up along the wharves and a spidery trestle across the shallow water of the Gulf busy with long lines of rail cars moving to and from the island. The short time between boat and train was occupied by a walk through the bustling business district.

"Why is it that this place is so busy and Tampa so quiet?" Tony asked.

"It's all because of pencils, if you want to know the truth," Jimmy told him. "See that big building over there?" he asked, pointing at a two-story wooden warehouse. "That's the pencil factory of Mr. Eberhard Faber. He came down here just to get all the cedar trees. This place is full of 'em, or used to be. They have to go a bit farther to find 'em now, but they still fill a train with cedar planks every few days and ship it north to make more pencils."

"That and the train, I guess," Tony rejoined. "That's why all the ships call here."

"I think that's how the North won the war," Jimmy added laconically. "They had more pencils."

"You know," Tony said when they had seated themselves in the last car of the train, as far as possible from the smoking, belching locomotive, "I have an idea what that fellow is up to and why he's wanting our land. I'll have to check it out to be sure, though. I think I may learn something in Gainesville."

Arriving in that city, Tony noticed only a few new buildings since his earlier stay, but Jimmy was impressed. "This is the kind of place Tampa could be, with people building and investing. This town is growing, you can feel it. "

"Come on, we've got to find Trout. He's probably out of town somewhere." Tony said and headed toward the livery stable, which could usually double as a great source of information on comings and goings.

Four hours later, the two rode their rented horses up to a dusty and familiar-looking camp, where the evening cook fire was only beginning to flame brightly in the evening cool.

"Rilly! What you doin' back here?" It was Sam Lewis, the former slave, who spotted his former work mate first.

"Hello, Sam! It's good to see you," he said, shaking his extended hand with both of his. "Everything all right with the crew?"

"Right as rain. Trout's gone up to Waldo, tryin' for a new contract. Seems we's gonna be busy as ever and this time it looks like its gonna' be some new track, no more of this ol' fix-up stuff. They'll be plenty of work for you and your frien', too, if'n you like."

Anthony took a moment to introduce Jimmy to the crew, proud to show off his strapping cowboy uncle.

"You gonna' be laying some new track, Sam? Where to?" Anthony asked when all the handshakes were done.

"Well, Trout says they's a Mister Plant who wants to put the track all the way to Tampa. Wants to start on it this year. Says he got plenty of money to make it happen, too."

There was a momentary pause, as Tony and Jimmy stared at one another, mouths open, followed by a whoop neither one could contain.

"Ya-hoo! We got it! We did it! We ought to buy more!" The words tumbled out in a jumble that only the speakers understood.

Sam stood looking at the two in wonder, dancing like kids at a Christmas tree, shaking his head slowly. "I don' know jus' what I said, but I guess it was the right thing."

•

The rest of that year passed like a whirlwind for the Crews boys, who tried to stay ahead of the burgeoning real estate boom. After twenty years of languishing in an economic pit, a new railroad building boom was promising to pull Florida to prosperity. Tony and Jimmy rode back and forth around the state, from the inland port town of Sanford on the St. Johns River, to Tampa, more than a hundred miles by horse. Somewhere along that line, they knew, Mr. Plant was going to build a railroad under a contract with the state. He would get most of the land along the right-of-way, entire square miles on alternate sides. The Crews boys figured to get as much as they could of the rest.

Back and forth they rode, from tiny sawmill settlements to surveyed townships, talking to local people, and listening to the debate about which route would be followed. In a new village called Acton, a group of British businessmen were confident that Mr. Plant would also bring the railroad to their new settlement. They had set about building a tidy community between Lake Parker and Lake Bonny in Polk County and soon erected some houses and a fine chapel. Promoters of the venture traveled in England, recruiting their fellows to join them. One who had been impressed was Alexandra, Princess of Wales, who had made a gift of some church fixtures which they proudly displayed.

Others in villages to the south toward Bartow were sure the railroad would pass them by well to the north, but they would be patient. It was in Bartow that the Crews boys first heard of the rich mineral strike which had been made near Fort Meade.

"It's pebble phosphate!" a man told them on a sidewalk next to the general store. "They say it's good for fertilizer. All you got to do is pick the rocks up off the ground. They tell me a wagon-load of the stuff could bring twenty dollars, or maybe more, if you could get it to market. Some even say there's lots more, buried in the ground. Sooner or later, they're bound to put the rails through here, just to haul the stuff out. You ought'a buy a piece of Fort Meade land before the price gets too high."

Talking up a storm, Jimmy and Tony bought all the land they could, not just phosphate land, but cattle and town-site land, too. Most they bought with little or nothing down and promises to pay more than it was worth. They went back to their friendly banker in Tampa and borrowed against the equity they had in their land there to add more to their holdings, but the parcels were always carefully chosen, and most along the expected line of the railroad.

"You know, Tony, we're taking a big chance, you and me," Jimmy said one November evening after they had arrived back in Tampa. "If Mr. Plant runs out of money and the railroad doesn't come through, we'll never be able to make the payments on the first piece of land and we'll lose it all. By my count, we got thirty-one tracts, close to nine thousand acres between us. It could all come to nothing, and we'll be back to chasing cows."

"Don't talk about it, Jimmy. I was just sitting here wondering if we could sell one of the horses to buy that section next to the river property. The price has gone up so much, though, I don't think it'd be enough to get the man to talk to us."

"You boys been buying land here?" asked the man at the next table. "Sorry, I couldn't help but overhear what you said."

Jimmy looked at the stranger, a rough looking sort. "Yeah, you heard right, Mr..."

"Foreman. Bill Foreman. I just thought you might want to know, before you get in any deeper. We got word here today from the Army... Fort Brooke's closing down. The Army's pulling out of here..."

"Where did you hear that?" Jimmy asked with a start.

"It's true," the stranger said. "Fort Brooke's being de-activated. You can see the notice posted on the gate and the post office. They're gonna' be selling off all that land. Sixteen square miles."

The news about Fort Brooke was soon confirmed, and the Crews boys retreated to their rented room in a state of shock. It was obvious that selling those big parcels of land would drive down prices again, not to mention the withdrawal of the entire garrison, which was the biggest customer for most of the local merchants. It was a combination that could kill a settlement, quickly.

After a long silence spent staring at the walls of their boarding house room, Jimmy spoke again. "D'ya think this fella' Plant will still want to build a railroad here if there's no town?"

"Maybe you and I ought to go visit this Mr. Plant and see if he's for real."

"I guess we should have done that in the first place. What if we find out he can't keep the contract? What would we do then?"

"Start selling land, I guess."

"You're right, we ought'a take a ride back up to Sanford and find out what's going on."

"Jimmy, let's get some sleep. We'll hit the trail in the morning."

Several days of riding along what they supposed was the route of the train line showed them little new. In Acton there was worry about competing developers with a rival community called Lakeland, almost within shouting distance. The two groups were both planning to lobby Mr. Plant to build a station on their property.

"They better hope that's all they have to worry about," Jimmy said, as they departed the next morning, headed east.

They spent several days on the trail, crossing over the Ridge and on into Orange County, without any sign of a rail line being built. No surveyors, no foresters, no gandydancers, no locomotives.

It was not until they reached the village of Orlando, only twenty miles south of Sanford, that they stumbled upon a crew working on rail line and got some news. Tracks had already been run south past Kissimmee and were being extended, but the effort was behind schedule. Mr. Plant, it seemed, was at the state capitol in Tallahassee, trying to get more time to complete the line. He was expected in Sanford the next day. If they were lucky, they could catch him.

When they finally arrived at the Sanford rail yard, it was a beehive of activity. Steamboats were offloading tons of new rails, hundreds of men were busy loading trains and sawmills were busy cutting huge logs into serviceable ties. It took the two little time to locate the plush private car housing the visionary behind all the activity.

"What can I do for you men?" a voice stopped them in their tracks. "If you're looking for work, you need to see the hiring office, at the depot..."

"We're not looking for work, we came to see Mr. Plant," Jimmy said to the burly Irishman who blocked the steps to the car.

"Why would you be needing to see Mr. Plant?" he asked. "He's a very busy man."

"Because we own a lot of land that he may be wanting to cross. We may be able to offer him some help," Tony said quietly.

"There's been nothing but a parade of men coming here to try to get Mr. Plant to build the line their way. I doubt very seriously whether he's going to have time to..."

"Mac, it's all. right," came a call from inside the car. "Show the gentlemen in. I have a moment now."

Henry B. Plant revealed himself to be a pleasant man and he listened closely while the two told him of their property in Tampa and along the line of the route. They carefully avoided mentioning that they had just acquired most of it and were mortgaged to the hilt. While they talked, Tony couldn't help but steal glances around the car, which reminded him of the interior of the opera house he had been in once as a child in Philadelphia.

"So, Mr. Plant, we're not so much concerned about exactly where your railroad will go, but rather just wanting to make sure that it does," Jimmy finished up.

"Well, I can see your concern, I really can, and I've got to confess to you that I share it."

"What?" Tony interjected. "Do you mean there's a chance that you won't build the railroad to Tampa?"

"Yes," Plant replied. "But it won't be because I didn't try. You see, when I set out to build a railroad system, I bought this old line called the South Florida, and I bought an old charter to extend the rails down to Tampa. I also hired Colonel Henry Haines to run the rail-building operation and a finer man could not be found. He's got the men working twenty-four hours a day in shifts. Blacksmiths are forging spikes, sawmills are cutting new ties, everything is going along as fast as can be hoped."

"My trouble is," Plant continued, "the contract with the state says I've got to be completed into Tampa by the end of February 1884. That only gives me three and a half months to get there, or lose the land, under the terms of the charter. Without the land, I can't finance the construction. I got surveyors and a crew heading to the Tampa end with wagons of supplies now, and a ship full of rails on its way, too, but east of Tampa the line goes through lots of cypress swamp. It's going to take a lot of work to get through, with plenty of bridge work. The problem is, I can't even get started on that part yet. I have another crew cutting through a hill of solid clay on the ridge halfway between here and there, but the work is slow going and it's holding up the line. Even if I had all the track down to there, I couldn't get past that point with a locomotive."

"I know that country, sir," Jimmy responded. "I spent a lot of time hunting cows north of the big lake Kissimmee and crossed that ridge many a time. There's very few ways around it and they're all wet."

"Do you know a man named John Trout, sir?" Tony asked suddenly.

"Hmm, Trout? Yes, Trout… I think there was a man by that name that bid on the rail work…"

"That would be him, sir. Is he here?"

"No, actually, we hired another company. Is he a friend of yours?"

"Let's just say, sir, that with your permission and Trout's help, I think I can promise you to have a track laid across Polk County before your deadline."

"Son, if you can do that," replied Mr. Plant slowly, "I'll owe you, and Mr. Trout, a large debt of gratitude. You have my permission, just let me know what you need, within reason, and it's yours."

"All I need right now is a ticket to Gainesville, sir," Tony told him.

The next afternoon, the two found themselves back at the camp at Arredondo, a short distance outside Gainesville. All was as they had left it in the spring, and they waited until nearly dark before the crews returned from their jobs, with big John Trout in the lead. Tony was surprised to see that only two crews of men were along. There was no sign of Sam.

"Mr. Trout, we need to talk to you. We got a job that needs to be done," Tony called as soon as they were within earshot.

"It's good to see you, Rilly," Trout said when he gripped the younger man's hand, "but I'm afraid I don't have that job I promised ya. I already had to let a crew go and next week, another. I'd like to help…"

"Can you call the other crew back? We've got work aplenty and it's got to be done on the quick."

"Work for who?" Trout asked Tony with a puzzled frown.

"Henry B. Plant. Building a real railroad."

"I tried to get his work, but he hired a crew a' gandydancers out a' Georgia."

"Well, he needs you now. Get your men back if you can. We're going all the way to Tampa."

Within a week, all three crews had finished up the work around Gainesville and were standing at a construction site in northeast Polk County. Col. Haines had at least two hundred men slowly cutting the banks deeper through the hard-packed red clay, using pickaxes and shovels. They had learned through trial and error that dynamite was almost useless in the soft, sticky clay. Once loosened, the material was being shoveled into mule-teamed wagons for removal. Piles of spoil stood to the side. It was obviously a big job, and slow going. Trout shook his head slowly as he stared at the job ahead.

"You know what you got us into, Rilly?" Trout asked, "There's still twenty feet of clay to be moved to get down to reasonable grade along this whole mile before we can even start to lay tracks, and it's a long way still to Hillsborough." Trout turned to Tony, a look of doubt on his face. "This here Polk's a big county. Too big, most say and we're still way up in the corner of it, by the map. I think you jus' bit off more 'n you can chew."

"Trout, I just sold you to Mr. Plant as the best team of gandydancers that ever swung a hammer. We can do it, Trout," Tony assured him. Jimmy stood to the side and listened. "You get the men to work helping the crews here for now and give me Sam. Jimmy and I are going to ride ahead just a little bit and see where the survey goes. Sam can go with us. We may need him."

On horseback, the three rode rapidly westward, following a line of survey stakes. A few miles down the survey line, the ground was level and low, but dry. The surveyors had gently curved the route to thread its way through the lakes that seemed to occupy a third of the countryside. Tony dropped from his horse and Sam slipped off behind him.

Jimmy sat astride his horse and scratched his head. "Well, Tony, what you got up your sleeve that Mr. Plant's railroad men haven't already thought of?" he asked.

"Sam," said Tony, ignoring the question, "If you had to build a line, really fast, over this country, what could you do different?"

Sam stood and pondered a long moment, looking ahead at the distant country and back at what they had crossed. "First start buildin' some bridges across these mires and sloughs..." He paused for a long moment, glancing forward and back at the lengthy line of stakes that marked the intended route. "I guess," he said at last, "that a man could skimp some on the cross ties, send a crew ahead an' rough-cut some from trees, just to make it go faster and then jack in the replacements from the sawmill. That way you could have the grade laid out afore the train can haul in all those fancy ties. Just load 'em up with rails. You still got to put down those down the same, but it would save lots'a time."

"Would a track like that hold up a train, Sam?" Tony asked doubtfully.

"Not for a long time, but we had to do that once back in Waldo," Sam replied

Tony's eyes lit up as he pondered this solution. "You know, Mr. Plant showed me the terms of that contract and it didn't say anything about how long the track had to last!" Suddenly, he leapt upon his horse. "Jimmy, you carry Sam back. I've gotta' ride fast. Sam, get a crew, you pick 'em. Get what axes you need from the stores at the clay cut, tell 'em I said to do it. Start cutting those temporary ties you talked about. I'll tell Trout. And hurry! We've got a railroad to build."

By the next morning Tony was back in Sanford, and after explaining the solution to Plant, the idea was approved. By the time he got back to Polk County, Sam's team had already made visible progress and there were thick but rough ties of pine lying along the route the rails would follow, as teams of gandydancers and mules hauled new ties forward from the end of the freshly-laid tracks. A train full of shiny new rails idled at the chocks as it was unloaded. They would beat their deadline after all.

Plant made plans to ride over the new temporary rails to Hillsborough County, but as soon as the inaugural train had passed, crews would be hard at work reinforcing the line with proper timbers and solid ties to support the heavier use ahead. Henry Plant would keep his contract and Tampa would have its railroad.

As the new line arrived, towns sprang up and prospered. Villages called Campbells, Lake Locke, Emmaton and Davenport sprung up south of Kissimmee. Farther west on the arcing line, Auburndale, Wahneta Junction, Fitzhughes and the British settlement of Acton also got their depots. On January 23, 1884, the rails reached the new station at Lakeland. In Hillsborough County, the rails passed through a town known as Cork, rising on the former site of a Seminole village called Itchepucksassa. Within a year the citizens would rename their growing town "Plant City" in honor of the man who turned it into a boom-town.

Later that month the line reached Tampa and the port town became an overnight success. Tony, Jimmy, Sam and Trout, along with the rest of their crew, watched the celebration, part of a crowd that included every soul in the town.

"Here." Tony said that evening, slipping an envelope into Sam's hand. "Take this with my thanks. Quit railroading and go find that farm where you can have your family together. That's the most important thing in life."

"Thank you, Rilly," Sam answered with a smile. "You're a good man, Sir. I will take your advice."

●

After having languished by the bay since 1834, Tampa's population surged from some 800 persons to two thousand. Within a year, two telegraph lines were laid to the town and in 1885, work began on a streetcar system, followed quickly by an electric company.

By the time a second railroad company reached the town from the north in 1890, along with the first telephone lines, the town had grown to more than 6,000 citizens and the Crews brothers had never missed a payment.

The Horn of Coral
April 1894

JACOB GREGICH WAS IN AN ORNERY MOOD, and that wasn't a good time to be around him. Jake, also known as "Gamble" to a few of his friends, had a leaky boat. To Jake, that was just not a tolerable situation. The sun blazing high over Key West was making it clear that the stuff in the bottom of his 30-foot cat boat wasn't rainwater. It was sloshing back in forth in the gentle swell that lapped against the side of the wharf.

"Well," he decided after a few minutes of contemplation, "nothing to do but go have a drink and think about it." Sponging, which occupation had been on his mind the last couple of days, would have to wait until the boat was fixed, which would further have to wait until Jake was good and ready.

Jake wasn't typical of the spongers of Key West, who prided themselves as sober, industrious, and God-fearing. Jake, for personal reasons, was none of the above, and as a result, wasn't used to carrying on with the usual crowd at the sponge docks. Jake wiped the sweat from his beard stubble with the back of a large, tanned hand and turned to glance up the street toward Mallory Square, where his favorite watering hole stood among the low wooden buildings that made up Florida's largest city, counting almost 18,000 citizens. Watering holes, despite the devout nature of most of the spongers, were in no short supply, but Gamble Gregich had his favorite. In this shady place the bartender and most of the regulars spoke English. With its population of Cuban cigar workers, Bahamian fishermen, wreckers, and Caribbean islanders, salted liberally with sailors and immigrants from around the world, only about one in five of the folks around Key West spoke the "national language."

"A slug o' rum," Jake told the bartender as he slid his broad, muscular bulk onto one of the several empty wooden chairs. Overhead, an electric fan turned lazily. It was one of the best benefits that the construction of the new electric power plant had brought, in Jake's opinion. The alternating current was controversial, and some folks said it would be the source of fires that would destroy the town, but Jake figured it had already been used in New York for three years and that city was still standing.

Pushing the short glass of rum over the bar toward Jake, the bartender cautiously opened his familiar topic. "Seems the sponge fleet is cleaning up these days, huh?"

"I reckon so," Jake mumbled. "Like to have a piece of that myself."

"Well, weather's been good for two weeks, ain't you going back out?'

"Cain't right now. The *Jackie M* 'as sprung a leak and I'll have to haul her out. Need a couple of hands to do it right and ever-body's out sponging," Jake replied.

"You need a hand, Mister?" came a voice from down the bar. "Not meaning to listen in, but if you need a hand, I can do it and I need some work."

Jake turned slowly toward the sound and took a good look at the skinny stranger who sat alone with a glass of beer and a stack of empty peanut shells.

"Who are you?" came his gruff reply.

"I just got into town," came the drawled reply. "Folks call me "Whistle" sometimes, 'cause I can do that, but my real name is Hannibal Johnston."

"With that handle, I can see why folks prefer Whistle," Jake said. "You know anything about boats?"

"Worked on 'em most of my life. I just got down here from Baltimore. I used to go scalloping and crabbing and fishing up there, but this winter

I decided I needed a change of scenery. I can fix a boat, too, s'long as the timbers are solid. I can't work on any rotten wood."

"The *Jackie M* ain't rotten, I just run up on the flats a few days ago and must'a kinked a hole somewhere," Jake replied. He took another sip of his rum while he eyed the younger man steadily.

"Tell you what, Whistle," Jake said at length. "You meet me right here tomorrow at sunup and we'll see what you can do with a boat. If you're any good, I'll pay you. If not, don't waste your time or mine."

Key West's sponge industry was a thriving concern and perhaps the most successful line of work in the state, bringing in rich revenue. The sponge docks featured a row of competing warehouses, and as the sponges came in from the fleet they were placed in piles while a sort of silent auction took place. Bids were written on slips of paper and placed on the piles by the bidders.

Once sold and taken inside the warehouses, the sponges were cleaned, bleached. and trimmed by crews of workers before being bundled into bales and shipped to markets around the world.

So it was that the next morning the unlikely duo of Jake and Whistle ambled down the gritty street to the sloop *Jackie M*, a typical cat boat, her single mast set near the bow, ready to hoist a gaff-rigged mainsail. Before noon they had walked her close to the beach and by means of her lines and mast, turned her so that she lay on her side in an ebbing tide. There they could wade in the shallow water around her bottom tightening and caulking every small seam that looked questionable, which was most of them, in Whistle's opinion. His professional work impressed Jake, although he was loath to say so, because he knew that any praise he gave him would drive his price higher.

"Alright, then, Whistle, she's looking good as new and I don't see any sign of a leak," Jake said the next morning as they inspected the results of their efforts. "What say I teach you a little bit about sponging."

"Yes, sir, I'm ready when you are."

"We'll leave tomorrow. Spend the rest of the day getting yourself in order, we're likely to be gone a few weeks, maybe longer. I'll see you here at daybreak."

•

A week later found the *Jackie M* and her crew of two working the shallow flats and reefs near Anclote Key, 200 miles away and north of Tampa Bay. Whistle had been a quick study and had learned how to discern the difference between the valuable grass sponges, the fine sheep's wool sponges and the worthless loggerhead sponges while peering into the clear water using a "waterglass." This curious instrument was nothing more than a bucket with a glass bottom, allowing spongers to scan the sea floor in search of their prey.

Once Whistle had spotted a good sponge, Jake went after it using a sponge hook, in his case a pole of almost 30 feet in length, with an iron hook which he used to pry the sponge from the bottom and haul it into the boat. There the gelatinous mass would sit and slowly dry, emitting a very foul odor by the second day as the living tissues of the animal decayed.

Whistle was amazed at the variety of life he observed through his waterglass, a revealed panorama of sea fans, anemones, stripped and spotted fish of every shape, oddly-branching corals, sea feathers and sea cucumbers, all in a brilliant array of colors. His exclamations at the beauty quickly decreased at the grunting responses of his companion. "You seen 'em once, you seen 'em all," Jake told him.

Fine weather persisted for most of their trip, only a few cloudy and rainy days making their work more difficult. Once or twice during their wanderings they encountered other spongers and compared their successes. "Just the two o' you, working alone, and that tiny boat?" one asked them from the side of a well-equipped 44-footer with a crew of eight men.

"Yeah. We're all we need," came Jake's reply and Whistle began to understand that he had been taken for a bit of a ride, in more ways than one.

"Well, good luck, you'll need that too!" came the reply.

It was the spongers' credo that they wouldn't set sail for home until the boat was full, a process that required plenty of sponges. Each evening the *Jackie M* would make for the shore, where they had constructed their corral, or "crawl," as the spongers pronounced it. There they would dump their dying load in the shallow water and allow the restless sea to begin the long process of rinsing them.

They lived mostly on a diet of beans, rice, and whatever fish they managed to catch on a baited hook they trailed behind them as they worked. Each evening Jake would celebrate the day's haul with several "snorts" poured from his generous supply of rum. Whistle imbibed more modestly and marveled at the older man's constitution.

"So if'n you're from Baltimore, how's come you talk like a Southerner?" Jake asked him one evening as they relaxed on the beach, watching their boat bobbing gently in the small waves.

"I'm not really from there. I was born on a farm up in north Florida. My daddy fought for the Confederacy in the war," Whistle replied. "I just couldn't imagine living on a farm my whole life, so I ran away when I was 'bout 14 and ended up working on boats up there in Baltimore."

"Well, I'm glad that worked out for you," Jake replied. "You don't miss your family?"

"I miss my momma a lot," he answered wistfully. "My daddy was a hard man, so I don't miss him too much. He lost his arm in the fighting and he never really got over all that he saw."

Jake gave a characteristic grunt in reply and dropped the subject.

After each week of sponging, they returned to their crawl and spent a full day pulling out the 300 or so good sponges they had found, beating them with bats until they had removed most of the pulpy flesh. Then they strung the remaining fibrous material on thin lines and hung them up to dry. This process was repeated, and the resulting dried sponges squeezed into the tiny hold or piled onto the deck until at last the boat was, in Jake terms, "stuffed to the gills," and couldn't contain another sponge.

"Well, time to head for home," Jake said when the last of the cargo had been crushed aboard. "Still several hours o' daylight and we can beat offshore during the night."

Whistle, much less ebullient than he had been at the beginning of the voyage, nodded his agreement. "Let's go," he said.

December 1894

"I don't know, Tony. I don't think this is gonna' end up too good," Jimmy observed, rubbing his frozen fingers vigorously, trying to get the blood flowing. "I just don't think these trees can take this kind of cold." He had just used his knife to slice open an orange, stirring the slushy interior casually.

It was only three days after Christmas, but the cold that had settled in on Florida was only slowly loosening its grip. At least riding a horse was warmer than sleeping on the ground, Jimmy thought to himself, as he repositioned himself on his familiar saddle.

Tony looked down the long row of young orange trees that Jimmy had indicated, his breath forming a dense cloud in the morning chill. Already he could see that some of the tender leaves that crowned the four-foot-tall trees were wilted and blackening after two frosty mornings. He just shook his head, offering no response. After four years of effort, their newest investment was at serious risk. Who knew, he thought, that it would get this cold in Florida? According to the newspaper the previous afternoon, temperatures had been measured as cold as the upper teens around the farming country east of Tampa.

Planting warm weather crops that could flourish in Florida's mild winter climate had seemed an obvious choice for the thousand-acre tracts they owned across the middle of the state. Although most had risen only slightly in value, those closest to rail stations had gained great worth. Putting them to work, they knew, would only increase their value, and hopefully turn a handsome profit in the bargain. Their lands in Hillsborough and Polk Counties had seemed to offer the best opportunities.

Much of the land was already being used for turpentine production. They passed hundreds of tall Long-leaf pines marked with "cat-faces," large diagonal gashes that seeped thick resin all summer. Caught by narrow strips of metal driven into the tree, in warm weather the sap slowly oozed into waiting terra-cotta pots hung on nails. In the chill the sap was as hard as a macadam road. Still, they could see thousands of stumps where the trees had been cut after succumbing to the bleeding. The long, straight "heart pine" boards milled from the center of the trees was as hard as stone and impervious to insects. Between the turpentine stills and the sawmills, the once-vast forests of stately pines were quickly being reduced.

The Crews boys' new orange grove was only one of a hundred that had been planted around the state during the previous few years. The railroads were hungry for new winter-time crops to transport to the booming northern markets. Oranges, grapefruit, tangerines, pineapples, and bananas were sprouting from plantations across the state. None of the optimistic farmers, though, had expected the arctic blasts which had invaded. Citrus groves had been planted as far north as Jacksonville, where the telegraph operator had reported that the temperature had fallen to only fourteen degrees.

Riding eastward during the next two days as the weather slowly warmed, Tony and Jimmy could only observe the devastation done by the cold. There was nothing to be done to save the fruit, which had just been "coloring up" toward its attractive and marketable state, but now was dropping from the trees to form an autumn-like litter on the ground. The real and growing worry they both shared was that the trees themselves were damaged, a fear that increased with each passing day as they saw the blackened leaves dropping from groves of citrus along their way. In places they could see that the very trunks of the trees, even in groves older than theirs, had split open to reveal the white heart of the tree, a sure sign of death.

Four days riding took them past Lakeland and deep into Polk County, where they turned south along the Ridge, a line of low hills nesting numerous lakes in the valleys between. The deep sandy soil, well drained, was ideal for growing citrus and here they had used one of their incidental tracts to plant a small grove of grapefruit at the town of Keystone, near the former site of Fort Clinch. As they rode over the heights of Windy Hill toward the settlement, they overlooked the broad expanse of Crooked Lake, overflowing into a broad sheet-flow marsh that bled its waters westward toward the Peace River.

"That's a pretty sight," Jimmy observed as the sun sparkled on the surface of the lake almost two hundred feet below.

"Yeah, it is." Tony nodded, "and when they ever get a railroad down this ridge, you can bet this land'll be worth something more."

Another hour's ride brought the two into the community of Keystone, where, to their surprise, the condition of their grove was much better than expected.

"Yeah, seems we got a warm drift off the lakes during the early morning hours and that seemed to keep the temperatures up here," one of the local burghers told them. "Some of the growers have concluded that we are frost-proof. We're glad to know that we got a special place here!"

None of the small group gathered at the local inn that evening for grub and gossip could know that the great freeze of 1894 would be only the first of a series that would end all thoughts of growing citrus in northern Florida and drive the banana and pineapple growers completely out of business.

February 1894

Julia DeForrest Sturtevant Tuttle surveyed her guests from the head of her table before calling her informal gathering together with a word. "Gentlemen," she began, "We have tried for several years to convince Mr. Henry Flagler to extend his railroad to Biscayne Bay, without results. Now, I believe success may be within our grasp."

Murmurs of question passed over the small group of landowners, but they knew that, if Julia said so, something must be up. Julia Tuttle was the undisputed leader of the tiny village of Fort Dallas. Her home, which had risen from the ruins of the former Seminole War fort, perched where the Miami River found its way to the mosquito-infested shores of Bay Biscayne. The bay was a beautiful but isolated backwater, virtually unreachable by land. Julia had called it home since 1891, when she arrived with her son and daughter and two Jersey cows. Although it could claim no more than two dozen settlers, it was one of the largest villages on Bay Biscayne, second only to Cocoanut Grove, another three miles to the south.

Bay Biscayne was a popular winter retreat for a handful of wealthy yachtsmen who attended the Biscayne Bay Yacht Club there and providing anchorage at their basin on the site of the old lighthouse on the southern end of Key Biscayne. Those blessed souls whiled away their time fishing for pompano and kingfish in the waters of the bay or socializing in the presentable inn which had been erected in Cocoanut Grove. That, to Julia Tuttle, was a world away. Her sights were set on the world of business and enterprise, and she was determined to bring that world to life in her village of Miami.

The Miami River was the water outlet of the eastern Everglades, passing through the scant miles of sandy dunes which held back the flowing pressure of that vast marsh. The south side of the river mouth just across from Julia's restored fortress was the home of Mary and William Brickell and there they maintained a small store. Seminoles still residing in the watery interior often made their way down the cascading rapids to trade at Brickell's Landing. Brickell and Tuttle had conspired to plat a town site spanning both sides of the river, with 640 acres on each side. She had met with Flagler a year before but could not convince him to extend his line south from Palm Beach, despite an offer of half the land held by both her and the Brickells, a square mile on the bay and river.

Here by her endless promoting of the beauty of the area she had lured others to stake their futures to the promise held by Biscayne Bay and she had a deep wellspring of enthusiasm. Her only real asset was the land she had claimed and unless the area grew, it would remain virtually worthless. The town was her dream, a personal quest to build a community where others saw none. Julia Tuttle was nothing if not determined.

It was a chilly February morning when she had summoned her conclave.

"As all of you know, two big freezes in two months have wiped out most of the citrus," she told the group. "Nearly every tree in the state is frozen, from Palm Beach and Okeechobee, all the way to Jacksonville. Mr. Flagler's railroad is dependent on citrus shipping. These freezes are going to cost him a great deal of money," she said.

"How's that going to help us?" one man asked. "If he needs money, why is he going to spend more of it?"

"He's loaning money to farmers all over the state to help them replant," the confident Mrs. Tuttle replied, with a steady gaze at the questioner. "His agent, James Ingraham, will be here tomorrow. Mr. Flagler's sent him to check the freeze damage around here. I want each of you to have some of your fresh vegetables and produce ready at Brickell's store when he arrives. I've got a special treat in mind."

Two days later, following his brief visit to Miami, Mr. Ingraham returned to booming Palm Beach to report to Mr. Flagler on the conditions he had found.

"It seems to be in good shape, no sign of freeze damage down there, and I must report that the pineapples were excellent. By the way, Mr. Flagler," Ingraham said as he concluded his report to the railroad magnate, "Julia Tuttle sent you this box. It's a gift of some sort."

"Mrs. Tuttle been trying to convince me for years to run my line to Biscayne Bay," Flagler observed of his persistent pursuer. "That place will never be more than a fishing village, but I told her I might bring the railroad there someday if she could give me one good reason to do so."

With that, Henry Flagler opened the small box Julia had sent him, looked at the contents and smiled. "I think she's beaten me at my own game," he said with a grin, tipping the box to show his associates. There, on a bed of damp cotton, was a fragrant branch of delicate orange blossoms, undamaged by the frosts which had struck the northern parts of the state.

The following April 15, sixty-six miles of new track laid south of Palm Beach carried the first steam locomotive into the future city of Miami on the shore of Biscayne Bay and Florida's long frontier was pushed farther south.

December 1896

The sunny morning that the *Three Friends* had left behind on Key Largo had long since faded to inky darkness and that was just what the group of plotters aboard the chugging tugboat wanted. The young moon had set hours after the sun and only the light of the stars guided them toward their intended destination. Ahead a long coastline was barely perceptible, but they were aware that it was full of danger. For most of the sixteen men crowding the deck of the steam tug, it was hoped to be a day of destiny. Below their decks and hidden under canvas at their feet lay cases of ammunition and boxes of repeating rifles, enough to supply a hundred men. Boxes of gunpowder and nitroglycerin lay barely concealed. Their cargo and the fourteen who would go ashore were there for only one nefarious purpose: the destruction of Spanish property and the support of the Cuban rebels in their fight for independence.

Running arms, known in the trade as "filibustering," was not work for the faint of heart, but the captain of the *Three Friends* was up to the task. Napoleon Bonaparte Broward was no stranger to fighting and violence and wore his politics on his sleeve. He was a born risk-taker. As the three-term sheriff of Jacksonville's Duval County he had proven himself a man of passion, a rough-and tumble sort who never hesitated to take on big challenges. Using his boat as a "filibuster" to supply the rebels of Cuba was just the sort of risky activity that stoked his imagination.

Broward had spent much of his youth on boats, after his family lost their farm in the aftermath of the Civil War. He had lost his parents, moved to Jacksonville, and worked the river boats, becoming an experienced hand. He traveled up the east coast of the United States, spent two years in New England and returned to Jacksonville to pilot boats across the treacherous sand bars at the mouth of St. John's River. It was a lucrative occupation and Broward grew to love the nicer things in life. The death of his wife in childbirth and the loss of his infant son, gave him a tough perspective on life. Two years later he remarried but stuck to his life on the water.

He had been picked by party bosses in 1888 to serve as sheriff of Duval, Florida's most populous county, after his predecessor was ousted after a major jailbreak. Broward thrived in the bare-knuckles world of politics. He had built a machine that swept friends to influential positions, but in 1894 a split in the party meant the end of his faction's success and he was back to the water.

Broward and his partners had built the *Three Friends* themselves after he had lost his position as sheriff and were barely half-way done when the steady drumbeat of anti-Spanish propaganda, led by Jose Marti and his allies, turned into armed insurrection in Cuba. The opportunity to run guns across the water was lucrative, comfortable, and in Broward's mind, politically acceptable.

As the shore drew closer in the darkness, the band of Cuban rebels on the tugboat watched for a signal from the land and every available eye was scanning for signs of danger in the form of Spanish patrol boats. At length, a flickering light flashed from the dark shoreline, and they made their way toward their expected rendezvous.

Drawing close to shore near a point at first light, they dropped anchor using a rope hawser, in case they needed to "cut and run," and hauled a look-out aloft in a chair to keep an eye out for patrol boats. Anxiously they watched as a longboat began pulling from shore to receive the cargo.

"¡Dése prisa! Consigue estas armas cargadas, vamos!" came the word in Spanish and the operation was begun.

Twenty minutes later the first light of morning had barely spread across the sky when the unwelcome call came.

"We've got company, smoke about eight miles west, looks like it's heading this way. I can't be sure, but it looks like a cutter!"

"Let's go, let's go! Cut the anchor loose!" Broward shouted and the desperados scrambled, a half dozen jumping into the boat with the last few weapons and quickly the tug began to make way back to sea as the longboat pulled for cover on shore.

They were barely around the point and angling for sea when the cutter was seen to be pursuing. "Come on baby, you can do it!" Broward said, patting the side of the wheelhouse. "Keep stoking that fire, we've gotta keep running, we're not nearly out of Cuban waters yet. They can't chase us all the way to Florida, but if they catch us here, we're dead men!"

Steadily the Spanish cutter gained on the tug, but in the end the long lead proved enough and as the coast was disappearing behind the *Three Friends* the cutter broke off the pursuit. It had been a close call, but there was always another night and another chance to run guns from Florida. Napoleon Bonaparte Broward would be back.

The Broken Eggshell
March 1897

A BONY FINGER POINTED toward the green horizon. "See that flock over there, circling?" a voice said quietly.

"Sure, I can see 'em," came the reply. "Is that where we need to go?"

"That's where we'll find the rookery."

The two figures in the small jack boat sailed into the narrow slough from the broad, shallow waters of Florida Bay. The southern tip of Florida was cooled by an early spring breeze and the sun sparkled on waters that offered a colorful mosaic to the eye with their varying depths and bottom covers. It was a day in paradise, but the pair had other things in mind, too busy to notice the beauty around them.

A short way up the slough a small cove, a hundred yards of open water, was ringed with dense banks of mangrove trees. The leathery leaves and multiple trunks of the thickets were white with the droppings of thousands of birds and the very air was a cacophony of their calls. Broad nests of sticks and leaves perched on every available space, where eggs were warmed by the late-morning sun. Other nests were filled with squawking young chicks of the snowy egrets that shuttled back and forth with meals of fish, snakes, and frogs to feed their growing broods. It was a spectacle unknown in Europe, where the fashion of wearing an "aigret," or hat plume, had started.

Anchoring their small sailboat, the two men slipped the hawser on their rowboat and entered the bayou quietly. Once within the small cove, the two picked up their shotguns and took aim. "Let's do it!" one said, and they began shooting at the adult birds, often killing two or three with a single blast. The flocks rose in panic, but the shot found them in the air as well and birds fell like stones, fluttering and struggling in the black waters of the cove. Reloading as fast as they could, they fired until targets were scarce. Two minutes of shooting had killed more than 150 birds.

Leaving their guns aside, the two plume hunters began gathering and clubbing the wounded birds, rinsing the blood from their feathers before dropping them into the bottom of the boat. Using a pole, they knocked those they could reach from the depths of the mangroves. The hungry young birds squawked in their nests, but the men ignored them, quickly setting themselves to work plucking the long breeding plumes from their prey, tossing the bodies to the waiting alligators. Two hour's work produced a respectable pile of snow-white plumes up to two feet in length.

Above in the nests, some hundreds of abandoned chicks and eggs would soon perish, but the plume hunters had their haul: four pounds of plumes, worth their weight in gold as ornaments for women's hats.

Originally only a small accent of stone and feather placed upon a hat, the style had become a competition for the most exotic feminine bonnets created from long plumes, entire wings, and even whole desiccated birds. From the 1880's the fashion had expanded, so that by 1895, there were no more rookeries remaining on the Gulf coast north of Tampa Bay and none within easy reach of any population center in the state. Plume hunters, eager to cash in on the "gold rush" fever, were pursuing the last of the great birds deep into their hidden domains in the Everglades. Great and snowy egrets, little blue, green and great blue herons, Roseate spoonbills, the few flamingos and all manner of wading birds were slaughtered and were being pushed to the brink of extinction.

March 1898

"Daddy! Daddy! Can I go? Please?"

Tony Crews turned around to see his little, brown-skinned beauty chasing him up the street, her long dark hair flying from side to side as she ran. With a smile he paused, then ran back to meet her, swinging her slight form high into the air, before wrapping her in his arms.

"Where are your shoes, young lady? Do you think I can take a ragamuffin to town to do business? What would people think?" he teased. "Now let's go get you dressed properly and then we'll ask your mother if you can come along with me."

Together they walked, hand-in-hand, back toward the big house facing the bay shore. An improbable couple, she had to stretch to reach his hand, her four years leaving her a bit short of altitude. Her father was understanding, though and by the time they reached the front walk, he had again swept her up and carried her through the gate and up the broad stairs to the huge porch. With a playful swat on the bottom, he sent her scrambling inside, while he waited on the porch, leaning against one of the row of gleaming white pillars.

" Amanda wants to come with me, sweetheart. Is that all. right with you?" he called, through the open window.

"Sure, Tony. Just make sure she doesn't get into trouble. And make her wear some shoes, for heaven sakes! That child just won't keep a pair on her feet!" came the response from inside.

"Oh, and one more thing..." The door swung open, and Marie Crews stepped through it and planted her arms around his neck. "Take this along, too!" she said, giving him a kiss.

Tony returned the kiss with a smile, happy to be alive. More than loving Marie, he admired her. Since they had first met, he had never stopped being impressed by her. She was a striking woman, tall, lean and dark-skinned, with a high forehead and prominent cheekbones and an independent spirit to match her looks. She told him it was because she was part wild Indian, but he doubted the story. More likely Spanish, he thought.

"By the way, I told Jack that he could go sailing with Tom," Tony said as Marie disappeared back into the house. "They said they were going fishing, but I think he really just wants to get on the water."

"Tony, did you ask him if he had finished his homework? He's got to keep up his studies if he's serious about being an architect."

"No, I didn't. I guess I figured he wouldn't have asked if he wasn't done. I'll talk to him about it this evening."

As he waited on the porch in the sunshine, he reflected on his good fortune. He had been in Tampa fourteen years and had made a great success of himself, as had his uncle Jimmy. Although they no longer thought of themselves as "the Crews Boys," they were still family, and everyone knew it. Jimmy's house was just up the street a few blocks, far enough away to be respectable, but close enough to be handy. Tony and Jimmy had both married within a year of their success, in the heady days of boom-time Tampa. The city's population had blossomed to twenty-five thousand and the boom just kept on, with only brief pauses when the country's economy went sour.

Florida had grown apace of the city. To the east, Hamilton Disston's dredges had indeed opened the Kissimmee River, as well as Lake Okeechobee, to steamboat service. Although he had died young, Disston's estate now controlled millions of acres of land throughout the state, including the southern part of the Hillsborough peninsula on the west side of Tampa Bay, where the fledgling town of St. Petersburg had been founded. Steamboats had navigated the waterways, opening the flow of commerce, only to be made obsolescent by the rapid expansion of the railroads, which girded the state like a fine web.

Florida oranges, grapefruit, and tangerines, as well as tons of fresh winter vegetables, rolled to northern markets by rail. New citrus groves were being planted throughout the peninsula, despite the damage done by severe freezes, especially in the north.

Florida had weathered the economic panic of 1893 and since had experienced a boom of prosperity of magnificent proportions. Growth and tourism were paying off in buckets. Entrepreneurs like Henry Plant and Henry M. Flagler were pushing the railroads into the farthest corners of the state. In each new significant town, a large public hotel provided the draw for tourists, who poured south for the warm winter weather. Flagler had been so successful with his chain of hotels at places like St. Augustine, Ormond, and Palm Beach, that he now owned more than 40,000 rooms.

In addition to Henry Plant's first railroad, others had reached the area, including the Florida Southern Railroad, which had built a line from Lakeland down the Peace River all the way to Punta Gorda, linking the villages of Bartow, Fort Meade, and Zolfo Springs, along with a string of smaller settlements. The trains also carried the valuable cargo of phosphate from the Peace River area, which some called the Bone Valley, to the Port of Tampa, where it was loaded onto ships to be used as fertilizer in the Midwest and around the world. Florida was a place of prosperity.

Tony still owned most of his land, having taken some early profits on a few pieces and keeping the rest to lease, or develop. He had built a cigar factory for a Cuban company on one piece, a business block on another and a few warehouses on a third. Most was still in cattle, some citrus, even there remained some good lumber still to be cut. The income was steady and that's what gave him his great confidence.

Tony had been lucky enough to meet Marie Powell just after she arrived in Tampa. She had come on one of the first trains to arrive, with her father, a widower. She was just seventeen. They had moved to Tampa from a north Florida town called Starke to follow the boom in search of a better life. Although they had arrived virtually destitute, Tony wasn't deterred by the family's poverty. After all, this was America and he had just come from poverty himself. Besides, one look at Marie, with her slim, feminine figure, nearly coal-black, waist-length hair and her gorgeous smile and he was completely taken.

Their courtship lasted six months and he could hardly wait to be married. She had proven a great match for his spirit, with an unpredictability all her own, enough to keep him on his guard, he thought with a smile. Their son Jack was now a strapping boy of twelve and now little Amanda was four. She, especially, kept him young.

Now, with his daughter's hand in his, they walked a short distance to the streetcar along the bay shore, gleaming rails set in a broad street of red bricks lined with new houses. Tony surveyed the scene with a sense of pride, for he had been involved in the campaign for the bond issue that had provided for the street paving. It had already paid off for the town.

It was a sunny Saturday morning in March and the sun sparkled on the blue-green waters of the bay as they rode the streetcar into town. "Daddy, what's that boat?" Amanda asked pointing out at a large ship in the distance.

"That a livestock ship, honey. It carries the cows we sell to Cuba and other places. Those ships over there carry freight between here and New York and Philadelphia." Then, turning around, he pointed out a building ahead, ornate Moorish spires like minarets looming over the shops in the foreground. "See that big building over there?" he asked, and his daughter nodded. "That's Mr. Plant's hotel. That's where the businesspeople stay when they come to visit and where I go to meetings with the Board of Trade. And see those big buildings over there in the distance? Those are cigar factories. Lots of men work in there." Amanda stared at the massive brick boxes with the high windows, casting shadows across streets lined with a web-work of electric, telephone and telegraph wires. The city was everywhere filled with amazement for the young girl and her eyes took in every detail.

Minutes later, they stepped from the streetcar in front of the Tampa Bay Hotel, built to impress visitors with the great expectations of Tampa's future. Inside the grand lobby, Amanda marveled at the vast interior, much as her father had at the opera house in Philadelphia a generation before. Hundreds of craftsmen from Europe and America had labored over the intricate stone, plaster and woodwork, delicate arches, and decorative rococo trim.

Built of red brick, the four-story Tampa Bay Hotel was modeled after the Alhambra, the great structure built by the Moors in Granada, Spain, during their reign over that land. Its five hundred rooms covered an area two blocks long. It was a magnet attracting the upper crust of American social life, as well as a steady stream of visiting European royalty. Surrounded by lavish tropical gardens filled with peacocks and flowers, the hotel featured a dining hall that seated six hundred fifty persons. The entire building was wired for electricity and electric lights and featured a pair of elevators, the first in Florida, for passengers and freight.

The foyer of the hotel led to a two-story rotunda, lavishly furnished. Thirty thousand yards of red carpeting, furnished with a blue lion motif, had been purchased at Christie's in London and installed on the public areas. Furnishings came from the collections of European royalty, including Queen Elizabeth, Queen Victoria and Mary, Queen of Scots, Napoleon Bonaparte, Marie Antoinette, Louis XIV, Louis Phillippe and Queen Isabella and King Ferdinand of Spain. Henry Plant had sought to build one of the most palatial hotels in the world and he had succeeded.

In keeping with the strict social rules of the hotel, Amanda was brought to the nursery, while her father entered the reading room, set with plush wing-back chairs, and reserved for men only.

"'Morning, Will," her father said to a gentleman seated before a cup of coffee, a folded local paper on his lap.

"Have you read the *Tribune* this morning, Tony?" Will asked when they had finished working over a set of contracts. "It looks more and more like we might end up in a war with Spain over the *Maine* explosion. I just can't believe they would blow up our battleship right in Havana harbor. It makes no sense. I suspect Jose Marti's got something more to do with it. Anyway, the New York papers are backing him, agitating for a fight and President McKinley is said to be about to give up on peace talks."

Florida had been caught up in the politics of the bloody Cuban revolution for years, but now the *New York World,* owned by Joseph Pulitzer and William Randolph Hearst's *New York Journal* led the nation into a war mood, whipping sentiment with sensationalized stories of atrocities in Cuba under the Spanish. The two papers fed the revolutionary plans of Marti and other ex-patriot Cuban revolutionary leaders. Tampa's fifteen-hundred expatriate Cubans gave them an enthusiastic welcome with each new visit. Tony's cigar factories had paid handsome rents while Cuban cigar workers within contributed ten percent of their wages to the revolution. Even that marginal involvement made Tony uncomfortable.

"The local Cubans I talk to are all for it, but they've wanted to get us involved in their fight for independence for years, anyway. I don't like the looks of things," Will concluded.

"I think the *Tribune* had it right," Tony responded, shifting in his chair, "when they said that the only ones who could profit from the explosion were the Cuban rebels. I don't think Spain would do something so stupid as blow up our battleship in Havana harbor and provoke us into a fight they don't want and can't win. Jose Marti may think that those papers want

Cuban independence, but they don't. What those men want is Cuba controlled by us as a new territory, maybe another state. Their chant about "Manifest Destiny" gave us a war with Mexico, and they got Texas and California. They're the same sort who wanted a war with England over the northwest Canadian territory. Spain's got their colonies, and those fellows want 'em. I just don't think it's worth the fight, but some of the New York papers say it's part of our "manifest destiny." It seems that we've just now got this state straightened out and growing. We got over that panic in '93 all right, but war with Cuba could set everything back twenty years. That's our best market for cattle."

"I think you're right, Tony, but there's not a whole lot we can do about it except get ready. The big question is, if war comes, what's it going to mean here and what happens if Cuba becomes a part of the United States? You're well connected with politics around here. What I want to know is, what should I be doing?"

"I wish I knew, Will. I just wish I knew."

•

"I'm worried, sweetheart," Tony said to Marie that night after the children were safe in bed. "I think this will turn into a real war with Spain over Cuba any time now." The couple sat together in an upholstered love seat she had ordered from a Sears & Roebuck catalog and a brass electric lamp casting a pool of light at their feet. The room was warmly decorated, with thick drapes framing tall windows. The thought of war seemed especially distant to her in the comfort of the setting.

"Darling, why do you worry? Do you think the Spanish would attack us here?"

"It's not that, really," Tony responded, giving her hand a squeeze and turning to gaze at her. "I just don't believe in war. My father died in a war, and I want a better future for my children. Jack's twelve already. I don't want to see him conscripted to go and fight because some publisher was trying to boost his circulation."

Marie gazed out onto the street, where a long row of gas lights curved away into the darkness, marking the margin of Hillsborough Bay. Her thoughts, too, were on family.

"Tony, I received a letter today. It's from my younger brother in Ocala. He says he has learned that my grandfather is not well," Marie said. "I would like to go to see him."

"You've never spoken of your grandfather before," Tony said, surprised at the idea. "I didn't even know he was alive."

"I didn't tell you about him," Marie said, looking away from Tony again, staring at the distant lights. "I never knew what you would make of my family. I've always told you that I'm part Seminole, but you laughed about it." Marie turned back to Tony, looking him in the eyes, watching his reaction. He gazed back, a curious expression on his face.

"My grandfather is half-blood Miccosukee," she said after a long pause. "His father's name, and my mother's maiden name, was Booker, but his mother, my great-grandmother, was called Nighthawk. She was full-blood Miccosukee. Her daughter was called Katrina, but she died young, of yellow fever. My grandfather named his own daughter, my mother, Katrina in her memory. She died when I was eight. My grandfather is called Eastwind. John Eastwind Booker. He still lives on an island where he moved after the Civil War. It's in a lake, on the other side of the Ridge. He never leaves there. He says that it's sacred ground for our family."

Tony looked at Marie, reading the worry on her face, understanding the fear she had carried inside for so long and the longing which made her open up to him now.

"Marie, you know I love you and I don't care who your people are," Tony said. "We have two beautiful, healthy children, a good business, everything we could ask for. I wouldn't care if you told me your father was really Jesse James. I love you and nothing else matters."

Her arms found their way around him and she held him close, savoring the sense of relief mixed with love, which drew them closer.

"I want the children to see him, too, before it's too late," she told him. "I haven't seen him myself since I was a little girl, before my mother died. My father refused to take me to see him, but my mother always told me I should be proud of who I am."

"And so you should," Tony responded, holding her close. "But how can the children meet him. I thought you said he doesn't leave his island."

"He doesn't. But we could go there... Oh, Tony, the children could handle a break from school, it would be educational. Jack especially would love the adventure and deserves a chance to meet him before he's gone."

Tony's mind turned back to the time he had spent hunting cows in the pine flatwoods of the Kissimmee Valley beyond the Ridge. He would love to see it all again himself but didn't relish the thought of bringing his young family into such an unpredictable setting. For a long moment he said nothing, then Marie looked up at him, her dark eyes filled with a silent pleading.

"You're right," Tony said. "He does deserve to see his only great-grandfather and you deserve to see him, too. We'll go right after summer." Then, as an afterthought, he added, "war or no war."

War did indeed seem imminent, with the Congress pushing for a fight. In April, President McKinley bowed to overwhelming public opinion and requested a formal declaration of war. In Key West, fear of Spanish warships drove fishermen and spongers northward to safety, with the spongers establishing themselves at Tarpon Springs, close to their new shallow-water sponge beds.

Henry Plant went to Washington to make his case for Tampa as a war port, speaking with the cabinet and War Department officials. His efforts proved effective. On April 15, Adjutant General H. C. Corbin ordered a camp prepared in Tampa, to provide for the housing of five thousand soldiers. Soon after, trains loaded with troops and supplies began to stream into Tampa for later boarding on steamships of the Plant Line. Tony Crews' lands were among those available and he was soon moving cattle into stockyards to make room for tents.

Soon the trains began to arrive, and it was clear that the army would not be stopping with five thousand soldiers just to garrison the city. It was an invasion force that was assembling, and Tampa had been chosen as the point of embarkation. On April 22, as if in celebration of the date, twenty-two troop trains poured into Tampa.

Plant's investment in the construction of a port at the end of his spur line, incorporated as the Port of Tampa, meant he had sole control of most of the shipping capacity in the area. His single-track system to Tampa was continually crowded with trains and a premium was charged to accept carloads of supplies from other railroads for transport the last few miles from the switch yard onto Plant System tracks to the docks.

The United States Congress formally declared war on April 25 and quickly appropriated money for big shore batteries at Jacksonville, St. Augustine, Fernandina, and the new town of Miami, which the railroads had reached only scant years earlier. Within weeks, Tampa's population of twenty-five thousand was nearly overwhelmed by the arrival of over forty thousand troops, support personnel, reporters and other camp followers. Henry Plant's hotel, normally closed for the summer after April 10, was filled to capacity with military officers and war journalists. Soon the troops were being billeted not only in Tampa, but on available land in towns throughout the area.

As before, Tony found himself on the right side of the new boom Tampa was experiencing. He leased land to the government at good rates and still found himself making more money than ever. Other small business blocks he owned were flourishing as well and building continued. Labor was in short supply and Henry Plant ordered a special train from Ocala filled with workers for Tony and other Tampa businessmen. Tony soon had a number of them employed erecting new blocks of stores in the business district.

The huge new military camps posed serious sanitation problems and services were strained. Disputes soon broke out between the city and county government over the licensing of saloons and other entertainments. Fears and rumors of an outbreak of Yellow Fever soon had many residents hoping for a quick dispersion of the troops, yet it seemed soon as arriving troop were settled into new camps, new trains arrived with still more troops.

The problem wasn't unique to Tampa, but a few miles to the east in Lakeland the situation included a social twist: it was there on the shores of Lake Wire that the Army had encamped the 10th Cavalry Regiment. Made up entirely of black soldiers, led by a handful of white officers, the 10th was equipped with twelve hundred horses. The legendary "Buffalo Soldiers" had been appointed Provost Guard, responsible for maintaining discipline among the troops. Gentile southern sensibilities were shocked at the sight of mounted black soldiers arresting white soldiers on the streets for violations of military decorum.

The citizens of Tampa pitched in where they could help, organizing baseball games, picnics, and church services for the troops. Cigar factories, filled with enthusiastic Cuban workers, donated tens of thousands of cigars to the soldiers and the icehouse distributed barrels of cold water. Tony kept his crews working overtime, loading and unloading trains, warehouses, and ships, organizing and moving thousands of tons of critical supplies when all seemed to be disorganized chaos.

By June, order began to emerge out of the confusion, even as word spread that a huge invasion fleet was assembling. On June 7, Tony had fourteen teams of mules pulling wagons from his warehouses to the long docks, where eighteen troop transports were lined up, loading the long columns of riflemen, artillery, and cavalry.

Through the midst of the crowded docks strode an energetic colonel bearing a distinctive mustache and round eyeglasses, determined to get his company of cavalry decent accommodations on one of the newer ships. Tony watched with some amusement as the shouting of the military officer rose even above the din and confusion of such a large movement of humanity. Tony noted the eventual success of his efforts and thought to himself that such determination in the face of bureaucracy would be even more formidable in combat.

The hurry to board the ships was followed by days of waiting in close quarters in sweltering heat as rumors of Spanish cruisers lying in wait were explored and found baseless. Finally, shortly after midnight on the morning of June 14, 1898, an impressive flotilla of thirty-five military transports left the port of Tampa, bound to liberate Cuba from Spain. More than sixteen thousand troops were on board, and they were comforted by the presence of an escorting fleet including four tenders, a hospital ship and fourteen warships. It was by far the largest single movement of men and military equipment that Florida had ever seen.

More than twelve thousand troops remained in Tampa after the fleet had sailed and more were arriving daily. The nation's attention was focused on the reports and sketches of war correspondents accompanying the troops to their invasion points and the swift victory that followed.

In a matter of weeks, the Spanish forces in Cuba were routed and Spain, her fleet destroyed in far-away Manila Bay, sued for peace. Among those lionized as heroes in the American press were the men of Colonel Teddy Roosevelt's Rough Riders, immortalized by reports their dismounted charge up San Juan Hill. Tony recognized the mustachioed image of the man he had watched taking charge on the docks.

Accolades also fell upon the Buffalo Soldiers of the 10th Cavalry, whose troops earned five Medals of Honor. Spain's colonial empire was smashed, Cuba was liberated, and the dreams of America's expansionists were stoked to new heights, but Tony felt that he had done his part and planned to keep a promise to his wife. He was busy arranging to leave the last days of the 19th century behind to journey deeply into the past.

October 1898

It was the first crisp autumn morning and a perfect day for traveling. Cognizant of the summer heat, Tony had delayed their trip, sacrificing a few days of school for a trip that would be equally educational for his children.

Leaving his superintendent in charge of the affairs of his businesses, Tony brought the family to the Tampa station and together they boarded the eastbound train. Jack and Amanda peered curiously from the windows as they left the town behind and rolled through open fields, small towns and dense forests. Marie sat quietly with her thoughts and Tony, respectful of her need for privacy, turned to the most recent northern newspapers he obtained from the porter.

Three hours later, they stepped onto the platform at a village called Haines City. Tony looked down the track at the high banks of clay, so patiently removed by hand labor and teams of animals years earlier and felt a wave of nostalgia for his railroad days. He recalled that the local settlers had renamed the place from Clay Cut to Haines City, after the railroad agent, in a political effort to get a station. That idea had paid off, and the clay banks now hosted a tidy and growing community. Tony wished his Uncle Jimmy could have been there with him and wondered what had happened to Sam and Trout and the other men he had worked with. But then a persistent tug at his sleeve brought him out of his reveries and back to reality and he looked down to see the puzzled face of Amanda staring up at him.

"Are we gonna' see my grampa' now?" she asked. Tony smiled down at her.

"Yes ma'am, we sure are, just as soon as we can."

In Haines City, Tony purchased three of the finest saddle horses available and a pack horse to carry their bags and the gifts they had brought along. Jack had become adept at riding on the family lands and Amanda clung tightly to him as the two bounced along the trail together. Tony smiled at Marie, who continually glanced back from her lead position to monitor the progress of the two youngsters behind her.

The trip to the remote island campsite took a full day of riding, following a crude road which led south along the ridge before heading east on a slender trail into the upper Kissimmee Basin. Marie's brother had described it in detail in a letter and Marie's memory of her visits as a small child helped to locate the right lake in a land where the horizon, viewed from the ridge, was filled with sprawling blue pools. Marie pointed out the broad blue oval, with a long arm stretching northward and Tony felt a momentary wonder, as his own memories of days on the prairie were again jogged.

The changes that had come over most of the state weren't evident on the east side of the Ridge and Tony thought about how much the state had changed since his arrival almost thirty years before. Tampa had been a village and was now a city. The same was true of other towns around the state. Change had come from nature as well and Tony thought back to his cruise on Lake Alachua during his railroad days. Only a few years earlier, the entire lake had disappeared in a week, leaving the steamboat *Chakala* high and dry as the waters suddenly flowed into a sinkhole and were swallowed by the aquifer. It was reassuring to see a place that was still much the same.

Late in the afternoon, the unlikely foursome came to the trail's end, where it disappeared into the waters of a lake. All around them was a deep forest of cypress and maple, bay, and sweet gum. Marie boldly forced her horse into the dark water and the family followed. Two minutes of wading the animals brought them to shallower water and then Tony knew that he was twice blessed as he recognized the low hammock which suddenly appeared through the trees.

As soon as they were on dry ground, Marie dismounted and whistled a clear, trilled call. Instantly it was answered and moments later, an old man approached them on foot. Tony stared closely at the man while he conversed with Marie, speaking in a strange language. Tony listened to her respond in the same tongue, again surprised at what he didn't know about his own wife. At length she turned to Tony.

"This is Itchee Billy," she said. "He lives here. My grandfather is also here, but he is not well. We should take care not to disturb his rest," Marie said to the children, as Tony began to help them from their horse. Tony exchanged a quick glance with Marie and took the children by the hand.

They walked past a long, low, crescent shaped mound which occupied most of the hammock and Tony's memories of an evening long ago came flooding back. Before them was a simple thatched chickee, a dirt floor surrounded by elevated planks for sleeping and working. Palm fronds covered its roof and inside was an old man, sitting on a simple mattress, while a small fire smoldered nearby. He smiled when they approached and reached his hand toward Marie. She quickly took it and knelt next to him, giving him a warm hug. Tony stood near the entrance with the children, awaiting a sign to enter.

After a moment's pause and the exchange of a few words, Marie arose and beckoned her family into the room. "Grandfather," she said with a look of pride on her face, "I would like you to meet my family. This is my husband Tony and my children. They have been looking forward to meeting you."

Still unsure what to do, even after all the anticipation, Tony stepped forward and offered his hand to the man called Eastwind and gave a sort of an awkward bow. John Eastwind Booker broke into a wide smile.

"It's OK, son, I don't bite," he said. "Have a seat and let me get a look at the children."

"You speak English!" Tony said, forgetting to hide his surprise and Marie burst into laughter.

"Of course, I do," Eastwind replied. "I lived for many years on the outside. It is only by choice that I am here and speak in the Hitchiti tongue of my ancestors. Let me see my great-grandchildren," he said, and patted the seat at his side, beckoning the children to come to him. Jack was there immediately, staring wide-eyed at his first real Indian. Eastwind smiled at the boy and lay his hand upon his head. "You must be Jack. I have heard that you have learned to fish and swim and can sail a boat and ride a horse. The blood of our ancestors flows true in your veins."

As Jack sat in silent awe, Eastwind turned his gaze upon Amanda, who stood shyly behind her mother, unsure what to make of the wrinkled old man. The level rays of the dying sun shone on his face, and it seemed to her that he glowed with a strange, red color, like a man made of light, not ordinary at all, but magical. At length she gathered her courage and stepped slowly forward. Eastwind waited patiently, admiring her delicate features.

"Don't be afraid, Amanda" he said to her. "Come sit by me and I will tell you a story of a princess who lived here a long, long time ago." Turning to where Marie and Tony now stood hand in hand, watching the meeting of generations, he told them "Make yourselves comfortable. Billy will make you some supper and make you a bed for the night. I'll just sit with the children until then and we'll speak later."

With that, Eastwind turned his full attention to the two young people who sat with him and began to spin tales of times long ago and the deeds of their ancestors. The presence of his grandchildren seemed to invigorate the old man and his voice soared and swooped with the characters of his tales. Tony and Marie slipped quietly out of the chickee and went to find Billy, who was just finishing his work with their horses. In the fading light they stood near the ancient mound and gazed at the long stretch of golden water. Behind them a great horned owl began its rhythmic hooting. Marie looked up at Tony, standing in the last glow of evening and was very proud.

"Thank you for bringing us here. It means so much to me..."

"Marie, I would take you to the ends of the earth if it would help make you happy. This place is but a little way and I am learning as much about myself as I am about you and your family. I love you more than I can say..."

Late that evening, as the children lay dreaming, the four adults sat around the smoking fire, which was fed with herbs to repel the insects. In the distance they could hear the mournful howling of the coyotes. Between long silences, Marie and Eastwind spoke of family members and Eastwind told many tales of his parents and the Seminole wars of Osceola. Marie listened intently, determined to remember as many details as possible.

"When I was a young man," he told them, "My father decided that I should see more of the world than our little cabin and the forests and hills. He had taught me to speak and read English. From his books, I learned history and arithmetic. I was ready to see the world. He cut my hair and together we walked to Fort Brooke. We bought new clothes, and I went to a private school for two years. Eventually, I traveled to Jacksonville by ship and to New York."

"When I returned to Florida, I took a wife from among the Miccosukee people, who still live in the Everglades. We had a daughter, whom we named Katrina in honor of my sister who had died. My wife died when our daughter was two." Nighthawk paused for a few long moments as the memories flooded back.

"I brought my daughter to my parents, and they raised her as I could not. I joined the army. When the Civil War broke out, we were evacuated to Pensacola, but then I was sent back to south Florida to help the navy with the blockade. We sailed the coasts looking for smuggling ships around Estero and down to the Ten Thousand Islands. When my enlistment ran out, I decided I had seen enough of the white man's world to last me, and I came back here to stay. When my daughter was ready, my parents brought her to a school to learn the ways of the world. She married a white man. They were happy for a time and gave life to you, Marie, as you well know. You are her pride."

"My parents lived out their lives near here. They died happy, in their own time. I buried them with my own hands and scattered the soil of their resting place to the four corners of the land. Now, all of my people have gone, except for you and your children."

Marie struggled to contain her emotions as he spoke. She already knew some of the old man's history, but some was new to her. For Tony, the entire story was a revelation, and he was moved to hear it.

"Your mother was a beautiful woman, Marie," Eastwind continued "Katrina had the fire of all our ancestors in her. It is a shame she died so young."

"I was only eight years old..." Marie said, staring at the fire. "My father loved her, but he didn't really want anyone to know she was an Indian. I think he was ashamed."

There was a long silence before Eastwind responded. "You have much to be proud of, for our people's blood is a thing of strength. It took great courage to settle this land with only the simplest of tools. Those qualities will bless you and your children and generations to come."

"On this island," he continued, "is a mound of ceremony, where many generations of our people came. Others, too, were here before us. This is sacred ground. I am the caretaker and when I am gone, Itchee Billy will be the caretaker. Then, perhaps, there will be no more..."

"Tomorrow, you will stay here and rest, and we will talk some more. Then, the next day, we will take the children to the sacred hill, to give thanks and ask for the blessings of our ancestors upon them."

With that, the old man bid them goodnight and settled into his crude bed. Tony and Marie slept with a dream as magical as those of their children and awoke refreshed and renewed.

Two days later, Eastwind sat upon the back of one of their horses and beckoned out at the distant horizon. Hours of riding and walking had brought them to the summit of the highest hill on the Ridge, from where they gazed down through the ancient, towering pines at a thousand square miles of open range, rolling hills and clear lakes. The ground at their feet was deep sand, with only sparse, stunted oaks, prickly pear cactus and other desert-adapted plants. It was an oddly alien landscape, Tony thought.

As they stood on the hilltop, Tony became aware of a fluttering in the bushes and a persistent call of a bird. Eastwind, without speaking, mimicked the bird call. Within moments, there came a fluttering of wings and a family of beautiful blue scrub jays gathered only ten feet from them, watching them curiously. Eastwind reached into his pocket and removed a few morsels of food, holding them in his open palm. Fearlessly, a scrub jay alighted on his hand and pecked at the food there, calling to its family. Jack and Amanda sat enthralled, silent, as the birds came, one by one, to eat from the palm of the old man. He poured a few morsels into Amanda's hand, and they came to her as well, one perching on her shoulder as another ate. Then, in a swirl of color, they were gone, retreating to their home in the fastness of the scrub. Silence returned to the hilltop.

"This is the sacred hill of our ancestors," Eastwind said at last. "Here they came to give thanks for their salvation from the floods and the winds. Here they gave thanks for the success of the hunts and the growing of the crops. And here they asked the favor of the ancestors upon the generations to come." With that, he lowered himself slowly to the ground and called the children to his side.

Staring out at the horizon to the west, he said in an even voice, "If you look very closely, you can see the people of a thousand pasts moving together beyond the trees. They are your people. These things will be with you all the days of your life and will be your strength in times of trouble." Jack and Amanda stood as if entranced, while in their mind's eyes they recalled the stories he had told them. Time immemorial swept past and they could see the mammoths and the tigers, the human hunters, and the great storms.

Then, turning to Jack, Eastwind spoke again. "You need a name that is yours and yours alone. You are very strong and will grow wise and patient. You have a Miccosukee name you do not know, and it is Heart-of the-bear. Keep it as your own."

Then he turned to little Amanda, who stood staring wide-eyed at her grandfather. "And you, young lady, have a special name, too, because you are the first of all the generations to come. Your name is Wind-rider. You are one foreseen, as an eagle which comes from afar. Your children shall do great things." Then he turned toward the horizon and called out in a language both strange and wonderful and it seemed to Tony that the words were as old as the hills themselves.

They camped there and spent the night together high on the hilltop, watching the meteors burn across the black velvet sky while a million stars pinwheeled overhead. Eastwind told tales of the animals and people seen in the night sky, though they were very different from the ones that Jack had learned from his books. Tony and Marie listened in silence as generations of knowledge changed hands to yet newer keepers. Late into the night the voice of Eastwind counted out the lore, with an occasional contribution from Itchee Billy. Jack and Amanda questioned each tale and Eastwind carefully explained how the fox outwitted the lion and how the ancient people escaped from the flood on the sacred hilltop.

The next morning dawned with a pastel blush and Jack arose to watch the stars fade against the growing light. His mind was a swirl of competing thoughts and unasked questions, but he knew the answers would have to come from within.

The family made their breakfast over an open fire, baptized by the smoke into a new consciousness. Jack watched each move his great-grandfather made with reverent awe, like a novice prostrate before a master.

After their good-byes they parted company, each concealing their emotions beneath a mask of cheer. Tony gave Eastwind one of the horses for his return home. Since the gifts and most of the supplies were gone, they had little use for it, and they watched as Eastwind mounted the animal and waved as Billy led the way on foot back down the eastern trail toward the prairie and their island home.

The small band watched silently as Eastwind's frail form was lost in the trees, knowing that they would likely never see him again. Tony at last broke the spell with a bit of a cough and said to no one in particular, "well, we've got a long way to go."

Somewhat reluctantly the family began their trip, putting their backs to the trail that had just carried Eastwind away. They slipped silently through the pine forest to a lake which wrapped around the western foot of the hill. After a brief stop to water the horses, they headed on to the west and north across the flat land, past Cow Ford, where the army had built a corduroy road across the swampland and so on to the higher ground on the other side.

After a night spent at a hotel in Florence Villa, the company continued to a train depot in the town of Lake Alfred. Tony had soon sold the horses, much to Jack's regret. By nightfall they were safely aboard the train to Tampa. Tony noted with satisfaction that the train included many cars loaded with military supplies, some, no doubt, headed for his warehouses in Tampa. In the darkness they passed through Lakeland and Plant City, arriving back in Tampa before dawn. They had traveled only four days but, Tony thought, had passed through a thousand years.

March 1900

"I know it's a bit of an expense, Tony, but the committee is unanimous that you should be part of the Florida delegation and the president himself has backed the idea."

The speaker grinned and leaned back in his chair, tapping a bit of ash from his cigar as he waited for Tony's response, hoping he had closed the sale.

"I realize that it's an honor, Victor..." Tony began.

"Then you'll go! That's great, Tony. I know you'll enjoy Philadelphia and the company of our delegation and get a chance to renew acquaintances with Governor Roosevelt of New York. Didn't you meet him when he was here?"

"Not really. I only watched him from a distance," Tony replied, recalling the hard-driving figure determined to get his troops accommodated on the ships before sailing to Cuba.

"Well, this time you might. He's going to be speaking in nomination of the president."

Tony, normally not much interested in politics, was swept up into the hoopla of the Republican National Convention. Tony reflected that his long-time membership in the Republican party was really a relic of his family's anti-slavery leanings during the Civil War. It hadn't done anything to smooth his business success in Tampa, where all the political leaders were Democrats.

Despite his misgivings, Tony went to the convention and realized only much later that he had also witnessed two historic events that heralded coming changes to American politics. The first was the selection of Teddy Roosevelt to fill the vice-presidential role under William McKinley, following the death of Vice President Garret Hobart the previous November. The second was even more significant, although little thought of at the time: Mrs. W. H. Jones of Salt Lake City, Utah and Mrs. J. B. West of Lewiston, Idaho had served as alternate delegates. It was a chink in the political armor that had made politics a man's world.

May 1901

"This stop, Jacksonville! All off for Jacksonville!" came the shouts of the conductor down the narrow aisle of the rail car and Joachim Burtin quickly gathered his possessions and herded his two children before him as they followed their mother toward the exit. Standing on the platform blinking in the bright sunshine, he quickly inventoried their few bags, making certain that nothing had been left behind. Then turning toward the station as the conductors busied themselves with the few new passengers, he led his small group across the board platform and down onto the dusty street. Here, he hoped, he could at last find work and an opportunity to raise his family without fear of persecution.

Burtin had fled Odessa, in the Russian Empire, after mobs had burned his elderly father's clock shop to the ground during one of the anti-Jewish pogroms that followed the assassination of Tzar Alexander II. His father had buried a small number of coins that he had been able to save over the years and he dug them up to press into his son's hand. "Go," he had told him. "Go to America. Take Sara and the children and be safe. You have your trade and your hands.

"But father, what about you?" Joachim had replied. "You cannot stay here."

"I am an old man, and the mobs cannot hurt me. If they kill me, what do I lose? Soon I will be dead anyway. You have your future and your children to think of. Now go!"

Joachim had obeyed because it was what he had always done. His father's word was law. Escaping from Russia, the family had traveled on foot, on river boats and in wagons, always moving westward, where he knew he would find America. It had taken two years to get to France, from where they were able to book passage on a sailing vessel. Three years working in a watch-repair shop in Norfolk, Virginia had left him with limited skills in English and scant resources, but the owner had died, leaving him without a job. Here in Florida, he hoped, he would have the opportunity to build a new life for his family. He led them past the fancier hotels and paused in front of a small boarding house. There he hesitated. Would they allow him to stay, with his strange accent and his sons in tow? Would they turn him away because he was a Jew? Steeling himself, he told his family to wait and stepped through the door into the dark interior.

"Howdy, what can I do for you?" came a disembodied voice across the room. Joachim blinked, trying to adjust his eyes from the dazzling sunlight. He could see nothing.

"I would like a room," he said. "I have my wife and two sons with me."

"We've got one, dollar and a half a day, or two-and-a-half if we feed you," said the man emerging from the shadows behind a low counter. "Grubs not fancy, but there's enough of it."

"Yes, thank you," Joachim said and pulled his small purse from the pocket of his worn jeans. "Here is your money."

"Just sign the book here and head upstairs to room three. Where you from?" the man asked.

Joachim looked up at the kindly, gap-toothed face that had come into focus and hesitated for a moment. "Virginia," he replied.

"That don't sound like no Virginia accent I ever heard," the man replied, the smile fading only slightly.

"I... I come from Europe," Joachim told him hesitatingly. "We left there years ago. Sorry my English is not good."

"Well, your English may not be very good, but your money's just fine," the innkeeper smiled again. "Welcome to Jacksonville."

As the group settled into their room, Joachim thought again of all the changes he had led his family through. Trying to get his boys into school in Virginia had been difficult and now they were eight and ten years old.

They needed to continue their studies to be successful in America, of this he was sure. Getting them accepted had meant compromises. His sons Lejbovich and Burilo had been called Lee and Rudy. If it helped them avoid being beaten by rough boys, it was worth the sacrifice of tradition, he thought.

It was in the booming town of Jacksonville that he hoped to turn the last of his father's savings into the goal that had been impossible in Virginia. Here he would open his own watch-repair shop and use the good skills that he had learned from his father for his own benefit. Exhausted, the family settled down for an afternoon nap.

"Get out! Get out, hurry!" came the shouts, accompanied by a pounding on the door of their room. Joachim roused himself, still groggy with sleep. Dim sunlight poured in through the window. "It's only been an hour," he thought to himself. "We have paid for our room, what can be the problem?"

"Daddy! The sky is full of smoke!" Rudy called from the window. "Something is on fire!"

Joachim turned and strode the three steps to the window and thrust his head out into the afternoon heat. A thick wall of smoke boiled across the street only a block away and a dense pall was spreading across the sky, already blotting out the sunlight. Quickly he organized their bags and the family hurried down the single flight of stairs, through the lobby and out into the street. There they joined a throng of people, horses and wagons, all of which seemed to be caught up in a rush to escape the smoke.

For the next five hours the family struggled to stay together as they were swept along in the chaos ahead of a fast-spreading conflagration. They stood on a corner three blocks away and watched as the raining embers ignited the boarding house they had just fled, which was soon engulfed in a fireball. Hurrying away, they saw other buildings smoldering on both sides as the wall of flame leapt high into the sky.

By nightfall they had walked for miles, past the boundaries of the town and into the surrounding fields. They were part of a tide of humanity fleeing the destruction of Jacksonville. They watched the wall of flames and the massive column of smoke through the long evening and the flickering flames and stench lingered through the night.

Before the sun could rise again, the fires had largely burned out, leaving a landscape of smoldering ruin. Florida's largest city had been burned to the ground, leaving its ten thousand citizens homeless.

Joachim stood in the crowd near the banks of the river that morning, sadly surveying the scene. His stomach grumbled from hunger, but he ignored it. His focus was once again on his family and the disaster he had led them into. A tear streaked the soot on his face, but he swiftly wiped it away. Barely enough money remained in his purse to keep moving and too little to build. What good, he wondered, could come to him now?

December 1902

The thundering blast of the shotgun was still echoing across the river when two colorful birds fluttered lifelessly to the ground at the foot of the sabal palm. Hurrying forward, the two boys who had wielded the gun quickly snatched their prey from the ground and held them up by their wingtips to admire the plumage.

"Wow, I haven't seen any of these before, have you?" the older lad asked his brother.

"Never! I can't wait to show them to father!"

Together they raced back toward their cabin on the Macclenny Road, and their mother watched their approach through the small kitchen window.

"Did you boys have fun with your new Christmas shotgun?" she asked them as they came dashing breathlessly into the room.

"Look what we got! Both with one shot!" The younger boy said excitedly, holding up his specimen, displaying a brilliant lime green bird with the bright orange and red head. A short, curved beak gave it an exotic look.

"Why, I haven't seen any of those since I was young!" their mother responded. "That's a Carolina Parakeet."

"We got two of 'em," the older boy told her happily. "Now you can have a fancy hat!"

"Well, maybe I can. We'll have to see what your father says."

The three gazed down at the still forms of the two birds, taking in the beautiful coloration.

"You'd best go wash the blood off them a'fore it dries," their mother told them.

"Yes ma'am," the older one said, "but we can still go out and get some more birds before it gets dark…"

"Just be back in an hour, 'cause I'll have supper on the table soon and you need to get washed up a'fore you can eat."

With their shotgun in hand, the two boys dashed back out the door and were soon stalking more birds to add to their growing Christmas list. The Carolina Parakeet, North America's only native parrot, once common across the eastern United States but now reduced to a handful of birds, would soon be extinct, joining the iconic Passenger Pigeon.

The Slide Rule
April 1903

"HEY, JACK, ARE YOU COMING OR NOT?"

Jack Crews looked up from his papers, where he had been carefully recording notes from his textbooks, comparing them with lecture notes and performing the slide rule exercises.

"No, I guess not." He replied to the shouted question. "I'm not done yet. Go on ahead and maybe I'll catch up."

"Not a chance!" responded the enthusiastic young male voice from outside his window. "We're taking Tommy's trap! We'll see you when we get back."

Jack gazed for a moment out the open window, where the spring breezes were tossing the newly-leafed branches of the trees amid bright sunshine. Then, with a deep sigh, he returned to his books.

The steady clatter of hooves and wheels on brick streets made a background to the sound of mockingbirds singing, but Jack was determined to complete this course. It threatened to turn into a stumbling block in his ambition to become an engineer and he was not one to react kindly to roadblocks. It seemed to him that only minutes had passed, but the sun was slanting low through the window when he heard the jubilant voices of his friends returning through the dormitory halls.

"Jack, you have missed the most marvelous sight!" one told him, as they burst back into the room with the enthusiasm of a winning baseball team. "We just saw one of those horseless carriages!"

"Really?" Jack replied with a note of interest. "I heard there were some in town, but I haven't seen any of them yet, except in the newspapers.

They still haven't made them any more reliable than they did years ago, I guess. I read in the newspaper about a man in Jacksonville who built himself one."

"I read that too, but his runs on a steam engine. This one was powered by gasoline. I think that's where the future will be. In fact, I think I'm going to try designing them when I complete school."

"Then you'd better get to work on your studies, William, or you'll be ready to retire before you graduate," Jack responded, closing his own books at the recognition that peace would not soon be restored in the room.

The spring soon flew by in a rush of youthful exuberance and his high school graduation was a relief. Jack was finally able to spend his summer weekends working at his father's firm while taking classes at St. Leo's College. The college, run by a religious order that had also constructed a European-style monastery north of the city, was the best educational institution around and well suited, Tony thought, to help rein in some of Jack's enthusiasm and help keep him out of trouble. Since Tony had no plans for further construction, which would have been good practice for his son, Jack spent the time working on maintenance and proposed remodeling of some of the older storefronts that his father had built in the 1890's. Afternoons passed in relaxation, since Marie insisted that her son was not yet to become a slave to business but should enjoy some of his youth.

Business had remained good for Tony and Tampa had continued to prosper. After Jacksonville had been mostly destroyed by a fire two years earlier, Tampa had taken on new economic importance in the state. Henry plant's Port of Tampa had become one of the busiest in the region. On the city's east side, the prospering cigar factories had formed the basis for the development of a substantial Cuban neighborhood, which was known as "Ybor City," after Vincente Martinez Ybor, owner of several of the operations. The city, recognizing their economic impact, had gone so far as to purchase and donate land and buildings to Ybor and other manufacturers to encourage them to expand their businesses.

During school breaks, Jack continued his love affair with sailing and spent many hours cruising alone on the bay or racing with other yachts from the local club. It was there, where the blue Tampa Bay met the bluer Florida sky, that Jack first saw Kate Morris, crewing on a boat that challenged him to race. With a crew of two, the other boat gave Jack a slight handicap in weight but gained by virtue of the extra hands. He watched as the young mate expertly trimmed her sails. Jack worked hard to overcome the lead, but they countered his every tack on a close haul around the upwind mark to leave him in their "dirty air," then sprinted ahead after making the turn. Jack pulled alongside to offer his congratulations as they headed back toward the marina.

"Nice job, you two. The boats make a fine match, you just handled yours better."

"We had an advantage," the young man replied. "My sister sailed every summer at Cape Cod and she's probably better with a sheet than anyone on the bay. By the way, I'm "Snooker" Morris and this is my sister, Katie."

"Pleased to meet you both. I'm Jack Crews," he responded, and his eyes met Kate's. He was even more impressed than he had been before. Kate smiled demurely, blushed just a bit and glanced up at her sails. Jack suddenly realized he had been staring and looked away, but resolved to learn more about his new discovery.

Within the hour, they had tied up their boats at the marina, packed their sails and lines and met at a little restaurant nearby at Jack's suggestion. They chatted for hours over a lingering lunch. Within weeks, Jack and Kate were practically inseparable, sailing nearly every afternoon and spending their weekend evenings together. In August, the two celebrated Jack's eighteenth birthday with a trip to Clearwater and a sail to nearby Caladesi Island in the Gulf.

Marie watched the progress of their relationship and smiled to herself. Yes, indeed, Jack was a determined young man, she thought to herself.

One Monday morning late in August, Tony stopped his son at home before breakfast. "Jack," he said, "I'm leaving this morning for Boston. I have to take care of a bit of business and pay my respects to the family of a friend who passed away."

"Who is it, Dad, someone close?" Jack asked, almost afraid at what he might hear.

"It's Frederick Law Olmsted. You never met the man, but he and I became close friends during my trips on business. I first met him in Philadelphia, but we got together whenever I had the chance to catch up with him. He was a landscape architect."

"I never knew that you were friends with him!" Jack said. "He was very famous. I've read about him, even in my textbooks. He designed Central Park in New York, Prospect Park in Brooklyn, the US Capitol grounds and dozens of other parks... even entire towns," Jack said.

"More than that, he was one of the most brilliant minds of our times and could sort out the most complicated problems in a short time. He had amazing insight. I've learned a great deal from him. He'll be missed, but I believe the things he achieved will always be appreciated."

"Is there anything I can do?"

"Just watch over the business. I'll be back by next Saturday and you can have the following week off."

Jack took the work seriously. Given a chance to watch the operations of the entire company from the nerve center at the age of eighteen, Jack reveled. Each morning he received the reports of the foremen and supervisors, telling them to treat him exactly as they would his father. He listened attentively to the weekly report on the livestock and which ranges were being used. Each day, he was updated on the prices at auction received the day before in cities around the country. He reviewed the books at the elbow of the accountant and visited the factories, warehouses, and retail properties to inspect conditions. He took careful notes, and each evening compiled them into a diary.

The following Friday, his father returned. Tony picked him up at the station, driving a handsome matched team of horses. Together they drove over the brick streets to the office, where Jack reviewed the activities of the businesses. Tony was impressed at the effort Jack had put into his records and his report.

"Dad," he said, when he had finished his report, "I think this week has been helpful to me. I have decided that, more than ever, I want to design and build new things. I can't see myself sitting in this, or any, office, managing the routine affairs of a business. I want to create whole new projects: buildings where none exist, maybe even monuments, fountains, and parks, like Mr. Olmsted. I want to take an idea and make it become a reality."

Tony looked thoughtfully at his son for a moment, his emotions mixed, but realizing that Jack would have to follow his heart, just as he himself had, years before.

"Well, son, if that's what you want, that's what I want you to do, too. So first, finish your school and then you can decide where to build your dreams."

•

Jack Crews returned to college and studied hard but spent his free time with Kate. His restlessness came to a head only two weeks later in September. He had decided that he had had enough of studies to last him a while and announced his intention to go to work for Henry Flagler. His engineering degree would be delayed by his decision to study part-time and work full-time.

"I've applied for a position and have been accepted. You know that Flagler is rebuilding his Palm Beach hotel, The Breakers, after the fire and he needs help. I can continue to study, work on the hotel for a while and then maybe get transferred and apprentice under an engineer. I want to learn the railroad business, Dad. After all, there are fortunes being made in transportation."

Tony looked dubiously upon this new adventure, but acknowledged that he, himself, had never completed school, having quit after his eighth grade. At that, he had more than twice the education of the average citizen. Now Jack was almost nineteen and had been through twelve years of school. He had earned a right to begin making some decisions for himself. Marie simply smiled a bittersweet smile and kept her own counsel.

Kate was more than a little upset when she learned of Jack's plans, which would take him to the east coast, far from her eyes. Weekdays away had been hard enough. This was too much. Her reaction to the announcement was a retreat to the porch, where she pouted invisibly, staring at the starry night sky. There was a tear in her eye when Jack found her and pulled her to face him.

"Don't worry, sweetheart. I'll be able to travel back here on the train during holidays. It won't be long, anyway and you'll be out of school, too. Then we'll have plenty of time together."

Kate stared deep into Jack's eyes, trying to read the deeper meaning of his words.

"I'll miss you, Jack and I'll be here waiting when you come home, at least until school is out in the spring," she told him.

Jack puzzled over her words the next day on the long train ride to Palm Beach. Soon, though, he was immersed in work, learning about Flagler's operations there. He kept records, worked with architects, and helped not only with the new and tremendously-improved Breakers, but also with a stream of maintenance and expansion projects.

Soon he was shuttling up and down the coast, from the Ponce de Leon and Alcazar in St. Augustine, then back to Palm Beach and Miami. At each turn, new improvements were needed, and Jack learned as much about architecture and building design as he had from all his books. He filled his evenings with independent study, knowing that he would want his degree soon.

Jack's travels visiting the depots of Flagler's line brought many surprises and a few new friends and acquaintances. Among them was Jo Sakai, a recent graduate of New York University, who lobbied Jack for improvements to the small depot at a stop called Yamoto Colony. Flagler had been granted thousands of acres of land from the State of Florida as incentive to build his railroads and created the Model Land Company to hold and sell to people who would develop them.

Young and ambitious, Sakai had purchased a thousand acres and recruited six hundred young Japanese farmers to move to Palm Beach County. He gave Jack a quick tour of his lands, which they were busy clearing land for the crop of pineapples they would plant. He was convinced that fertile soil and temperate climate of Palm Beach County would be ideal for the crop and the demand of northern markets would soon guarantee a steady return on his investment. Jack made sure the improvements were approved.

December 1903

The Christmas break was a welcome relief for Jack. Since the hotels filled rapidly for the holiday season and construction work was impossible, Jack got the week before Christmas to spend with his family. He arrived back in Tampa on Friday, December 18. There to meet him at the station were Kate and Amanda, the latter looking more grown-up than ever, Jack thought.

"Mom told us she got your wire and asked us to come meet you," Amanda said. "Welcome home! And Merry Christmas, too!" she added, with her typical bubbly enthusiasm very much in evidence. Kate's own reception was more subdued, but she gave Jack a quick embrace and a peck on the cheek before smiling at Amanda and walking toward the street.

Jack quickly hefted his bags and followed, Amanda peppering him with questions about his job and Palm Beach and the shops and hotels there. Jack answered politely but wondered at Kate's behavior. Perhaps it's because of Amanda's presence, he thought and decided not to worry overmuch about it.

When they pulled into the carriage house, Jack could already see his mother waiting on the back porch with a smile on her face. "It's so good to have you home again, Jack," she said, wrapping him up in a mutual hug. "I suppose you're hungry and tired. Go get yourself cleaned up and I'll have a little something you can eat before dinner, if you promise it won't spoil your appetite."

"You know me, mom. I could eat your cooking all day and still have room for a slice of your pumpkin pie."

When Jack returned from his room, he found the women assembled in the parlor. "We have a little surprise for you," Marie said, barely unable to contain a secret, "but we can't really tell you until your father is here."

"Mom!" Amanda interjected. "Be careful, or you'll give it away already!"

"Nonsense, Amanda," she replied smiling. "I just wanted him to wonder a little beforehand, that's all."

Jack looked from one to the other with curiosity, but they just grinned like the cat that had swallowed the canary. Kate's knowing look gave away nothing more and Jack wished he could have a moment with her in private, to find out what she was thinking.

Small talk covered the silent standoff for the few remaining minutes, until an unfamiliar rumbling halted at the curb outside. Amanda bounded onto the sofa to peer out the windows into the evening light, calling "He's here!" even as she ran toward the front door. "Plenty of youth still left in the girl," Jack thought to himself and grinned as he rose with the others to follow. Before they were out on the porch, Tony had already bounded up the steps excitedly.

"Hey, everybody, look at this!" he shouted, and the group nearly collided in the doorway. "Jack! I almost forgot you were here! Sorry, everybody, I just got a bit excited."

Jack's gaze had already traveled past his father's outstretched hand where he could see a shiny new Model A Ford parked at the curb. Already Amanda was climbing onto the passenger seat.

"Look, Jack! It's the best thing you ever saw!" she called.

"Dad! You bought an automobile! I can't believe it!" Jack said, clasping his father's hand and slapping an arm around his back.

"If you think that's tough to believe, then I don't know what you'll make of this, son," he answered. With his left hand, he brought forth a copy of the evening paper. "I just heard the hawkers when I left the office, and I could scarcely believe it myself!"

Jack took the proffered paper and opened it, holding the front page for all to see. There, on the side of the page, was a story headlined, "First Powered Flight Achieved." Jack looked at his father and then quickly scanned down the page. Not once, but four times, a gasoline-powered engine had lifted the glider into the air. The inventor brothers, Orville and Wilbur Wright, had done themselves what the War Department had failed to achieve.

"This changes everything!" Amanda said in awe, having hurried back to see what had distracted everyone's attention from the automobile. Marie looked at her with a puzzled expression and looked again at the paper, trying to fathom the deeper meaning of the story. Even Jack, though impressed, didn't see the significance that his sister read into it. It was more like a stunt, he thought. Interesting, but probably nothing more would come of it.

Kate had been invited for dinner and soon the family was gathered around the table, while Amanda bubbled about the future uses of powered flight. "You know, just as they keep improving automobiles, they'll do the same to these flyers. One day, people won't use horses at all and then, maybe one day, they won't use automobiles, either. Maybe they'll just fly wherever they want to go."

"You could be right," Tony agreed, with a bit of a lop-sided grin.

"Tony, really! Don't you think that's just a bit far-fetched?" Marie objected. "After all, this machine they built is already broken after four flights. And why on earth would anyone want to fly anyplace they could safely go on a train or a boat!"

"Mama, maybe people will want to fly just to see what things look like from the sky," Amanda interjected.

"Maybe so, young lady," Marie answered, "but one of them will not be me, I assure you! Now, eat your dinner before it gets cold."

Jack listened to the conversation, but his thoughts were more on Kate, who sat across the table and stole furtive glances at him, while pretending to be entranced with the conversation. "I've got to find out what's on her mind," he told himself and resolved to do it right after dinner.

"Tomorrow's Saturday, Jack. I'm not expected at the office, but perhaps you and I could take a drive in the Model A. I'll show you how it operates,"

Tony said after dinner, when they had stepped into the drawing room to talk, seated before a warm fire.

"Thanks, Dad! I'd like that! In fact, if you wouldn't mind, maybe you could drive Kate and I to town? I was planning to take her to see a moving picture, if she'd like to go. They are showing *The Great Train Robbery* at the nickelodeon."

"That sounds like an entertaining day for you and Kate. You deserve a chance to enjoy each other's company. Fine, then. I'll see you at breakfast. I'm sure you'd rather spend a few minutes alone with Kate tonight and I get the feeling she'd rather be with you, too," Tony said.

Jack wasted little time in getting Kate alone and the two stood on the porch, taking in the deep chill of the December night. "I've really missed you, Kate. Palm Beach is a lonely town, when you are still here in Tampa."

"I've missed you, too, Jack. I really have," Kate said, looking up and staring deep into his eyes for the first time. "I've wondered if you really felt about me as I've grown to feel about you during these past months."

"Well, Kate, I guess there's something I should tell you, because I don't think it's fair to keep it a secret from you," Jack said. Kate turned her head away, afraid to hear the words that might follow.

"In fact, it's so tough for me to say it, that I thought I'd better just let you see for yourself." With that, he tapped her on the shoulder, and she slowly turned back to face him. There, beneath his broad smile, partially hidden in the shadow of his hand, a tiny twinkle reflected the light of a thousand stars in the moonless night sky.

"Oh, Jack! Oh, my..." Her arms flew around his neck and tears of joy streamed down her face.

"I think that I'm...supposed to ask you, if you would consider being my wife..." Jack stammered, as Kate tightened her grip on him. Then, suddenly, she pushed away, holding his shoulders at arm's length.

"Jack, don't think you ever need to worry about the answer to that question."

"Umm, don't you want to look at the ring...?"

"I don't care about the ring, Jack. I only care that we will spend the rest of our lives together. I love you."

"And I love you, too, Katie," he said and kissed her passionately.

The Christmas holidays seemed all too brief for the couple, but Tony and Marie smiled more than they could remember and stood hand in hand watching as Jack and Kate strolled from the house to walk along the Bayshore Drive in the bright sunshine of Christmas day.

It was to be a long engagement. The following months seemed to creep by for the young couple, though in reality they were a whirlwind.

For Tony the year ended on a less-satisfying note, when his worries about the empire-building dreams of many politicians, who justified seizing lands and the breaking treaties and with their chants of 'Manifest Destiny," nearly led to war with Colombia. The assassination of President McKinley had elevated Teddy Roosevelt to the presidency. Roosevelt was a firm believer in American supremacy, and he wasted no time in moving to assure that the United States would control world trade routes.

Since helping to eject Spain from its American colonies, Roosevelt had eyed the floundering private French project to build a canal between the Atlantic and Pacific. Colombia, though, controlled the isthmus that separated the oceans and was demanding control of the completed canal. American interest in a competing project across Nicaragua had helped to drive the price asked by the French investors down and now he needed only complete control to justify the investment.

Roosevelt struck by supporting rebels in the isthmus, blockading the Colombian fleet and moving to recognize the province as the nation of Panama. He immediately signed a treaty securing the rights to finish a canal. The promise of a new connection to Asia would soon bring repercussions to Florida as well.

Shortly after his return to Palm Beach, Jack was transferred into the railroad division, and he enjoyed the new challenge. Although Flagler's Florida East Coast Railroad had been completed along the entire Florida Atlantic coast, maintenance of the heavily used lines was a constant task. After a period of orientation, he was sent on to Miami. There, he was assigned to a team of engineers and surveyors working on Flagler's newest dream.

Based upon little more than eccentric faith and the confidence which comes to men who had achieved great success, Flagler had determined that he should build a railroad to Key West, ninety miles out to sea. The island town was a significant stopping point for ships trading with South America and the islands and President Roosevelt's determination to build a canal across Panama would make it the closest east coast port to the Pacific. The railroad would multiply its value.

Beginning at the end of the current line in Homestead, it would require one of the most expensive investments in rail construction ever attempted. Miles of bridges would link the chain of small islands stretching to the southwest and enclosing the pastel-colored waters of Florida Bay. There seemed to Jack no more peaceful place on earth.

May 1905

Guy Bradley took his time guiding the jack-boat along the shallow shoreline, while his friend Hannibal Johnston scanned the trees with his binoculars. The Ten Thousand Islands of Florida's southwest coast were a tangle of bayous and inlets, some leading to open water, while others lead into mazes of mangroves that a man might get lost in for weeks.

Their sprawling roots and fallen leaves provided a rich habitat for juvenile fish and crabs and feeding grounds for the birds.

Peering through his glasses, Whistle searched closely for any sign of egret rookeries. Those would be the places to look for the poachers.

"Seein' anything?" came the question in his ear. Whistle lowered his field glasses without turning his head, maintaining his gaze on the shoreline four hundred yards away.

"Nothing yet."

"Sooner or later, though, we'll find 'em," Guy replied laconically. "There's only so many places where they can still get to the birds."

The morning sun was still fighting its way through a bank of clouds, giving the shoreline a hazy, water-color appearance. Yet somewhere in there, or along this stretch of coast, plume hunters were at their ugly work destroying the last of the rookeries. Guy was determined to find them before they could complete their slaughter. He turned to his partner, who was now eyeing the shoreline through his new telescopic rifle sight, checking to make certain that the morning's dew hadn't fogged the lens.

"It's good that you keep that thing handy, Whistle," he said. "We may well need it when we find the bastards."

"I'm sure they ain't just gonna toss us their guns and fix us breakfast," Whistle replied, setting down the long rifle and picking up one of the shotguns from the gun rack. "It's just you and me out here and the Coast Guard boat don't usually pass by here more'n twice a month. If a shooting war breaks out, we need to be prepared."

Guy Bradley was the deputy sheriff and warden hired by Monroe County to begin to protect the last of the bird rookeries and Whistle had offered to sail with him up the coast to try to stop the pillaging. Guy was a reformed former plume hunter himself. Whistle was just sick of the destruction. The European fashion of plumes on ladies' hats showed no sign of abating.

New state laws had also been enacted to try to protect the birds, yet populations were still tiny and some thought that no recovery was possible. The showy birds of the Gulf Coast and tropical waters were likely to follow the passenger pigeon and the Carolina parakeet into extinction. Yet bird protection societies were emerging nationwide touting the idea of counting birds on Christmas day, rather than shooting them and the idea seemed to be catching on.

The hard-charging President Teddy Roosevelt, an avid hunter, was perhaps the last who would be suspected of working to protect the nation's wildlife, but he knew that many species had been pushed to the brink. Encouraged by the sympathetic ear in the White House, conservationists began a campaign for protection laws. Congress finally acted in 1901, granting the president the authority to protect a variety of national monuments and nature preserves. Less than two years earlier Roosevelt had used his new executive authority to create the nation's first bird sanctuary on Pelican Island in the Indian River.

Indiscriminate shooting had also wiped out most of the cormorants, anhingas, ducks, osprey, eagles, cranes and other Florida birds. Even the songbirds had been decimated, but the worst destruction had been done by the plume hunters. Gone were the days when the sky would be filled with great whirling flocks. Now, scattered refugees sought out the few places where they could escape the reach of man. Yet the poachers were clever and difficult to stop.

Late that afternoon the warden and his navigator cast a weather eye about and decided that the night would be placid. Choosing to stay away from the mosquito-infested shoreline at dusk, they dropped their anchor in the flats about two miles offshore. From that point they could also watch for any suspicious coastal traffic until the sky darkened. Slinging their hammocks under the boom of the boat, they found themselves a comfortable night.

It was almost first light when Whistle opened one eye, peering into the gloom. A light fog seemed to enclose them, and the waning moon had long since set, but something was happening, out there in the darkness. Was that a voice he heard? Alert now and sitting up in his hammock, he strained to make out any muffled sound, but heard nothing more. Then again through the darkness came the sound of a voice and the squeak of an oarlock. Someone was moving around out there, and they were likely up to no good.

"Psst, Guy. Wake up, keep quiet," Whistle whispered to his companion.

"I heard it too," came the muted response.

As quietly as possible the two slipped from their hammocks and stashed them away and by the time the first blush of dawn was upon them, they had drawn their anchor and were drifting in the barest of breezes, sails down, toward the coast. The sea was a glassy sheet, a slight swell disturbed by only a slender line of ripples that caught the early light, the wake of a passing small boat. They could see that it had headed in close to shore but could not make it out against the dark tree line.

"Let's creep in there and see what's up," Guy suggested. Whistle nodded his agreement. As quietly as possible they raised their jib from its boom, knowing that they were going to make themselves very visible in the process. The light breeze freshened just a bit as the dawn began to spread broadly across the sky and their jack-boat began to make way toward the shore. Whistle used his glasses to scan along the mangroves, but still nothing was visible.

"Damn, I can't see a thing, but I know they're in there and probably up to no good," he said at length. "Keep heading us toward that creek there," he added, indicating a dark line between two of the small islands. Guy steered the boat ahead, still listening for any sound that might tell them the whereabouts of the strangers. They soon drew within two hundred yards of the shoreline and steered for the narrow pass, without detecting a sign of another boat.

"Boom!" came the retort that echoed across the water and a squawk rose over the bay as a cloud of birds were frightened from their roosts and rose into the air.

"That wasn't far away!" Guy said excitedly.

"Get down!" Whistle almost shouted. "It wasn't far, in fact it was mighty close!" He reached out and poked his finger into a quarter-sized hole that had appeared in the hull between the two of them. "They're shooting at us!" Guy nodded, grim faced, keeping his wits about him and his hand on the tiller.

"Keep your course and toss all our gear against the gunwale there, keep crouched behind it. I'm getting out the rifle," Whistle told him. "It might have been a trick of the light and the fog, but I think it seemed a bit thicker right behind that point of the mangroves. It might have been a bit of smoke."

Lying on his stomach and peering over the bow, Whistle endeavored to keep his profile low, so as not to present a target, but he knew that whoever had shot before hadn't missed by much. Slowly he slipped his own rifle and scope before him, scanning for a target in the growing light. Although he could see nothing, he noticed suspicious ripples coming from the very point he had indicated before. Someone was there and they were up to no good.

"Before they were hoping to scare us away. Now they know we're serious and we're likely going to have to fight this out," Whistle said quietly. He kept his eye glued to the scope, hoping to get off his own shot as a warning, at least. Slowly their boat drifted ever closer to the narrow pass where he knew the poachers were hiding. At one hundred and fifty yards, the shot would be fairly easy if they were in a killing mood.

"Drop the stern anchor and toss me that bullhorn," Whistle said, and Guy pitched it forward. "Whoever's in there, better put down your weapons and come out where we can see you. Orders of the Sheriff."

A long silent wait brought no reply. Whistle watched through his scope and saw no further movement beyond the tell-tale ripples on the water, which seemed to diminish. It would be suicidal, he knew, to try to enter the pass without seeing their opponents. They waited.

At 7:30 am., after several more calls for the surrender of the fugitive shooter, the pair pulled up anchor and sailed south, hoping to head off any escape around the south end of the islet. It was a dangerous game of cat and mouse and a futile one. Rounding the far end, they found the back-bay empty. Whoever had done the shooting had likely eluded them through a shallow-water passage. Both men knew that, sooner or later, they would be back.

June 1905

The chugging engine of the broad-beamed boat pushed it steadily through the transparent green-blue waters of the Gulf of Mexico as the men aboard watched the green coast-line sweep slowly past their starboard. Behind them were Key West and Fort Meyers, Sarasota, and St. Petersburg. The village of Clear Water Harbor had been briefly visible before they passed around the long, sandy keys that sheltered it. With the passing of each landmark, they knew that their long journey was closer to its end. Each man was lost in his thoughts when at last the lighthouse that marked the Anclote River came into view. The captain changed course sharply, following the bend of the river to the southeast and at last a scattering of low, white buildings could be seen against the green backdrop of the bayou.

"There it is, Dmitri, our new home." The speaker turned back to him as he spoke and flashed a broad smile. "Once we are sure of our work and have earned enough money, we can send for our wives and things will be set right. Until then, we have much work to do."

Tarpon Springs was not much more than a collection of warehouses, a scattering of residents, a small hotel and a railroad station, but for these hard-working men, it was the promised land. Once only a sheltered resort for a handful of winter visitors, its future was changed when turtle-fishermen from Key West had accidentally snagged their nets upon banks of sponges. In a dozen years the sponge fleet of Tarpon Springs had grown to surpass Key West, Havana and other Caribbean towns as the most important source of the material.

Dmitri looked at his friend Markos and then gazed past him at the line of clap-board buildings that marked the waterfront of Tarpon Springs. "I am ready, Markos," he replied. "It's not as beautiful as our village in Greece, but here we may find prosperity. I can hardly wait to get into the water and see if these stories are true. If the sponges are as they say, it won't take us long to make our fortunes here."

Also watching from along the low gunwale were more than a dozen of their compatriots, recruited by the promise of sponge beds far, far richer than any they had ever worked in the distant Mediterranean.

Watching their approach from the dock was a man who shared their excitement for the moment. had arrived from Greece full of experience and had been a sponge buyer for years. Now he worked for John Cheyney, a Philadelphia banker convinced that sponging was going to be a very profitable business for himself and his experienced Greek employees. Both men had seen the wealth of valuable sponges that were being brought ashore from the bars just offshore. Spongers were now concentrating on harvesting, hauling the fresh sponges only as far as shore, where other crews manned the "crawls" where they were cleaned and dried.

From there the bounty was hauled by wagon to Tarpon Springs auctions and onto trains toward the major northern and global markets.

Waiting on the dock and adjacent warehouses were not only other new employees from Greece, but the machinery that would make them the most efficient in the area. Air pumps, hoses and hard-hat diving suits filled the crates piled there. Soon they would be installed on a boat that Corcoris had purchased for $125, and they would finally have access to the deep-water sponge banks they were sure filled the off-shore waters, beyond the reach of the pole-hooks.

The brave men who would use the new equipment knew the hazards. They would risk their lives to find a modicum of security and prosperity for their wives and children, strapped into a heavy helmet and lead-weighted boots. Alone and deep below the surface, their survival would depend upon the fragile stream of air pumped down from the surface. There, a puff of smoke in the intake, a kink in that stiff hose, or a leak in their helmet would leave them dependent upon the swift action of the crew on the winches to haul them to the surface before they died. Already the divers had learned that to spend too much time below the surface risked the feared but little-understood malady they called "the bends," which left many of their fellows permanently crippled with searing pain in their joints. Others simply died of the embolisms

The bounty of the sea was quickly proven as the deep waters produced a wealth of quality sponges. By the end of the year, more than five hundred Greek spongers would arrive in Tarpon Springs, soon to be followed by the families they had left behind. Dreams were coming true.

July 1905

Guy Bradley knew that plumes of Florida's wading birds brought a rich price on the market, as much as $20 an ounce, equal to that of gold. As a guide and plume hunter, Bradley had led a Frenchman named Jean Chevalier on a hunt that had bagged thirty-six different species of birds, almost fourteen hundred in total. But Bradley was an honest man. Once the laws had said that the birds were to be protected, he realized that he had helped to drive them almost to extinction. Now, for the stipend of $35 a month, it was his job to help undo the damage by protecting the few remaining birds and teaching everyone he encountered about them. Deputy Bradley took his game warden responsibilities seriously. He believed in what he was doing,

Guy's background as a plume hunter also gave him an advantage that other wardens didn't have. He could think like them. Although his friend and one-time companion Whistle had moved on to other pursuits, Guy used his small boat to patrol alone along the length of the Keys and Cape Florida, hoping to stop the slaughter of the remaining rookery birds.

Today, having heard gunshots, his mind was principally on the outlaws of the Smith family. He had encountered them before: the belligerent Walter Smith, a Civil War veteran always ready to fight and his two sons, cut from the same cloth. Neighbors of sorts in the small community of Flamingo, they were well known as poachers. Bradley had arrested Walter once before on poaching charges and his older son, Tom, twice.

"You ever arrest one of my boys again, I'll kill you!" Walter had threatened him. Bradley didn't doubt that he would try, but Guy Bradley had a job to do. He knew that he was hated by all the plume hunters in his range, which included all of south Florida, from the Ten Thousand Islands, across the Everglades and down to Key West. More than 6,000 square miles of territory to cover and he was doing it alone.

The previous year had been a frustrating one for Bradley. He had been monitoring a secluded rookery that he called Cuthbert, where hundreds of the rare snowy egrets still nested. Each time he had visited, the numbers had seemed to increase. His efforts were paying off, he thought. Then he arrived for a check and found hundreds of slaughtered birds lying deplumed in the water under the trees. He suspected that he had been followed and his suspicions led to his neighbors, the Smiths.

This particular summer day found Bradley at his home at Flamingo, on the tip of the peninsula facing the broad Florida Bay and the distant Keys. It was a rare day off and he enjoyed it until he heard the sound of gunshots from not far away, coming from the direction of one of his rookery sites. Grabbing his rifle, he climbed into his small sailboat and cruised the two miles to the rookery, surprising Walt Smith and his boys once again as they were loading newly-killed birds into their boat.

"Well, looks like you fellas are rather slow to learn," Bradley said as he dropped a bead on them. "I told you it was time to find another way to earn a living, 'cause this one's coming to an end."

The three Smiths turned to glare at him. All had side-arms and Walter picked up his rifle. "Bradley, what did I warn you about messing with my boys? You come around here looking for trouble, you're gonna get a belly full of it!" the elder Smith growled.

"Say what you will, Walter, but I am afraid that I am gonna' have to arrest you and your boy Tom, since he's already been arrested twice before. I might let your younger son go this time, if he'll promise to stay out of trouble and he can take your boat home."

"Dammit, Bradley, you make one move toward my boy, I swear to God I'll put a hole in you!" Smith told him. Bradley didn't flinch, but pulled the handcuffs from his back pocket, still holding his rifle in his right hand.

Smith took the opening, raised his own rifle and fired. Bradley staggered back, a hole in his chest. Looking down, he placed his hand on the bleeding wound, looked back at Smith with a stunned look on his face and fell backwards into the water. He struggled and attempted to stagger back to his boat tied up nearby. The Smiths stood and watched him go.

"I don't think he'll be so quick to mess with us anymore," Walter said. "Let's finish getting' these birds loaded."

Guy Bradley's body was found the next day by a search party led by his brother. He had floated ten miles and bled to death in the water. Hearing that Bradley had died, Walter Smith sailed down to Key West and turned himself in, claiming he had fired in self-defense. He waited five months in jail, unable to post the $5,000 bail.

Guy was laid to rest in a shell mound on Cape Sable, not far from where he lived and died. Friends and admirers erected a small monument, which bore the inscription:

"Guy M. Bradley, 1870–1905

Faithful Unto Death as Game Warden of Monroe County

He Gave His Life for the Cause to which He was Pledged"

•

Despite the prosecutor's proof that the deputy's gun had never been fired, a jury of local men acquitted Smith of murder. While he was in jail, however, Bradley's family took what revenge they could get when his two brothers-in-law burned Smith's house to the ground.

The Rivet
October 1905

THE YEAR OF 1905 WAS A HAPPY ONE for Jack Crews, who started his work in the Keys. He worked with the surveyors, boring holes in the sea bottom to test densities and wading through tangles of mangrove roots and trunks on the desolate islands. In the lower keys, he saw his first key deer and marveled at the miniature wonder, no bigger than a large dog. He learned, too, to avoid the salt-marsh crocodiles, which wandered along the mangroves, or sunned themselves on the beaches.

Kate continued her education at Tampa College and Jack took every opportunity to visit, using his train pass privileges exclusively for trips back home. After each short visit, Jack was expected back at Key Largo, where work was just under way on the construction of the "Overseas Railroad." Jack continued his studies part time, taking a leave of absence to complete his final semester, before returning to the project that had absorbed his imagination.

June 1908

On a bright Saturday morning, the sixth of June of 1908, Jack and Kate were at last married, with all the pomp and circumstance that the growing city of Tampa could produce. The marriage of a son of one of the city's business captains was no small event and flowers filled the big church, while the sound of a new pipe organ rang out. The reception at the Plant Hotel was one to remember, as well and a photographer hired for the event filled the room with smoke from his flashes. Tony watched the scene unfold with a sense of pride and hope well founded. Kate blushed when he raised a toast to the grandchildren they would bring him. She was more than a bit relieved to step onto the train and escape the congratulatory crowds, alone at last with Jack.

A week after their marriage, the young couple arrived at their first home, the modest cabin of a flat boat which floated in the warm waters of Florida Bay. That evening they stood on deck as the full moon rose above the dark water, casting a million sparkling diamond lights across the surface of the bay. On the horizon, a line of dark islands disappeared into the distance, only a solitary light bearing testament to human habitation. Although they were to share the boat with four other engineers and three hands, the others had taken their leave on shore for the week, and it seemed to them that they were the only people in this watery world.

"I'm so glad to be here with you, Jack. This is the happiest time of my life," Kate said as they stared at the magical scene before them.

"I'm happy, too, darling. I'm glad that Mr. Flagler gave permission for you to be here with me. I'm sorry we don't have a little dream house on a beach somewhere, but it means the world to me to have you here."

After a long silence, Jack spoke again. "You know, darling, that I never wanted to build railroads for a living, but I have to admit that I love the challenge of building this line over the water. They say he's crazy, you know, people in Miami and even Palm Beach. They call it 'Flagler's Folly.' Some say it can't be done at all, but I know it can."

"Jack, if you say it can be done, I believe it," Kate said and gripped his hand tightly.

•

Jack worked hard during the long summer months and into the fall, winning a series of promotions. The project moved forward slowly, as a constant succession of new problems were encountered and overcome, but it was the optimism of the age, as much as Flagler's own determination, which made the workers sure of eventual success.

Everywhere, America was expanding and the cry of "Manifest Destiny" was bearing fruit around the world. Theodore Roosevelt had taken the White House for his own full term and had expanded upon the Monroe doctrine of America for the Americans. He had encouraged a revolution in Columbia's isthmus and recognized the new nation of Panama three days later. Now, he had set the nation to work completing the long private efforts to build a canal there, to more closely link the Caribbean with America's new Pacific possessions. It would be the cement that would bind the new American empire, beginning to rival the size of even Britain's broad domains.

Flagler was eager to be part of the blooming optimism, even at the age of 75. His new railroad to Key West would provide the closest US terminal to the new canal at Panama and he had no reason to believe that the same enthusiastic prosperity that had followed the rails to Ormond, Palm Beach and Miami wouldn't travel on to Key West as well.

Florida's sub-tropical climate had shown itself to be usually suitable for citrus and Flagler reaped the benefits of vast new plantings along the length of the Atlantic coast. Named after the long lagoon called the Indian River, the oranges, grapefruit, lemons, and tangerines would find ready markets in the growing cities of the north. Bananas were found to be more susceptible to the occasional freezing temperatures and fell from favor with the growers. Jack's friend Jo Sakai's pineapple plantations, too, failed, after a blight attacked them, but across western Palm Beach County, vest new plantings of sugar cane replaced them, and Flagler's business thrived.

Back in Tampa, Tony Crews had decided that his good fortune would allow him to retire at the age of fifty. He gradually liquidated his real estate holdings, realizing that managing the properties would become a hindrance for his plans to travel. Gradually the ranch lands, citrus groves and phosphate properties followed the cigar factories and stores into other hands. Tony was content to invest his funds in stocks and bonds and let others build and devise the future.

October 1909

"Amanda! What are you doing here in the Keys?"

"Hi, Jack! I just happened to be in the neighborhood, and I thought I'd stop in and surprise you."

Jack smiled across the fast-diminishing gulf of water between his work boat and the dock, where his little sister stood grinning at him. No longer a little girl, Amanda had become a young lady. Then realizing that other men along the rail had joined him in staring at her, he conceded that she was not just a lady, but beautiful as well.

Springing to the dock, Jack swept her into his arms, glad to be reunited with his only sibling, whom he hadn't seen since the previous Christmas.

"I sent a wire to Kate last week but asked her to keep it a secret." Amanda said, wrapping her arms around Jack's waist and kissing him on both cheeks. "I took the train down and the railroad made all the arrangements like I was an owner. I've already been to the house and Kate has prepared a nice dinner, so I promised her I wouldn't delay you."

"No problem. I'm so hungry I could eat a horse, anyway," Jack answered, as they began walking the short distance to the bungalow which overlooked the surf of the Atlantic beach. "How have you been, Amanda? I guess you're out of school now?"

"Oh, yes. I'll go back for the spring term. I don't think I could last through college, though."

"Now, don't be too hard on schooling, Amanda," Jack chided her. "Anyway, you're a genius, so you never needed to worry about studying."

"Oh, please!" Amanda retorted. "It has been a grind all the way through, but for now, I'm as free as a bird."

"Anyway," Jack said, "I'm sure you have learned a lot at school that you can use in the future."

"I have, Jack, it's true. For one, I have learned to operate a typewriter. I plan to be a writer and I believe typing will be a great help in my work."

"A writer! And what is that you will be writing about, young lady?"

"For one thing, Jack, I plan to write about why women should be given the right to vote. And, of course, there is much to be said about the situation in Florida, including the terrible destruction of the birds and animals and the forests and the Everglades…"

"Wait! My little sister is a suffragette? I didn't know you even thought about politics and such."

"I do now. I might even learn to fly an aero-plane one day. I have learned quite a bit since you left home, Jack Crews and don't ever you forget it!"

"Hey, you two! This doesn't sound like the kind of loving reunion I expected!" Kate called from the window of the bungalow as they mounted the steps to the porch. "I hope you're not getting off on the wrong foot already."

"Not a chance, Kate," Jack replied with a smile. "My baby sister is just straightening out my primitive, condescending way of thinking of her."

"See, Kate, there he goes again! He always calls me his baby sister"

"And I always will, even when you're old, grey and wrinkled!" Jack shouted, sweeping her off the floor and spinning her around, only to plop her down in front of her chair at the dinner table.

"Just you wait, Jack Crews," Amanda said, smiling as she smoothed her dress. "There will come a time when I'll get even with you for this mistreatment you heap upon me at every opportunity."

"OK, time for a truce!" Kate interjected. "Now sit down and enjoy your dinner, which I have worked on all afternoon!" She smiled, amazed at how the arrival of Amanda could suddenly cause Jack to lose his normal reserve and revert to his youth.

"My sister doesn't believe she's a genius, Kate. That's how stubborn she is."

"Because I'm not a genius, Jack" Amanda replied adamantly.

"No, Amanda, you really are a genius," Jack responded. "Tell me, what's two hundred seventeen times twenty-six point five?"

"Five thousand, seven hundred and fifty," Amanda replied with only a moment's hesitation. "Point five, of course."

"So how did you know the answer, Amanda?" Jack asked as Kate's eyes widened in surprise. "It would take me at least twenty seconds to do that on paper."

"I don't know, Jack," Amanda said, looking at him intently. "I just know numbers. There's a beauty in them and they just sort of fall into place in my mind."

"See, Kate? She could do this sort of thing when she was seven years old."

"That's proof enough for me!" Kate said as she carried platters of food from the kitchen to the dining table. "You are a genius."

"So, how are Mom and Dad doing?" Jack asked between bites of baked red snapper, with sliced tomatoes and peppers.

"They're fine. Dad's still trying to sell off the rest of the land and says he can't wait for the day he can leave Tampa a free man and not have to worry about what's going on while he's gone. Even though he lost a lot in that railroad stock crash two years ago, he still wants to invest in other businesses. He's just a lot more careful. Mom doesn't say much except "your father knows best." I think they'll probably sail to Europe on one of the new ocean liners. I think she's ready to go anywhere he wants, but she definitely wants to keep the house. She says she wouldn't mind traveling, as long as she can come back home again."

"I'm not surprised," Jack said. "I really don't think you could force her to leave him for more than a day or two. She even hates it when he has to travel on business."

"How about you two? Mom wonders if you are ever going to get around to starting a family."

"Amanda Crews, how can you speak so bold!" Kate burst out, an astonished look on her face.

"Oh, come on, Kate, I'm sixteen years old now. I'm practically an adult."

Kate's surprise had changed to a deep blush and Jack grinned across the table at her. "Now you see why we were tussling on the way home. Amanda's more than a handful now, she's a boatload! Since little sisters are so much fun, Katie, maybe we should just plan on having all girls..." Jack said, shaking his head.

"You better watch out, Jack," Amanda said evenly. "I know stuff about you that you wouldn't want repeated!"

•

"I've really got to work tomorrow, but maybe you two could just enjoy the beach," Jack said that evening as the trio enjoyed the ocean breeze on the front porch. "On Saturday, if you're interested, I can take you on a tour of our work. I could borrow a sailboat and we could go to Long Key and take a picnic lunch."

"That sounds great," Amanda answered, staring up at the starry dome overhead. "You know, I don't think I've ever seen as many stars as this. Is it because we're so far south?"

"It has more to do with the lack of lights and the clear air," Jack responded. "Even from Miami, you can't see half as many."

Suddenly the night sky was lighted by a dazzling flash of light as a meteor plunged to its fiery death far to the east. "Wow!" Amanda and Kate said in unison.

"That was a big one," Jack said, staring at the spot where the object had disappeared in a shower of orange sparks.

"I wonder if it's some kind of omen," Amanda said to no one in particular.

"Do you believe in that stuff?" Kate asked, looking her way.

"I do," Amanda replied without hesitation. "I can't tell you why, exactly, but I do. My grandfather once told me to always trust my feelings, because they were there to help people. He told me I had special powers I didn't even know about."

"Your grandfather said that? The one who lived on the island in the swamp? Jack told me about him."

"He said that Jack and I were very special and represented all our ancestors in Florida," Amanda continued, her voice almost a monotone as she strove to recall those events of so long ago. "I believe him."

"Well, I'm impressed," Kate said with a smile and turned to Jack. "Why didn't you ever tell me that part of the story?"

"There's more to tell, too and someday, maybe I will," Jack said mysteriously. "Maybe I will."

Saturday dawned bright and clear, and the three adventurers headed out before the sun had pulled itself from the horizon, taking advantage of a gentle breeze that had blown through the night.

"Let's head out into the Atlantic side for a change," Jack said as they trimmed the sails on their southwest heading. "It's a fine day."

"Let's not, Jack," Amanda said. "I think I'd rather not take chances. You know how quickly the weather can turn in the summer."

"All right, if it makes you nervous, we'll stay on the lee side," Jack replied and kept his heading along Florida Bay. "Scaredy-cat," he couldn't resist adding.

"I'm not afraid of anything, just playing it safe, OK?" Amanda answered, looking away. Jack wisely decided to let the matter drop.

As was their usual practice, Jack took the helm while Kate crewed, trimming the sails with her usual expertise. Amanda leaned back in her perch near the bow, taking in the beauty of the turquoise waters. "Look, dolphins!" she shouted, as a pod of the sleek mammals began leaping and cavorting out in the bay.

Florida Bay was a large expanse of shallow water, sheltered and embraced by the ninety-mile-long arm of the Keys. Peering down into the crystal waters, Amanda could see an endless procession of coral heads and sandy bottom, filled with schools of silvery fish that darted and wheeled beneath their hull. As the depth of the water changed, the water changed its colors from pale greens to deeper blues, running through a pallet of pastels. "This is such a beautiful place, I can't believe I've never come here before," she said.

Sailing along the island chain, Jack pointed out the massive structures they had erected, products of the engineering efforts of his team. "Those supports are buried several feet deep into the fossilized coral at the bottom of the sea. They have to support the weight of a locomotive passing over, four times a day," he said.

Amanda could see the product of all his efforts and the obvious pride he took in pointing out the advantages of the system they had used. As she watched him, she could see how much he'd changed since their childish rivalries at home and how he had become a man of real vision, dedicated to his work.

"You really love this job, don't you, Jack?" Amanda asked him when they had stopped for lunch, wading ashore through the warm waters to picnic on a sandy strand.

"I didn't think I would after the first month, but I do. Yet, a part of me really wants to create buildings, classical designs, or even skyscrapers. I wish I could have been in New York, working on that new Singer Building. Can you imagine, it's forty-seven stories tall? I can't grasp building an office five hundred feet in the air. Someday, if I get my wish, I'll be building things like that."

Amanda contemplated Jack's dream of magnificent edifices, comparing it to her own ideals of writing great books and shaping public opinion. Both are worthy, she thought, but still... She shivered suddenly and glanced around. "Jack, I'm cold. Can we go back now?" The afternoon had worn on as they basked in the warm waters and lounged on the beach talking and the sun had started its descent.

"What's the matter?" Jack asked. "You were ready to go to the ends of the earth a minute ago. You're not getting ill, are you?"

"No, I don't know. I just got a sudden chill, I guess. Maybe I am coming down with something. I just want to go back."

Jack looked at Kate, who shrugged her shoulders. "It's OK with me. We can come out here any old time. It's her vacation."

Jack turned back to Amanda, who had already begun to gather their things, quickly putting the remains of their picnic back into the basket. "OK, kid, we'll go," he said, then looked up at the sky, feeling a sudden chill himself. A thin veil of clouds had covered the sun and he could hear the surf breaking on the Atlantic side of the island. With a sudden sense of urgency, he hurried to gather and fold the blanket they had sat on during their picnic and grabbed the last few objects from the sand.

Glancing up, noticed movement in the thickets of mangrove, which made a tangled web of roots and branches nearby. Looking closely, he saw the shapes of land crabs crawling among the branches, seeming to compete for the highest perches, jousting like ancient knights in their armored shells.

"That's strange. I've never seen the crabs climb up the trees before," he said.

"Come on, Jack, let's go," Amanda called from the boat, where she was already tugging on the anchor line, ready to cast off. Jack hurried to take his place at the tiller, while the women lifted the light weight from the rocky bottom. Even before the sails were raised, they were drifting away from the island, pushed by an easterly breeze. Even from a distance, Jack could still see the activity in the trees, and it gave him a cold feeling.

Two hours of sailing found them more than halfway home, amid stiffening breezes. The normally calm waters of Florida Bay began to show whitecaps as the wind increased and their small boat skidded over the water at top speed, heeled well over, despite their positions on the windward side of the vessel. All three of the young adventurers leaned well overboard, helping to keep the boat balanced as Jack stayed near the sheltering shore of the islands.

By five o'clock, they were just five miles from home, with only a final stretch of unprotected water between them and safety. A fitful rain fell from leaden clouds which had swept from the Atlantic.

"When we clear this last island, we're going to catch some bigger surf coming through the channel from the Atlantic side," Jack called above the sound of the wind in the rigging. "I'm not sure how rough it's going to get, but I want to make sure you two are hanging on tight. Take these lines and tie yourselves to the boat. That way, if you fall overboard, we can at least pull you back aboard."

Kate and Amanda did as they were told, tying double loops around their waists and making the other end fast to the base of the mast. As soon as they cleared the end of the island, Jack's prediction came true, and the waves grew in intensity until they broke over the bow of the boat and began to fill the cockpit with water.

"Kate, see if you can reduce the sail a bit more, so you can help bail," Jack called. With quick, seemingly telepathic coordination, Jack brought the bow into the wind and waves, while Kate took a further reef in the mainsail. The jib had already been reduced to a tiny triangle, but the boat had continued to fly along the water before the wind.

As soon as she was done, Jack swung the tiller and they quickly fell off the eye of the wind, resuming the boat's beam reach across the face of the strengthening gale. Kate scrambled into the cockpit, where she quickly employed a small pail and began to lighten the load of water aboard. Amanda continued to cling to the upwind rail and watched as the wind pushed the mast toward the water with each fresh blast.

"Jack, I don't think we're going to make it back to the dock like this," Amanda called at last, as the port rail of the boat dipped enough to allow the backwash of the waves to flood back into the cockpit. "Why don't you try for the tip of the island, and we'll see if we can tie up and wait out the storm."

"Amanda, you know more about sailing than I thought," Jack shouted back. "I had just decided to do that." Amanda looked ahead to where, in the distance, she could just make out the outline of buildings in the small work camp. One of them was the secure bungalow that Jack and Kate called home. May they see it again soon, she prayed.

As soon as the boat drew near the tip of the island, the waves abated slightly, even though the wind now raged in a shriek through their rigging and a stinging rain began to fall. Jack gave Kate the helm and scrambled forward to man the anchor as she brought the vessel as close to the mangrove-covered shore as possible. He tossed the anchor and grabbed an extra coil of rope, making it fast to the bow cleats. Then, with a leap, he plunged into the frothy water and struck out for the shore.

"Jack!" Amanda screamed, terrified.

"It's OK, Amanda, he's got to do this, or we'll never make it. That anchor alone will never hold us in this wind!" Kate shouted.

Within two minutes, Jack made it to shore, tying the rope around not one, but a series of sturdy mangroves, before plunging back in, following the iron-taut rope back to the boat. Quickly he grabbed the end of a second coil which Kate tossed to him and repeated the process.

"Untie yourself from your safety line, Amanda and give it to me," Kate shouted. Quickly Amanda complied and just as quickly the third line was coiled and tossed to where Jack was plunging into the water. Heading back to the shore, he pulled the third line farther up the beach, creating a strengthened pivot for the bow.

"Now, if only the cleats will hold," Jack gasped as he huddled, drenched, in the bottom of the cockpit while he tied a back-up rig around the base of the mast. Kate had stripped the last of the sails and the wind made a terrifying howl as it clutched at the mast and rigging, alternately screaming and sighing. Amanda huddled in the bottom of the open boat and breathed a silent prayer. The bare mast remained standing.

For six hours the wind shrieked over their heads, slowly clocking from due east to south, pushing the small boat perilously close to the shore. "Only one line holding us now, because of the angle," Jack observed as the light began to fail. Finally, as they were enveloped in total darkness, the wind slowly began to abate. They spent the rest of the stormy night still huddled together, chilled by the rain. By dawn, the wind had died enough that the group could free the boat from its moorings, raise a reefed main and sail the following wind back to the settlement.

The dock was partly gone, so they tied the boat between two remaining pilings, far enough from the wrecked remains of other boats to be safe. Forced to swim to shore, they comforted themselves with thoughts of warm baths and dry clothing at home. Before they got there, however, they were met by several people who had been checking the damage.

"Thank God, you're all safe!" one man told Jack. "We had almost written you off as lost. We haven't seen Johnson or Lind since before the storm. They were checking that new cross-bracing work on section thirty-four. From what we can tell, most of that section is down. Your place took a pretty good hit, too."

Jack ran ahead, only to find his bungalow in ruins. The roof was gone, as were some of the windows. Most of the walls were standing, but much of what they owned was missing or ruined.

Kate quickly caught up with Jack and stood looking at their home, almost in a state of shock.

"Well, at least Mr. Flagler had the buildings insured," Jack said at last. "Anyway, with what we've saved, we can build ourselves a home, like we've always talked about. We just won't do it here, OK, honey?"

Kate didn't answer but remained frozen with an expression of shock on her face. After a moment, Amanda put her arms around her shoulders and comforted her. "At least you weren't at home when it happened," she said.

December 1911

Work soon resumed on the Overseas Railroad, despite the damage of the hurricane of 1909 and another one the following summer. Henry Flagler was a determined man and would not allow the threat of repeated hurricanes deny him his goals. Jack continued to work, directing the drilling of new pilings into the bottom of the sea, or supervising the bolting of the giant trestles that would bear the trains.

By the end of 1911, work was nearly completed on the line. At the family's traditional Christmas dinner, Jack had a proposition.

"One of my gifts to you for Christmas dinner this year is a special trip. I've talked to Mr. Flagler, and he's agreed to give me passes for the whole family to come down to the Keys on the inaugural run of the railroad."

"Jack, that is a great idea. I would love to be there," Tony said, then turned to his wife.

"What do you say, Kate. Fancy a little vacation to take a look at Jack's handiwork?"

"I think it's a splendid idea. When will it be?"

"Next month. You'll have to ride the Atlantic Coast Line over to Winter Park and meet the special train coming from Jacksonville on the twenty-first. I'll meet you in Miami and we'll go on from there together."

As planned the family was reunited in January and rode together down the line, over the seven-mile bridge and two dozen more, admiring the spectacular views of the sea, which dressed itself for the occasion in a thousand shades of blue.

When the train chugged into the island city of Key West at 10:43 on the morning of January 22, 1912, it was met by musical bands, firecrackers, and an enthusiastic crowd. Many Conchs in the crowd had never seen a train, let alone ice, which was brought for the fishing industry.

Henry Flagler and his wife, Mary Lily, were cheered from their places of honor on the platform and anyone associated with the company found himself thanked and congratulated repeatedly. Jack soaked up the attention, basking in his moment of triumph.

"Now I can die happy," Flagler said when his time came to speak to the crowd. "My dream is fulfilled."

"You know, dear," Tony said to Marie as they sat watching the speeches and celebrations, "Henry Flagler is eighty-two years old. He makes me feel a bit guilty for retiring from business at such a young age."

"Oh, don't be silly, Tony," Marie responded, with a twinkle in her eye. "Old Henry would have retired, too, if he'd had me to retire to."

The Canvas Patch
December 1913

"DAD, I CAN'T BELIEVE you're going to let her go through with this!" Jack shouted, as the two men stood side by side on the open field. A loud roar almost drowned out his words, but Anthony turned slightly and looked at his son.

"And just what would you have me do, Jack? Jump up there and drag her from the cockpit? You know your sister has a mind of her own..."

Jack sighed in desperation and watched the improbable scene unfold. Gradually the deafening noise subsided as a clumsy-looking biplane moved down the pasture away from them.

"I learned a long time ago that to oppose Amanda's desires is simply to make her more determined to achieve them," Anthony said as softly as possible over the diminishing roar of propellers. "Now, if she wants to learn to fly, she's going to learn to fly and there is not a thing you, or I, can do about it." He turned back to watch the small plane, which by now had reached the end of the field and turned back toward where the two men stood.

Jack glanced over at his father, seemingly calm and realized that he was holding his breath. Despite the cool exterior, inside he was a mass of nerves.

The distant rumbling of the aircraft's engine built to a screaming, high-pitched whine as the plane lurched forward, building momentum as it raced up the pasture, bouncing from ant-mound to hillock on the uneven ground. Then, with a bound, it soared into the air and Jack found his heart in his throat as he watched. With a rush of noise, it passed overhead and headed off to the east. Anthony and Jack stood for a long moment watching it go and then slowly turned and walked back to the car.

"Well, I trust you had a view as good as ours, standing there on her flying-path," Marie said as the men approached.

"It's called a run-way, Mother," Jack said, rolling his eyes slightly and winking at Kate, who sat beside her in the rear of the open car.

"Nevertheless, I can tell you I didn't feel safe at all, not even from this distance. I am so worried about Amanda! I still can't believe that I let you drag me out here to see this. If I was only safe at home, I could be pretending that she changed her mind, and I wouldn't have to know any better until she was safely home again."

"Now don't worry, Marie. She's safe. Captain Jannus is a fine pilot, with a good reputation. I believe he even studied under the Wright Brothers," Anthony responded, trying to calm his wife's worries, even as he wrestled with his own.

"That's a small comfort. Remember, just a few years ago, Orville crashed his own plane and killed his passenger? He's lucky to be alive himself! I really should have put my foot down. I can't believe I let her do this! She's just so headstrong... I've always encouraged her to do for herself, but this time she's just gone too far... Oh, Anthony, what if she likes it! She'll be wanting to do it again and again! I really couldn't take that..."

"Now, Mother, please try to calm down!" Jack said at last, almost against his own best judgment. "After all, this is Amanda's life to live. If she wants to fly aeroplanes, then I think we should just give her our blessings," he said. "Or she'll beat them out of us," he thought to add, but stopped himself.

Anthony and Jack settled themselves into the front seat of the machine, which was Jack's newest joy, a 1913 Cadillac Model 30 with an electric starter. It was a fine December morning, and the sun was quickly removing the chill as they sat patiently, scanning the skies for any sign of the noisy machine that had carried the youngest member of their family high above the safety of the ground.

"I think I hear them," Kate said after a long silence. "Over that way."

Jack stood in his seat and turned to look, squinting into the bright sunshine. "There they are!" he said at last, pointing at a distant dark spot against the blue. "See, mother, I told you she'd be fine."

Within a few minutes, the dot turned to a noisy contraption which buzzed low overhead and the foursome could make out the tiny, waving arm of Amanda as it turned and began an approach to the field. At last it touched down, bounced a bit and settled onto the grass, taxiing directly before the Cadillac before turning neatly back to face the runway. With a final cough, the engine stopped and Amanda and the pilot, a young man named Tony Jannus, began to extricate themselves from the flimsy-looking canvas and wood contraption.

Before they could jump to the ground, the other four were already approaching the plane, Jack in the lead, while Marie cautiously brought up the rear, as if afraid to approach the monster for fear of being snatched up and carried to the heavens.

"That was grand! You wouldn't believe it, Jack!" Amanda gushed. "Dad, I saw our house and we flew out over the Hillsborough Bay and McKay Bay and the river, and I could see the entire port... It was terrific! You should try it, Jack! You'd love it, really you would"

"Maybe I will someday, Amanda," Jack said, grinning from ear to ear at his sister's jubilation.

"Now don't you even think about it, Jack!" Marie said firmly. "You children will be the death of me."

"Well, I'm glad you had such a wonderful time, Amanda," Anthony said with a smile, trying to sound as reasonable as possible. "Now that you've gotten this out of your system, perhaps things can begin to get back to normal around here..."

"Oh, Dad, don't be silly!" Amanda interrupted. "Of course, this isn't something you just 'get out of your system,' And I am more certain than ever that I want to learn to fly one myself. And Captain Jannus has said that he is sure that I could learn how. Isn't that right, Captain Jannus?"

All eyes turned toward the tall, dark-haired man who was busily tying the craft to a series of anchoring lines. He straightened himself with a smile and cleared his throat. "Of course, I said that any healthy person with good eyesight and balance could learn to fly a plane. Certainly, Amanda could become an excellent pilot, given time and correct instruction..."

"I hope this conversation can wait until we get home, Amanda, for I have worked up a great appetite just watching you fly through the air," Anthony said. "Let's get aboard the car and I'll drive us out for a nice lunch. Oh, and a good day to you, Captain Jannus. Thank you for seeing my daughter safely back to earth."

January 1914

The visionary Henry Flagler had lived long enough to see his railroad completed and died a happy man but without his driving passion the operations of the Florida East Coast Railroad took on a routine. Jack took advantage of the slower pace at the business to make a visit to his parents in Tampa. As always eager to participate at any event of note, on this cool morning he stood with his wife and family at the foot of Lee Street at the Hillsborough River, near the bustling heart of the city. They were part of a throng of two thousand that crowded the waterfront. Thousands more waited across the river, or on the smart stone bridge overlooking the scene. The onion domes of Henry Plant's hotel served as a dramatic backdrop to the scene.

"Here he comes!" Amanda shouted, pointing at the shape of the flying boat skimming low over the water of Hillsborough Bay. It was January 11, 1914, and the City of St. Petersburg was flexing its economic muscle. Promoting the town that called itself the "Sunshine City" was part of the mayor's job, and he was enthusiastic. The local newspaper, the *Evening Independent*, had coined the slogan and pledged to give away its papers the next day if the sun didn't shine before noon.

Having led the successful effort to create the new county of Pinellas on the long "Hillsborough" peninsula across Tampa Bay, the city fathers were renewing ties with Tampa and Hillsborough County in dramatic fashion. They had contracted with entrepreneur Percival Fansler, who had hired Tom Benoist and his Benoist Aircraft Company of St. Louis to provide the world's first scheduled airline service, two daily round-trip flights to Tampa. The plane carried only a single passenger along with the pilot, none other than the intrepid and popular Captain Tony Jannus, but it was hoped the service would become popular with businessmen in the two towns.

After much anticipation, the gathered crowd let go a lusty cheer at the sight of the plane approaching over the water and cheered louder as it climbed to one hundred fifty feet before settling down onto the river and taxiing up to the specially-constructed landing dock. Captain Jannus had just made history and the cities of the bay would long mark the occasion.

"Isn't it exciting? Imagine, soon, airplanes will be competing with trains!" Amanda said as they watched the ceremony at the landing. St. Petersburg's mayor, A.C. Pheil, was addressing the crowd. He had successfully bid four hundred dollars for the right to be the first passenger and was basking in the attention of the crowd and the press.

"Amanda, dear, I hardly think that the act of ferrying a single passenger across Tampa Bay by air qualifies as competition for trains," Marie said with a skeptical smile as she watched the proceedings.

"But don't you see, mother, that this is just the first trip?" Amanda countered. "No one has ever offered a regular passenger service before! He already has two planes, and they'll fly *twice a* day, on a schedule! Dad could fly to St. Pete for business and fly back two hours later! He only charges five dollars. Think of it."

"I can think of it, dear and I think it would be very handy if I had need to travel to St. Petersburg every day, or even occasionally," Jack said.

"When I think of the future, I can imagine bigger aeroplanes, that can carry several people at a time," Amanda said. "I think that the St. Petersburg-Tampa Air Boat Line could become a start of something much bigger. Someday people will travel all over in planes."

"I'm sure you're right dear," Kate said. "I just can't think of why people would want to endure all that, just to get across the bay, when a boat or train would get them there safer."

Amanda rolled her eyes, giving up on convincing the older generation that much would ever change. Then, with a roar of approval, the crowd cheered and waved their hats in the air, as Captain Jannus returned a salute in triumph from the cockpit and prepared to depart with his first westbound passenger.

Anthony found himself comparing the moment with the arrival of the first train in Key West and realized that maybe, just maybe, his daughter was right. He had expected the invention of powered flight to bring changes, but this was something he hadn't considered...

A week later, Amanda had just returned from her lesson at the flying field when she noticed the young man parking a bicycle at the top of their walkway. "Dad, it's Western Union!" she called. "I think you're getting a telegram!"

"Well, hellooo!" the young delivery man said, as Amanda opened the door.

"Hello to you, too," she replied. "I can sign for that, thank you."

"Say, aren't you the girl who's taking the flying lessons? I've heard all about you. Do you really think you can learn to fly one of those planes?"

"Yes, that's nice and of course. I'll take the telegram now," Amanda replied matter-of-factly, handing the young man his pen, and holding out her hand for the envelope.

"I sure wouldn't be afraid to try it, if I had a chance..."

"Good day," Amanda said, closing the door and rolling her eyes. "Boys," she thought to herself. "They have every advantage and never make use of them. Girls have to work for everything, while everyone else tries to hold them back..."

"What is it, Amanda," Anthony asked, entering the room.

"It's a telegram, all right. It's for you."

Quickly Anthony opened the envelope and read the brief message inside. "Oh, no," he said quietly.

"What is it, Dad?"

"Jack's lost his job with the East Coast Railroad. I was afraid this might happen when Mr. Flagler died last year. Without a visionary, there's no need for engineers to build new projects..." He paused for a moment, considering the situation. "Well, I guess we'll just invite them back to Tampa. They could stay here for a while, until he finds new work. After all, we've got lots of room, right? Did the messenger who brought this already leave?"

"I'm sure he's gone, Dad, but I'll look to see," Amanda responded, walking back to the door.

"Hellooo again" the Western Union boy said, as she swung the door open. "I thought you might want to send a response, so I waited. Besides, I thought you just might like to go see a "movie" at the nickelodeon with me on Saturday?"

"Well, aren't you smart!" Amanda replied with a smile. "Now, if you'll wait here a bit longer, I'll bring you the response to the telegram."

A few minutes later Amanda reopened the door and handed the young man the folded message. "My father has an account. Here's something for your trouble," she said and handed him a half dollar.

"Hey, four bits! Thanks! Now, what about that movie on Saturday?" he asked with a charming grin.

Amanda hesitated for a second, impressed by the brash young man. "Sorry, chap. I'm busy this weekend and the next few. Check back in a few years, though, and I might take you up on it." She turned and closed the door, leaving the disappointed young Romeo alone.

Jack and Kate arrived on the train two weeks later, with several large shipping crates full of all their earthly possessions. Their move into the big house on Bayshore Boulevard was as smooth as could be expected, though the house seemed smaller than ever to Amanda, who was beginning to realize that it was time to spread her wings in other ways.

May 1914

"Get off the boat now, or go up with her, that's yer two choices," shouted the man aboard the motor-vessel that had drawn up alongside the sponging schooner, and his words were enforced by a mob of twenty-five men who were scrambling aboard the '*Amelia*', all of whom brandished weapons. At his shouts most of the crew of the *Amelia* quickly fled to the dock, leaving their personal belongings in their quarters below. One of the hands, a black mate by the name of John Manis, refused to leave without his few family heirlooms and dove below decks instead to retrieve his belongings.

The terrified crew of Greek and black deckhands and spongers had already watched from a distance as their captain, Harry Bell, had faced a mob of five hundred on the dock earlier that day. Some had fired shots at him after he jumped into the water to swim for his life. Wounded in the knee, he had been rescued by the sheriff and was being held in the jail overnight for his own protection.

Now many of the same violent crew had returned on a late-night visit, determined to finish what they had begun before. The Key West Conchs, jealous of the success of the Greek hard-hat divers, and many convinced that their weighted boots were destroying the sponge beds, were determined to drive the interlopers out of Florida waters once and for all.

It took only a moment for the mob on the boat to toss their lighted bundles of dynamite aboard the *Amelia* and draw their boat away before they began to explode. It was the unfortunate fate of John Manis to be caught below-deck, and he was killed during the resulting fire that burned the vessel to the waterline.

The *Amelia* wasn't the only Greek sponging schooner burned that fateful day, as another armed band surprised the crew of the *"Louise"* in the darkness of the Marquesas Keys a few dozen miles to the west. There they forced them into their life-boats and looted the vessel before setting it ablaze. The long-standing "Sponge War" between the Greek immigrants and the jealous Conchs had taken a yet more violent turn.

October 1914

After their move back to Tampa, Jack soon found employment in Tampa, working with a local engineering firm. Kate assumed many of the household responsibilities that Marie had previously supervised, and the two women got along well. Marie, in fact, was surprised to feel a pang of disappointment when Jack announced late that year that he had found a house for rent and the two would be moving out.

In the fall of 1915, Jack began work for the state of Florida, reviewing the existing road network. The exploding population and the growing popularity of automobiles had finally forced the state to take responsibility for its highways. Soon he was helping to design concepts for a new network that would build upon the scattered county systems. The necessity of traveling gave him the opportunity to see more of the state but left Katie alone in Tampa for long periods and her friendship with Marie continued to grow.

Amanda continued to pursue her twin loves of writing and flying, offering her works to the popular women's magazines. She sold two articles to *The Ladies' Home Journal,* an intellectual magazine aimed at women. She met with enough success that she was encouraged to pursue writing as a career, leaving her many suitors pining hopelessly after her.

In the growing community of Miami that Jack and Kate had left behind, a boom of prosperity followed the arrival of James Deering, a bachelor who had made millions in the farm equipment business. Impressed with the great palaces and art works of Europe, he had chosen the town of ten thousand residents as the site to create his own vision. After buying several acres along Biscayne Bay, Deering hired hundreds of European craftsmen and a thousand local workers and began to erect his grand "palazzo," which he called "Villa Viscaya," in Italian renaissance style. More than three hundred fifty acres of ground, including ten acres of formal gardens, created the setting for the home, which he was soon filling with an elaborate collection of art masterpieces. It was a landmark of cultural significance, which helped to create even more interest in the fast-growing community.

The Suffrage Pin
April 1917

ON THE SIXTH OF APRIL, Florida and the nation went to war. Floridians, like most Americans, had wanted no part of Europe's wars, but powerful isolationist sentiments were finally overcome by German submarine attacks on neutral shipping and the sinking of the passenger liner, *Lusitania*.

Tens of thousands of young men volunteered to fight for Democracy, in the "War to end all wars." The American Expeditionary Force, or AEF, filled scores of troop ships heading for the trenches of France and Belgium.

Amanda, as a pilot, was excited to see the tremendous military buildup in aviation and volunteered her services as an instructor. "I'm sorry," she was told, "but the military will use only qualified military instructors."

"Well, then, take me into the military. There's no law that says a woman can't join," she responded.

"Young lady, such things are just not done."

Dejected, Amanda watched from the sidelines as new airfields were created and staffed and thousands of young men learned her skills. "None of them will ever be as good a pilot as me," she told herself and pushed the limits even harder in the cockpit of her rented plane.

In the spring of 1918, Amanda flew her rented biplane 50 miles to the fast-growing town of Arcadia, on the Peace River. There the military had built Carlstrom Field and Dorr Field as training facilities. She attracted quite a bit of attention by doing a barrel roll over the field at five hundred feet and only grinned and waved when army pilots overtook her and gaped to find a young girl at the controls.

"Young lady, if I ever hear of you doing such a thing again, so help me, if I have to chain you to your room, you won't leave this house again until you're sixty!" Anthony raged when he heard the story from a military officer.

"I'm sorry, Dad, I didn't mean to upset you. It was just an impulse," she told him, apologetically. She couldn't help adding, "But don't worry. After women get the vote, we'll still let boys fly planes."

Amanda's statement proved prescient, for in August 1920, after decades of campaigning by determined "suffragettes," the 19th Amendment to the Constitution of the United States was ratified. She and millions of other women were finally given the right to express their opinions in the form of a vote.

November 1921

"This is an opportunity that cannot be surpassed anywhere in the entire State of Florida, folks!" The voice, amplified by speakers on a car behind him, echoed along the Hillsborough River waterfront. "Now, you don't have to take my word for it, you can ask any one of the two hundred smart buyers who have already purchased a piece of their future in sunny Florida, right here. And you can trust me when I say that you'll never again see prices like these on land like this. Just twenty dollars today will hold your pick of these choice lots..."

Jack leaned against a tent pole at the rear of the crowd, listening to the animated pitch of the real estate salesmen, who formed a tag-team of nonstop hype before the curious onlookers. Even as he watched, others strolled over to take advantage of the free orange juice and listen to the sales line. The postwar optimism seemed to make the salesmen even more believable. Victory had brought the public an almost unlimited faith in the future of the country.

America was strong, the common thinking went, and investing was the way to get wealthy. If you couldn't afford to invest, you could borrow enough to do it. Next year, the stocks, bonds, or land will surely be worth more, the common thinking went and then you could sell at a profit.

Jack had left his temporary office at the lunch hour, sneaking into the roadside tent to see what all the tourists were flocking to. Everywhere he turned, it seemed, there were tourists arriving in their autos or piling off the trains, filling every available space. They came from New York and Pennsylvania, from Ohio and New Jersey. They had all read the glowing stories in their hometown newspapers and heard the radio broadcasts. Florida was the land of milk and honey and the tourists flowed like a river to taste it.

Florida had few hotels and unprepared for the onslaught, lodgings were scarce. Along the margins of the new highways there sprang up "campgrounds" with banners calling them "Tin Can Tourist Camps." There the Model A's and shiny new Buicks gathered in the evenings, large cans of water and gasoline strapped to their running boards to supply them on their way. Many drivers brought tents. In the evenings, some made their dinners from still more cans warmed over campfires. They would happily sacrifice to enjoy the winter warmth and explore this new frontier.

Jack had been at work for long stretches, supervising the building of a new network of state highways. He had watched as the road, popularly called the Orange Blossom Trail, had filled with cars almost before its completion. Each new road, it seemed, opened another path for a growing invasion of the state, the likes of which Jack had never imagined.

In inland Polk County, local bond money had built one of the first and best, systems of macadam-surfaced roads in the state and led to a rapid spurt of development, leading a newspaper editor at the Polk County Democrat to boast that the expansive county was "an empire." Soon they referred to it as "Imperial Polk County." Other local jurisdictions had quickly followed the example, but it was the involvement of the state that had finally opened the much-needed network of intercity highways. Now, long stretches of fresh black asphalt, wide enough for two cars to pass, were girding the state. And it seemed to Jack that everywhere an automobile could go, someone was selling lots. The frontier state was being rapidly settled.

The pace of the emerging boom was breath-taking, as the population of the state seemed to grow by half again overnight. Tampa's population soon leapt to over fifty thousand citizens, making it second only to Jacksonville, with one hundred twenty-nine thousand. Florida was experiencing unprecedented and historic, growth.

In north-central Florida, citrus was king, pushing out the ancient scrub along the sandy hills around Orlando, Leesburg, and Clermont. New towns and fast-growing settlements sported names like Orange City, Citra, Winter Garden, Fruitland Park, Tangerine, and Groveland.

Agriculture drove Florida's economy and the state's products rolled north by rail, filling the tables of northern homes with winter fruits and vegetables. To the south, twenty years of effort by a series of Florida governors had laced the wild Everglades with canals, slowly draining thousands of square miles of sawgrass marsh. Dikes rose around the margin of Lake Okeechobee as the waters of that vast but shallow inland sea were harnessed for irrigating the expanding miles of sugar cane fields. Settlers poured into areas around the Big Lake and towns like Belle Glade, Moore Haven, Pahokee, South Bay, and Clewiston flourished.

Amid all this, the fastest growth and speculation was focused on the town of Miami and the area they called the "Gold Coast." There, along broad bays and saltwater lagoons, dredges were at work deepening the shallow estuaries while workers erected miles of sea walls to retain the newly-formed lands pumped from bay bottoms.

The new "Dixie Highway," the brainchild of developer Carl Graham Fisher, was being built from the far Midwest down the length of the east coast to Miami. Fisher's own private "American Riviera" of Miami Beach, just across his bridge from the city, was being constantly expanded by the work of dredges. Once the outcast fringe of civilization, those on the mainland had long ignored it as uninhabitable.

Gone were the impenetrable thickets of mangroves, the cactus and palmettos that had defined it. The crocodiles, nesting birds and the rich nursery of the fish, shrimp and crabs were now obliterated, leaving not a trace of their former existence. It had for millennia provided a reliable refuge for the thousands of leatherback, hawksbill, and green sea turtles. They had survived their travails in the wilds of the open ocean to return to their natal sands to repeat the holy cycle. No more. The barrier islands had become home to a growing array of resort hotels and apartments. Polo grounds and golf courses sprawled across the narrow strand of dunes, hosting sporting events and spectaculars.

In Miami itself, a single street of crude frame buildings only twenty-five years earlier, new multi-story buildings sprouted at a rate of one a week. The very face of Florida was being rapidly changed by the hand of man and Florida's population was rapidly approaching a million people.

"Sometimes, Katie, I wonder if we're doing the right thing, trying to open Florida so fast," Jack said as they relaxed in the glider on the porch of the big house on Tampa's Bayshore Boulevard after a family dinner. "It seems that all people want to do is buy, buy, buy. Prices keep going up, but it doesn't slow them down a bit. In fact, they just seem to buy faster."

"I can answer that question," Amanda offered from her place in a rocker nearby, not waiting for Kate to respond. "Of course, we're not. We're ruining Florida."

Kate gave her a knowing smile and Amanda ran with the story. "As fast as people can get to it, they destroy it. I've flown pretty much everywhere within a hundred miles of here and all around, there's destruction. Huge mine pits, forests cut down, smokestacks and pipes spewing filth. And it's getting worse."

"But Amanda, people need those jobs," Jack interjected. "Don't you know there are thousands of men out of work since the shipyards closed down after the war? And now, with the cigar strike, there go another ten thousand men idled. This town's in trouble. I don't know, really, what's good or bad, but I worry about where all these new people are going to work, what the economy is going to do…"

"Destroying nature isn't going to help, Jack," Amanda replied. "You know that already, without me saying it. It's getting harder and harder to find fish in the bay and the water in the river smells funny. I just can't see an end to it."

Kate had been listening to her passionate sister-in-law but thought maybe it was time to chill the conversation. "Well, we both know you two aren't going to solve it here, don't we? Can't we talk about something a bit happier?" she said.

"Oh, yeah, Jack," Amanda began, "this may not be much happier, but I think you might want to know, since you build roads. Do you remember hearing about that Mr. Gandy, over in St. Pete?"

"You mean George Gandy from Philadelphia? The one who calls himself a 'transportation expert?'" he asked, his fingers making quotation marks in the air.

"Yeah, that's him. Well, he's started talking about building a bridge across Tampa Bay again."

"Are you serious, Amanda? I thought that idea died years ago, when Bernard Baruch and the War Industries Board denied the permit," Jack said.

"He's going to build it now. At least, that's what he says. I heard about it when I was in St. Pete last week. He spoke at a meeting there and told the board of trade that he would build it and operate a street-car on it."

"It's a good concept," Jack said. "It would surely shorten the trip over there. It takes three hours to drive around the bay, but I'll bet you could drive across it, on a good road, in half an hour."

"You can still fly it in twenty minutes, Jack," Amanda said.

"Only if you have a plane, Amanda," he retorted. "The airline didn't last so long, after all."

"Now what are you young people up to?" Anthony asked, as he and Marie walked onto the porch from the house. "I know you must be plotting some new mischief. I can tell by Jack's tone of voice."

"Dad, have you heard about this George Gandy who wants to build a bridge across Tampa Bay?" Jack asked.

"Yes. In fact, I met the man, at a luncheon downtown," Anthony answered. "He was president of the Gulf and St. Pete Railroad. According to what I heard, he used to work for Hamilton Disston and was married to his daughter, but she passed away several years ago. They call him "Dad." Remember, before you get too excited, that he's been talking about this toll bridge for years now. It's hard to tell if he's really got the wherewithal to do it, but he seems quite serious."

"Boy this guy really gets around, doesn't he?" Kate interjected.

"Any man who has a dream that he wants to make come true needs help. I'm sure he's only doing his homework," Jack said, smiling at her.

"Either that, or he just likes to go to luncheons," Amanda observed.

"Dad," Jack continued, ignoring his sister's sniping, "do you think you could arrange for me to meet with him? I'm really interested in his project."

"I thought you just said you were tired of building roads!" Amanda said.

"This isn't just a road, Amanda," he answered. "It's a bridge and there's no one else in Tampa with my experience at building bridges."

Before Jack's brief vacation was up, he had met with Mr. Gandy. A few months later, he had given his notice at the State Road Department and was working on designs for the new bridge. Along the way, he learned quite a bit more about Mr. Gandy. He had envisioned the bridge as far back as 1902 but knew that the small population wouldn't make the deal feasible then. He waited but was caught in the material shortages of the war and couldn't get permission. Then, the post-war recession had halted his plans.

When the economy improved and he finally got his permits, the Wall Street investors Gandy was counting on demanded control of the project. He canceled the deal and set about finding other sources of the money. His salvation was Eugene Elliott, a self-styled "financier" from Philadelphia. His job, according to a few wags, wasn't to sell the bridge, it was to sell Gandy. He set out to convince the public that the bridge would be built, even if he wasn't sure of it himself.

Gandy was not a tall man at five foot two inches and was not automatically the sort of man who could inspire others to invest in something simply because he said he was going to do it. He sported a bushy mustache and Van Dyke style beard that gave him a bit of an imposing appearance, though more bulldog than Great Dane. Although Gandy was a millionaire, Jack soon learned that he had no intention of building his bridge using his own money. In fact, he hadn't invested a penny in the project.

He was convinced that the bridge could be built with the money of investors and that the tolls would pay them back.

"If that bridge is ever built, by myself or anyone else, it will be by some fellow who gets behind it like I have and never quits," Gandy said adamantly.

Jack had misgivings about the duo, and especially Elliott, who traveled along with Gandy to sell stock in the venture. He struck Jack as being particularly shady, yet he couldn't find anything but intuition to pin his hesitation on. Nevertheless, Jack was designing real structures, instead of just laying pavement.

When necessary, he also found himself attending the various luncheons, dinners, and meetings alongside Gandy, explaining the construction techniques necessary to span the bay. He also listened to the sales pitch generated by Mr. Elliott. It was a traveling road show, but it worked and soon stock had been sold to the tune of nearly two million dollars.

Kate was overjoyed at Jack's new job, for it brought him home to Tampa, rather than the constant traveling he had endured. Amanda, too, was pleased, for before long, she was able to pilot Jack on his first ride in a plane, traveling to a meeting in St. Petersburg. Her skills also came in handy as Jack closely scanned the clear bay waters from the air, searching the bottom to make sure that there were no obstacles in the proposed route for the bridge, which had already been selected. In August, she demonstrated her barrel roll for Jack, leaving him quite pale. "That was my way of celebrating the passage of the 19th Amendment," she told him, when they were safely on the ground. "Votes for women at last."

"Hooray," Jack responded. "Just make sure we both live long enough to see them used, OK?"

The following spring, as Amanda and Jack returned from another excursion over the bay, Amanda spotted a second plane approaching, which crossed before them and circled to come up on their wing, in a military-style move. Amanda grinned at the second pilot, who waved a jaunty salute, before putting his craft into a steep, swooping dive to low above the bay.

As Jack gave Amanda a hand with the tie-downs back at the field, they heard the shrill buzz of the other aircraft approaching and stopped to watch its perfect landing. Quickly the aircraft taxied toward where they stood and stopped its engine. From behind the stick there emerged a tall young man, who approached them with a smile.

"It's nice to see you in the air again, Amanda. It's been quite a while," he said.

Amanda looked closely at the dark-haired, handsome young man, but could not recall where she might have met him. Another pilot, surely, she would have remembered. "Who are you?" she asked abruptly.

"I'm sorry, I should have introduced myself. My name is Martin Wilson. Captain Martin Wilson, formerly of the US Army Signal Corps. I saw you fly once before, while I was in training at Arcadia."

Amanda blushed briefly at the memory. "Well, Captain Wilson, you seem to know who I am already. Let me introduce you to my brother, Jack Crews."

"I'm very pleased to meet you," he said, warmly shaking Jack's hand.

"It never occurred to me that I might someday meet any of the people who saw that stunt in Arcadia," Amanda said. "Sorry about all that."

"Oh, actually, we had already met when I saw you there and I knew immediately that it was you."

"We have met before?" she asked, a bit puzzled.

"Most definitely," he answered her, trying to suppress a grin. "And I saved the four bits. Do you think you might be interested in that movie now?"

•

From that date forward, Amanda and Martin were virtually inseparable, flying together, dining together and dancing together. Amanda was completely smitten by the dashing young man and Jack and Marie smiled as they watched the blooming courtship. The summer flew by, and the young couple's whirlwind romance ended in a Labor Day proposal.

"I can wait until June if I have to, Mother," Amanda said several weeks later, as they sat together on the porch on a calm Monday afternoon, "but I don't have to like it. Oh, Mom, he is so wonderful... Was it like this when you met Dad?"

"Yes, dear," said Marie, her mind drifting back across the years, "and despite the few difficult times we've had in between, it still is."

"Then I'm surer than ever that he's the man for me. Did I tell you that he was born in St. Augustine? He says his family has lived there for a long time, since before the American revolution. His great-grandfather was English and owned a big plantation."

"Oh, dear, he's teasing you! Everyone says that. 'Oh, my people came over on the Mayflower,' things like that."

"No, Mom, that's not what he says. He says his mother's family were farmers from Madeira, an island someplace near..."

"It's near Spain, dear. Well, if that's what he says, then I'm sure it must be true. I'm just glad you're happy, dear. That's what matters the most to me."

The peace of the afternoon was disturbed by the sound of Jack's big Buick rounding the corner and accelerating toward the house.

"I wish Jack would drive more carefully! He scares me when he races around in that thing," Marie said.

"Oh, Mom, that's nothing! If you want to see really fast cars, you should go with him to see the races on the beach at Daytona, like I did. They go over a hundred miles an hour, just a blur going by..."

"Mom, Amanda! Is Dad home?" Jack shouted excitedly, bounding up the steps to the porch.

"No, dear, he's gone to town. Is something wrong?" Marie asked, rising from her chair.

"I just heard the word at the yacht club, where they got news by telegraph. There's a hurricane in the Gulf and they think it's coming this way. This one is big, not like that tropical storm we had last week."

"Oh, God, what should we do, Jack? I don't know what to do for a hurricane..." Marie began turning for the door, then back again.

"The first thing to do is not panic. Amanda, can you go to my house and get Katie? And bring all the food, blankets, and medicine you can carry. Here, take my automobile," he said, tossing her the keys.

Quickly Jack climbed the steps to the porch and put his arm around his mother. "Now don't worry, Mom, we'll be all right. After all, I've been through these things before." Then, suddenly remembering, he turned back to Amanda, already behind the wheel of the Buick. "Oh! and tell Katie not to forget to bring me some extra clothes!"

By the time Anthony returned from town two hours later, the family was gathered in the house, hurriedly making what preparations they could. Using lumber he found in the garage, Jack had boarded over the larger windows, attracting the attention of the neighbors, who also raced into preparations.

Anthony considered the danger they would face in the big house facing the bay. Built over a sort of half-basement, the main floor was elevated several feet above the street. The lower level would offer protection from the wind, but if the wind pushed the water into the bay, it would likely flood. For the first time he was truly in fear for the lives of his family.

By early evening a premature darkness had descended and as the wind had begun to rise the waters of the Bay were whipped to a froth. Soon they topped the Bayshore Boulevard and poured into the lower level of the house despite their best efforts to hold them back. They retreated to the main floor as the house rocked and groaned, timbers creaking loudly with each new burst of wind. Anthony left the family huddled in the hallway to peer out the front windows and watch as the storm seemed to lift the raging waters directly from the bay, sucking it skyward.

Nightfall masked the sights of the storm, but not the terrifying sounds. The electric lights had failed and only a kerosene lamp held the darkness at bay as the winds raged overhead, reaching a roaring crescendo before slowly beginning to subside. The house stood.

The following morning, the family emerged to find Tampa in ruins. Some of the houses along the Bayshore had been lifted from their foundations and tossed like toys. Downed trees and power lines blocked the streets and a twelve-foot storm surge had damaged thousands of buildings. Ballast Point had been severely damaged and ships at the piers had been piled upon each other, the docks, and the shore, making an intimidating heap. Tony shook his head sadly as he surveyed the mess with Jack once the streets had been cleared.

"Don't worry, Dad, it will all be cleaned up and fixed up faster than you can imagine. This town's got spunk. And thanks to the solid house you built, we're all OK."

It was another reminder that nature still had the upper hand in Florida and hurricanes were a fact of life.

•

As Jack had predicted, Tampa was quick to rebuild and repair and the cleanup from the storm put many of the unemployed to work, at least temporarily. But the city had suffered yet another blow to its economy and it was thanks to the continued influx of the "Tin Can Tourists" that the city worked its way out of its slump. A building boom in small, roadside inns, called motor-hotels, or 'mo-tels', had helped keep the tourist trade thriving.

By the following year, George Gandy had lined up the necessary financing for his dream of a bridge across the bay and soon Jack was busy supervising real work, instead of just designing and drawing a "hurricane-proof" structure. He took time off in June, though, for the marriage of his only sister and followed the couple from the church reception to the airfield. There they climbed aboard their rented plane for a trip to St. Augustine to visit his family before flying to New York for their honeymoon.

"Now go make some babies!" he shouted as he threw rice into the cockpit of their plane as the luggage was loaded.

"You should talk, Jack Crews. Go make some yourself!" Amanda shouted back at him.

Katie, standing a short distance away, blushed when she heard the taunting. "Why can't you two behave like normal adults," she said to Jack, who was still tossing rice at the fuselage.

"Who says adults have to be normal, Katie?" Amanda shouted from the plane, moments before the engines coughed to life.

The Black Stone
January 1923

"I DUNNO' SAM, I DON'T THINK WE'RE REALLY SAFE around here anymore." Wilkin Watson shook his head slowly and looked down at the ground. "The Ku Klux Klan done held a big cross-burning las' week over to Gainesville and they's been stirrin' up trouble for a long while now. This story about that white woman getting raped by a black man, I don' know if it's got a lick of truth to it."

Sam Lewis tilted his hat back on his head and glanced around. The green walls of forest that encircled the scattered houses of the community of Rosewood suddenly seemed ominous, rather than sheltering. Were there men out there right now, watching them?

Rosewood was a tight-knit community and just the place that Sam Lewis had figured to be safe to stay during his stints to work on the railroad in years past, sending his cash money back to support his growing family. He had made plenty of friends there and hadn't expected to find it troubled on this visit.

"When those men killed Sam Carter three days ago, we knew it was bad. He hadn't done a thing wrong," Wilkin continued. "I don' even know if that Fannie Taylor lady was telling the truth when she said she was attacked, but I know Sam Carter didn't do nothin' wrong. Now he's dead."

Sam thought about the terrible mob justice that had been dispensed by bands of white vigilantes in recent years. Every black man and woman had heard the stories. The Klan made sure of it. He knew about the big battle in Ocoee barely two years earlier that left the black community destroyed and several people dead. He had heard about the four black men dragged from a jail and lynched by a mob in MacClenny. He knew about the lynching of a black man in Wauchula, accused of assaulting a white woman. He had heard about the black man burned at the stake in Perry, where the mob also burned the church, school and masonic lodge. Now the violence seemed to be drawing closer.

Sam had good reason to be worried. Nearby, a group of Klansmen plotted their activities for the night and Rosewood was their target. If there was a rapist hiding among the blacks there, they would be sure to find him. He would be dead by dawn, they muttered.

It was the gunfire that woke Sam from his sleep, and he immediately recalled the fearsome sound of the Civil War skirmishes that had awoken him during his childhood. A steady barrage of shots pierced the night as a large group of men laid siege to the home of Sylvester Carrier nearby. They were convinced that he was hiding an escaped convict, who was almost certainly guilty of the crime. Sylvester's mother, Sarah Carrier, had confronted the men after they shot her dog. She died in a hail of gunfire, standing on her own porch. Sylvester returned fire and killed two of the attackers before he was also killed. Others in the house continued the defense and the attackers eventually withdrew, leaving scattered bodies behind.

Sam didn't wait to hear what had happened but followed the example of his father sixty years earlier. He fled into the woods, joining most of the residents of Rosewood.

Behind him the violence raged. The following day, the mob returned and burned the Carrier home to the ground. By nightfall, an assembled army of more than two hundred vigilantes attacked the village of Rosewood, slaughtering anything that moved and burning every building they encountered. By morning, only a general store and a single house remained of the town. John Wright, the white owner of the store, had hidden several his customers inside the locked building, confident that his presence would keep it safe. He stood guard outside as the riot raged.

Sam and hundreds of other fugitives hid in the surrounding woods until the following afternoon, when two train conductors, John and William Bryce, arranged for their rescue. Most fled to northern cities without spare clothing or cash. Sam managed to make his way south, where his family awaited him on the shores of the Big Lake Okeechobee.

November 1924

It was a crisp fall day as Jack stood once again in triumph, watching as Governor Cary Hardee cut a rope of flowers and the first cars began to roll across the bridge he had helped to construct across Tampa Bay. The cities of Tampa and St. Petersburg were forever linked, drawn closer together than anyone had ever been imagined. Anthony and Marie stood with Kate, beaming proudly as their son basked in the achievement. Amanda and Martin couldn't join them, as they were living in St. Augustine, where Martin worked in his family's pharmacy.

Jack missed his sister's easy smile and constant ribbing. He thought of her concerns about Florida's nature often and especially the previous month, when D.P. Davis had held a real estate auction, not of land, but of the bottom of Tampa Bay and a few low, marshy islands. He planned to dredge the bay bottom and fill in the land to build houses. People believed him, buying out the first block of three hundred lots in less than three hours. Already dredges were at work and brown silt stains spread across the blue water of the bay as the "Davis Islands" became a reality. Recalling Amanda's warnings of how Florida was being ruined, Jack admitted to himself that she was right.

The following days brought Jack a renewed sense of drift. "I've got to do something different," he announced to Kate and his parents a week later as the four dined at a popular restaurant in Ybor City. "I mean, I'm tired of building bridges and certainly roads, too. I still want to put up buildings, real buildings that people can use. You built lots of them, Dad, even our house, your house, on the Bayshore. It stood up in the hurricane when others came apart. The factories, the stores, they're all still standing. Sure, some were damaged, but they were all repaired, and they'll be there for years. That's the kind of things I want to build."

"But, Jack, dear," Marie said to him, "You've built bridges that will stand up, that people will use for many years to come. You've got a lot of good work to be proud of."

"Not really, Mom. Someday, storms will come that will tear those bridges away. Even if that never happens, they'll need newer, bigger bridges, better materials. They won't last. No, that's not what I have in mind, but I'm not yet sure what it is yet..."

"Well, dear," Kate said, glancing at Anthony, feeling like she was leading the charge, "Florida is a growing place. People are putting up buildings faster than anywhere in the world. If you want to do that, this is the time and place."

Kate was right, Jack realized. Instead of slowing down, as he had expected, the numbers of tourists pouring into Florida had increased and thousands decided to stay. New towns and subdivisions sprang up everywhere, seemingly overnight. Tampa was growing much too fast, he thought. He was ready to leave the city and strike out into new country.

"Jack, I've got a suggestion for you," his old college buddy, Tommy, told him one afternoon as the two couples sailed on the bay. "Some friends of my family from Bartow invested in a new town at Lake Wales a few years ago. It was planned as a "garden city." Now it's a boom-town. It's real pretty country and you need a change of scenery. It should be a good place for a guy like you to make a splash. I would imagine that there will be some call for a good architect and structural engineer. There's always a need for new buildings in any new town. Why don't you give it a look?"

"I think it's a great idea, Jack," Kate told him, eager to see his fire rekindled.

It was only two days later that Jack and Kate packed a lunch and set out in their Buick, driving east from Tampa toward the center of the state.

They found the town rising among the lakes and pine-covered hills of the ridge. The area's first enterprise, a turpentine still and sawmill, was little more than ten years old, but now two railroads and the new Scenic Highway were delivering hundreds of newcomers eager to invest in building a town from scratch.

Jack was pleased to see that a young engineer named Allen Carleton Nydegger had carefully surveyed the town-site, laying out a sensible pattern of streets while preserving the lake shores for public use. The clear delineation between proposed commercial and residential areas made a pleasant change from the random development which Jack had seen in his travels around the state.

Kate immediately took a liking to the place as well and Jack made an inquiry at the new board of trade. Architects from nearby Lakeland. and as far away as New York, were already busy erecting elaborate commercial buildings in the town, he learned. Jack's notice, though, soon brought him an offer of work. "If you can build a bank as well as you can build bridges, son, you're the man for me," one business leader told him and within the week, he was busy designing the new structure, while Kate settled them into a suite of rooms at the Lakeshore Hotel.

On the weekend, they drove through the beautiful hill country around the town, taking in the vistas of tall pines and orderly rows of young citrus trees along the Scenic Highway. "You know, this place is about as different from Tampa as you could get and be this close," he told Kate one afternoon. They had spread their picnic lunch on a blanket cast under the trees on the top of a high hill overlooking sprawling Crooked Lake and were enjoying the views and breeze. "If one really decided to, this would be a nice place to raise a family, away from the crowds..."

Kate looked at him slyly, trying to understand what he was saying. "Are you saying that you think that's a good idea, Jack?" she asked him.

"Well, Katie, I know we've tried and after all these years, I don't think it's possible. I mean, at first, we didn't want children and then when we thought we might be ready... I'm very happy with you, though. What I mean is, I'm not unhappy that we never did, but sometimes I wonder what it might have been like to have a son or daughter..."

"Jack, I've always wondered if you might have a sixth sense," Kate said, looking out at the distant horizon, where the land fell away to the coastal plain. "I know your sister does. It saved our lives in the Keys. I thought you might and now I'm almost sure of it. I've got something I've been waiting for the right time to tell you, Jack, but I can't think of a better time than this." She looked at Jack again and the words just poured out. "You can stop wondering now. We're going to have a baby."

•

That Christmas was the most memorable holiday yet. The family gathered in Tampa, Anthony, and Marie excited about news of their impending first grandchild. Amanda arrived with Martin, both bubbling over with excitement at Kate's big news and let the word of that expected event soak in a good while before she broke her own big news.

"Mom, Dad, I want you both to hear this at the same time. I didn't call you last week because I wanted to see Jack and Kate's faces, too. Martin and I are going to be parents!"

For Marie, the news of her impending double-grandparent status was too much. She fell into a chair, smiling a lightheaded grin. "I can't believe it!" she said, "after all this waiting!"

Anthony, too, smiled broadly, reveling in the moment. Amanda thought he looked terribly distinguished, as a grandfather should, with his grey hair shining in the light of the fireplace. "It's hard to believe," she thought to herself, "that he's already sixty-one. He's always seemed so young to me."

The Carved Bird
February 1925

AS THE WEEKS AND MONTHS flew by, Jack quickly fell into the pace of his new life and spent much of his spare time supervising and working on the construction of a comfortable home near tiny "Crystal" Lake, a beautiful spring-fed pool surrounded by ancient live oaks in the heart of the growing town. Kate's nesting instinct drove him onward, as she walked through the unfinished structure, describing how each room would look when it was done. Boxes soon piled up in one corner of their rented rooms, filled with the curtains, wallpapers and carpets she had chosen for their new home.

Jack's work week was filled with overseeing work on the bank, making hundreds of small changes necessary to make the design come together as he intended. Buildings, he soon realized, with their need for plumbing and wiring, bearing walls and sight lines, were much more complex than he had remembered. Time and again he changed the layout of the offices to suit his client, only to discover that dozens of other changes were then required.

Jack was soon pulled into the activities of the business community at the Board of Trade, where he was delighted to meet the noted economist, Roger Babson. A neighbor of Bok's, he was busy developing a suburban community on the nearby shores of Crooked Lake. "We're changing the name to Caloosa," Babson told Jack with a serious look. "Can't have anything crooked around, because I'm planning a bank and it might give the wrong impression," he said, before breaking into a grin.

Jack's search for further work to follow the construction of the bank led him to a meeting with a man who proved to be well acquainted with his work. It was the late spring of 1925 and Jack was in shirtsleeves, busily at work in his offices pouring over sheets of design changes for a new building. A lone ceiling fan turned lazily overhead, stirring the afternoon warmth. The door opened and gentleman entered, wearing a three-piece pinstriped suit. His entire manner gave him a serious air.

"Good afternoon, young man. If you are Mr. Crews, you are an engineer of some repute if I may pay you a compliment."

"Thank you, sir. I'm John Crews, but everyone calls me Jack," he replied, rising to shake his visitor's hand.

"So I have heard. I'm very pleased to meet you. My full name is Edward William Bok, though my friends in the United States call me Edward."

Jack's smile froze on his face and an astonished look replaced it. "THE Edward Bok?" he replied.

"Oh, have you heard of me before?"

"Of course, Mr. Bok! It's a great pleasure to have you in my office. I've read your autobiography. Your story of immigrating almost penniless to the US, becoming a writer and a magazine editor..."

"The Ladies Home Journal," Bok interjected, "for thirty years, which was quite long enough for a man to be devoted to a single task in a short lifetime."

"Oh, I understand completely," Jack said. "In fact, it seems that I have already spent too many years building bridges and have now chosen to concentrate on houses and office structures."

"A decision I can fully appreciate."

"By the way, Mr. Bok, I am also familiar with you through my sister. Your magazine purchased some of her stories."

"Indeed? And if her last name is Crews, as is yours," he paused briefly as Jack nodded, "then her first name would be Amanda."

"That's right! I'm amazed that you would remember her!"

"A talented young writer and destined to tell much of Florida's tale, I would guess. I'm disappointed I've never had the opportunity to meet her. Perhaps that is a situation you could help me remedy."

"I'm sure she would jump at the chance," Jack said, but added, "well, perhaps she wouldn't jump at the moment," he grinned, "for she'll soon be a mother."

"Well, that is delightful news!" Bok replied. "Please send her my kindest regards and tell her that I shall look forward to meeting her and her newest blessing."

"I shall!" Jack replied before remembering his manners. "Forgive me, Mr. Bok! Please take a seat and tell me how I may be of service to you."

Bok settled himself into the wooden straight-backed chair and began to explain his need.

"I have a home, recently constructed at Mountain Lake, and have purchased the top of the highest hill there, called Iron Mountain," he began.

"Yes, only two miles from where we sit, isn't it?"

"That's correct. I have retained the firm of Frederick Law Olmsted, Jr., who landscaped Mountain Lake and my home, to design a park or sanctuary there. This country has done much for me, you see, and I would like to return the favor, by giving something of myself and my native land to it. I conceived of this project during my walks on the hill. It was intended to become more homesites and a citrus grove, but I find it much to attractive a site for such mundane uses."

"The Olmsted firm is an excellent choice. His work with the McMillan Commission is legendary. The White House grounds, the Vanderbilt estate in Asheville, so many famous parks…"

"I see that you are very familiar with his work. I could not have thought to select another. I'm glad that you know of him."

"I have met him once, when I was a child. My father was a friend of his father and traveled to his funeral a few years ago."

"I'm pleased to hear that. His father was a man of rare brilliance, capable of doing most anything he set his mind to," he said. "Except farming," he added with a grin. "His son learned the trade from him and has his good instincts. He has assigned his assistant, Mr. William Lyman Phillips, to supervise the work."

"Then how could I possibly be of assistance to you?" Jack asked.

"We realized that our sanctuary needs a focal point and his suggestion of a statue of me is out of the question. I believe we need a large monument. I have begun to contact architects and engineers for my project," he continued, "to find who might be willing to labor in harness, so to speak. I know that you have done so before, working with other engineers on your bridges."

"I have and would do so again for the right goal."

"I'm delighted to hear it. At any rate, I have decided to build a monument for the park. Not an ordinary monument, you see, but a "singing tower," a carillon.

"Oh, like the campanili in Italy?"

"Similar, but with a vast range of bells. They will carry three or four octaves, such as one might find in my native country of Holland. I envision a tower of perhaps one hundred feet of height. As you can well imagine, I have just begun to think about selecting a master architect. However, I would like to employ such local services as I may, and I would be most pleased to be able to recommend you."

"Thank you, Mr. Bok. I am honored to be considered. I will look forward to hearing from whomever you select."

Jack smiled to himself as his visitor left, hoping that he had at last found his dream project, something that would stand for a long, long time.

Two weeks after Mr. Bok's visit, he had the opportunity to tour the grounds of the developing sanctuary and take in the magnificent views it offered of the surrounding lower countryside. He walked about the gardens with Olmsted and Phillips as they discussed Olmsted's concepts of blending space and form. "It's about preserving the long views as much as the wooded areas. Each place needs a purpose," Olmsted told him.

•

On the fourth day of July 1925, Kate bore a son, whom they named Anthony. "It's a strong name," Kate told him, and Jack smiled, knowing his father would be pleased.

A week later, Jack was summoned to a meeting in Philadelphia, where he met Milton B. Medary, the renowned architect Bok had chosen to lead the design work for his tower. Jack was delighted to be given an opportunity to work on a dramatic project, though only as it began to unfold did the scale of the undertaking become plain to him. Assembled at that meeting were some of the great architectural talents of the day, including Samuel Yellin and J. H. Dulles Allen. Together with John Taylor of the bell founders and William Gorham Rice, who was an authority on carillons, they talked of their ideas for the project.

Jack was amazed when he began to understand the scope, scale and level of artistry which would be required. No mere church-steeple, as he had imagined, but a magnificent structure, designed to rival the awe-inspiring beauty of entire cathedrals, would rise upon the top of Iron Mountain. Quickly Jack attempted to dispel his preconceptions and embrace the grandeur of what they would build.

The long train ride from Philadelphia to Lake Wales brought him near to St. Augustine, so with the permission of Kate, who had the assistance of an around-the-clock nurse, Jack changed trains in Jacksonville and detoured to see his sister. He arrived in St. Augustine in time to catch a taxi into town and gawked like any tourist as they drove past the great hotels and the historic old houses and shops of the ancient Spanish town.

His timing was nearly perfect, for only hours before his arrival, Amanda had delivered a beautiful baby girl, whom they had already named Katrina. Martin stood proudly holding the peaceful, dark-haired newborn, while Amanda beamed from her bed, as proud as he had ever seen her.

"Katrina's a pretty name," Jack said, as he touched his niece's tiny fingers, which clutched his own reflexively.

"It has a special meaning, you know," Amanda said.

"I think I remember what that might be," Jack said. "Our grandmother, whom we never met, was named Katrina, after her aunt. Eastwind told us the story." Even as he recalled that night, long ago, nearly lost in his memory, he had a sudden realization.

"Hey, do you remember that time, when we were little children, and we went to visit our great-grandfather?"

"Of course, Jack. I'll never forget it."

"Do you remember where we went?"

"Not really. I remember it seemed a very long way from home. We rode a train and horses..."

"Do you remember the island and the big hill?"

"Sure! I remember that we stood on the hill and watched the sunset and it seemed we could see for a thousand miles and at night there were stars that filled the sky, like diamonds, they were so bright..." She suddenly had a faraway look on her face, as her mind's eye relived the experience of her childhood. "After everyone else was asleep, I woke in the middle of the night and looked at the stars. Suddenly, one of them fell across the sky and it left a beautiful trail of sparks. I was afraid, just for a second and then I realized that it was what Eastwind had told me about and so I closed my eyes and went back to sleep."

Jack looked at his sister curiously. "What did Eastwind tell you?"

"I can't say, really. I can't remember his exact words, only a special sense of wonder, of never being afraid again of what might happen to me, because my children would do amazing things. As I grew older and met Martin…" She paused to smile at her husband, who tenderly cradled her newborn. "I realized that I felt the same about my future children and grandchildren. I knew that they would all find something special in life, for they would be special, too. And now I can finally look at her face and see she is special. She's a promise for the future, better than we can see today. She'll do great things."

Jack looked at his sister with a new appreciation, for there were deep currents beneath the still waters of her words.

•

Home at last in Lake Wales, Jack spent what time he could with Kate and Anthony, while he began the first work of testing the soil that would support the great tower. He watched as the leaders of the design team walked the site, taking careful measurements and expanding upon their earlier ideas.

Anthony grew strong and healthy, and Jack loved to take him in his arms and show him the world, walking around his own small yard and later, around the shores of the little Crystal Lake, while the child gaped at the trees, the water and the birds. Anthony and Marie began to make the train trip from Tampa to visit at least once a month, while often traveling to St. Augustine as well. That Christmas, as had been the tradition each year of his life, Jack's family was united again at the big house on Bayshore Boulevard in Tampa and the holiday seemed brighter than any he could remember.

"We've got something we wanted to tell you," Anthony said in an offhand way as the group relaxed before the fireplace after a big Christmas meal.

Jack immediately looked up from a piece of pumpkin pie, which he was trying to tempt Anthony into tasting. "What is it, Dad," he asked, a bit apprehensively. He had come to understand his father's warning signs too well, he thought.

"Your mother and I have been talking and we've decided to sell the house," he announced. "I just thought you might like to know, before our last Christmas here is over."

"But why, Dad?" Amanda immediately began, but Jack already knew the answer. The house was large, far bigger than they needed. It was a house for children and the birth of Anthony and Katrina had only driven the point home to them. The children now would live in other places, have other lives.

"We just think it best, Amanda," Marie replied. "It's just a surprise now, but you'll get used to it. Besides, we'll be much closer to you. We've decided to move to Winter Park. It's almost halfway between Lake Wales and St. Augustine. There's nothing to keep us in Tampa now, since your father's business is sold. Winter Park is a lovely town."

"You're right, Mom, you don't need to be here," Jack said at last. "Wherever you two are will be home to me. I don't care that much about the house, especially."

The next morning Jack stood for a long time in his room on the second floor after the bags had been safely packed in the car and tried to absorb the details of the room, the smells, the way the light warmed it in the morning. He knew that the house was a part of him and that, in a way, he would never leave it behind.

Time seemed to fly for Jack after that. Kate was a natural mother and spent her time catering to Anthony's every cry. "You're going to spoil that child, Katie and if you do, I'll never forgive you," Jack said, but Kate just smiled.

"If I'm going to raise him, he's mine to spoil, Jack Crews and I'll deal with the consequences."

Jack's pride in parenthood couldn't detract from his pride in having been selected to work on the team building the tower. He worked under the direction of engineers William Gravell and I. H. Francis and was soon humbled to realize that his knowledge of engineering paled before their lights. He watched as they established the parameters of the design: supporting a total of fifty-one bells, ranging in size from the gigantic "bourdon" bell, which would weigh twenty-three thousand four hundred pounds, down to the smallest, at only seventeen pounds. All told, they would span four octaves. The Taylor foundry in Loughborough, England, would cast the bells and duplicate each of the smallest thirteen, so that two bells would be rung together. That would give them more resonance and eliminate the otherwise tinny sound they would produce.

When ranged upon their supports, the bells would require a space thirty-five feet in diameter, fifty feet from top to bottom. The lowest bells, it was decided, could be no lower than one hundred fifty feet above the ground. The tower would be an impressive structure, indeed.

The engineers carefully calculated the wind resistance needed to withstand the inevitable major hurricanes before determining the size and depth of the foundations, based in part on Jack's work at the site. Then, as the various calculations were placed on paper, the form of the structure began to emerge before their eyes.

To the engineering drawing, Medary applied the architects' greatest skills, and gradually a graceful, tapered design was formed upon paper, which changed from a modified square with recessed corners to a delicate octagon two-thirds of the way to the top. Tall Gothic arches would contain open grills adorned with mosaics, which would allow the sound to emerge from the tower. "It's beautiful already," Jack said when he first beheld the grace with which the structure took shape on the page.

"Form follows function, as you know, Jack, yet the form may always be modified beyond its requirements, in order to please the eye," Medary told him.

Jack was especially impressed to see the work of Lee Lawrie, the sculptor chosen to ornament the tower. His elegant designs reflected the nature of Florida and included dozens of kinds of birds, delicate, detailed plant life and sculpted bands of friezes, finials, and cresting, all carved from Georgia marble. In Jack's mind, he was participating in the building of some ancient monument, a kingly castle perhaps, or a Taj Mahal. The tower, he realized, no matter what he may do with the rest of his life's work, would be his crowning achievement. It was not only the building of which he had dreamed, it was a work of art on a massive scale.

Jack's work proceeded against the backdrop of a tremendous land boom. The population of Lake Wales, only about seven-hundred and fifty in 1920, had grown five-fold in five years, with thousands more in the surrounding communities. Hundreds more were arriving each month. Across the state, the situation was much the same, as tens of thousands of people poured into Florida, driving land prices to ever higher levels in a wave of speculation. People who had made great profits on earlier purchases bought even more, using land as collateral, or buying on the margin. It was a dream come true for Florida's developers.

In Lake Wales, the experience of boom-town Florida inspired local businessmen to greater efforts as well. In three short years, the commercial section tripled in size and houses sprang up by the hundreds in the new neighborhoods. "This town needs a first-class hotel," they agreed at the Board of Trade. Since no powerful railroad magnate was there to build one, they determined to do it themselves. They formed a corporation and began promoting the idea. In a few short months, bonds were sold, and construction began on an eleven-story hotel which they dubbed the 'Walesbilt.'

The same bubbling optimism was running through the veins of Florida's business leaders and speculators alike. The new American architectural concept of a "sky-scraper" was a symbol of that enthusiasm. In booming Jacksonville no less than nine new towers were begun in a single year, changing forever the skyline of the once-sleepy port town. In Tampa, St. Petersburg, Miami and dozens of smaller towns across the state, similar projects sprang from the ground like so many sprouts.

The Walesbilt soon dominated the compact downtown area, a monument to the high aspirations of the city and the state. By the time the structure was nearing completion late in 1926, Edward Bok's new tower on Iron Mountain was beginning to take shape, a giant framework of metal on the horizon, pointing toward the Florida sky.

December 1926

"It really is going to be magnificent. I can hardly wait until you can come see it. I can give you a tour of the work and you can imagine what it will be like. Riding the work elevator to the top is so spectacular, you can literally see for forty or fifty miles on a clear day, maybe more. One really clear evening, we could see the sun reflecting in the water of the Gulf of Mexico, like a second sun."

"It sounds wonderful, Jack. I am so glad you are finally getting to work on the type of project you've always wanted," Marie said, rocking slowly as Anthony slept soundly in her lap and Katrina napped in a crib next to her. It was a beautiful Christmas season, she thought, and the family was together, just as they had been in the house on Bayshore.

"We'd love to go see it sometime, Jack, wouldn't we, Amanda?" Martin said.

"You bet! I think what we'll do is fly down that way when I get a break, maybe at Easter this year. Do you think you could meet us with your car?"

"Sure, Amanda. Just let me know and I'll be there! If I can't make it to meet you, I'm sure that Katie could, right, Katie?"

"Oh, sure! It'll give me a chance to drive the Buick. Jack never lets me behind the wheel!"

"Jack!" Amanda scolded him, "is this true? I thought you were an open-minded man."

"I am and she does. Drive the car, that is. In fact, if she drives it any more, I'll have to get her one of her own."

"Now there's an idea!" Kate piped in. "Maybe a new Cadillac, like the one we saw last week! Or that fancy Lincoln."

"See what I mean, Martin? She's just as difficult as Amanda," Jack said with a grin.

"Jack, you better watch out, or you'll regret saying those things!" Kate said, smacking him with a pillow.

"I've still got you topped, Jack," Martin said. "Try buying her an airplane."

"Yeah, tell me about this plane," Jack responded. "Do you really own it?"

"Well, not really," Amanda said. "I am making the payments, though. I use it at the institute to teach the students, so it really pays for itself, if I count my wages as an instructor."

"So, the Embry-Riddle institute really is attracting students?" Jack asked her.

"Yes, it really is," she replied. "Are you surprised? Everyone says that the demand for pilots is going to grow fast, now that the Ford Tri-motor is becoming so popular. People who wouldn't have dreamed of flying are doing it, because the planes are so safe."

"Well, I'm still not convinced," Marie told her. "I wish you had found some other type of work."

"Oh, Mom, you really shouldn't worry. Nothing bad is going to happen to me."

"Every time I think of you, I worry just a bit," Marie said. "When we heard about the hurricane in Miami in September, we thought of you and the storm you went through in the Keys. And every time I hear about an airplane having an accident, I think of you."

Anthony smiled at the debate, relaxing in his easy chair in the corner. "How do you get to work from St. Augustine, all the way to Daytona Beach?" he asked Amanda. "Isn't that a long drive?"

"I only teach three days a week, Dad and I fly back and forth. It only takes half an hour. Anyway, we hadn't told you yet, but," she glanced at Martin, who smiled and nodded, "we're going to be moving to Daytona anyway, so we'll be a lot closer to you and Mom. I'm going to miss St. Augustine, but it will really be better. Martin is going to be opening a new pharmacy there."

"Oh, Martin, that's wonderful news!" Marie said. "When will this happen?"

"I complete my training as a pharmacist in March. I think we'll be opening about the beginning of June."

"That's great! I know you two will miss having your family so close, though."

"Yeah, but we'll see them often enough to stay in touch."

"What about St. Augustine. I thought you both loved it there?"

"St. Augustine is really pretty, Mom, but I'm afraid it's going to be ruined. There was a Mr. Davis who came there last year and was going to fill in part of the river, just to make room for more houses. People there loved him and said it would be great, but I would rather have the river, myself. It never happened though. He was going broke, I guess. He died last summer on a ship to Europe. They said he fell overboard."

"Hey, everybody," Jack called from across the room, "it's almost time for that radio show you wanted to hear. Do you remember where to tune to get it, Dad?"

The following day, Jack drove the Buick so Kate and Martin could take in the sights in Winter Park. The kids were safely ensconced in the care of their grandmother, giving the young couples a chance to relax for a few hours. It was Christmas Eve, a Friday morning, as they cruised down the thriving main street of the town, flanked by smart shops on one side and a broad stretch of park on the other. A small choir sang Christmas carols for a gathered crowd, while shoppers rushed to purchase their last gifts before the shops began to close.

"This is a pretty place," Amanda pointed out. "I'm glad Mom and Dad chose to move here. Hey, Jack, why don't you park, so we can explore some of those stores."

A few minutes later, as they wandered through bright shops, Jack pulled his sister aside. "Amanda, I've been wanting to ask you something, but I haven't had a chance until now."

"What is it, Jack?"

"Have Mom or Dad said anything to you about their financial situation?"

"No, I've always assumed everything is fine. After all, Dad was very successful in business."

"Well, it's probably nothing, but I remember Dad had once told me that he had put most of his money in railroad stocks. I know they had a pretty sharp sell-off last year. I just don't know if he got hurt."

"Well, I guess no news is good news, huh?"

"I hope so, kid. I really hope so."

The Cypress Knee
March 1925

"THERE IS IT, SIR. I knew when I saw it that I should let you know before I did anything. It's a whole lot of lumber!"

The voice that carried through the dense stand of forest came from the foreman of a crew that was cutting down and "hauling out" thousands of big cypress trees. His muscular arm was still extended upwards, finger pointing through the thin canopy of pale sprouting cypress "needles" and festoons of Spanish moss.

The Overstreet Land Company had made a good deal of money tapping sap for turpentine from thousands of longleaf pines on the higher part of the land just outside the newly incorporated town of Longwood. Now the Cypresses were being addressed.

The cypress trees generally stood in marshy ground and often in a couple of feet of water. When the foreman had done his job, most of the trees then visible would be sliced into tens of thousands of board feet of sturdy cypress planks and posts, which for generations had been the most popular, or at least most widely-used, building material in the entire state. It was a useful harvest.

The man to whom the words were spoken were none other than Moses O. Overstreet, a Florida state senator and owner of the company. He leaned back, gazed upwards at the branches which seemed to conceal the true top. He turned and stepped away from the tree again, raising his arm to measure the tree against a walking stick he was carrying. Then he turned his wrist, marking with his eye the same distance on the ground. In a minute he had paced and calculated the height.

"A hundred ninety feet, at least," Overstreet said. "Probably a good bit more. But I'm glad you didn't cut it, 'cause it's probably hollow anyway. Most of 'em are long before they get anywhere near that size. I have to say that I've never seen its equal anywhere."

He turned again and found a pathway around the massive cypress, quickly finding the typical opening into the dark interior. He peered inside but saw nothing but weathered heartwood and a thick layer of decaying detritus, leaves and moss probably deposited by the wind. He turned back to his foreman. "Tell the boys if they spot any other giants, don't cut 'em until I approve it."

As the foreman went back to his job, Overstreet turned and walked back toward his late-model roadster, pondering what should be done with the discovery. Somehow, he knew, this tree had some potential.

June 1927

Jack sat before his tilted drafting board, the tools of his trade surrounding the broad sheet of drafting paper upon which he worked. Slide rule, straight-edge, compass, triangle, each was as familiar to him as his own fingers. Those tools had given him a successful career and his tangible work was all around him. The state had grown and grown mightily. The scale and scope of Florida's real estate boom of the 1920's was difficult to grasp.

In the first five years of the decade, his small town of Lake Wales had grown from a tiny village of a few hundred to more than five thousand. Yet it was only a reflection of what had happened elsewhere. In December 1924, twenty thousand people poured across the border into Florida each week, many lured by the legislature's new constitutional amendment prohibiting state inheritance and income taxes.

In Miami, taxable property values had swelled by 560 percent in five years. During that time, paved road mileage in the city had increased from thirty-two miles to four hundred twenty, while the city's jobs payroll grew 2,499 percent. Miami had been pinched by its own success in 1925, when the Florida East Coast Railroad had declared an embargo on shipments of building supplies to south Florida because its railroad cars were being used as warehouses, instead of being returned to the system.

Then, in 1926, a disastrous hurricane had again slowed the boom. In addition to major damage in Miami, the storm had caused an even bigger disaster at Moore Haven, where the Lake Okeechobee dike failed, loosing a tidal wave that drowned three hundred. More than six thousand were injured in the storm.

Now, Jack thought, the effects of what had happened in Miami seemed to be spreading. He was grateful to have employment working on the great "Singing Tower," but already he could see that his duties were coming to an end. Soon he would have to find other work. It was time to get busy.

The Rusted Nail
September 1928

SAM LEWIS SCANNED THE GLOOMY MORNING SKY as he ate his simple daily breakfast. Eggs were plentiful, thanks to the yard full of chickens outside his simple frame home. Corn ground into grits could be purchased cheaply enough at the local store and had a way of sticking to his skinny ribs. He was grateful for the meal, for times were often hard for the elderly sharecropper and the three generations of descendants that shared his two-room home. He had built it with the help of his two sons from rough-sawn cypress. Huge logs cut from cypress domes in the surrounding Everglades had provided the material for every building in their village of Chosen.

Sam glanced back outside through the open door and had a good view of water. The house sat beside an overflowing canal and most of what passed for a yard was also submerged. The chickens had only a small patch of dry ground around their hen house.

As he savored the last morsels of his meal, he turned his eyes to the surrounding fields, source of the vegetables that provided the family's meager cash income. Those crops would soon be loaded onto trains to be shipped to northern markets or trucked to the growing markets in Palm Beach or Miami.

Sam presided over a household of nine souls, including daughters-in-law, grandchildren and his first great-grandchild. It was to the little ones that he felt devoted. Sam spent many days with the children, telling them stories and teaching them to read, for there was no school nearby and the family owned only a small skiff for fishing. Too small to ferry the children to school, they used it to pole over the waters of the Big Lake, or drift down canals draining from the weirs in the dike, in search of catfish, bream and bluegill, or even an occasional big mouth bass.

Everywhere there was water, Sam thought. It was Water to him. At eighty-two years of age, he thought of it with a capital letter, because Water had seemed to represent everything good and bad in Sam's life. His oldest son had drowned on a fishing trip, three years earlier, but it was Water that had provided for his family's escape from danger when they had fled a mob, years before, and Water that brought the abundant life forth from the rich muck soils of the Everglades. Those soils, lying as much as twenty feet deep atop the ancient limestone, had been laid down by Water in the past and were replenished every year in the floods that swept down the Kissimmee River into the Big Lake, Okeechobee. Water was life, Sam thought.

The road outside Sam's cabin was "improved," meaning that, as a "secondary" road connecting to what passed as a "highway" nearby, the state had dumped and graded out enough canal spoils to elevate it above the flood. Although it was usable most of the year, today its muddy, puddled surface was barely fit for walking, but it was Sunday and time to take the children to church.

Sam's life had not been easy. For twenty years following the end of the Civil War, he had made a good living on the farm in north Florida before the death of their former owner and benefactor, Rebecca Lewis. Sam's father Willie had been granted the land legally but found it impossible to obtain a deed from the county. When his parents had died, Sam and his family had been besieged by both the terror of the Ku Klux Klan and a series of repressive laws passed by former Confederates who controlled Florida's government.

Sam had seen mobs of men on horseback and heard the tales of lynching of blacks accused of infractions. He had seen the burned crosses, remains of the fiery warnings meant to terrorize blacks into submission. He had heard that his elected representatives were blocking laws to stop the lynchings. The world seemed stacked against them.

At length Willie decided to gather the rest of his clan and flee. They had moved first to Freedtown, an all-black community not far from the site of the Dade Massacre north of Tampa. There they farmed the rich soil and became part of a prosperous community with the assistance of sympathetic white neighbors. While his wife and children remained at Freedtown, Sam sometimes found "cash work" on the railroads, living near Gainesville for years to help support the family by sending money home.

In 1894, the series of big freezes put an end to the farming operations at Freedtown and the community was abandoned. Most of the freedmen moved into nearby Dade City, but there was little work for them, and hostile whites often threatened violence. Eventually Sam and his family had retreated to the shores of Lake Okeechobee, or what the locals called the "Big Lake." Here, in a community of other former slave families, their presence was welcome and the big companies that owned the land had plenty of work to be done.

Driven from the land he had once owned, Sam realized that he lived day-to-day much as his slave ancestors had. It pained him, but it seemed that the chance of the family owning land again was slim.

Florida's great land boom had followed the arrival of the railroads, and huge jumps in population had fueled speculation that had inflated the cost of housing and land in leaps that defied imagination. Prices, even for the muck lands, had risen again and besides, the big farms weren't selling any land. Most had been carved from federal and state land grants years before and were held by big companies that shipped their crops northward on the trains.

Brokers bought property for a dollar an acre in the coastal communities, then re-sold it for double in days. Some properties changed hands several times in a week, each time doubling in price. It was a frenzy that was unprecedented, and the wealth of northern cities was being invested in the blooming promise of the newly-civilized tropical paradise.

South of the Big Lake, the new "Tamiami Trail" highway now bisected the Everglades and linked Tampa and Miami. It also provided access to the once-remote village of Naples. Built in part by an advertising mogul named Barron Collier after the state ran short of funds, he had financed it in exchange for a pledge to create the new "Collier County," and he was reaping the benefits. His advertising touted the health advantages of the sunny southern climate and the gleaming modern cities that seemed to sprout like weeds. The nation was enchanted by the Florida miracle.

For Sam and his family, though, the boom had brought little change to their lives. They remained, as always, tied to the land from which they scraped their living. For them, the weather was the more pressing concern. Months of almost unceasing rain had already fallen and today the sky promised more. For the few crops sprouting from the fields for the expected winter harvest, more rain was not welcome. Most fields were now too wet to plant and would have to wait until dryer fall weather, hopefully only weeks away.

Sam glanced repeatedly at the sky as he strolled with his family down the narrow dirt lane toward the African Methodist Episcopal Church, walking in the lightest of drizzles. His seventy-two years had slowed his gait and his great-grandson Jimmie pulled on his fingers to hurry him along. Sam knew that Jimmie was used to the cajoling of his two older sisters, who alternately smothered and ignored him. "Now, don't you be in too big a hurry, child. The good Lord will wait a minute for an ol' man like me," Sam said, smiling at the boy. Then, turning, he glanced over his shoulder to the road behind, where his granddaughter Elizabeth followed, holding his new great-granddaughter, and keeping an eye on Sarah and Pearl, already five and seven. His younger sister, Mary, held their hands, trying to keep them from soiling their best clothes, using a steady barrage of scolding and instructions. Sam smiled to himself but felt a paternal worry.

"Somethin's not right about this day, Mary. I can feel it in my bones," Sam called and stopped walking, to let the rest catch up.

"What 'you saying now, Sam? You don't feel good?" Mary asked him, keeping her eyes on the young ones.

"No, I feel fine. I jus' got a funny feeling, that's all. It's too cool for September and the sky looks funny," Sam said, poking his cane into the deep brown soil of the road for balance as he looked up. The shallow ditches at each side were filled to overflowing with murky rainwater, which lay listlessly, in no hurry to flow away into the surrounding Everglades.

A few blocks away, water also lapped high on the far side of the muddy dike that marked the edge of Lake Okeechobee. The dike had allowed farming to claim the rich, peaty soil. Now, at the end of summer, the pancake-flat, four-thousand square miles of surrounding countryside was also filled with water, all of it slowly, ever so slowly, trickling into the larger canals intended to drain the marshes. As the summer monsoon rains came to a climax, the level of the lake behind the dike was higher than the land by more than two feet. It would take months of drier winter weather for the water levels to drop and still some would remain to irrigate the spring planting.

Mary paused beside the old man, his wizened figure stooped from a lifetime of hard work. She looked at him closely, then turned her attention to the sky. "It do seem a bit strange, like God put a lid on it. I can't hardly see the sun," she observed, pointing. "Just sorta' dim, there."

"Well, if I had to guess, I'd say somebody's gonna' get a hurricane," Sam said. "Maybe the preacher knows somethin' about it."

Morning services were a joyous time for the families who worked the sugarcane and vegetable fields. The church was filled with workers, enjoying the social highpoint of their week, when work was set aside and family, friends, song, praise, and a church meal were the order of the day. Many in the congregation were Bahamian, come to help cut the sugar cane. They spent only a few months in the community of Chosen each year for the cane harvest before returning to the islands. Sam Lewis, though, knew many of them by name, calling greetings at the door of the church.

Sam wasn't the only one who had noticed the strange sky that morning, and one congregant shared news he had overheard on a radio while in Palm Beach on Saturday that a big storm was moving through the Bahama Islands. He had also brought back a newspaper that carried notice of the devastation of Puerto Rico on September 13.

Talk of a hurricane made many nervous. Only two years had passed since the "Great Miami Hurricane" had swept near the big lake on its route north, devastating that city, killing hundreds, and tarnishing the state's reputation as a tropical paradise. Although it had passed the southern side of the lake, it had burst the dike at Moore Haven and the town was flooded out.

"I have heard about this storm, children," the traveling preacher told the gathering at the start of the service. "The weatherman in Palm Beach says it's going to pass us by over the ocean. But I want to make sure you all get home 'fore we get rained upon again, praise the Lord."

"Amen," the congregation answered, thankfully.

A steady rain was falling from a leaden sky as they made their way home after the service and the wind came in fitful bursts. Everyone pitched in to get ready for the storm, rounding up the chickens and putting hoes and shovels under the floor of the house. They brought out the solid shutters that fit over the openings that passed for windows, tying them to the post and beam frame of the house.

Drying the children's Sunday clothing before a slow fire kept Mary busy for the next hour as Sam sat on the porch of the home, within sight of the low dike at the big lake. Dark tiers of clouds scudded rapidly past, and the wind rose to a witchy moan as it swept through the trees. Sam could hear the big gusts coming and then sweep over the house, which responded with creaking. The gusts were getting stronger.

"Mary," Sam said to his sister, finally seated in her favorite rocker nearby, "do you 'member when we was hiding from those soldiers during the war, back up to Baldwin?"

"Sure, I do, Sam. You kept tellin' Mama not to worry, 'cause you was gonna' take care a' her, if you had to fight the whole army," she answered.

"Well, this time, Ma, I'm not sure I can do it. We're fixin' to have us a hurricane, real bad." Mary looked at her brother and nodded. He had never been wrong about such things, as far as she could remember. "That ol' dike ain't likely to hold back that lake too long and if it busts nearby, there ain't no other high ground around here," Sam continued. "We needs to be ready to move these chil'rens, but I don't know where we can go. All we has is one boat, but it might hold them up."

"If'n you say so, Sam, tha's what we'll do, when the time comes."

•

Lake Okeechobee was an inland sea, the vast, shallow basin that caught the waters of almost a third of the peninsula. The efforts of Disston's dredges had done little to lower the lake's level. It had once spilled its liquid bounty into the Everglades in a "sheet flow" of water, a river that ran a foot or two deep and eighty miles wide. Now the waters were held back by a low dike of muck and mud dredged from the lake bottom, allowing it to pour forth through a series of canals.

The Everglades, only slightly lower than the Big Lake, pushed against the coastal dunes to the east, where it had once spilled over low falls to form the Miami River. To the south and west, it reached the sea through thousands of bayous, mixing gradually with the waters of the Gulf of Mexico to form a gigantic nursery for both birds and fish.

The ring of towns and villages along the south shore had grown up dependent on the Big Lake. All were agricultural towns, serving the vast ring of freshly-plowed muck lands of the northern Everglades. Submerged for a thousand centuries, they were arable only because the dike and canals kept them slightly above the water table. Hurricanes were a constant threat.

Few in Florida were aware that the approaching storm was not an ordinary hurricane. It was a monster, a storm that had crossed the entire Atlantic Ocean from the Cape Verde Islands before it struck Puerto Rico. The U.S. Weather Service issued warnings based upon wireless communications with operators across the Caribbean, as well as ships at sea. This time there was a sense of urgency in the warnings, due to the intensity of the storm.

The devastation in the Antilles had been remarkable, especially on Guadeloupe, where twelve hundred had been killed. When it hit Puerto Rico a day later, it left hundreds of thousands homeless and "at least three hundred" more dead. At landfall in Palm Beach County, winds approaching 175 miles per hour would rank it as one of the ten most powerful ever recorded to strike the United States. Yet there was no way to measure a storm, so a hurricane was a hurricane in the minds of most.

Across South Florida people took note of the change in the weather. Thousands took shelter in churches, schoolhouses, and solidly-built homes. Along the shore of Okeechobee, few took the threat lightly. Most sought the protection of substantial buildings. A steel barge, brought in loaded with equipment to dredge canals and build a roadbed for the new State Road 80 along the south end of the lake, was anchored to the mouth of the canal by four two-inch-thick steel cables. More than two hundred white citizens sought shelter in its dark and cavernous interior. For other whites and the poor blacks and farm workers from the Bahamas, Jamaica and elsewhere, the only shelters were their crudely framed wooden houses, or the churches.

By that evening the storm had smashed ashore at Palm Beach and the wind at Chosen had already risen to a gale. Rain came in great driving slashes, drops moving so fast they stung bare skin like stones. The Lewis family huddled in their two-room shelter, only the feeble light of a kerosene lantern holding the darkness at bay. Sam's great-grandson, Otis, barely sixteen, had sneaked out to check the dike, feeling his way partly on hands and knees through the gloom. After only a few minutes he ran breathlessly into the house. The tiny structure creaked and groaned as the wind mounted outside

"The lake's all white, big waves, Grandpa!" he reported, drenched and dripping muddy water. "They're splashing over the top of the dike! That water come up even as I sat there for a minute," Otis reported. Already lapping over the threshold of the front door, it soon began to fill the room, rising an inch every five minutes or so. Sam pushed the table against the interior wall and put the smaller children on it.

Outside, the storm seemed to redouble in fury, the wind rising to a shriek, seeming to pause a moment before rising still higher. The family was huddled in the lee side of the house an hour later as the wind rose to a deafening crescendo. The house groaned and rocked like a thing alive, testing the strength of the solid cypress timbers that formed its frame.

Without warning, the planks of the house suddenly burst open, and a wall of water crashed through, throwing Sam and Mary against the back wall, which collapsed in turn, followed by the roof. Sam gasped in a lungful of air as the roof and walls became a dark tangle, converted in an instant from a shelter to a trap sprung upon them.

Sam struggled to rise and felt a sharp edge slash his shoulder before being pushed under again. His lungs ached as he strained, attempting to push the wall upright, lift the building from upon his family, yet the weight of tons of water fought with him. He felt along the flat surface amid the surging water and was suddenly thrust through a window opening. His head popped above the surface, and he called out. He received no response but the shriek of the wind that tore his breath from his lips.

Frantically Sam tried to find footing in the crashing flood but was being swept rapidly southward. Around him large pieces of his home spun in the flood, and he struggled to avoid being crushed between them. He groped frantically in the waters, cutting his hands and arms, calling the names of the children, but could find no trace of them. The rain stung like stones against his face as he struggled, weeping for his family.

Still instinctively working to survive, Sam clung to a slab of wall that swirled in the powerful current until it smashed into a cypress tree, slinging him away like a rodeo bull. The current tugged and pushed him like a thing alive, pinning him to another tree. Sam managed to grasp a limb, his feet swept behind him and heaved mightily to pull himself from the torrent. His frail muscles no longer had the strength to swing a sledgehammer, but they gave him a chance to live as he hoisted himself, shivering to the lee side of the tree, praying that it would stand against the onslaught.

Just as he feared his strength would fail, the wind suddenly abated. In minutes the raging howl faded into the distance and an unearthly calm descended upon the scene. A few stars appeared in the sky overhead, but the new moon had already disappeared. Sam peered into the darkness and called out for his family. Listening for a response, he heard a distant wailing, a mournful sobbing, and a call for help from deep in the sawgrass marsh. Others were still alive, but he had no way of reaching them.

Then, across the vast, flat landscape, Sam heard the roar of gusting winds and the storm's eye-wall drew swiftly onward. In a rush it was over him and the winds roared with incredible force, even stronger than before, but from the opposite direction. The tree he clung to creaked and the top suddenly fell, tearing free with a terrible cracking groan. Sam strained to hold onto his only hope.

For another hour he tried to hide his head between his arms but was slowly fading in strength, and at last his feet slipped from their perch and he fell into the dark churning water. Surprised to find that his feet touched bottom, he realized that the water level was dropping. Even as he struggled to force his way behind a stump, it fell further and was soon only waist deep. Although he could not know it, the powerful surge of wind-driven water was abandoning the south end of the lake, only to repeat the floods in the low-lying north end of the Big Lake.

All through the night the winds raged until, shortly before dawn, they began to abate. When a pale dawn appeared through the deep layers of clouds, it provided Sam more than enough light to see the horrors that surrounded him.

The flood waters still covered everything but a few battered cypress trees, but upon the surface a mass of debris piled in huge drifts against them. Jagged broken lumber, tree limbs and sheet metal heaped ten feet high in places. The landscape was a tangle of fallen trees, flattened cane, dead livestock, and scrap wood from every imaginable sort of building. Bodies could be seen floating in the flood waters.

Sam waded in hip-deep water, reversing the direction he had blown during the storm. Dazed with shock and bloody from his injuries, he looked in vain for his family, his home, his street. Everything was covered with water. After an hour of searching, he realized that the dike, too, was gone. His former home and town were now part of the Big Lake.

Two hours after sunrise, exhausted and hungry, Sam found a solid resting place in the form of a set of steps rising out of the water. He lay atop them, sobbing, but sitting up occasionally to call out the names of his missing family. It was almost noon before he heard a voice answering. It was Otis. He slogged his way through the flood and clambered up beside his great-grandfather and they hugged as tears streamed down his face. "Momma's gone," he told Sam. "I found her. I left her on a piece of roof down by where Jones's house was, up against a tree. I can't find the others. Maybe they'll come back here to the church."

Sam looked around, shocked to realize that the wooden steps they perched upon were all that remained of their church. His daughter was dead, the children were all missing and now, this. With a mighty effort he gathered his composure. Better to be strong for Otis, he thought. At least they had each other.

"When the water goes down, we'll give her a decent funeral, Otis. Now let's see if we can find anyone else."

Throughout that day, Sam and Otis wandered, hungry and thirsty, searching for survivors of the storm. By evening, a band of a dozen survivors had gathered at the site of the church and an informal morgue nearby, assembled on a slab of rooftop, held the remains of three dozen others. They had survived a tragedy of unimaginable magnitude. Most of the inhabitant of Chosen, and virtually every member of their church, had drowned in the flood.

Nearby, the barge full of white settlers was still afloat, but such had been the fury of the winds and waves that two of the steel cables that held it in place had parted. The remains of the schoolhouse and the churches were tattered posts and scraps, all that was left of Chosen. The scene was repeated in nearby South Bay, Pahokee, Bean City, and other farming settlements, all drowned in the catastrophic surge.

The second morning after the storm, a boat appeared, and a jug of water and a ham hock were passed to the group. More help was coming, they were promised. The state was sending trucks, but they were having trouble getting through because all the roads were flooded. It would be better to try to get down to Moore Haven, as that's where help could be found, they told them. Tramping through the slowly receding waters, the small group of survivors left their dead behind and began to head toward salvation.

It would be weeks before most of the victims would be recovered from the sawgrass and thickets of the Everglades, where they had been carried by the winds. There were bodies everywhere, and volunteers began the difficult task of collecting them. Three-fourths of the dead were seasonal workers from the Bahamas or other islands. As bodies were recovered, Sam and Otis took turns looking at the rows of former friends and neighbors, renewing their pain before they finally found Sarah and Pearl. Like more than two thousand others, their bodies were loaded onto trucks a week later to be taken to West Palm Beach, where they were buried in a mass grave. Others, unclaimed, were piled upon huge pyres and cremated.

Although they searched every available moment and asked everyone they knew, Sam and Otis could find no trace of the rest of their family. They mourned together for the lost children.

For generations to come, farmers plowing the rich soil of the northern Glades would occasionally find the bones of livestock, wild animals, and too often, those of the people of the farming towns, hardy pioneers who had been lost and were soon all but forgotten.

December 1928

The great Hurricane of 1928, coming so soon after the earlier storm, had a bad effect on Florida's real estate market. Prices became soft, and then began to drop. A few cautious bankers became worried about the many outstanding loans they had made on sketchy collateral. Some began to call the notes, forcing the borrowers to sell more land and other assets to try to satisfy their banks. The boom was coming to an end.

For Jack and his team, however, work had pressed forward on the great tower. Huge blocks of Georgia's pink marble and tan Florida coquina rock, the same used on the Castillo de San Marcos in St. Augustine, had been quarried and carved into thick walls and delicate ornamental details. Craftsmen from Europe and America had labored to complete the vast array of sculpture, engraving and wrought iron work.

Jack took several walking tours of the gardens with William Phillips as the two became good friends, watching the progress as moats were dug, creating a beautiful reflection pool. Enormous polished-brass doors were constructed to be placed at the entrance to the tower. At last, all was in readiness. Soon the guests would begin to arrive.

January 1929

The lush vegetation of North Florida filled the window of the luxury rail car, sliding past in a quickening blur. Calvin Coolidge turned his attention briefly across the aisle to where his wife rested comfortably on a settee, her nose buried in a book.

As President of the United States there had been many requirements for travel and even a pleasant winter vacation in Florida came with official duties attached. He re-read his notes of the remarks he would give at two very disparate dedications in the next two days. The events, although very different in nature, seemed somehow related. Both Florida landmarks he would visit were lofty and somehow represented ideals worth striving for. He struggled to encapsulate his thoughts in the fewest possible words and no one who would witness either event would expect more. It was not by accident that he had earned the moniker "Silent Cal," and he would do little to disprove it.

At last, the train slowed to a crawl, stopping at the bustling station of Sanford, where a band and a motorcade of vehicles awaited. After a brief drive the party arrived at a small park in Longwood, where the president would perform a brief dedication of a six-acre park, a gift to the town from State Senator Moses O. Overstreet. It would mark in perpetuity, he said, the home of the largest tree known to exist east of the Mississippi River. Forever after to be known as 'The Senator', to prior people it had long been known as the Father of the Forest.

•

The next day was the first of February. On that cool Friday morning President Calvin Coolidge gazed at the multitudes gathered upon the hilltop before Edward Bok's great tower. Roads for miles around were clogged with parked vehicles and throngs of people had walked for miles to reach the great landmark.

Jack sat with pride at the foot of the tower, next to the dais with many of his co-workers. The vast crowd of some 50,000 people had traveled from every corner of the state on a rough assortment of paved and clay roads. Others had come from across the nation to witness the moment. The entire extended Crews family and even Tony's uncle James, had joined them to share Jack's moment of triumph.

The tower dominated the landscape from its place on the crest of the hill, a soaring monument to the ideals of freedom, peace and beauty. Its dazzling pink marble and coquina were ornamented with representations of the spectacular environmental blessings of Florida, crowned by massive sculptures of the birds that symbolized the state in the minds of millions. At its base, an enormous door of polished brass bore representations of the story of creation. It was awe-inspiring and the tens of thousands of guests swirled around it in solemn reverence.

The official dedication was a memorable moment. Edward Bok solemnly addressed the crowd, sharing the story of his arrival as a penniless immigrant who spoke no English and how it was that America that had allowed him to flourish and contribute so much to society. The Mountain Lake Sanctuary and its Singing Tower was his gift in return. Forever a place of refuge and repose, it was a place where the cares of the world could be left behind, to allow the peace of nature to refill a soul left empty by the pressures of modern living. It was a token of thanks from a grateful man.

Bok also revealed the creation of a foundation that would maintain the tower and the Mountain Lake Sanctuary, keeping access free for all time. Then he repeated something his grandmother had said to him and her descendants many years before: "Make you the world a bit better or more beautiful because you have lived in it."

As Jack expected, when he finally took the podium, Coolidge was spare with words, but acknowledged that America was changed by modern conveniences and that citizens now had more time to enjoy such sancutaries. He recognized Bok as an exemplary American, remarked on the talents of the architects and builders and dedicated their great achievement as Edward William Bok's gift to the American people. It was a place for meditation and peace.

The visit from a sitting US president to the Sunshine State was an event not soon to be forgotten and Coolidge made the most of it as well. Coolidge and his wife were each invited to plant a commemorative palm tree near the reflection pool and toured the great tower with Bok as the gracious host. The group paused at the far end of the pool, where the calm waters reflected the inverted image of the tower as swans glided gracefully and flamingos waded in the foreground. The cameras of the press documented the moment for readers across the nation. The Singing Tower was a new landmark, a symbol of Florida that would draw visitors like a magnet.

•

The next day was a happy one for the Crews family, gathered in Jack and Kate's home in town. A large midday meal became a thanksgiving of sorts, filling the void of those they had not celebrated together as they had pursued their several lives.

"Anthony, stay out of that candy, you've already had enough," Kate called from the kitchen as she cleaned up after the feast. "Why don't you give that piece to Katrina? She's being so good."

"Here, Kate. I'll finish cleaning these things," Amanda said to her. "You should be taking it easy anyway since you're in a family way. Why don't you go referee and make sure they're not going to get into trouble."

"Thanks, Amanda, but I hate to leave you working in my kitchen..."

"Don't worry about it. We've almost got it finished now. Just get out of here and relax. You, too, Mom. Go ahead and spend some time with the kids. You don't see them often enough, anyway."

A few minutes later, as Amanda stacked the last of the big pots on the sideboard, Jack wandered into the kitchen. "It's great that you could come for this. I really did want to see you here before we finished up."

"I'm glad I could make it. Things have been really busy at the school and Martin's store takes most of his time. But we both love it, anyway."

"I'm glad to see you happy," Jack said and paused.

"There's something else you want to say?" Amanda said, more a statement than a question.

"No, it's really something I want to show you. Back at the tower. Do you think we could ride back up there for an hour or so?"

"Sure, Jack," she replied, a curious expression on her face. "I'm sure Mom and Kate would be willing to watch Katrina for a while."

"Then let's go now. I don't know if we'll get another chance."

Within the hour, the two had driven the three miles up the curving road to the top of Iron Mountain and walked the wooded paths through Frederick Law Olmsted's garden sanctuary, past the great tower to a point facing the western slope. The huge crowd of the day before was gone and an almost church-like silence lay over the hilltop. There, Jack halted, and Kate stood at his side, staring across the land toward where the sun was beginning to descend toward the horizon.

"It's so beautiful, Jack, but it seems strangely familiar..."

"It is. It's different now, for then it was only sand and these tall pines..."

"Oh, Jack! This IS the place!" Amanda blurted suddenly, as recognition came to her. She turned and looked at her brother, who wore a look of satisfaction on his face. "I never thought I would know where it was!" she said. She paused for a long moment, looking around before speaking again. "When did you realize..." she began.

"About two years ago. Everything is so changed now, with the gardens and now the tower, but when I stood in this spot, I knew this was it."

There was a long silence as they stood side by side, their memories flying back across the years to the last time they had been there together as children.

At last Amanda broke the silence.

"Eastwind gave me a name, Jack. And you, too. A Miccosukee name," Amanda said, with tears in her eyes. "And he gave me something more, something that I have always carried with me."

"What was that, Amanda?"

"A sense of who I am, and who I represent, and what I have to offer my children and their children..."

Jack stared at his sister for a long moment, wondering at the remarkable things she held inside. "You have great gifts, I know," he said, "and you have never failed to use them."

March 1929

"Prices are heading down fast, Tony. I think we both dumped our real estate just in time."

Tony looked at the speaker and nodded grimly. In his mind, Zebulon Curtis was an operator. He had made a great deal of money by being very up-beat about the future of Florida and selling up the prices to unrealistic levels. Now he had turned against the very thing that had made him a rich man.

"I saw that sales had petered out and I just couldn't get my prices anymore," Curtis continued without encouragement. "I was used to making triple, or at least double money, within three months' time by flipping these lots. Ya' can't do that anymore, so I just pawned off my whole sub-divisions on some Yankees. I figg'ered if land ain't making me money, invest in stocks. At least Wall Street is run by smart people, not like these yokels around here."

This was just the sort of thing that had Tony silently fuming. To his frustration, he had found himself seated with Curtis at the Chamber of Commerce luncheon once again. He was sure that he was being targeted for some sort of investment scheme but was dodging it as best he could.

"I wish you luck, Zebulon. You seem to keep on your feet, so I guess you're ahead of the crowd on this one," Tony replied as he picked up his hat and stood. "I've promised my wife that I'm not pulling a dime out of the bank. I think I'll be fine. Good day." With a quick gesture, he turned and walked away, leaving his coffee and half-smoked cigarette behind.

"So long, Tony. I'll see you at next week's meeting," Curtis called behind him.

Tony walked slowly along the Hillsborough River, enjoying the fresh spring day. He had indeed sold most of his land before the prices had begun to slide and for that he was grateful. How Curtis had learned so much of his business was what had left him aggravated. He was glad that he had sought out the safety of the Citizen's Bank and Trust, a solid Tampa institution, and put a significant reserve away for the future.

The matter had been swept from his mind before that evening. A delightful meal with Marie soon had him relaxed. Sitting on their broad front porch following dinner, conversation turned to the future.

"So, what do you think of a cruise?" Tony suggested. "We could head up the east coast, maybe see Charleston, Washington D.C., New York, even Boston. Some of the men at the Chamber come down from up there and brag about their hometowns. I've barely been up north since I came down here from Philadelphia."

"Whatever you want to go see is fine with me, dear," Marie replied, glancing up from her knitting with a mischievous smile. "I am ready to go wherever you like."

"Honey, I am so glad I married you, you have never once let me down," Tony said. "I think I'm the luckiest man on Earth."

"I guess that makes me the luckiest woman, then!" Marie offered, her smile turning to a grin.

Tony stood and leaned over his wife's chair to give her a kiss and looked at her lovingly. "I have always done my best to provide for you and the kids. I think that we've finally arrived. Now let's take some time and go enjoy life."

"That sounds wonderful, Tony. You have certainly earned it," she said. "My job now is to make you the happiest man on Earth."

Tony grinned right back. "Give me your hand, beautiful and let's see if we've got what it takes!"

The Stock Certificate
September 1929

"HI, JACK, HOW ARE YOU?"

"I'm fine, Dad. I hope I'm not interrupting."

"Not at all, son. Thanks for calling. You remind me that this damned telephone is good for something pleasant, once in a while. What's the occasion?"

Jack paused for a moment, then went on. "Is Mom alright? I always worry about her."

"She's fine, yes. We're both fine. You and Kate and Anthony, too?"

"Yes, we're doing well. Work's a bit slow, but I'm recruiting some new clients now, so it should be picking up."

"So, what's up? Planning to drive over for the weekend to surprise your mother?"

"I wish I could... maybe it's possible. I'll have to talk to Kate and make sure she doesn't have plans with the kids. Really, though, I was calling to pass on a tip."

"What sort of tip?"

"Do you remember I told you about Roger Babson, who built the bank and Webber College here, and his own little village of Babson Park?"

"Well, sure. He's the economist, right?"

"That's him. I saw him last a few months ago, but I read a story about him in the paper this evening. He's advising his clients to sell everything and get out of the stock market. He pointed out that lots of people have bought stock on loaned money. He says we are primed for a stock price crash, and that it could lead to a serious recession. I guess he sees what is happening in Florida with the banks and land prices and thinks it will spread."

"That's a grim prediction, Jack. Do you think he's right?"

"He could be, Dad. He's smart about finance and has his ear to the ground. And he's widely respected. He said all this in a speech today and the stock market in New York fell about three percent in a couple of hours."

There was a silent pause for a moment.

"Dad, I know you got hurt when the Citizen's Bank failed in that run in July. I don't know how bad and it's not my business, but I love you and don't want to see you caught again."

"Jack, I thank you for your concern and the tip. But I want you not to worry about me, or your mom. You have your own challenges to deal with. Besides, President Hoover said he's not at all worried about the lenders supplying money for stock purchases. In fact, that's the only thing that might help them buy up some of these depressed stocks and get things going the right direction again. Doesn't that give you some comfort?"

"Not enough, Dad," Jack replied. "Just be careful. I love you."

"I love you too, son. Give my love to Kate and the boys."

"Please pass mine to Mom. Tell her I promise to bring the boys over soon."

October 1929

Tony sat calmly in front of the radio, listening to the bad news that poured in from New York. The entire nation would soon find out how dependent it had become on the world of high finance. Nothing could have fully prepared Florida or the world for the financial crash of 1929.

Tony clearly grasped that the nation, and apparently the world, had caught a contagion that had begun with Florida's real estate speculation bubble. Florida's deflating land prices had sparked the growing sense of unease that soon turned to panic. Fear soon became a self-fulfilling prophesy. Capitalism's reliance on private finance was dashed upon the rocks of the great Stock Market Crash.

In a matter of days, billions of dollars of assumed worth vanished as the sell-off wiped values from the books, hurtling the entire nation into an economic tailspin.

March 1930

"It will indeed be a city in a garden, and an attractive place to build a home and raise a family. Mr. Phillips will supervise the plantings."

The words, spoken by the renowned Frederick Law Olmsted Jr. to the gathered members of the Lake Wales Board of Trade, raised Tony's hopes, as did the agreeing nods of the men in the room, each eager to find good news and hope amid the gloom of the sudden economic downturn. The city's flow of new residents had ground to a halt, and real estate prices had fallen.

Tony was cheered that Olmsted himself had been retained to design the future expansion of the city and could now present the results of his genius of design. Displayed maps showed new curvilinear streets lined with trees, and planting had already begun along many existing streets and in the parks that wrapped the lakes. Lake Wales was to become a garden city to match Olmsted and Phillip's beautiful work at Bok Tower. Bok himself had died two months earlier, only a year after the completion of his monumental construction. He had secretly offered to pay for Olmsted's work in the city, on the condition that city fathers keep the matter private. "I really don't want the people to know that I am back of it," he had written. His dream of making the world a better place would be continued.

November 1930

America's powerful corporations, their source of capital depleted by the collapse of their stock prices, had sought to maximize profits and restore faith by laying off employees by the thousands. Yet people deprived of their incomes no longer purchased products, and the effect was a downward spiral into economic disaster. The wheels of commerce were swiftly grinding to a halt.

For Tony Crews, the crash had been a personal calamity. His various investments were virtually wiped out, although because he had invested his cash rather than borrowing to buy, the stocks he owned were still his and he owed no one.

Although he had been able to sell a portion of his stocks during the panic, he soon realized that taking as little as two cents on the dollar was a fool's game. He had put a stop to it. His losses in the bank panic were now multiplied. Although he was one of only a relative handful of Americans who had significant investments in stock, he still had some cash and a home. Others were not so lucky. Yet for Tony the strain of a failure he blamed on himself was too much. He became increasingly despondent, and his health gradually declined as his depression worsened. In early December he suffered a fatal cerebral hemorrhage. Marie found him sitting in his favorite chair before the fire in their quiet home in Winter Park, a look of peace on his face. Christmas would never be the same for the Crews family.

With no need for engineers and desperate to support his growing family, in March Jack finally found a temporary, part-time job in a sawmill, convinced that work as an architect was nonexistent. Florida's boom had let him down. Kate, Anthony, and baby John, born in 1929, would have to make do with little.

Large numbers of unemployed men were soon wandering the streets seeking any available work, and conditions continued to deteriorate. In the next two years shantytowns sprang up in parks, under bridges and anywhere land was unguarded. Popularly known as "Hoovervilles" in recognition of the seemingly futile policies of President Herbert Hoover, they soon became targets of police crackdowns, as frustration, heaped upon hopelessness, led to senseless violence.

By spring work was completed on the Empire State Building and, months later, the George Washington Bridge opened, spanning New York's Hudson River. Jack watched from a distance, reading about the new engineering milestones, and gazing at the incredible photographs while struggling to find enough customers to keep the sawmill operating.

The Tin Cup
April 1932

"I'M GOING, MARTIN, and I think that if we just show up, they will see how desperate we are, and they'll come to their senses." The tinny voice on the telephone couldn't mask the speaker's passion, and Martin was moved. "We can't afford to wait another thirteen years to get those bonuses they promised us. Most of us will starve to death by then!"

"I don't disagree, Rudy," Martin replied, "but I am lucky enough to have a job, so I can't get away to go to Washington. I'll tell you what, though. I can afford to put two dollars in the hat to help you and the boys get up there. That's about all I can spare and keep my own family fed."

"Thanks, Martin. I do understand about the job, don't let go of it. The two bucks will be a big help. We've raised almost fifty already, but I think we'll have at least thirty men from our Legion post heading up, and they're expecting thousands from across the country. I never thought that I'd see this sort of reunion of the AEF, but it's happening."

"I'm glad I can help a bit, Rudy. By the way, how's your family?"

"Well, my mother died two years ago. My dad finally gave up on his watch shop. Not enough business to make it worthwhile. It was his pride for almost 30 years. Anyway, he's too old to be working now, so I'm hoping to help him with the bonus. My brother is out of work now too. We're going to make it, though. How's yours doing?"

Martin shared his story of the failure of the family pharmacy in Daytona Beach and his eventual good fortune in finding work with Pan-Am in Miami. It had taken calling on some of his own buddies from the Great War, but they had responded with loyalty and made work for him until a real position had opened up.

Hanging up the phone at the end of the call, Martin shook his head sadly, recalling the hardships endured by the men of the American Expeditionary Force in the Great War. Although he had spent most of his time flying above the trenches or resting in warm houses, he still identified with the doughboys. They had headed to Europe full of enthusiasm, eager to defend democracy. There many of them had been crippled and thousands of their friends killed by poison gas and charges into machine-gun fire. Life in the cold, muddy trenches alone had been enough to rob many of them of their health and vitality. Now they were suffering again, and Martin shared their sense of desperation.

"Honey, I wanted to tell you that I have a debt to settle," Martin told Amanda that evening. "I need to take two dollars out of our savings to give to Rudy and the men from the American Legion post. They're heading to Washington to try to get their bonuses."

"If you think we can spare it, that's fine with me, darling," Amanda replied. "As long as we have enough left to feed Katrina and she's starting to outgrow her smock again."

"I know. Hang on, Sugar, we'll get through this mess."

•

Rudy Burtin and his companions happily accepted the support of friends and patriots grateful for their service and by the hundreds they boarded trains, cars, trucks, and buses to descend upon the nation's capital. Tens of thousands of veterans of the Great War gathered in Washington, many with their wives and children in tow, reuniting with their former units through the help of veteran's organizations from around the country. Homeless, out of work and desperate, they erected tents or built rough shelters and dug latrines in green lawns. Theirs was a shantytown in the city. They demonstrated and petitioned the president and Congress to speed the issuance of their service bonuses. The nation watched to see if Congress would agree, but the authorities were not in a mood to compromise.

President Hoover had been elected by a wide margin and had taken office in March of 1929, months before the crash and felt that he had a mandate to deal with it on his own terms. America's heroic army waited in the squalor of their poor shanties only a few blocks from the splendor of the Capitol and the White House while the government set about ignoring them.

The summer months brought a noticeable stench from the camps of the self-styled "Bonus Army," where the shanty town facilities were primitive at best. Government had done nothing to help alleviate the situation. Hoover grew increasingly impatient with the vast campsite. He had expected them to give up after a short stay, but that now seemed unlikely. He decided it was time to send them back home.

•

"It was bad, Martin," Rudy reported by telephone a few weeks later. "You probably remember Major General Smedley Butler, from the Marines? He's retired now, but he came to our camp to back us and said getting our bonuses was only fair, considering our situation. We thought we were winning, and that Hoover would come around. Then they sent in the police, and they started roughing up the boys, telling them they were trespassers, and they would be arrested. Some of the guys fought back and the cops just shot them down. I heard that there were quite a few shot, and a few died, but rumors were flying around the camp, and nobody could be sure."

"Then," Rudy continued, "a couple of days later the Army showed up. We were all cheering and waving flags. We just knew they were there to defend us, and they had tanks, too. We figured the Army was on our side and we knew the police wouldn't try anything with the Army around. Then they fixed bayonets and came at us. They charged us with cavalry.

They gassed us, set fire to the tents... it was terrible, just a one-sided riot. Lots of the men were running to try to get their families out of the way while the single guys tried to hold back the charge with whatever they had. They ended up burning the place to the ground."

"My God, Rudy, it's still hard to believe it really happened in America," Martin replied when his friend's story had ended. "We saw the stories in the newspapers here and let me tell you, people were shocked. I saw that General Douglas MacArthur was ordering those charges and that he claimed your men wanted to overthrow the government, that you were out for revolution."

"That's a lie, Martin. All we want is a chance to live our lives and feed our families."

"I'm just glad you and your men made it back safely."

"Yeah, we were lucky. Some of our unit had bad bruises, a few cuts and a broken arm, but we're all still alive. But I'll tell you what, Martin, these boys don't forget and they're not forgiving."

•

The violence of the Bonus Army eviction was repeated across the country as local and state authorities attempted to drive the legions of homeless from their Hooverville camps under bridges and in public parks. Not only around the nation but around the globe, the interdependent economies of the industrial world had unraveled. It was a situation fraught with hazards for government, as normally-loyal citizens began to feel betrayed, placing the blame squarely at the feet of their elected leaders. Storm clouds were gathering as Anarchist, Fascist and Communist movements gained strength in Florida, America, and around the world.

February 1933

Martin's thoughts were deeply focused on the diagram of a new aircraft engine in his manual when he heard the knock on the door of the apartment. The squeaky hardwood floor of the walk-up apartment complained as he rose and walked the few feet to the door, where he was surprised to find his brother-in-law.

"Jack! Come in! It's so good to see you again. I'm really surprised that you're in town."

"Thanks, Martin. I didn't really plan to be here, but one thing led to another...is Amanda home?"

"No, she said she was going to pick up some groceries to fix us some dinner tonight and she's got Katrina along, too. She should be home shortly. Can I fix you a drink?"

"What have you got?"

"I've got some good Spanish wine and real Cuban rum. Not bad, eh? So much for prohibition. The stuff just pours in from the Bahamas and the government can't stop it."

"I guess I'll have the rum, Martin. I really feel like a stiff drink. I've been hitch-hiking and riding buses for a week."

Martin and Amanda's small apartment in Miami was at least a secure home, Jack thought. They were fortunate to have found relative security after the failure of his family's pharmacy. Being hired by Pan-Am and returning to flight as a relief pilot was a godsend and now Jack needed one of his own. His long wandering in search of a job had brought him near at last to the southern end of the state, but no closer to the work he needed.

"You know, I wonder why they haven't given up on prohibition already?" Martin said, breaking the silence as they sipped their drinks. "It's been over ten years and all we've gotten out of prohibition is gangsters, smugglers, and moonshine. Anybody who wants a drink can still get one."

"It makes about as much sense as anything else the government does," Jack replied, swirling the brown liquid slowly in his glass as if contemplating a mystery. "It looks like this time, though, they are going to pass that amendment and repeal the prohibition. It's only logical."

A brief silence followed as the two men sipped their drinks and Martin recognized that Jack had something weighing heavily on his mind. At last, he spoke up. "I'm really worried, Martin. I can't find any work. I've been all over the state. On my way south I stopped in Palm Beach, Fort Lauderdale, Hollywood, and every town in between and there's just nothing going on. And I mean nothing at all. I didn't just look for work as an engineer or architect. I tried to get a job picking oranges. For every man they need, there are five hundred waiting for the job. It's really hopeless."

Martin looked at Jack and another moment of silence passed between them before Jack spoke again. "The hardest part is what to tell Kate. Our savings are almost gone, Anthony's seven, John's going to be four this year and they're both growing like weeds. We can't even afford to buy them enough clothes."

"I wish I could get you on with the airline, Jack, but it's the same there. Too many people need jobs and not enough people can afford to fly. If it wasn't for the government mail contract, I doubt we'd still be in the air."

"I understand, Martin. I'm just glad you've got a job. We are happy for both of you."

At that moment, the kitchen door opened, and little Katrina strode boldly into the room, followed closely by Amanda, her arms filled with packages.

"Here, let me help you with those," Jack said, rising from his chair.

"Nonsense, Jack," Amanda said, dropping the bags onto the counter. "Just give me a hug. It's so good to see you!" Jack wrapped his arms around his sister's waist, and she gave him a kiss on the cheek, before looking at him face to face, perceiving the worry written there.

"How's it going, brother?" Jack glanced away, not wanting to lie to her. "Not so good, huh? Don't feel bad, Jack. It's not your fault. It's the times. We'll make it through, though."

Jack sat back down as Amanda turned away, unwilling to let her brother see the tears that formed in her eyes.

"Hi, Uncle Jack," Katrina said shyly, peeking at Jack from the corner of her eye.

"Well, hello, princess!" he said, happy for a distraction. "I brought you something!" he said and pulled an orange from his jacket pocket.

"Thanks, Uncle Jack!" she said. "Can I eat it now, Mama?"

"Why don't you wait until after dinner, dear," Amanda answered, and Katrina ran to set the orange by her place at the table.

"Would you like a drink, dear?" Martin asked, as Amanda began to unpack the grocery bags.

"Just a little wine. Sorry I'm late, guys. The buses were running slow today. It seems there's a run on another bank."

"Not ours, I hope!" Martin said, looking up from where he was carefully pouring Amanda's wine.

"No, we lucked out again, but I'm not sure how," she answered, before glancing back at Jack.

"It seems we've stayed just ahead of the failures, Jack. Last time Martin got a funny feeling and moved our account a week before the bank failed."

"We're about to run out of banks," Martin observed. "It seems a town this size ought to be able to support at least one solid bank."

Conversation over the dinner was subdued, but Jack was focused on the meal. Amanda watched him closely, realizing that he probably hadn't eaten a square meal in days. She made herself a mental note to do some extra cooking the next day.

"How's Kate doing, Jack?" she asked him as they were clearing the table. "I haven't talked to her since we were up there at Christmas."

"She's fine. She's got her hands full with Anthony, but he's really a good boy. He just has so much energy. I swear, if we could hook him to a dynamo, he'd power the state."

"How's Mom?" she asked, hesitating.

"As well as can be expected. She seems happy in the house in Winter Park. Without a mortgage, she's says she's making it just fine on the money from Dad's insurance and the little bit of dividends that the stocks still pay. They are almost worthless, but I figured the remaining stocks were probably just as safe as a bank these days. Who can really tell?"

"Jack, what are we going to do?" Amanda asked after dinner as Katrina retreated to her room with the orange to get ready for her evening bath. "Martin and I are lucky, because he's working, and we still barely get by. Miami is getting to be a desperate place. People are talking about how capitalism has failed, and it scares me. This country is ripe for a revolution."

"I know, Amanda. I only hope that things will get better. I think it was a good thing the elections were happening, because it gave people something to focus on besides overthrowing the government. I think most Americans still have faith, as long as they can vote and change things."

"Yeah, at least we can all vote," Amanda said, winking at Jack, who smiled back.

"You know, I have always been a Republican, because Dad was a Republican," Jack said. "I don't know if he really knew why, just that that's what people in Philadelphia were then. But I voted for Roosevelt in the election."

"We did too, Jack. I took a good look at the Hoovervilles along the highway and decided it was time for a major change."

"It's funny you said that Amanda, because I was just thinking that I'd slept under a "Hoover Blanket" so long now it must say "Miami Herald" in reverse across my forehead," Jack responded with a wry grin. "But you have work and it's still bad, huh?"

"It's been hectic," Martin answered. "It seems like we never really got unpacked after our move to Miami before it was Christmas. And now it's February already and Amanda's still got work to do. But we don't regret a minute of it, Jack. I feel very lucky to have gotten the job, after the pharmacy failed. I love working for a real airline. I really think this is the wave of the future."

"I'm sure you're right, Martin," Jack answered, before glancing at Amanda. "Do you regret being the housewife, while Martin does the flying?"

"No, I don't really mind. I just wish Dad had lived long enough to see me do it. But someday, I'll be flying again too."

•

Jack spent the next day combing Miami for work, part of a restless throng of thousands of unemployed men. Another day's fruitless search only served to continue the slow erosion of his self-esteem. That evening, Jack returned to his sister's home, grateful for a place to sleep.

"Jack, I talked to one of the supervisors at the airfield today," Martin told him. "I think I can get you work, at least for a day. One of our guys is in the hospital. It's just a few hours of sweeping up and maybe loading mail bags, but at least it's something you can earn a couple of bucks at. I was lucky to get it for you, because we must have at least thirty men a day ask for work. We try to save any work we have for family, though."

"Thanks, Martin. I appreciate it. At least maybe I can earn a bit to help me get back home. I know Kate must be beside herself, worrying. I stayed up late last night and wrote her a long letter, telling her how things were here. I'm sure it will cheer her up a bit, just to hear that you are doing well."

"Jack, we've been talking," Amanda said. "Why don't you and Kate move to Miami? I know the situation isn't any better here for work, but you could move in with us and save some money. Katrina wouldn't mind giving up her room for you two and the kids could sleep in the dining room. It would be crowded, but we could work it out."

Jack looked at his sister's smiling face and at Martin, who gave him an encouraging look. "I don't know..." he began.

"Think about it, Jack. After all, Kate's probably lonely by herself, anyway. This way she could spend time with Amanda and the kids would have companionship."

Jack paused, looking at the floor. "I really appreciate what you two are offering to do for us," he said. "I have been worried what we would do when the savings ran out. We've got enough for three more mortgage payments, plus groceries. After that, who knows? But, moving in with you here, I don't think..."

"Just wait to think it over, Jack. That's all we're asking," Amanda said. "Don't decide tonight. Wait until you get back home and talk things over with Katie."

Jack spent the next day working in the hangar at Pan-American, the struggling young airline which was hauling passengers and mail to Latin America and a handful of American cities. His initiative in making some repairs at the hangar got him a second day's work as well, but then he was back on the street, competing with the unemployed masses.

"Jack, I know you were planning to leave today," Martin said the next morning, "but you ought to wait until tomorrow and go with us to see Roosevelt tonight. He's only going to be here a few hours and how often do you get the chance to see the future President of the United States?"

Jack thought for a moment, then agreed. "What the heck. You're right. Kate isn't expecting me for a few days. I voted for the guy, maybe we'll hear him say he's gonna' do something to help the unemployed."

That evening they traveled along North Miami Avenue to the band shell at Bayfront Park, where a crowd of twenty thousand had gathered to greet the next president, the man who had defeated Hoover in a landslide. Franklin Delano Roosevelt was the hope of the people but had yet to spell out details of his plans and programs. He was barely more than two weeks from assuming the presidency of the United States.

An almost carnival atmosphere prevailed among the gathered crowds in the warm February evening. Everyone in town, it seemed, had come to see the president-elect. The wealthy and the politically-connected, seated upon the bandstand and the desperate and hungry, gathered on the lawns. More than one hundred and fifty police officers mingled with the crowd, observant for any sign of attempts to disrupt the speech. At last, at nine o'clock, the presidential motorcade arrived, and President-elect Roosevelt could be seen seated on top of the back seat of an open car, which stopped in front of the bandstand. A cheer came from the crowd as he grinned and waved. "Can you see him, Katrina?" Martin asked, holding his daughter on his shoulders.

"Yeah, Daddy. Is that him in the car there?" she asked pointing.

"That's him, dear," Martin said. "The next president of the United States and he's right here in Miami. You'll remember this night the rest of your life."

Amanda and Jack stood side by side as Roosevelt spoke through a microphone he was handed and communicated his empathy for the unemployed of the nation, now totaling fifteen million. Jack was inspired by the sight of the man and the sound of the voice he knew only from the radio. It gave him encouragement to know that Roosevelt had been so close to him, had seen the crowd, had grasped the desperation on the faces of so many.

After a brief speech, received with enthusiasm by the crowd, the president prepared to leave.

"Let's get closer, so we can wave at his motorcade when he leaves for the train station," Amanda said and Jack led the way, snaking through the masses of humanity toward the curb. After a minute or so they were only a hundred feet away. Jack could see the president shaking hands with well-wishers, see him reach to accept a telegram, see him bend to read it in the dim light...

"Bang!" came a sudden report and a scream. "Too many people are starving to death!" came a shout over the crowd, even as more shots rang out. People dove in panic, huddling on the ground, but Jack remained standing, his body a wall between the disturbance and his sister's family. There, on the bandstand, he could see a woman, grasping the arm of a small man who clutched a revolver. Even as Jack watched the taller woman pushed his arm into the air, seeking to prevent his firing. Yet the man bent his wrist and continued to fire the weapon, until at last others came to her aid and wrestled the gun away from him.

Jack looked quickly to where the president-elect was still seated on the back on his car, as the driver was hurriedly attempting to drive away from the scene. "Get him out of the crowd!" shouted the Secret Service operatives, waving them onward. "Stop the car!" commanded the president, looking back at the scene. There on the ground lay his good friend Anton Cermak, the newly-elected reformist mayor of Chicago, seriously wounded. Jack sprang forward, even as the crowd was still rushing away from the scene. Quickly he bent over the form of a woman bleeding from the abdomen and attempted to help her. All around him was blood and panic.

The crowd, comprehending that the shooter had been captured, halted its flight to watch.

"Kill him!" someone shouted, and others took up the chant, bent upon revenge. As Jack worked to assist a doctor who appeared, he saw the police quickly drag away the perpetrator, a tiny, frightened-looking man.

Jack looked up to see that the president's car was directly alongside him. "Please, help place that woman in the next car. I'm ordering the motorcade directly to the hospital," Roosevelt told him, and Jack complied, carefully helping to lift the woman. Even as they completed the task, Jack could see that the wounded mayor was being placed into the president's car, as Roosevelt quickly bent to aid his friend. In a moment, they drove away, hurrying to seek help.

Jack turned and realized that the crowd was still there, engaged in thousands of excited conversations. Women wept, people hugged one another and a few still called for revenge upon the arrested gunman. Nowhere, he realized, did he see his sister, or Martin, or Katrina.

Slowly he began walking north along Biscayne Boulevard, part of a wave of humanity moved by the great tragedy they had witnessed. "Jack! Jack, over here!" he heard and turned to see Martin waving from across the street. There at his side were Amanda and Katrina, standing in near darkness close to a building, out of the stream of people. Jack hurried to their side.

"I guess this wasn't such a good idea, Jack," Martin began. "If I had known that someone would start shooting, I would never have brought them here, or you either."

"Don't be silly, Martin. No one could imagine that such a thing could have happened in Miami. Thank God the president is OK."

"Are you sure, Jack?" he questioned. "I couldn't tell in the confusion. Someone got shot, I think."

"He's OK. He spoke to me, as cool as if he was ordering bread at a bakery. His only concern was for the wounded. At least two people were shot pretty bad."

"Oh, God, Jack, you've been shot too!" Amanda suddenly cried out, reaching toward him and Katrina froze, a frightened look on her face.

Jack looked down at himself and realized that he was covered in the blood of the victims. "No. I'm fine, it's not my blood. Don't scare Katrina. Let's go home and I'll get cleaned up."

●

Later that evening the group was safely at home unwinding from the ordeal and turning the events in their minds.

"What really scared me, Jack, was the crowd," Martin said. "They turned into a mob. If the police hadn't gotten that man out of there, I think they would have killed him."

"People are strange, Martin," Jack said. "Most people lose their heads in an emergency and just react to their emotions. Others stay calm." After a pause, he added, "I sure am glad Roosevelt is going to be president."

●

News of the tragedy in Miami swept over a stunned nation, yet another blow to the morale of a country already staggered by the depth of its desperation. Six people had been wounded, including the president's driver, who had been shot in the hand but still drove to the hospital. The president remained in Miami until the following day, when he was told that two seriously injured were stabilized. The injury to Mayor Cermak, the crusader from Chicago, was the greatest blow to the new president. His friend and ally would die of complications only two days after Roosevelt's inauguration.

Two other names were long remembered because of the shooting. Guiseppe Zangara was a diminutive, deranged immigrant. Only five feet, one inch tall and weighing one hundred and five pounds, he had suffered a long-untreated series of physical and mental health problems. He had purchased the "Saturday Night Special" at a pawn shop on North Miami Avenue for eight dollars only a short time before the shooting. He would be executed for the crime only weeks later. He was unable to accomplish his goal only due to the actions of Mrs. W. H. Cross, the wife of a Miami physician. She had seen the gun, grabbed the arm and prevented him from aiming. It was an act that would have great implications for the future of the free world.

March 1933

On the fourth of March a nationwide radio audience tuned in millions of tube sets to hear the inaugural speech of Franklin Delano Roosevelt as President of the United States. Listening at their radios, along with thousands of other Floridians, were Marie Crews in Winter Park, Jack and Kate in Lake Wales and Martin and Amanda in Miami. Of the entire family, only Martin had a job, but all clung to the slimmest thread of hope.

Roosevelt's reassuring bass tones emerged through the static as Jack carefully turned the dial to catch the signal.

"First of all, let me assert my firm belief that the only thing we have to fear is fear itself. Nameless, unreasoning, unjustified terror," he told them. "This nation asks for action and action now," he said, as millions nodded their heads. "In the event that Congress shall fail... I shall not evade the clear course of duty that will then confront me. I shall ask the Congress for the one remaining instrument to meet the crisis: broad executive power to wage a war against the emergency."

It was a message filled with hope, intended to begin the long process of rebuilding peoples' confidence in the future, in America, in themselves. The words of the president gave them all reason to believe that, at last, something would be done about the calamity which gripped them.

Within days, events in Washington would begin to unfold which would have a tremendous influence on the course of events in Florida. Two days after taking office, Roosevelt's first emergency order took effect, closing all the banks in the nation, giving them a chance to reorganize. During the brief banking holiday, he placed an embargo on the export of gold. Congress convened and immediately passed an emergency banking bill, which made the decrees law and gave the president power over the Federal Reserve.

The Treasury Department was empowered to license banks and soon they reopened with strengthened public trust. Federal insurance of bank deposits soon gave a new measure of confidence to the public and bank deposits began to rise again. Federal regulation of the securities industries began to restore confidence in the stock markets as well.

Of more immediate importance to Jack and Kate was the creation of the Home Owners Loan Corporation. It gave them a chance to refinance their mortgage and avoid foreclosure. Jack watched in hope as tens of thousands of men lined up for a chance to work for the new Civilian Conservation Corps, limited to men eighteen to twenty-five years old.

January 1934

"It's not a lot of work, but it's something," Jack told Kate one evening at the dinner table. "It might help us get through this mess before we run through all our savings."

"Jack, whatever you think you can do to help Mr. Pope and earn a few dollars is fine by me. I'll help any way I can," Kate replied earnestly. "We are in this for the long haul. We've got kids to feed. I will sweep streets if that's what it takes."

"Don't even think about it," Jack told her. "I will find full-time work soon, one way or another. This little job is just a stop-gap, I know. Anyway, if Dick needs my help, how can I refuse? He's a neighbor, goodness knows, and he's seen hard times like the rest of us."

"What exactly has he got planned now?" Kate asked.

"He's building a garden on Lake Eloise, just this side of Winter Haven. He calls it "Cypress Gardens," and he's going to charge people to come and see it."

"Do you really think that will work?"

"Who knows?" Jack replied. "If there's anyone who could get it to work, it's probably Dick. He's quite the promoter, you know. I heard he closed his first real estate deal when he was twelve, back in Iowa. He learned real estate from his dad."

"I guess if it brings in some tourists again," Marie added after a pause, "it would be a good shot in the arm. We haven't seen any around here for quite a while."

"That's his goal, I guess. We'll see how he does."

February 1935

The Crews family, like all Floridians, continued to struggle through bad times. Yet, new Federally-funded jobs brought new hope and a slowly-improving economy. The CCC began reforesting logged lands and constructing parks. The Withlacoochee Land Use Project, begun in January of 1935, put hundreds of men to work as foresters, surveyors, and engineers to work in the rural areas of Pasco, Hernando, Sumter and Citrus counties, where extremely high unemployment had led to starvation. The stated project goal was the creation of a vast improvement program spanning over 100,000 acres of riverine lands, designed to protect both nature and the works of man. The real mission was a return of hope.

A virtual alphabet soup of Federal programs soon began to employ the nation in putting muscle back on bone. Help for Jack finally came in the form of the National Industrial Recovery Act, which included minimum wage and maximum work hours regulations. More importantly, it established the Public Works Administration, with a budget of more than three billion dollars to build roads and public buildings. Within weeks, Jack had been hired to help supervise construction of a new "Federal Highway" down the east coast of Florida and later, a series of bridges.

Across Florida, the Works Project Administration began organizing the construction of hundreds of libraries and post offices. Large numbers of young men were soon employed building a broad array of public works projects. Near Sebring, teams of Civilian Conservation Corps workers, supervised by Jack's friend Phillips, were busily constructing a new park with cabins, trails, and boardwalks through a cypress swamp. It would become Florida's first state park.

Not all the president's plans came to fruition, however. In response to requests from Florida promoters, he approved a plan to start construction of the long-sought "barge canal" across Florida, even though railroads had made the idea obsolete fifty years earlier. Soon after the construction began, however, Congress exerted its authority and again stripped funding for the project.

A letter finally brought Jack more opportunity and he resumed his familiar position of designing and supervising part of a giant bridge project. The Federal Emergency Relief Administration, another of Roosevelt's wide array of Depression-fighting weapons, had determined that a highway should be built parallel to the railroad in the Florida Keys. By way of fulfilling its primary goal, the "Overseas Highway" would employ thousands, with preference given to the World War veterans of the Allied Expeditionary Force, who were still awaiting their promised bonuses. Rudy and his Bonus Army veterans were given hope at last.

With the new work, Jack and Kate were able to maintain their home in Lake Wales and provide for the needs of Anthony and John. On his occasional furloughs at home, they often spent two hours driving sixty-five miles up the scenic "Orange Blossom Trail" through Haines City, Kissimmee, and Orlando to visit Marie in Winter Park. Although she had only a few friends there, Jack could not convince her to leave her home and join them, for she preferred to surround herself with her remaining memories of Tony.

September 1935

"Have another game, Rudy? Or another beer?" asked the lanky fellow reaching toward the tub full of bottles in the ramshackle dining hall. In his other hand he held a dart, ready to stroke it toward the horsehair board that hung a few feet away.

"No, I think I've had enough, Billy. You beat me two in a row. I think I'm going to just kick back and relax for a while, maybe read a bit and hit the hay. Tomorrow's Labor Day and I think some of the boys are going to spend it fishing. I can't remember the last time we had two days in a row off work."

"Now don't start complaining," his friend replied with a grin. "At least we got work and plenty of it, thanks to Roosevelt and his programs. Beats the days we spent camped in Washington hoping for our bonuses."

Like Rudy and Billy, most of the work crews were veterans, members of the former Bonus Army, beaten by MacArthur and finally employed by the government on road-building projects.

"Don't worry, I'm not complaining," Rudy replied as he made his way toward the door and his own tent and bunk. As was his habit, he stopped to check the chronograph to re-set his watch, which always seemed to run slow. As he turned the winding stem, he glanced up to check the barometer as well.

"Hey, Billy, have you seen how much the glass has dropped? It's nearly down to twenty-nine point six."

"Yeah, they say there's a tropical storm out over the Bahamas, but its gonna' hit Cuba. Nothin' to worry about."

"I don't know, Billy, that's really low for just a tropical storm that's not even close. Must be something else going on."

"Well, it's nothing you can do a thing about, so just get some sleep. Maybe you'll get lucky tomorrow, and we can all have a fresh fish dinner."

"Have a good night, Billy."

Rudy lay in his bunk an hour later, still not ready to sleep. The night was calm, but when he peeked out through his mosquito netting the black moonless sky revealed not a trace of light. No stars were visible and there was not a sound of life. Rudy sighed. Matecumbe Key seemed a tropical paradise. Lime trees, hedges of guavas, tall coconut palms and the tangled roots of the mangroves formed their shelter. Old, fossilized reef rock with a thin coat of shell, ground to sand by ancient waves, lay underfoot.

He lay back down and tossed fitfully, his memories of the Great War often intruding into his thoughts as he attempted to sleep. "The War to End All Wars," they had called it then, and he had believed it. His youthful optimism had come home badly dented, but it was not until he had seen the newer and younger US Army overrun his camp in Washington that he had let it fall away forever. His cynicism had been slightly softened by Roosevelt's turning of the ship of state, but he was not yet ready to believe.

In the middle of the night, still awake, Rudy dragged on his worn jeans and stumbled the few paces back into the mess hall. Holding his kerosene lamp before the glass, he stared at the face for a moment in disbelief. "Twenty-nine point four-six," he read slowly to himself. "Must be broken, I guess, or somebody's having a bad time tonight."

•

"Get those men out of there now!" Jack shouted into the single working telephone as he paced back and forth at the end of the cord like a watchdog on a leash. A thin stream of wan light filtered through the open window. "These storms are nothing to fool with, trust me! There is no safe place anywhere down there!"

"But Jack, you've got to realize that it will take hours," came a response. "We've got lots of men in the camps on Islamorada and Windley Key. Some of them came to Miami yesterday to see the ball game, but the rest are taking a couple of days off for Labor Day weekend. There's not many here and we've got tools to move and cranes to park..."

"Forget those stinking cranes and tools, tell them to drop what they're doing and run! They've sent a train south from Miami. It should have left already. Tell them all to get aboard and get out of there. That goes for the locals too. Anyone who will, just get them out of the way of that storm!"

"But Jack, isn't it just a tropical storm and heading south of us? That's what we heard a couple of days ago."

"Alex, you'll have to trust me on this. We just had a plane fly over here dropping hurricane warning leaflets from the Weather Bureau. It's intensifying fast and it's turning your way! I was down there in a storm before and it's not safe. Just get them out!"

Jack hung up the phone, almost angry at how complacent people could be. They just didn't know hurricanes like he did, he thought. Now he had hundreds of men working the project, nearly a hundred under his direct supervision and all were in harm's way. Construction of the new parallel highway hadn't bridged the gaps between the islands in the Islamorada area. The train would be their only way to safety.

Carefully Jack recalculated the time it would take to back the train down there and return to Homestead. It was already just after noon. "It's just not enough time, unless the storm slows down," he thought. Silently he began to pray for a miracle.

•

By late Monday afternoon in Homestead, the storm had not been felt. Only a blanket of cirrus clouds banked high in the sky spoke of rain nearby, while a fitful breeze stirred the palms and hibiscus bushes. Forty miles south, though, down the chain of Keys, the storm had already begun to arrive in earnest.

Rudy had awakened that morning with a sinking feeling, as a steady breeze and bursts of stinging rain had begun to sweep the tiny island that held their camp. Just across the water on Upper Matecumbe Key he could see the camp hospital, the converted Snake Creek Hotel. He knew that it would probably be the best place to be if a big storm was coming, but the water was too rough to try rowing across.

By noon, the wind had risen only a little, still not much more than a gale, but the waters of the Atlantic side of the island had built to a frightful churn and large waves battered the exposed side of the island. Word was passed around the camp to expect a train, which was being sent south. The men were told to seek shelter on the lee side of the railroad embankment, a twenty-five-foot-high wall of rock intended to keep the trains above the water. "That's a solid barrier, it should be good shelter if things get rough," he thought. It would have been effective against artillery. Nature would throw a different challenge.

The winds had risen, and the sky had darkened, but still there was no immediate threat. As the locomotive chugged slowly along the single track pushing a string of nine cars, people clambered aboard at every stop. Yet by 4:00 in the afternoon, water was lapping over the tracks in many places as the storm surge arrived with the howling winds.

Already the waves were racing in a fast torrent between Matecumbe and Upper Matecumbe Key and the ragged clouds were swept before the winds, sailing far away to the southwest. Darker masses lurked to the east and south, behind a thin shield of driving raindrops. In the tangles of mangroves, tiny sand crabs clung to the upper branches, competing for space.

By late afternoon the winds had risen to a terrifying shriek. Rudy, Billy and two dozen of their co-workers had fled the shelter of their "canteen" as the timbers creaked and canvas shredded. They fled to the lee side of the rail embankment and there they were sandblasted by fine particles driven by the swirling winds. They watched as the waters crept ever higher toward their tenuous shelter. The raging seas flowed through the pass between the islands like a torrent. They huddled and watched in horror as the rising waters and pounding waves tore down the trestle that carried the tracks across the channel.

"Now the train will never get here," Billy shouted against the wind.

"Hang on, Billy," Rudy called back from his position only three feet away. "We'll get through this!"

"My family came from Ireland, Rudy and I always heard about the howl of the banshees coming to take some poor soul to purgatory," Billy shouted across the scant two feet that separated them. "I never heard them howl like this before."

Farther north in Key Largo, the long-delayed rescue train was slowly chugging southward, its long string of cars pushed by the old steam locomotive. As it rolled, a few of the Conchs, stranded far from their usual shelters, decided to get aboard. It was a fateful decision. Even as Rudy and his friends huddled by the track, the train was struck by huge waves topping a massive storm surge. Billions of gallons of sea-water pushed over the tracks. The train foundered, then toppled into the surf as the rail cars were swept away. All aboard were drowned in the raging surf.

Meanwhile, Rudy and his friends watched in horror in the evening light as the dark shape of the hospital began to crumble, the walls buckling under the assault of wind and water. The men knew it held about fifty patients. Half were men, mostly co-workers from the highway crews, but a few were from local "Conch" families. A dozen were children. He had presumed they were safe. In less than a minute it was gone, only roofs and floating timber visible on the tossing waves.

Some of the men shouted prayers, begging for a miracle as the storm raged. Yet still the shrieking winds swept over them, and the cold chill of wet night took their toll. Some lost their grip under the force of surging waves and were swept away. Rudy clung determinedly to a small shrub, its roots buried deeply in the sand and gravel.

Then with a final surge the waters crested furiously, and huge waves broke over the top of the embankment. Millions of gallons of water poured down upon them and no one could survive the onslaught. In less than a minute the thrashing group of men were swept far into Florida Bay and the dark water made their graves.

In those few short hours, Jack's long efforts in constructing the overseas railroad were undone, as bridges crumbled under the assault of the surf. More than four hundred people were drowned. Key West was returned to its isolated status as an island city.

December 1935

"Well, Jack, I guess you were right about your bridges after all. They were temporary. You always seem to be right," Amanda said, trying to help cheer Jack from his gloom as the family gathered at Marie's at Christmas time. Martin sat silently listening, swirling his glass of ice and rum.

"Good point, but there's no comfort in that. I did predict, I just never thought it would happen so soon, or that so many people would be killed."

"That's just part of life, Jack. As a pilot, I always admired Wiley Post," Amanda said from her chair near the fire. "I felt just as bad when he went down with Will Rogers as if it were my fault. It never should have happened..."

"Will you two cut it out? It's Christmas!" Marie shouted from the bedroom, where she was busy playing with John. "You ought to cheer up before the kids start thinking like that."

"You're right, Mom. We'll quit," Jack called and winked at his sister. Changing the subject, he turned to his former employer. "Did you hear about Dick Pope's gardens?"

"Is he the guy you worked with for a couple of months?" Amanda asked.

"Yeah, he's building what he calls a "tourist attraction" on Lake Eloise. He calls it Cypress Gardens. He was going to make it a public park, but lots of the folks in Winter Haven started calling him a fraud and the Canal Commission made him repay the loan and then the Feds pulled the workers that were helping to build it, so he's going to finish it himself and sell admission."

"Will that work?" Martin asked. "There's not so many tourists around here lately."

"He's not discouraged, and his enthusiasm seems to be contagious," Jack replied. "I have actually started to think he may be on to something. There are still plenty of people who make the drive to get up to the Singing Tower every day, so maybe he can beat the depression and get them to come to his gardens, too. It would be good to see things start to bounce back... Say, , now that Katrina's almost old enough to take care of herself after school, have you thought any more about going back to flying?"

"Oh, didn't I tell you? I've been flying more often lately. I've been getting brushed-up so I can go back to teaching. Amelia Earhart's been inspiring me, I suppose. I guess the world's not yet ready for women to fly airliners, but I'm going for a multi-engine rating. I sure would love to try one of those new DC-3's."

"Yeah, me too!" Martin added. "I saw in the paper yesterday that American Airlines is going to start flying them on long routes. They have a range of fifteen-hundred miles."

"Holy smokes! That's almost all the way across the country!" Jack observed.

"It's just a matter of time, you know, and we'll be flying them all over, down to South America, too," Martin said. "No more island-hopping."

Jack gave a strange shrug, halfway looked over his shoulder and then said, in a slightly lower voice, "I don't know if you are aware of it, but President Roosevelt has ordered some restrictions on the use of steel in construction. We've had to jump through a few hoops to get the material we need to go on building the new highway to Key West. Now that the train has been knocked out and won't be rebuilt, the highway is really needed."

"Why would he do that, Jack?" Rudy asked, as Amanda leaned a bit closer. "I thought he was trying to stimulate production, fire up the economy?"

"He is, but he's also trying to follow his own star. He obviously thinks that we aren't keeping up with the rearmament going on in Europe and Asia. Japanese troops are in China making war, you've got Stalin and Hitler running Russia and Germany and they have no love for each other. Germany still hasn't accepted how the last war ended."

"I guess he's got a point, Jack," Martin replied. "I talked to a couple of English pilots the other day. They're worried too. They said they listened to Winston Churchill's speeches. They told me he used to be Lord of the Admiralty, or some such title, and they say he knows his stuff about weaponry. He's a war hero, too. Anyway, Churchill says that Hitler is breaking the treaty, re-arming Germany, but the government there isn't listening to him. They said that Britain isn't keeping up. But all that still doesn't explain why Roosevelt would put a limit on the steel," Martin said.

"He is diverting it to shipyards," Jack replied levelly. "He's re-arming."

The three of them sat silent for just a moment, contemplating the future.

"Whatever happens," Amanda said into the empty moment, "we'll still be family. We're for each other and we'll take care of kids and parents." Both Martin and Tony smiled and nodded.

Into the room's warm glow came Anthony, wanting to say goodnight, homework behind him. His thick shock of dark hair, dark eyes set in an angular face, reminded Jack of himself when he was ten. He gave each a warm hug and his dad a kiss on the cheek.

"Hey, Dad, if you didn't get me a bicycle for Christmas, do you think I could have one for my birthday in July?"

"Why are you so obsessed with a bicycle, son?" Jack asked, smiling back at his son. "Don't you know that Santa will bring you whatever he thinks you really need and deserve?"

"Yeah, right, Dad!" he replied with a sarcastic tone, a grin spreading across his face. "I'm ten now."

"I hope you're not saying that you have lost faith in Santa Claus!" Kate said with a serious expression as she stepped into the room.

"Well, let's just leave Santa aside and say that if there's one thing I could use for Christmas it's a bike. Maybe I could get a job carrying papers, for one thing, or hit the library when I need to get books for school. You wouldn't have to drive me around all the time..."

"All right then, enough of this talk," Jack said. "Tomorrow's Christmas. I think you need to get yourself ready for bed and just wait and see what magic comes to visit during the dark of night."

January 1936

"Everything seems to be in order, Sir," said the clean-cut young man with the clipboard. "There's about fifty people at the gate and more still in their cars. Should we open up?"

It was a chilly morning, but the man he addressed was standing in a yellow suit cut in business style. His white shoes and a smiling demeanor radiated a confidence. "Yes, it's time, no sense in waiting a minute longer!" he said. Then he stepped forward to greet the small crowd that poured through the gate. The irrepressible Dick Pope was back in his element, and he would soon show the naysayers that he was as good as his word.

Pope's vision of Cypress Gardens had come to pass, finished by hired labor. The completed canals wound through the cypress trees and an electric boat carried visitors past elaborate plantings of tropical plants gathered from distant lands. Paved pathways were woven between grassy lawns and flowering arbors. It was a photographer's dream and Pope, ever the shrewd promoter, mailed packets of new photographs daily to northern newspapers, giving them full publishing rights. Always in the market for attractive material, the papers snapped them up and Cypress Gardens was soon becoming a symbol of Florida to rival the Singing Tower or Silver Springs.

May 1939

Amanda looked up from her work at the loud droning sound of a squadron of aircraft and wiped motor oil from her hands. Around her, the expanse of the airfield was an open vista. Above her head, more than a dozen bombers passed in formation. She watched for a moment, still impressed at the sight even though it seemed to be repeated daily. America had belatedly begun to rebuild its neglected armed forces and President Roosevelt had assured the nation that the best way to stay out of the wars that had engulfed Europe and parts of Asia was to present a show of strength.

As the squadron became shrinking specks, Amanda turned back to the small civilian plane she was tending. Changing the oil and filter were a familiar part of her maintenance routine and one she never neglected. Being able to fly the plane as a reward for her efforts made it all worthwhile, so while Katrina attended class at the junior high and Martin was off on a trip, she loved to sneak away to the airfield and keep her pilot's certificate fresh.

"I heard a rumor today at the airport," Martin told her that evening as they cleaned up after dinner. "They say that the Army Air Corps is going to build a new landing field in Tampa at the end of the Interbay peninsula. They plan to base some fighter aircraft there."

"Wow, that's not far from our old home," Amanda commented. "We used to sail around the point when I was a kid. I guess it makes sense, it's got water on three sides, so nothing in the way of the planes. Tampa just got that new shipbuilding contract from the government, too, and they are hiring hundreds of men at the yards. I guess the economy is finally coming back to life there. It's too bad Dad isn't around to see it all come back."

Martin paused for a moment, letting her digest her own thoughts before changing the subject a bit. "I see all these planes flying around every day," he said, "but I just hope we don't have to use them for what they are designed to do. The idea of dropping bombs on people isn't my idea of flying."

"Mine either, sweetheart," Amanda replied. "Let's just hope that all this building does what it's supposed to do: keep the peace."-

Amanda wouldn't be disappointed with President Roosevelt's emphasis on air power as a deterrent to war. In September that year Nazi Germany invaded Poland after forming a secret pact with the Soviet Union. The German's "blitzkrieg" form of war demonstrated the power of aircraft in a way that even General Billy Mitchell's sinking of anchored ships hadn't done. Aircraft were proving to be critical.

The Brass Shell Casing
December 1941

"IN FURTHER UNCONFIRMED REPORTS coming in from around the globe, it is understood that the Japanese raiders have also struck at British Malaya, Thailand and Hong Kong. We will continue to bring you news of the fighting at the Philippines and Wake Island, as well as Hawaii. Stay tuned for further details...."

"What does this mean, Jack? We are going to war now, aren't we?"

"Yes, Katie, I'm afraid we are. The president was right. America is just too involved in the affairs of the world to avoid something like this war. I hoped we'd never again see another world war, but now, it's here."

"Mom, Dad, what's the latest?" Anthony asked, walking into the room.

"Well, I guess you're old enough to understand, Anthony," Jack said, glancing at Kate. "The Japanese have attacked more of our bases in the Pacific Ocean, and British and Dutch bases, too."

"All the guys at school today were saying that we're going to go to war and kick the Japs six ways to Sunday. I think we ought to bomb Tokyo, just like they did Pearl Harbor. That'll teach 'em."

"Anthony, war is no game," Kate responded. "It's a terrible thing. We lived through the Great War before you were born. You should be glad that you're only sixteen and don't have to go. The war will be over before you're out of school."

"I wish I was old enough to go now, Mom. All the guys say so. We'd go show 'em. I'm not afraid of the Japs."

"Your mother's right, Tony," Jack added. "It's not at all like you think it is. And do me a favor, son? Don't say anything to John about the war, all right? He's just too young to be worried about things like this."

Far to the south in Miami, Martin and Amanda sat near their radio that evening, listening to the reports of the carnage in the Pacific.

"It looks bad, doesn't it, Martin?" Amanda asked.

"Yes, dear, it does look bad. We've got our hands full. I thought we might end up in a war with Germany and that didn't look good. Now, I don't know what might happen."

"I'm scared, Martin."

"It's OK to be scared, Sugar. I'm scared, too. We're just going to have to do what we do best and that's fly our tails off." He looked deep into Amanda's eyes, reading the unspoken message of her thoughts. "You can stop worrying about one thing, baby. I'm coming back to you." Amanda wrapped her arms around him and held him as if it would be the last time.

That next day, Martin turned in his resignation at Pan-American and reported to the US Army as a qualified pilot. Within weeks he was in training as a bomber pilot and was soon assigned to England. Thousands of other men, young and old, were lining up to join the military, destined for service in the far theaters of war.

Florida became a great training camp, as dozens of large hotels were converted into barracks, providing seventy thousand rooms to house trainees. Only months earlier Florida Governor Spessard Holland had presciently ordered the addition of an air wing to the fledgling Florida Defense Forces, called the First Air Squadron. Soon the first unit was organized at Morrison Field in Palm Beach.

Amanda, like thousands of young mothers left behind, found a way to contribute as well. Pan-Am expanded upon its contract to train British pilots, taking in hundreds of young Americans for training as well.

Amanda got her wish and began work with Pan Am at Miami airport, giving classroom instruction to pilot recruits. Soon she was watching her students go through the hurried program, take to the air, and leave to face the enemy. It was a job she now regretted, knowing that many of her young charges would not be returning.

May 1942

For the first time in years, jobs were abundant, and the American economy boomed as everyone went to work. Nowhere was the impact more evident than in Florida as the outlook suddenly shifted from depressed to prosperous. The state was changed by the war in a matter of weeks, shifting from an economic backwater depending on a few tourists and a handful of industries into a booming and very crowded, training base for tens of thousands of new military recruits and many of their families.

After work Amanda spent time with Katrina, helping her with her studies. Her teachers had identified her as a gifted student early in her education and had directed her into advanced courses, so that now, at age 15, she was performing at a college-level. She was Amanda's pride and joy and the focus of her life, keeping her from dwelling solely on her worry over Martin.

Jack's service in civil engineering made him valuable to the Army and he was soon working in a civilian capacity on coastal defense installations. Observation towers were to be built along the coasts, where civilian volunteers incapable of active duty could provide an essential service watching for ship activity and the enemy submarines which preyed on the coastal shipping. It was while he was away on an extended assignment that Jack got a painful phone call.

"Jack, It's Kate... Can you hear me OK?

"Fine, Honey. What's the matter? Is something wrong?"

"I don't know how to tell you this Jack, so I guess I'll just have to say it. It's your mother. I received a call from her doctor. He was at her home. He said she hadn't really been sick or anything, just a touch of the flu. He went by to check on her and found her. She's gone, Jack... Oh, Jack, I'm so sorry. I wish I could be there with you."

There was a long silence before Jack responded. "I know you loved her, too, Katie. She was a very good woman, who always wanted the best for her family and that included you and the kids. I'm sure I can get away from here. There's a train early in the morning, so I'll be home tomorrow. Just keep yourself together, for the sake of the kids."

They laid Marie to rest alongside Tony in a simple, private ceremony in Winter Park. The personal loss Jack felt after his mother's passing was not lessened by the deepening gloom of loss around them. Amanda, too, he noticed, seemed to have lost the spring in her step, but he knew they both had to do better for the sake of the children. Katrina and Anthony were both sixteen now, he thought, old enough to understand about life and death, but for John, it was a tough adjustment. Jack was quickly back at work and glad that the war effort was keeping him occupied, but he was frustrated that he couldn't do more.

Americans at home seemed to think that the war was far away, but that was soon dispelled. Coastal shipping provided easy targets, silhouetted against the bright lights of coastal towns and German submarines quickly struck the state. Only weeks after his return to the coast, Jack watched helplessly as an American freighter was torpedoed by a German submarine near Vero Beach. The crew abandoned the flaming vessel in the darkness of night while the coastal rescue services bravely rushed to their aid, despite the chattering of a heavy deck gun on the sub. The next day the smoking hulk lay on the sandbar offshore, a reminder of Florida's vulnerable position. It was one of two dozen sunk in Florida waters.

"This has got to end!" Jack told himself. "'We've got to go on the offensive!"

The military responded with a hurried system of anti-submarine surveillance using blimps based at Key West, Richmond, and Banana River Naval Air Stations. They effectively added to the activities of the ever-vigilant coastal observers, adopted a convoy system of shipping and ordered a night-time blackout. The First Air Squadron proved the effectiveness of their civilian aircraft in hunting submarines, radioing positions to Coast Guard cutters and Navy destroyers.

Within a few months, Jack's services were turned to the construction of airfields. Many existing airfields seemed to have been turned to military use and expanded. Even Lake Wales's small airport became an Army Airfield serving as an auxiliary for the III Fighter Command. Every significant city and town in Florida that didn't have one already was to get a field, it seemed to Jack, and his team of men worked rapidly, using heavy equipment to carve the runways out of rough woods, or fill in low land. Concrete and asphalt covered thousands of acres of Florida in a matter of months, while back home, his son John collected scrap metal, paper and rubber with the Boy Scouts.

Every Floridian found themselves caught up in the war in one way or another as the state became, in the words of some observers, "the world's longest aircraft carrier." Floridians were ready to face any enemy. Yet the word from the front lines seemed to be a drumbeat of bad news. For the early months of the war, everything seemed to be going against the Americans and their allies. Only General Jimmy Doolittle's daring air raid on Japan had lifted spirits and given young John encouragement in his fantasies of beating the enemy alone.

Then, at last, came the word of the enormous naval victory in the Battle of Midway. Four Japanese aircraft carriers had been destroyed and the might of Japan was badly dented. Florida air bases were commissioning thousands of young pilots who would fly the burgeoning aircraft production of America's industry. Now, slowly, the course of war would begin to flow the other way.

The Flag
July 1943

A SUMMER OF TRAVELING found Jack in South Florida, where he took the opportunity to visit Amanda. The long separation from Martin had taken its toll, he thought, for she looked tired and older than he remembered her.

"Have you heard from Martin lately?" Jack asked as they ate a simple dinner with Katrina.

"I get a letter almost every day. He can't tell me exactly where he is, but I know it's England. From what I gather he's flying daylight raids over France and Belgium. It's dangerous stuff, but he's good at what he does."

"He'll be home, Amanda. I just sense it."

"I don't know if Mom told you already, Uncle Jack," Katrina suddenly said, "but I'm leaving college at the end of next spring's term and joining the Women's Army Corps. I want to help end this thing."

Jack stared at the young lady for a moment, suddenly grasping that she was almost eighteen.

"I didn't realize that you were old enough already, Katrina. I guess I've lost track of time."

"She's a pilot too, Jack," Amanda added. "You knew I was already teaching her before the war. She's hardly been up lately, because we can't get enough fuel for the civilian planes, except for our volunteer flights on anti-sub patrol. But if she were a man, she'd probably be on her way to a war zone. By the way, what's Anthony doing? He's eighteen tomorrow, isn't he?"

Jack looked suddenly stunned. "Oh, my god, that's right! Tomorrow's the fourth of July already! I've lost track of time! I bought him a gift last week, but I haven't been home to give it to him."

"Why don't you give him a call?" Amanda suggested. "Go ahead and use our phone. He should be home now."

Within minutes, Jack had dealt with the array of operators necessary to complete the long-distance call and Anthony's strong, reassuring voice gratefully accepted his warm birthday wishes. Soon, Jack told him, he'd be home to see him.

"I may not be here next week, Dad," Anthony told him.

"Why not?"

"I've joined the Navy. I report for basic training on Monday."

"You've what!" Jack exploded. "Are you crazy? You can't just join the Navy! What about your mother? Who's going to be there for her?"

Even as he raged, he knew that he wasn't being rational. He just didn't want to accept that his son was an adult, going to war. He didn't want to accept the reality of the times. Anthony hadn't even had a chance to be a young man and enjoy his independence. "It isn't fair," he thought. Jack stood frozen for a moment, wrestling with his emotions, before Amanda broke the silence, placing a hand on his shoulder...

"Jack, you know he has to go," she told him. "He couldn't live with himself otherwise. We all have to do our part, in one way or another."

Jack paused and shook his head, trying to come to grips with the situation. After a moment, he brought the phone back to his ear. "Anthony?" he said.

"Honey? It's Kate. Anthony just handed me the phone. Are you OK?"

"I'm sorry, I yelled at Anthony. Tell him I need to talk to him again."

"He's upset, dear. He needs your approval."

"I know. And I need to give it to him. I'm so wrong about him. He needs to do what he knows is right. He needs me to be as strong as he is."

"Jack, can I have the phone for a moment?" Amanda asked and Jack relinquished the receiver.

"Hi, Kate, it's Amanda," she said. "Are you alright?"

"I'm fine, but now I'm worried about Jack. Is he going to be OK?"

"Hold on a second," Amanda said and turned back to Jack, who was sitting in his chair, his head in both hands.

"How could he do this, Amanda" Jack asked, his anguish clear. "He's just a boy..."

"He knows what he's doing, Jack," Amanda replied, understanding what he was going through. "I've talked to him about it. He knows the risks. We all do."

There was a long silence, before Jack finally found the words he needed. "I know you're right, Amanda," he said. "It's just so hard to accept. I love him so much. I love you so much. I can't stand the thought of..." There was another long pause before he spoke again, taking the phone from Amanda's hand. "Put him back on the line, Katie. Please? I need to talk to him."

Moments later, Anthony's voice came over the line. "Yes, Dad?"

"Son, I just want you to know that I'm very, very, proud of you. Do a good job and get yourself home safely, OK?"

"Sure, Dad. Don't worry, I'll be OK, no matter what happens."

"I love you, son."

"I love you, too, Dad."

February 1944

The times were not fair for the Crews family or millions of others around the world. The war raged and the young men and women were called from their homes to serve. Within weeks, Katrina had enlisted and soon she was back in familiar territory in Daytona Beach, part of Florida's first training class for the Women's Army Corps.

The shortage of pilots finally brought Amanda her chance to fly again, as Pan-American established an air transport route under military contract. Originating in Miami, the line hauled freight, mostly military supplies, to Brazil, then on to Africa, India, the Netherlands East Indies and on to Australia or the Philippines. Pan-American set up an "Africa-Orient Division" to coordinate the flights of the "Cannon Ball Express" between Miami and Karachi, India, covering more than eleven thousand miles in three and a half days. Another leg flew across Burma, "over the hump" of the Himalaya Mountains and into China. Elsewhere, Delta, National, Eastern and United flew from Florida under similar military contracts.

Florida's shipyards in Jacksonville, Tampa and Pensacola began to turn out the vessels needed to support beach landings in Europe and on far-flung Pacific islands. As the war raged on, the incredible buildup of military and industrial might began to have its effect and the fortunes of war turned inexorably in favor of the United States and its allies. Yet the victory was an expensive one.

"The Secretary of War desires me to express his deep regret..."

Kate's hand fell and her eyes turned upward, not wanting to finish reading the sentence she had begun. She stood on the porch of the house, surrounded by the fresh greens of the budding oaks and the blue view of Crystal Lake, but her every fiber was wrapped into a focus of denial, one which would be strong enough to undo what she was experiencing. Tears filled her eyes as she finally looked again at the scrap of telegram she had involuntarily crumpled in her hand. "...that your son, Ensign Anthony E. Crews, has been reported missing in action since January..."

"Mom? What's wrong?" John asked, stepping from the living room. He was a handsome young man of fifteen years, who tried to make his mother's life easier in the difficult times. Suddenly his gaze landed on the torn telegram envelope lying at his mother's feet and he recognized the look of agony on her face. "Is it Anthony, Mom? Has something happened to him?"

Kate reached out her arms, wrapping them around her surviving son. "It's not fair, John. It's just not fair. He's such a good son. He has so much he wants to do..."

John began a quiet sobbing, but then turned his face to hers. "He wanted to go, Mom, remember that. It was what he wanted. He told me before he went that he might not come back and that it was OK if that happened. He told me that I would just have to do twice as much and make up for him."

Kate looked at John, seeming so mature despite the tears in his eyes, being rational when she was devastated, practically incoherent. With a conscious effort, she tried to pull herself together, retreating from the precipice of despair.

"You make too much sense to be fifteen, do you know that?" she sputtered, wiping her eyes with the back of her hand. "He told you that, huh? I guess there are things I'll never understand even about my own family." She smiled the barest trace of a bittersweet smile, imagining her sons discussing the possibility of death in their room, late at night, or perhaps in the boat, fishing. She wasn't sure how, but it gave her comfort, to know that they understood life, perhaps better than she.

An hour later, after struggling to compose herself, Kate faced the toughest call she had ever had to make, finally reaching Jack at his current project at MacDill airfield in Tampa. He made it home that evening and Kate took comfort in his strong presence, for he shed not a tear. He had done his crying on the train and few around him wondered why. In these days, people understood. Death was all around, touching family after family.

It took a week of persistent telegrams and telephone calls before they confirmed their fears. Anthony wasn't coming home, even in death. He had gone down with his ship, somewhere in the far Pacific Ocean, half a world away. It would be a simple memorial service: a photograph, a flag, an honor guard. And so, they bid farewell.

December 1945

Peace had come at last to Florida and the world. Jack was free to leave his support work and return home to spend precious time with his family and rebuild the life they had known, with the marked absence of Anthony. Christmas was a time for muted celebration and Jack, Kate and John boarded the train to Miami for a reunion with Amanda, Martin and Katrina. Martin related stories of his service over Europe, focusing on the good experiences. Like most of the returning veterans, he was eager to forget the tragedy, pain and death and look to a brighter future.

Katrina, too, had stories to tell, but much of her service had been secret operations. "Can't you tell us a little of what you were doing, Katrina?" Amanda teased her. "I mean, after all, the war is over now, and I know you weren't building the atom bomb."

"I wish I could tell you all about it, Mom, but I have to be really careful. I know that sounds silly when there's no one here but family..."

"Don't press her, darling, you might not want to know what she knows," Martin chimed in. "With a "whiz-kid" like Katrina, it probably really is top secret."

Katrina looked at her father and a smile spread across her face. "I'll tell you what. If you promise not to repeat it and not get worried either, I'll tell you what I can, the unclassified part."

"OK, that sounds like a deal," Jack said. "I think we can all be trusted, even John."

"You mean especially John," Kate said. "I've never seen anyone as good with a secret as him." John merely smiled enigmatically and said nothing.

"Well, then," Katrina began, "when I first completed basic training, I was given a battery of aptitude tests. Then I was sent to some really intense classes in science, aerodynamics, physics and stuff. Then I was sent to work for a team of researchers. Since it seemed that everything was a secret in the Army, I didn't think much of what they said about it being a top-secret project at first. The background security checks did seem pretty detailed, though."

"I'll say!" Amanda volunteered. "I had these two serious-looking spy types going through all my files, checking your health records, asking about your flight training, a regular interrogation. They were here for two days."

"I heard about it from my friends, too," Katrina laughed. "They must have interviewed everybody I knew and half the people they knew. I later came to find out why. You know those "flying bombs" the Germans were launching at London?"

"If you mean the "buzz-bombs," I know about 'em," Martin said. "I saw one of them fly right over my squadron one day, coming over the channel. Scary-looking."

"Actually, not the V-1's, but the V-2's that came later. Those were true rockets. I can tell you that the Germans weren't the only ones interested in figuring out how to build them better. Before long, I was typing detailed notes about rocket systems and then, discussing them with the scientists. I traveled to Washington with them to look at captured German rockets. When Germany collapsed six months ago, we finally got our hands on whole systems. Now, we're improving them."

"Does this mean that soon we'll be flying around in rocket planes that are even faster than those "jets" they're building?" Jack asked facetiously.

"There's a big difference between a jet and a rocket, Uncle Jack," Katrina said. "Rockets don't need atmospheric oxygen."

"You mean..." Jack started.

"Exactly, Jack," Martin cut in. "What she's saying is that rockets aren't limited to the atmosphere."

"You mean they could fly into space?"

"Even to the moon, Jack. Even to the moon."

•

That evening, Jack found Amanda sitting alone, reading in a comfortable chair by the light of a lamp. She looked up when Jack entered the room, smiling at his mock-furtive glances to make sure they had the room to themselves. "I see we're alone at last. I've been waiting for an opportunity to share something with you," he said.

"Well, this seems the perfect time. I'm at the end of a chapter and ready to quit for the night," Amanda replied with a smile as Jack settled into a chair next to her.

"Remember, after mom died, you told me to handle the probate?"

"Sure, Jack. It made sense because you were closer to Winter Park. I hope you didn't mind..."

"Of course not. It's just something I felt that I had to do, anyway. I promised dad when I was a kid that I would learn about business, so one day I could take over for him. I always felt guilty because I never did. Then he retired and sold everything off and invested in stocks and got wiped out in the crash in '29, remember?"

"How could I forget. But you really shouldn't feel guilty, Jack. Dad was always proud of you. I'll always remember how he stood beaming a big smile every time you were marking some achievement or another."

"Thanks, Amanda. You make me feel better about it, I guess..." Jack hesitated, then began again. "But anyway, after he died, mom had the house all paid for, her savings, their Social Security and dad's life insurance.

All together it wasn't a lot, but it was enough to support her, modestly. She always said it was all she ever wanted, remember?"

"Oh, yeah. And I believed her. She was completely content with her few friends, her memories of her life with dad and a good book to read."

"Well, she did a bit of writing too, it seems. She left us quite a long letter that tells us some personal details I would never have guessed and lots of family history. I won't read you the whole thing now, because it's lengthy and you can read it yourself later. But I want to read just a part of it."

"Well, go ahead, then, Jack. I'll just sit here and listen."

"'I've left you a large envelope in the bottom drawer of dad's dresser,' he began, 'In it you'll find the stock certificates that your father bought when he retired. Most of them were worth very little after the crash, but they've regained some value over the years, it seems. I never touched them. I put them in your names because I thought that you two should have them, for the benefit of the children.'"

"That's all, Jack?"

"No, there's a lot more, mostly about all her keepsakes, our native heritage, sharing memories she wanted to pass along, stuff like that. But the envelope was the shocker.

"What was in there, Jack? Did the old certificates really have any value?"

"I didn't think so. I just had a broker trace them all out. A couple of companies went out of business completely. Some of the others merged or were bought up by other firms in stock swaps. One of them was worth six cents a share in 1931. Today, it's worth about seventy-five dollars. They're all still here in this envelope, Amanda," he said, pausing to look her in the eye. "They have a total value of almost two and a half million dollars."

December 1946

The post-war years brought a sense of plenty. The Florida economy, growing throughout the war, accelerated to near boom proportions. Tens of thousands of military personnel had passed through Florida during the war, and they apparently liked what they had seen. Thousands returned to try their hands at building a life in the "Sunshine State," as the new and widely-used promotional slogan proclaimed it. Housing construction expanded and the thousands of returning service men and women settled down to celebrate the peace by raising families of their own. The "baby boom" was beginning.

Coastal cities and towns that were formerly considered risky because of mosquitoes, floods and hurricanes became the new population magnets. Miami once again surged in growth and soon overtook Jacksonville, St. Petersburg and Tampa to become Florida's largest city. Other towns from West Palm Beach, south through Fort Lauderdale boomed in their turn. The town of Daytona Beach, already known for its auto races, became a popular summer resort.

With the boom in traffic on the "Tamiami Trail," Naples and Fort Myers began inexorable growth. Sarasota, already popular, became a mecca for northern wealth. Florida exploded with middle-class growth, her popular beaches and warm climate being the perfect antidote to northern winters. The state's population surged to two and a half million people.

July 1950

"Thirty seconds to launch. All systems ready," echoed the voice over the speakers outside the bunker. Katrina peered through a narrow slit at the graceful rocket poised on the tarmac before her and held her breath as the seconds ticked down. The finned shape of the German V-2 supported a smaller WAC Corporal rocket, developed by the US Army. It was time to test their theories, to prove that their two-stage mating was achievable.

"Three, two, one, liftoff, we have liftoff!" Immediately, a flash of light dazzled her eyes, followed moments later by the roaring sound of the engine. The tube of painted metal rose rapidly on a column of fire and began to trace a graceful arc into the afternoon sky. Upon the concrete pad a few hundred yards away, all that remained was smoke.

Katrina and her companions ran from their bunker, to gaze into the sky at the dwindling rocket. As they watched, the plume of flame trailing behind the projectile sputtered and died. Katrina held her breath, waiting as the rocket separated into two parts. Then, in a sudden flare, the second stage ignited, carrying the missile farther into the sky, a disappearing point of light against the blue.

It was a time for celebrating their success in launching the first rocket from Florida soil. After years of testing and developing prototypes in the desert, at last the American researchers had a permanent home in Florida and their work could be collected from White Sands, New Mexico and El Centro, California and relocated here to the tiny, once-inactive Banana River Naval Air Station on the sands of Cape Canaveral, a large expanse of coastal dunes and marshes jutting into the Atlantic Ocean.

An old lighthouse stood on a seven-hundred-acre site there, which the federal government had expanded to more than twelve thousand acres. That would provide room enough to grow, Katrina thought hopefully.

President Truman had ordered the development of the range, to allow the competing Army, Air Force and Navy rocket programs access to a common facility. With the cooperation of the British government, the testing range could reach to a length of as much as ten thousand miles.

Despite their success that day, Katrina and her entire team felt a sense of urgency, for as they worked, American troops were pouring into Korea as world powers confronted each other. The rockets they were building could have important applications in time of peace, or war, but Katrina prayed that they would need to be used only for the former.

August 1955

"They are killing our families." Rafael said in muttered breath. "How long can we allow it to continue before we act?"

The breeze that swayed the palms of Miami carried the soft words away, yet the hard reality of the argument was not lost upon the heart of his friend Ramone. The two sat fiddling with the remains of their sweet café Cubano as the smells of fresh baked bread swirled and mixed with the fumes of buses passing on 8th Street. The discreet conversation was not unique, but there was a certain fear that accompanied it.

"I can't disagree, Rafael, but what can we do from here?" Ramone replied "If we speak up, we may be deported back to Cuba and handed over to Batista's thugs. Eisenhower doesn't see what is happening, the Americans only care about stopping Communists. We are caught in a box."

"Batista closed the universities because students protested!" Rafael interjected. "They are brutes. They torture, imprison their enemies, or execute them. I am not going to sit down and let this go on. Just tell me when you have heard enough of the killing, the looting, the starvation of our own relatives there. Then we can talk again."

Miami had become home to waves of Cuban political refugees fleeing the oppressive policies of Fulgencio Batista, the strongman who had seized power on the island. Manipulating American interests in global politics, he had shielded his most self-serving policies behind his "Bureau for the Repression of Communist Activities." For Batista, though, that label conveniently fit anything that challenged his iron-fist grasp of the flow of kick-backs and lucre from cruise lines, hotels and casinos catering to wealthy Americans. After suspending the constitution, Batista had catered to the powerful gambling interests and Cuba became the domain of American gangsters. The United States government provided weapons and military support to the Cuban government but turned a blind eye to the terrible excesses. Yet student demonstrations and sabotage by peasants were fanning the flames of open rebellion.

Deep in the mountains of eastern Cuba, a band of revolutionaries led by a determined Fidel Castro were resisting Batista's military. Florida was the departure point for late-night drops of weapons from boats and planes, just as it had been sixty years earlier. A modern version of the "filibuster" boats illegally supplied a new generation of revolutionaries.

The Medal
October 1958

"WELCOME. I'M SURE THAT I DON'T HAVE TO REPEAT to each of you that what is discussed in this room is just as secret as the rest of your work, but I'll say it anyway. Any information released to anyone outside this program will go through official channels."

Katrina sat silently among the dozens of engineers, physicists and chemical engineers assembled for the meeting. She glanced discreetly around, pleased to see another woman and even an Asian face, among the group. A dozen black women, mathematical wizards employed as human "computers," sat in the back of the room. This truly was an assembly of the best, closed for reasons of security only. Quickly she returned her full attention to the speaker.

"The projects that each of you have been working on have now been folded into one," the man continued. "It no longer matters if you were working for the Army, the Air Force, or the Navy. Two days ago, President Eisenhower signed our orders, and we are all now part of Project Mercury. From now on you are authorized to share what you have learned with the rest of this team, and we expect each of you to do so, without hesitation. Your competition is over. This is now an American and civilian, project. Our goal is the same as before: to design the hardware that will place a man in space and return him safely to the earth. I have confidence that the people in this room, the best of America, can get the job done."

The chatter at the base cafeteria was animated that day, Katrina noted, as groups of newcomers filled the room. She watched as her own team members gathered in familiar groups, eager to discuss the anticipated changes. New arrivals seemed to be doing the same, perhaps reluctant to let go of traditional rivalries.

The growing Army program she had helped develop had seen its ups and downs, but now was being transformed. Their successful launch of an eighteen-pound satellite into earth orbit had been a satisfying achievement for her group only nine months earlier, but it had lagged Soviet efforts, which had already placed a live dog into orbit. Now, with the help of others, they would move toward a higher goal.

"Hi, I wanted to introduce myself," Katrina heard a man say and watched as he approached one of her own team seated at the end of her table. Katrina watched for the reaction of the man, whom she knew as a career officer. "I'm Otis Lewis, Jr.," the man said, offering his dark-skinned hand to the soldier. There passed an awkward moment before the officer rose and faced the black man, distinctive in a white lab coat.

"I'm sorry, I didn't realize that there were Negro scientists," he replied, ignoring the extended hand. "Just what is it you do?'

Mr. Lewis straightened himself and gazed levelly at the man in uniform. "I serve my country, the same as you do, sir."

Katrina rose and approached the two and quickly addressed Lewis, extending her hand. "Hi, I'm Katrina Crews. It's nice to meet you, Mr. Lewis. Won't you join us?" she said, indicating the far end of the table.

"Thank you, Miss Crews," he replied with a smile, "but my goal is introducing myself to my new co-workers. I know many of them will need a little time to get used to the idea of a Negro on the team. Old habits die slowly."

Katrina returned the friendly smile, impressed with his diplomacy. "Then come over here and let me introduce you to a few of my friends."

With appropriate decorum, Katrina introduced him to each of the men seated with her and then accompanied him around the room to introduce him to others she knew. Some were friendly, others reserved, but barriers were falling.

"Don't feel too badly, Mr. Lewis," Katrina told him later. "They gave me the same sort of reaction when I started working with them. I was part of the team during the war, but as soon as it was over, some of them seemed to think I should just go bake cookies or something."

"Trust me, I'm used to it, Miss Crews," Otis replied. "I appreciate what you are trying to do for me, but I will have to prove myself before they will come around."

"That will be a happy day," she replied, "and please call me Katrina."

"Thank you," he said, smiling broadly. "And you must call me Otis. My grandfather loved the name and even though he never saw an elevator in his entire life, he chose the name and insisted that my mother name me Otis, because he said I would go all the way to the top," he added laughing.

"Then we will be going together," Katrina replied. "So how did you come to be here, Otis? I must not have been easy."

"I joined the Army when the war started, and was sent to a place called Tuskeegee, where they taught me how to fly. I was one of the lucky ones, shot down a few enemy planes, and came home in one piece. Then they put me through college on the GI Bill. I guess I did alright there, too."

"They can't hold a good man, or woman, down forever!" Amanda replied seriously. "I've been working with rockets since the war and helped develop the Atlas D. It looks as though, with the latest refinements, it will be our bird."

"Congratulations!" Otis replied. "My work has been with materials, mostly for re-entry heat shields. If you can get 'em up, we can get 'em back down!"

Their friendship was lasting and together they helped to power Project Mercury successes.

The Transistor Radio
January 1959

THE SITUATION IN CUBA HAD DETERIORATED, and this time the United States was caught on the wrong side of history. On the first day of the new year, Batista fled Cuba. Castro and his revolutionaries marched into Havana and basked in the adulation of the long-downtrodden peasants. The rebels, though, remembered who had supplied the arms and support to Batista. Before the year was out, relations between the United States and the island nation were chilled.

September 1960

"Ship reports and those from land-based stations in the Bahamas indicate that the hurricane continues to move westward through the Florida Straits and is expected to enter into the eastern Gulf of Mexico, passing very near or over the Florida Keys."

"This can't be good," Jack muttered to himself as the radio bulletin squawked from the transistor set.

"Hurricane warnings are now in effect for South Florida from Palm Beach southward on the Atlantic coast and on the Gulf Coast of Florida from Fort Myers southward, including the Florida Keys" the voice continued. "Interests in southern Florida and along the northern Gulf coast should closely monitor the progress of this system and be prepared to take immediate action should hurricane warnings be issued."

"What's the latest word, Jack?" Marie asked as she entered the room from the kitchen, wiping her hands on a soft towel. The evening meal was behind them, but the threat of the storm was becoming much too real to relax. Hurricane Donna had churned across the Atlantic from the Cape Verde Islands and into the Caribbean, leaving a path of destruction behind.

"It's still a big one, if you can believe what they say. Winds are over a hundred and thirty miles per hour, but they think it will go on into the Gulf. They have a Hurricane Hunter flying around in it and they have it on radar now. It's only too bad that the Tiros weather satellite failed."

"Well, if it's still coming closer in the morning, we need to be getting ready," Marie said. "What can I do to help?"

•

The following morning was sunny, and the threat still seemed distant, but Jack would take no chances. He marked the latest position on his tracking map and realized that it seemed to be turning in the classic fishhook pattern. Jack thought back to the hurricane they had faced in Tampa twenty-nine years earlier and the one that had destroyed his railroad bridges. Always, it seemed, there was another storm to face, another challenge to rise above. This time, at least, they were on the Ridge, far above the surge of wind-driven flood that would strike the coast if the eye turned their way.

Florida's five million people were preparing for a hurricane, many of them for the first they had ever experienced. Windows were boarded and tubs were filled with water. Extra ice was made and packed into every space in the freezer and more sat in tubs inside refrigerators.

At Cape Canaveral, Katrina and her teams were busily preparing for a blow as the military evacuated aircraft to distant bases. The low-lying Cape would be vulnerable to a storm surge, too. It was obvious that something would have to be done to protect rocket components from future storms.

By evening the wind had risen and Hurricane Donna had described a broad curve across the middle Keys and into the lower southwest coast and was now heading a shade east of due north. If the arc of travel continued, the center would pass directly up the middle of the state. Jack turned his radio dial from station to station, listening first to WFLA in Tampa before straining to hear stations far to the south already overrun by the storm's fury.

During that long night they remained huddled on cots in the central hallway of their home as the storm shrieked and tore at the roof and walls. They listened to the local station of WIPC to find out what was happening in town, but the crunch of the back porch being ripped away interrupted them. It sailed like a kite across the neighborhood. They heard the glass breaking on the bedroom window and Jack reinforced the rope that helped to hold the door closed, keeping the winds from the rest of the interior.

During the long calm that marked the passage of the eye Jack dashed from room to room of the house, checking and reinforcing their defenses. It was a long, sleepless night, but by 3:00 am the winds slowly began to abate and by 4:00 it was clear the worst was over, and they collapsed in exhaustion.

At first light the following morning, Jack and Kate were already up, having slept no more than an hour. Leaves plastered their windows, so that they had to open the door to see the changed world. In silence they surveyed the damage. Debris covered the ground. The huge oak that shaded their front yard had lost a few limbs, but was still standing, unlike several others on the block. More than a foot of rain had swollen little Crystal Lake to overflowing, and a veritable mill-race was flowing from it toward the much-larger Lake Wailes nearby. It was a scene repeated across the state as rivers over-topped bridges and swelled far beyond their normal banks.

"We've got no electric power and probably won't for a couple of weeks," Jack observed, pointing out the tangle of broken wires that blocked the street in both directions. "We might as well plan to have some cook-outs!"

By afternoon the combined efforts of some of the neighbors had cleared enough of the street for Jack to maneuver the car the three short blocks to the icehouse. There he found a line that stretched around the building. The rumors flew about the extent of the damage, but most were relieved that there were no reports of deaths in the local area.

By that evening Hurricane Donna had moved on to the north, leaving the east coast near Daytona Beach. It had slashed diagonally across Florida and left little of the state undamaged, with only the Panhandle being outside the force of its damaging winds. Much of South Florida had been left awash in a storm surge of up to thirteen feet. Florida's nature was disrupted, yet it was the fearsome floods of the interior rivers that would elicit the greatest and most destructive, response from people.

October 1962

"I hope all your work with missiles don't end this way, Katrina."

A worried silence followed before she responded. "We have to have faith in our basic humanity, Dad. No one really wants to destroy the earth, even though we have the power to do it."

"My faith in "basic humanity" was shaken during the war, Sugar," Jack replied. "Hitler proved that madmen can and will do unspeakable things in the name of their perverted views of the world."

Both remained focused on the grainy black-and-white images on their television, where Walter Cronkite and a team of newsmen were reporting on the tense situation. It had been two days since President John Kennedy had shocked the world with a speech revealing that the Soviet Union was building facilities in Cuba capable of launching nuclear missiles, as well as bases for bombers. Either could strike any city in Florida within minutes and posed a threat to more distant parts of the United States.

For Floridians, the persistent problems of Cuba had risen to catastrophic levels. A single error of judgment by one of hundreds of people in critical positions might result in the destruction, not only of Florida and Cuba, but of global civilization.

An American invasion of Cuba was the subject of speculation. A failed counter-revolutionary invasion of the island nation by Cuban ex-patriots only eighteen months earlier had resulted in inflaming the already tense anti-American feelings among Cuban leaders. Their response had been to turn to America's cold-war foe, the Soviet Union. The two world powers seemed primed for war, which could easily result in a nuclear exchange that would destroy both nations.

Far at sea, a fleet of American warships was patrolling the Atlantic, ordered to intercept any Soviet vessel headed to Cuba and search them for weapons. At any moment such an action could turn into a shooting war. America was flexing its muscle. Kennedy was determined and Florida was the point of the spear.

"I saw a big military convoy on my way over here," Katrina said as the broadcast ended and as if to add drama to her statement, they heard the roar of jet engines as a pair of Air Force planes passed low overhead. "That's probably the new F4 Phantoms they are moving in," she added. "I heard that they can do better than twice the speed of sound." The noise was quickly becoming familiar as new squadrons were transferred to the bases of Homestead, MacDill in Tampa, Orlando's McCoy and others throughout the state.

"We can only hope that if the Russians launch their bombers at us, those boys can shoot them down," Jack said and shook his head worriedly.

For thirteen long days the two global powers stood eyeball to eyeball as Floridians stocked groceries and medical supplies. Some began hurried excavations of "fallout shelters" in backyards. Others fled to the questionable safety of distant cities. No one slept well as the phrase "we interrupt our regular programming for a special news bulletin" became familiar and a cause for a sharp intake of breath. Was this the dreaded announcement of war?

The crisis came to a boiling point when an American U2 spy plane, flying high above Cuba to photograph the Soviet installations, was destroyed by a surface-to-air missile. The pilot was killed, and many military advisers urged Kennedy to order a quick preemptive strike to take out as many Soviet missiles as possible. Kennedy refused to be pushed.

His counterpart, Nikita Khrushchev, realized that the order to shoot down the US plane had been issued by a field commander. At that he grasped that the high-stakes game of bluff and bluster could end suddenly. The destiny of the world might lie in the hands of one rogue pilot or general.

After much debate among cabinet and defense officials, President Kennedy dispatched his younger brother, US Attorney General Robert Kennedy, to a secret midnight meeting with a new proposal for a settlement to the Soviet ambassador. After a flurry of telephone calls, Khrushchev took the opportunity to disengage. Soviet ships turned around and Khrushchev announced that the nuclear-armed missiles would be dismantled and removed. The US in turn promised that it would never again threaten an invasion of Cuba.

It took months before the missiles were withdrawn and the world retreated from the precipice. Florida, and the world, had been spared.

March 1964

The community of Santos stood among the tall pines and spreading oaks just south of Ocala. With its three churches, rail station and an array of small businesses, Santos was prosperous and hardworking, the self-sufficient product of freed African slaves.

Avoiding confrontation with whites under strict "Jim Crow" laws, the citizens of Santos were surprised one morning to find government agents going door to door throughout the town, advising residents that the town was to be destroyed.

"But why?" was the most often-asked question. "Why do they need our land?"

It was a matter of "national security," they were told.

•

"Seriously, Mom. They plan to dig a ditch to replace the Ocklawaha River, so they can push barges across the middle of the state." Katrina folded the newspaper across her lap, a disgusted look on her face. "Isn't that just more of the same dumb destruction you always told us about as kids?"

Amanda glanced up from her magazine, a wry smile on her face. The family was enjoying a rare and relaxing Sunday together. "Yes," she replied. "I always told your grandfather that they were destroying Florida and that I could see it every time I flew over it."

"But isn't that river one of the most beautiful in the whole state? Isn't that where you took us camping and canoeing?" Katrina pressed her.

"Yes, sugar, it is, but it seems no one cares much for that sort of thing," Amanda replied. "They want their 'economic development.' That means that any development project they can build for private use with public funds is a good thing. They started this in the 1930's during the Great Depression. I thought it was dead, but it keeps coming back."

Most Floridians merely watched as a massive machine began the work of chopping and crushing miles of pristine riverine forest into wasteland. At Inglis on the Gulf Coast, a huge dredge was soon employed, and the blue-green waters of the sea were soon clouded with huge volumes of silt stirred by the machinery and flowing in the river currents. The rich scallop and sponge beds were soon suffering. Katrina wasn't the only one who had noticed the unfolding environmental disaster.

•

"It won't stand the light of day and once you take a good close look at it, Senator, I'm sure you'll agree," the voice on the phone said. "It's a threat to our fresh water, it's a threat to Silver Springs, it's destroying the Ocklawaha and the Withlacoochee and it's costing us millions of dollars! Why? There isn't even any serious purpose! There isn't enough barge traffic going around Florida to begin to justify it."

"Well, Mrs. Carr, I assure you that I will take a good look into it, but you must remember, this project is already funded by the government and well begun. Stopping this won't be easy."

"I understand that, Senator Williams, that's why I'm calling you, because you have always assured the public that you will look out for their interests. Now is your chance to do it. I would like to invite you to be the guest speaker at our public meeting next month, so you can tell everyone just what you have done to help stop it."

"I'd love to do that, but I'm afraid I have a conflict next month, Mrs. Carr. I'll be heading off to..."

"Then I'll put you on the calendar for the following month. I know our voters are eager to hear from you, with an election coming up."

"Yes, of course, Mrs. Carr," the slightly exasperated voice on the phone replied. "Thank you so very much."

Marjorie Harris Carr hung up the phone and smiled at her companions. "There's another one who's going to feel the pressure. Now let's all write some letters to the editors of that list of papers."

Marjorie Carr was a woman motivated and would prove herself a force to be reckoned with. Horrified at the sight of the "crusher-crawler," a massive machine that was grinding the Ocklawaha wilderness to mud and pulp, Carr acted. "Here, by God, was a piece of Florida, a lovely natural area right in my back yard, that was being threatened for no good reason," she wrote.

As others raised old opposition with fears of salt-water intrusion into the drinking-water aquifer, the very idea of turning the entire southern half of the state into a virtual island just struck many as wrong. Opposition mounted and President Johnson, sensitive to public opinion, began to withdraw his support, even as a few of Florida's elected representatives began to soft-pedal their own former backing. Others, however, stuck to their guns, mocking the natural lands as worthless "scrub" and the opponents as "tree-huggers."

Rallying supporters and organizations around the state, Carr continued to push and soon assembled a powerful force as a fledgling environmental movement took root in Florida's sand.

January 1967

Katrina made little effort to hide her tears as she turned away from the television. Around her, many of her co-workers were crying, others stoic in the face the tragedy they had all shared. On the television screen, the images of three lost heroes were outlined in black at the conclusion of memorial services in distant Houston.

The American space program had been an almost unqualified success. Seven Mercury astronauts had been launched from the Cape and safely recovered. Only the loss of a single capsule at sea had marred the program. Eight Project Gemini missions, with teams of two astronauts aboard larger craft, had proven hardware, rendezvous and docking techniques, tested astronauts and hardware in long-endurance missions and allowed for the testing of "Extra-Vehicular Activity" technology. EVA was essential, allowing bold astronauts to work outside their craft in space.

The first American in space, the first American in orbit, the first rendezvous and docking of craft in orbit, and the first "space-walks" were landmark achievements, and Katrina's mathematics had played a role in each one. Florida and her people had assumed a place at the front of a global effort.

Apollo was to be the crowning program and would allow Americans to achieve the goal of President Kennedy. Now everything seemed in jeopardy. For all the dangers the programs had overcome during flight, it was errors on the ground that had cost lives.

It had happened in only a few terrifying seconds and almost every person who worked at the Kennedy Space Center had known the victims and shared the pain of the disaster. The smiling faces of Gus Grissom, Ed White and Roger Chafee were seared in their memories. A flash-fire in an oxygen-filled capsule during a test run on the launch pad had killed the three in seconds. Katrina's pain ran deep.

Amanda had watched with pride Katrina's participation in the American space program as it grew through the successes of the Mercury and Gemini programs. President Kennedy's stated goal on "placing a man on the moon and returning him safely to earth" was a national call to achievement. His tragic murder barely three years earlier had solidified American resolve to achieve his goal and prove that ingenuity could conquer the harsh environment of space.

The Cape Canaveral Air Force Station and the adjacent, civilian John F. Kennedy Space Center launch facilities had grown from a remote outpost to a major installation. Sprawling across more than two hundred square miles of Florida's east coast, they incorporated more than a dozen launch complexes adapted for an array of space vehicles. President Kennedy had visited the site only a week before his assassination, re-committing the nation to the goals of space flight.

Rising above the horizon was the enormous Vehicle Assembly Building, where space vehicles of every configuration could be stacked and raised. It was one of the largest buildings in the world, enough to contain the massive Saturn V rocket assembly that was expected to carry men to the moon.

No longer flying herself, Amanda watched enviously as her daughter mingled with the men at the cutting edge of flight: not only the technicians who designed the "birds," calculated the stresses on the hardware, planned the maneuvers and programmed the flight computers, but the hardy men who would risk their lives to ride them to orbit and endure the fiery return to earth. It was that personal connection which had doubled the pain Katrina felt at their loss. The work was the focus of her life, a calling that had been preordained. It would soon allow her to re-double her efforts in memory of those who had died. Her business-like approach consistently impressed her superiors, and her imagination gave wings to her calculations, so that she soared with them.

"Orbital Mechanics are confusing at first for many people," she told her parents two months later over dinner. "When two orbital bodies rendezvous, speed and altitude are both factors, because the faster you go, the higher you go. If the docking target is behind me, I need to make a larger orbit by increasing my speed, in order to allow it catch up to me. Likewise, to catch up, I need to slow down."

"Don't even try to explain it, Honey," Jack said. "I'm just glad it's you and not me. My engineering was great as long as everything stayed in one place!"

Amanda just grinned at her husband and winked at Katrina. "You can't teach an old dog new tricks."

May 1967

"It's a disaster for the river, just like that crazy cross-state barge canal is for the Withlacoochee," Coleman observed. "I was out here last week with some friends from the Sierra Club, and they were telling me about this ditch."

The three friends in the small wooden boat sat motionless for the moment on the warm spring morning, three pairs of field glasses trained upon the activity a short distance away across the vast, watery prairie of the Kissimmee River. Shimmers of heat distorted their view, but towers of swelling cumulus clouds built themselves on the soaring thermal currents. Much-needed rain might be in the offing by afternoon, but the friends were much more concerned about what was happening before them.

The fish weren't biting, and it hadn't taken them long to determine the reason. Before them ran a tall bank of "spoil," sand and mud that had been dredged from the river and shaped by a squadron of earth-movers into effective dikes.

The Kissimmee carried the waters of a vast basin stretching south from Orlando and was the major source of water that fed Lake Okeechobee, which in turn had once spilled the excess over its low southern rim in a sheet-flow of liquid bounty to fill the coffers of the Everglades. In all that vast watershed were only a handful of people, but tens of thousands of cattle.

Nowhere more than a few feet deep, the broad river fell only about thirty feet in a hundred miles. It had once spread its nutrient-rich waters into the surrounding meadows and cypress domes, annually submerging a thousand square miles of surrounding marsh land. The shallow water was richly oxygenated, allowing it to support vast numbers of fish and in turn, birds. Cranes, herons, egrets, kingfishers, and storks feasted on the crayfish, frogs, minnows, and insects that proliferated in the late-summer floods, while bald eagles and ospreys hunted speckled perch, bream and bass from above.

Now the roar of distant machinery disturbed the normally-quiet marshlands. Thousands of ducks and wading birds had fled the arrival of the battalion of bulldozers, pans and dredges commanded by the US Army Corps of Engineers. No enemy but the liquid nature of Florida's environment confronted them, but the engineers were there to conquer and control. The floods resulting from the hurricanes of 1947 had won the funding from Congress and the effects of Hurricane Donna had spurred the work.

"It's not quite done now and already there are hardly any fish left." Coleman observed. "It only takes a minute to see that there aren't any birds and that's a sure sign."

Across Florida, the energies of humans had re-engineered the systems of nature. Water had been drained and re-directed, marshes and swamps bled dry, and streams converted to ditches. Thousands of acres of rich habitat had been logged of its cypress and pine forests and almost ninety percent of the unique desert-like Ridge habitat had been converted to subdivisions, parking lots and citrus groves. Many of the rare, endemic species that lived there had been pushed to the edge of extinction.

Downstream, the disastrous hurricanes of the 1920's had spurred the construction of the Hoover Dike encircling the big lake. It had replaced the original, poorly-constructed dike that had failed in 1928. The new construction, far wider and taller, diverted the excess waters into the westward-flowing Caloosahatchee River and the eastward-flowing St. Lucie River. The dredging and enlarging of those waterways had further modified Florida's natural plumbing system, dumping unwanted fresh water, mud and algae into the rich lagoons of the Gulf and Atlantic coasts. Meanwhile, the Everglades, deprived of their annual flood-borne flow of silt and detritus, were beginning to suffer. Repeated droughts were ravaging the once-rich habitat.

Now the "improvement" work was being continued upstream. The new C-37 Canal didn't follow the broadly-meandering course of the river, but instead cut across the countryside, converting the hundred and three miles of broad riverine oxbows into fifty-three miles of canal. Locals soon dubbed it the "Kissimmee Ditch."

The owners of the vast, surrounding ranches were happy to see the river basin drained and their prime pasture-lands improved. The waters, however, were being funneled into a deep and stagnant channel. Deprived of oxygen, the nutrients were converted to a noxious stew, an algae-ridden flow slowly crept down to the big lake.

"Richard, you're a scientist. Why don't you convince them they are killing the river?" his friend Pete asked. "Maybe there's a better way to do this."

Coleman scratched his head for a moment before replacing his broad-brimmed hat and considered the possibility. He was devoted to the outdoor life, having grown up in Clearwater, become an Eagle Scout and spent his youth roaming the lakes and rivers of the state by boat and canoe fishing. He wasn't easily intimidated, but this was a challenge that college hadn't prepared him for.

"They've already spent five years and millions of dollars on this, and you want me to convince them to "un-do" it?" Coleman replied, glancing at his friend. "I spoke to Ken and Helen Morrison about it. He runs the preserve up at the Singing Tower. He's a naturalist, and she's a teacher. They've been raising the issue too. But how do you stop the Army?"

"Isn't Helen the one who was involved in helping Marjorie Carr stop that Cross-Florida Barge Canal that trashed the Ocklawaha River?" Pete asked. "She's effective. You are too, I've seen you in action. Besides, you work for the Department of Agriculture, so you're on the inside. Put a team together, get the Sierra Club to back you. Maybe you can reach people."

"You know, Pete, I'm a chemical engineer and that's not the same kind of engineering these guys do. All I could do is show them the sort of destruction they are causing. They are the ones who would have to fix it."

"That sounds like the beginnings of a plan."

Coleman spent only a few days contemplation the issue before committing himself to a persistent campaign to shape public opinion, influence politicians and save the Kissimmee. It was easy to see that haphazard and unplanned development had created devastating problems for Florida's natural environment.

The Tamiami Trail had proven to be an effective dam across the Everglades, depriving the estuaries of Florida Bay of crucial fresh water even as it had drowned the "tree islands" that supported wildlife during the annual monsoon. A hundred thousand miles of random ditches and swales, intended to drain water from farms and pastures, diverted fresh water directly to the sea, reducing the recharge of the aquifers that supplied the state's homes and industry. Strip mining for phosphate and sand had disrupted surficial aquifers and springs, while the former had left behind enormous heaps of mildly-radioactive gypsum.

The people of Florida were beginning to stand up for their state and resist the powerful forces of development that had destroyed so much of it. The Kissimmee would be just one of a hundred battle-grounds in the effort to preserve the rivers, lakes, springs and cypress swamps that represented the natural treasures of the watery peninsula.

It would be almost twenty-five years before Coleman's efforts and those of thousands of like-minded believers, would bear fruit and a partial restoration of the Kissimmee River marshes would begin. Other habitats would fare worse fates.

June 1969

The sound of singing resonated through the old house.

"...Happy birthday, dear Ja-aack, happy birthday to you."

"Well, your singing hasn't gotten any better over the years, that's for sure," Jack winced, feigning an earache, and grinning at the assembled family.

"Quit griping, you old geezer, and cut the cake, or do you need someone to do it for you?" Amanda retorted, as Kate and Martin chuckled. "A body could starve to death waiting for a little nutrition around this place."

"See what happens, Kate?" Jack said, as Amanda popped her with a kitchen towel. "I warned you. As soon as you mature a little bit, they start treating you like you're helpless."

"Mature, hell, Jack Crews," Amanda replied. "You're eighty-three years old and you don't act a day over thirty. I'll let you know when you show signs of maturity."

The family had gathered again, after a long hiatus, at Jack and Kate's home in Lake Wales. It was comforting to Amanda that they still had the house and she felt it a connection to earlier times, when Jack had first constructed it, a time before babies, or grand babies...

"You better be nice to me on my birthday, Amanda, or I'll change my mind about the surprise I have for you," Jack said, interrupting her reverie.

"You've got a surprise for me? Don't tell me you've decided to take flying lessons!" she teased.

"No, I'm leaving the flying to the winged half of the family. But tomorrow morning, you'd better put on your jeans, grandma, 'cause we're going on a little trip."

"I hope we can trust you two alone for a while," Kate observed, laughing at the sibling barbs.

"Don't worry, Katie. Since he couldn't be here tonight, John's coming down from Orlando tomorrow to drive us. We're taking his Jeep."

"Well, that gives me some comfort. Now, here's some ice cream to go with that cake. And Jack, you can have seconds, since it's your birthday."

"You really seem to enjoy being around Amanda again, Jack," Kate said when they had retired to their own bedroom that evening. "I guess we should try to get together with them more often."

"I'd love to, Katie, but I know that we can't just go dashing off to visit them in Miami at our age. Everything we do has become a bit of a production."

"Well, I'm glad they're here for a few days, anyway. It does us both good and them too, I think."

"Katie, I think it helps me, too, because at this time of year, I always think of Anthony. Last week, on his birthday, it felt like he was so close, like he was still watching us, even after all these years..."

"I miss him, too, but we're lucky to have John and the grand kids and now, a great-grand baby.

"I never thought that we'd live to see it. We got kind of a late start at this family stuff, you know."

"Florida's been good to us, Katie. And we've been good to each other."

Smiling, she leaned over and kissed his forehead, before turning off the light.

•

"Just a little farther down this road and we should find a house and a barn," Jack said, consulting a hand-drawn map as the Jeep bounced along a pair of tracks cut deeply into the dark, sandy soil. Calling it a "driveway" was a stretch, but it led to a house. All around was dense tropical forest; bay, cypress and red maple competed for a living. Wild grapevines tangled their branches around each tree and stretched across the narrow ruts to scrape at them. Overhead, turkey vultures circled lazily among towering cumulus clouds that rose under the warm sun.

"There it is, I see it up there," Jack said, pointing ahead. "Stop over there, John. You can't see it well through the trees, but the lake is just past the house."

A few minutes later the trio was led along a dock and aboard a pontoon boat by a fishing guide.

"What lake is this?" John asked his father, who scanned the waters ahead like an eager child.

"It's Lake Pierce. Full of fish and alligators."

Amanda suddenly looked about her, aware of her surroundings, recognition spreading across her face. "I think I may suddenly understand why you've led us on this merry chase. I was beginning to think you were crazy, but now..."

Soon they were racing across the waters of a broad lake, cooled by the speed-induced wind. "There, you see where that long arm of the lake stretches away there to the north? That's where we're going," Jack called over the roar of the engine.

A few minutes later, their driver pulled alongside a primitive and decaying dock and tied the boat. "Well, this is it. I hope it's the place you're looking for," he said.

"Don't worry. This is the place," Jack said. "I knew it as soon as I first saw it."

"Oh my!" Amanda said, as they walked down a narrow path away from the dock. "This is really a jungle."

"Just a little bit farther and you'll see it."

"I wish someone would tell me what we're looking for," John said, following behind the two.

"It's a memory, son. Not just our memory, either. It's yours, too, even though you've never been here before." Jack stopped and turned to look his son in the eye. "This place is the memory of a thousand years. No, let's say ten thousand years before we were here. This is a sacred place. Look," he pointed. There, still half hidden in the woods, was a low mound of earth, stretching away through the trees in a gentle curve. Slowly they approached it and Amanda stood at the base of its slope, as if in a dream. After a long silence, she turned and walked a few feet, picking a place out of many, different in a way that only she could understand.

"Here was his chickee," she said. "And over there is the mound where he is buried. His name was Eastwind. He was your great-great grandfather, John. He was Mikasuki and Calusa and all the people that lived here before us. His blood is in your veins and your family's. This place is sacred for you and your children."

John stood in silence, trying to fathom the change that had come over his aunt, trying to grasp the full importance of the things she said to him. He had heard it mentioned that he had First Nations blood among his ancestry, but suddenly it began to assume more significance. Deep inside him, something was changing.

July 1969

"Thirty seconds and counting. Astronauts report 'it feels good,'" said a disembodied voice that boomed from speakers nearby. John stood in the hot July sun, much too excited to sit, while Kate and Amanda, Jack and Martin sat nearby in folding chairs, part of a crowd of many thousands.

"You know, Amanda," Jack said, "I can still see Dad's face the evening he came home clutching the newspaper with the story about the Wright Brothers' plane. He knew it had changed the world forever, he just wasn't sure how."

"He wasn't sure, Jack," Amanda replied, "but I was. I knew what would happen next. I have watched it unfold like a blooming flower."

"T minus 25 seconds..." interrupted the amplified voice.

"Why do you think it was so clear to you, Amanda?" John asked. "Was it just a premonition or something?"

"Twenty seconds and counting..." the voice echoed across the grassy marshes of the Kennedy Space Center.

"Eastwind told me when I was a child," Amanda continued. "He knew, and I knew, that we would fly. Not just us, but our children and grandchildren, maybe generations to come. Today is just another step on that path. It is only our destiny."

"T minus 15 seconds, guidance is internal." The voice boomed from the speakers, sounding cool and detached, but generating an undeniable wave of excitement as it counted down the seconds.

A few miles away, seated at a console, Katrina glanced up from the stream of telemetry to stare at the massive Saturn V rocket, the product of an almost frantic effort by the best science could offer. Despite having participated in test launches, she remained in awe of the vehicle that might carry three men to another world. She found it hard to breathe. Her every hope and dream seemed to be merging into this single moment in time.

Now, everyone was on their feet, watching the distant gantry tower and the gleaming missile that stood alongside. "Twelve, eleven ten, nine ... ignition sequence start... Six, five, four, three, two, one, zero. All engines running. Liftoff! We have a liftoff ... 32 minutes past the hour, liftoff on Apollo 11. Tower clear."

A loud popping roar shattered the peaceful morning with a force that each person present could feel deep within their chests, the sound of immense power. Five gigantic engines roared, seven and a half million pounds of thrust harnessed to carry these three pioneers to another world. Around the world millions of others were also holding their breath, watching the distant spire that glowed with a power fantastic to behold and sprang from the earth. Their fear was interrupted by reassuring voice of Neil Armstrong, professional, cool, and focused. "OK," he reported. "We've got a roll program."

All eyes strained as the rocket spun on its axis and roared skyward until the brilliant flames disappeared, leaving behind a streak of white billowing smoke, like a pillar mounting toward the stars. It bore with it the hopes and aspirations of a thousand generations. Yet as it rose far above the sandy ground of Florida and sped on its way to a distant world, Katrina breathed a silent and very personal, prayer.

Epilogue

Florida had proven itself to be an irresistible magnet and it grew in a sort of sad magnificence. Lured by the promotions of "theme park" attractions that sprouted across the center of the state, throngs of visitors came each month and many of them returned to snatch up a piece of this southern paradise. People poured in from both north and south to flood into small towns, turning them into cities.

Water was still often treated as an unlimited resource, or even a hindrance. As wetlands were drained, springs were diminished or ceased to flow. Places linked only a hundred years earlier by horse and wagon trails were now joined by multi-lane expressways and hurtling automobiles. The southeast coast, once home to tidy towns strung like beads along A1A, had become home to a sprawling urban landscape bristling with condominiums and hotels that stretched in an unbroken urban landscape for more than a hundred miles.

Narrow strands of shifting sands once home to shorebirds and nesting turtles became home to thousands of people in towers of concrete and steel. Hundreds of square miles of asphalt shed rainwater laden with heavy metals and trash into lakes, canals, and rivers

Beneath the onslaught of machinery, Florida's fragile ecosystems were crushed, and her wildlife dwindled. Decades of debate and sporadic action to restore the Everglades had resulted only in continued decline. Across the state, cypress domes and wetlands were drained and replaced with "mitigation." The runoff of urban landscapes was directed into fragile, once-pristine lagoons, polluting them with the murky waters. Algae blooms choked waterways and estuaries, fish and corals died, and power boats swept through the resting places of basking manatees.

As the population swept above twenty million, Florida's leadership remained closely allied with development interests and failed to deal with the growing calamities of water fouled with fertilizer and septage, air fouled by industry and autos and the ever-present bulldozers and dredges that shredded and fragmented the remaining pockets of undisturbed nature. Yet only a handful of voices were raised against the forces of "progress." It seemed that many of the people of Florida cared little for the irreplaceable treasure that nature had bestowed upon this special place.

•

Familiar with Big Tree Park due to her many day-time visits, Sara Barnes was comfortable enough with the winding boardwalk to use it at night. It was the perfect place to hide from family and at 27, Sara had made a habit, not only of sneaking away to hide, but of going to the park to use methamphetamine, which gave her a few minutes of addictive elation.

On this cool January evening in 2012 she took advantage of the empty park to slip right into the hollow interior of the name-sake feature, the tree known as The Senator. Inside, safe from prying eyes and the chill, she struck a spark and built a small fire for warmth and light, using a few sticks she had gathered. The flickering light gave the interior the appearance of a great cathedral and a wisp of smoke rose upwards as if drawn through a chimney, escaping high above. She smiled at the perfection of the moment, pulling out her cell phone to make a video of her fire. Then she began to slip into the comfort of her drug-induced fog.

It was a few minutes before she noticed that her small fire had ignited the several-inch-thick layer of debris that had gathered within the base of the tree. The smoldering, smoking fire quickly drove her out of the space, where she gasped for air. Within the tree, the contained heat of the fire was slowly igniting the ancient wood, rising to concentrate at the top of the hollow.

Sara looked around for a bucket or cup to hold water, but there was nothing to be seen. She watched the flickering coming from inside the tree and realized that she would be caught if anyone noticed it, or the smoke wafting from high above. Quickly she hurried back down the boardwalk and left the park.

Behind her, the flames continued to smolder and grow. The ancient, decayed heart of the massive tree was tinder dry and soon the flames began to creep upward. As the heat built, the entire hollow became a funnel of fire, drawing the heat and flames ever upward in a flaming spiral.

It was three hours or more before a passer-by noticed the smoke and called the fire department in the town of Longwood. They hurried to the scene, pulling their hoses along the boardwalk to reach the giant tree. The fire, however, had already done its worst and minutes later the top of the tree crashed to the ground. Streams of water from the outside were unable to reach the flames, contained within their wooden chimney. Before morning the 3,500-year-old monument to life had been reduced to a smoldering stump only twenty feet high.

Historical Figures Cited in the Book

(Listed in the order in which they appear)

Juan Ponce de León (1474 – July 1521) was a Spanish explorer and *conquistador* known for leading the first official European expedition to Florida and the first governor of Puerto Rico.

Jean Ribault (also spelled Ribaut) (1520 – October 12, 1565) was a French naval officer, navigator, and a colonizer of what would become the southeastern United States. He was a major figure in the French attempts to colonize Florida.

Sir Francis Drake (c. 1540 – 28 January 1596) was an English sea captain, privateer, slave trader, pirate, naval officer and explorer of the Elizabethan era.

Robert Searle (alias of John Davis) (lifespan unknown) was one of the earliest and most active of the English buccaneers.

Henry Woodward (c. 1646 – c. 1690), often referred to as Dr. Henry Woodward, was the first British colonist of colonial South Carolina. He established relationships with many Native American Indians in the American southeast. He initiated trade, primarily in deerskins and slaves, with many Indian towns and tribes.

Francisco de la Guerra y de la Vega (c 1620 – 1685) was the governor of Spanish Florida (*La Florida*) between December 30, 1664, and July 6, 1671. He participated in the war against the British buccaneers who sacked and plundered the province's capital, St. Augustine (*San Agustín*) in 1668

Sergeant Major Nicolas Ponce de Leon the Younger was the senior officer of the presidio of St. Augustine at the time of the attack by Robert Searle's pirates.

Corporal Miguel de Monzon was second-in-command of the presidio of St. Augustine at the time of the attack by Robert Searle's pirates, and the first to raise the alarm..

James Grant, Laird of Ballindalloch (1720–1806) was a British Army officer who served as a major general during the American War of Independence. He served as Governor of East Florida from 1763 to 1771

George III (George William Frederick) (June 4, 1738 – January 29, 1820) was King of Great Britain and King of Ireland from 25 October 1760 until the union of the two countries on 1 January 1801, after which he was King of the United Kingdom of Great Britain and Ireland until his death in 1820.

Andrew Turnbull (1718–1792) was a Scottish physician who later served as a British Consul at Smyrna, then part of the Ottoman Empire, in what is now Turkey. In 1768, he organized the largest attempt at British colonization in the New World by founding New Smyrna, Florida, named in honor of his wife's birthplace, the ancient Greek city of Smyrna on the Aegean coast of Anatolia

Ahaya Secoffee (circa 1710-1783) was the first recorded chief of the Alachua, a band belonging to the Seminole tribe. In some European sources he is referred to as Cowkeeper, since he held a very large herd of cattle.

Bernardo Vicente de Gálvez y Madrid (July 23, 1746 – November 30, 1786) was a Spanish military leader and colonial administrator who served as colonial governor of Spanish Louisiana and Cuba, and later as Viceroy of New Spain.

Arthur Middleton (June 26, 1742 – January 1, 1787), of Charleston, South Carolina, was a signatory of the United States Declaration of Independence.

Thomas Heyward Jr. (July 28, 1746 – March 6, 1809) was a signer of the United States Declaration of Independence and of the Articles of Confederation as a delegate of South Carolina.

Edward Rutledge (November 23, 1749 – January 23, 1800) was an American politician, and youngest signatory of the United States Declaration of Independence. He later served as the 39th Governor of South Carolina.

John Moultrie (January 18, 1729 – 1798) was a deputy governor of East Florida in the years before the American Revolutionary War. He became acting governor when his predecessor, James Grant, was invalided home in 1771 and held the position until 1774. Moultrie again became a deputy under his successor, Patrick Tonyn.

Patrick Tonyn (1725–1804) was a British General who served as the last British governor of East Florida, from 1774 to 1783. His governorship lasted the span of the American Revolution.

Frederick North, 2nd Earl of Guilford (April 13, 1732 – August 5, 1792), better known by his courtesy title Lord North, which he used from 1752 to 1790, was Prime Minister of Great Britain from 1770 to 1782. He led Great Britain through most of the American War of Independence.

Andrew Jackson (March 15, 1767 – June 8, 1845) was an American soldier, a Tennessean who served as the seventh president of the United States from 1829 to 1837. Before being elected to the presidency, **Jackson** gained notoriety as a general in the United States Army and served in both houses of the U.S. Congress.

Homathlemico (Unknown – April 6, 1818) was a Red Stick Creek warrior who moved to Spanish Florida at the time of the Creek Wars

Josiah Francis (c. 1770 –1818) also called **Francis the Prophet**, native name **Hillis Hadjo** ("crazy-brave medicine") was a religious leader" of the Red Stick Creek Indians.

Alexander (George) Arbuthnot (1748 - 1818) was a Scottish merchant, translator, and diplomatic go-between, on occasion, who had been present in Spanish Florida since 1803.

Robert Chrystie Ambrister (1797–1818) was a British subject, a native of Nassau in the Bahamas, and a Spanish subject.

Colonel Abraham "Abram" Bellamy (1752 – 1828) was an immigrant from South Carolina, where he had served under Gen. Francis Marion (the "Swamp Fox") during the American Revolution. He purchased land and with his son surveyed the area of Cow's Ford on the St. John's River to lay out a new city, which he dubbed Jacksonville.

John Brady (life span unknown) lived for a brief number of years at Cow's Ford, present day Jacksonville, Florida, where he operated a ferry boat across the St. John's River.

Sarah Waterman (c-1770 - September 04, 1820) was an early settler and the influential owner of an inn at the site of Cow's Ford (present-day Jacksonville, Florida).

Andrew Jackson (March 15, 1767 – June 8, 1845) was an American soldier, a Tennessean who served as the seventh president of the United States from 1829 to 1837. Before being elected to the presidency, **Jackson** gained notoriety as a general in the United States Army and served in both houses of the U.S. Congress.

James Monroe (April 28, 1758 – July 4, 1831) was an American statesman, lawyer, diplomat and Founding Father who served as the fifth president of the United States from 1817 to 1825.

James Gadsden (May 15, 1788 – December 26, 1858) was an American diplomat, soldier. and businessman after whom the Gadsden Purchase is named. James Gadsden served as Adjutant General of the U. S. Army from August 13, 1821 – March 22, 1822, and later as a member of the Florida Territorial Legislature.

Osceola (1804 – January 30, 1838) was named **Billy Powell** at birth in Alabama but became an influential leader of the Seminole people in Florida. Of mixed parentage, including Creek, Scottish, African American, and English, he was considered born to his mother's people in the Creek matrilineal kinship system.

Micanopy (c. 1780 – December 1848 or January 1849) also known as Micco-nuppe, Michenopah, Miccanopa, and Mico-an-opa, and Sint-chakkee ("pond frequenter", as he was known prior to being selected as chief) was the leading chief of the Seminole during the Second Seminole War.

Zachary Taylor (November 24, 1784 – July 9, 1850) was the 12th president of the United States, serving from March 1849 until his death in July 1850. Taylor had been a career officer in the United States Army, rose to the rank of major general and became a national hero after his victories in the Mexican–American War.

Abraham Lincoln (February 12, 1809 – April 15, 1865) was an American statesman and lawyer who served as the 16th president of the United States (1861–1865). Lincoln led the nation through its greatest moral, constitutional, and political crisis in the American Civil War.

James McKay Sr. (May 17, 1808 – November 11, 1876) was a cattleman, ship captain, and the sixth mayor of Tampa, Florida.

John Perry Wall (1836-1895) was a physician and mayor of Tampa, Florida (1878–1880). In 1859 he was a surgeon at Chimborazo Hospital in Virginia, where he served Confederate soldiers from Florida during the American Civil War.

Matilda McKay Wall (1851-1893) was the wife of John Perry Wall and the daughter of James McKay Sr.

David Mizell (1833-1870) was a cattleman and the sheriff of Orange County, Florida. He was ambushed and shot while crossing a stream with a posse while attempting to settle a dispute over cattle.

Moses Barber (lifespan unknown) was a slave owner and cattle rancher who came to the Kissimmee basin from Georgia after the Civil War. He was involved in a feud with the Mizell family, who were loyalist during the war and came to political power during reconstruction. The two families fought a bloody war over cattle.

Hamilton Disston (August 23, 1844 - April 30, 1896) was a real estate developer and heir of Pennsylvania industrial firm. He purchased four million acres of Florida public lands in 1881, which is reportedly the largest single purchase of land in world history.

John Eberhard Faber (December 6, 1822 – March 2, 1879) was a German-born manufacturer of pencils with major operations in New York,

Henry Bradley Plant (October 27, 1819 – June 23, 1899), was a businessman, entrepreneur, and investor involved with many transportation interests and projects, mostly railroads, in the southeast.

Alexandra of Denmark (Alexandra Caroline Marie Charlotte Louise Julia; 1 December 1844 – 20 November 1925) was the wife of King-Emperor Edward VII, Queen of the United Kingdom and the British Dominions, and Empress of India.

Henry Morrison Flagler (January 2, 1830 – May 20, 1913) was an American industrialist and a founder of Standard Oil. He was also a key figure in the development of the Atlantic coast of Florida and founder of the Florida East Coast Railway.

Mary Lily Kenan Flagler Bingham (1867 - 1917) was an American philanthropist and heiress who became notorious when she married one of the richest men of the Gilded Age, her first husband, Henry Flagler. She inherited his huge fortune, married again three years later, and died under suspicious circumstances. She left a portion of the millions she inherited to the University of North Carolina at Chapel Hill.

Julia DeForrest Sturtevant Tuttle (January 22, 1849 - September 14, 1898) was an American businesswoman who owned the property which is now downtown Miami, Florida. She is the only woman known to have founded a major American city.

Theodore Roosevelt (October 27, 1858 – January 6, 1919), was an American politician, naturalist, historian, statesman, conservationist, and writer. He served as the 26th president of the United States from 1901 to 1909.

Frederick Law Olmsted (April 26, 1822 – August 28, 1903) was an American landscape architect, journalist, social critic, and public administrator. He is popularly considered to be the father of American landscape architecture.

Henry Bradley Plant (October 27, 1819 – June 23, 1899), was a businessman, entrepreneur, investor involved with many transportation interests and projects, mostly railroads, in the southeastern United States.

Henry Morrison Flagler (January 2, 1830 – May 20, 1913) was an American industrialist and a founder of Standard Oil, first based in Ohio. He was also a key figure in the development of the Atlantic coast of Florida and founder of what became the Florida East Coast Railway.

Napoleon Bonaparte Broward (April 19, 1857 – October 1, 1910) was an American roustabout, river pilot, captain, and politician; he was a three-term sheriff of Duval County, elected as the 19th Governor of the U.S. state of Florida from January 3, 1905, to January 5, 1909. As governor he undertook a major effort to drain the Everglades to create land for agricultural cultivation.

Theodore Roosevelt Jr. (October 27, 1858 – January 6, 1919) was an American statesman, politician, conservationist, naturalist, and writer who served as the 26th president of the United States from 1901 to 1909.

William McKinley, (January 29, 1843 – September 14, 1901) rose through the ranks, having enlisted in the US Army during the Civil War and achieving the rank of Major. He was elected as the 25th president of the United States 1897, serving until his assassination in 1901.

Garret Augustus Hobart (June 3, 1844 – November 21, 1899) was the 24th vice president of the United States, serving from 1897. He died in office in 1899.

Mrs. W. H. Jones and **Mrs. J. B. West** (lifespans unknown) were the first women elected as voting delegates to a national political convention, more than two decades before women's suffrage.

Wright brothers – **Orville** (August 19, 1871 – January 30, 1948) and **Wilbur** (April 16, 1867 – May 30, 1912) – were two American aviation pioneers generally credited with inventing, building, and flying the world's first successful motor-operated airplane.

Jo Sakai (1874 – 1923) was an immigrant from Miyazu, Japan and a graduate of New York University who led a group of Japanese colonists to develop a 40-acres pineapple plantation at a place they dubbed "Yamato" in 1905.

Guy Morrell Bradley (April 25, 1870 – July 8, 1905) was an American game warden and deputy sheriff for Monroe County, Florida. As a boy, he often served as guide to visiting fishermen and plume hunters, although he later denounced plume hunting. In 1902, Bradley was hired by the American Ornithologists' Union, at the request of the Florida Audubon Society, to become one of the country's first game wardens.

John Michael Corcoris (September 17, 1877 – 1944) was a Greek businessman who came to New York City in 1895 to work in the sponge trade. In 1905, he introduced sponge diving to the Tarpon Springs area and recruited Greek sponge divers from the Dodecanese Islands. By the 1930's, the sponge industry of Tarpon Springs was very productive, generating millions of dollars a year.

John King Cheyney (April 1, 1858 – March 19, 1939) was a Sponge Company & Sponge Exchange founder, a local politician and a sponge industry promoter in Tarpon Springs, Florida.

Walter Smith (lifespan unknown) was a Confederate Army veteran of the Civil War. He became a plume hunter operating out of Flamingo, Monroe County, Florida, and was accused of the murder of Deputy Guy Bradley but was acquitted after claiming self-defense. He served only five months in jail while awaiting trial.

Antony Habersack "Tony" Jannus, more familiarly known as Tony Jannus (July 22, 1889 – October 12, 1916), was an early American pilot who flew the first airplane from which a parachute jump was made in 1912. Jannus was also the first commercial airline pilot.

Abram C. Pheil (February 12, 1867 – Nov 1, 1922) was a St. Petersburg businessman and politician. He was elected to the City Council in 1904 and was re-elected in 1906. He was elected Mayor of St. Petersburg in 1912 and served until August 1913.

John Manis (unknown – May 1914) was a crewman of the *Amelia*, a hardhat sponge boat operating in waters around the Florida Keys. He was murdered by rival spongers.

Harry Bell (lifespan unknown) was the captain of the *Amelia*, a hardhat sponge boat, He was assaulted and shot by a mob on the Key West docks but escaped with his life. His boat was burned.

James Deering (November 12, 1859 – September 21, 1925) managed the Deering Harvester Company and later International Harvester. He was an antiquities collector, and built his landmark home, which he called Vizcaya, on Biscayne Bay in the Coconut Grove area of Miami.

Carl Graham Fisher (January 12, 1874 – July 15, 1939) was an American entrepreneur who founded the present-day Indianapolis Motor Speedway. His trans-national Lincoln Highway project is largely credited with inspiring construction of the modern Interstate Highway system.

George Sheppard "Dad" Gandy (October 20, 1851 – November 25, 1946) was an American business executive and developer, president of the St. Petersburg and Gulf Railway, best known for constructing the original bridge linking Tampa and St. Petersburg, Florida.

Eugene Elliott (lifespan unknown) was a millionaire, self-styled financier and promoter who helped attract financing for the Gandy Bridge. In 1926 he was arrested on suspicion of murdering his wife on the day she filed for a divorce. He was charged with manslaughter, but the prosecutor's primary witness, a maid, disappeared.

Sam Carter, Sylvester Carrier, and Sarah Carrier (unknown - 1923) were among an unknown number of Black victims of a vigilante mob of Klansmen and White sympathizers who attacked and burned the Black settlement of Rosewood after false rumors of an assault spread through neighboring communities.

John and William Bryce (dates unknown) were two White train conductors who rescued numerous Black refugees of the massacre at Rosewood in 1923.

John Wright (dates unknown) was the White operator of a general goods store who concealed many of his Black customers inside his store, standing guard with a shotgun to protect them from a mob in Rosewood.

Cary Hardee (November 13, 1876 – November 21, 1957) was an educator, banker. lawyer, legislator, and the 23rd Governor of Florida.

D.P. Davis (1885-1926) was a real estate promoter who moved from Miami to Tampa after the passing of his wife, purchased three low islands at the mouth of the Hillsborough River and dredged the bay bottom to create the largest real estate development in the city to date. He was lost at sea during a transatlantic voyage.

Allen Carleton Nydegger (1886-1981) was a land surveyor who laid out the original town site of Lake Wales, Florida as a "planned city" following the concepts of the Garden City movement envisioned by investors in the Lake Wales Land Co.

Roger Ward Babson (July 6, 1875, Gloucester, Massachusetts – March 5, 1967, Lake Wales, Florida) was an American entrepreneur, economist, and business theorist in the first half of the 20th century. He is best remembered for founding Babson College. He also founded Webber College, now Webber International University, in Babson Park, Florida, and the defunct Utopia College, in Eureka, Kansas.

Moses O. Overstreet (October 10, 1869-April 16, 1955) came to Plymouth, Florida in 1898 from Georgia and engaged in the turpentine business.

Edward William Bok (October 9, 1863 – January 9, 1930) was a Dutch-born American editor, Pulitzer Prize-winning author, and social reformer. He was editor of the Ladies' Home Journal for 30 years (1889-1919) and transformed the architecture of American homes by popularizing the "living room" to replace rarely-used formal parlors.

Frederick Law Olmsted Jr. (July 24, 1870 – December 25, 1957) was an American landscape architect and city planner known for his wildlife conservation efforts. He was responsible for the McMillion Commission plan for Washington DC and several hundred other significant American landscapes.

William Lyman Phillips (June 11, 1985- October 18, 1966) was an American landscape architect and graduate of Harvard University. He worked under the direction of Frederick Law Olmsted Jr. for much of his earlier career before parting with the company during the Great Depression. His best-known works include Bok Tower Gardens, McKay Gardens, and Fairchild Tropical Gardens, all in Florida.

Milton Bennett Medary Jr. (1874 – 1929) was an American architect from Philadelphia, Pennsylvania, practicing with the firm Zantzinger, Borie and Medary from 1910 until his death.

Samuel Yellin (1884–1940), was an American master blacksmith and metal designer who created many fine iron sculptures and designs.

J. H. Dulles Allen (1979-1940) was a noted designer and ceramicist from Enfield, Pennsylvania. He created the remarkable ceramic art grilles that surround the bells of the Singing Tower.

Lee Oscar Lawrie (October 16, 1877 – January 23, 1963) was one of the United States' foremost architectural sculptors and a key figure in the American art scene preceding World War II.

Barron Gift Collier (March 23, 1873 – March 13, 1939) was an American advertising entrepreneur who became the largest landowner and developer in the U.S. state of Florida, as well as the owner of a chain of hotels, bus lines, several banks, newspapers, a telephone company, and a steamship line.

Calvin Coolidge (born **John Calvin Coolidge Jr.**) (July 4, 1872 – January 5, 1933) was an American politician and lawyer who served as the 30th president of the United States from 1923 to 1929.

Herbert Clark Hoover (August 10, 1874 – October 20, 1964) was an American engineer, businessman, and politician who served as the 31st president of the United States from 1929 to 1933. A member of the Republican Party, he held office during the onset of the Great Depression.

Smedley Darlington Butler (July 30, 1881 – June 21, 1940), nicknamed "Old Gimlet Eye", was a United States Marine Corps Major General who fought during both the Mexican Revolution and World War I. Butler was, at the time of his death, the most decorated Marine in U.S. history.

Douglas MacArthur (26 January 1880 – 5 April 1964) was an American five-star general and Field Marshal of the Philippine Army during WW II.

Franklin Delano Roosevelt (January 30, 1882 – April 12, 1945), often referred to by his initials **FDR**, was an American politician who served as the 32nd president of the United States from 1933 until his death in 1945.

Giuseppe "Joe" Zangara (September 7, 1900 – March 20, 1933) was an Italian immigrant and naturalized United States citizen who attempted to assassinate then-President-elect Franklin D. Roosevelt on February 15, 1933, seventeen days before Roosevelt's inauguration.

Anton Joseph Cermak (May 9, 1873 – March 6, 1933) was an American politician who served as the 44th **mayor** of Chicago, Illinois from April 7, 1931, until his death on March 6, 1933.

Mrs. W.H. Cross (lifespan unknown) was the wife of a prominent Miami physician. She was present at the attempted assassination of President Franklin D. Roosevelt and may have prevented that outcome by grabbing the arm of the shooter.

Winston Leonard Spencer-Churchill (30 November 1874 – 24 January 1965) was a British politician, army officer, knight, and writer. He was the Prime Minister of the United Kingdom from 1940 to 1945, when he led Britain to victory in the Second World War, and again from 1951 to 1955.

Richard Downing (Dick) Pope Sr. (April 19, 1900 – January 28, 1988), was a real estate promoter, investor, and developer. He was the founder of Cypress Gardens in Winter Haven, Florida.

Spessard Lindsey Holland (July 10, 1892 – November 6, 1971) was an American lawyer and politician. He served as the 28th Governor of Florida from 1941 to 1945, and as a United States Senator from 1946 to 1971.

Marjorie Harris Carr (March 26, 1915 – October 10, 1997) was an American environmental activist who campaigned to block the construction of the Cross-Florida Barge Canal.

Dwight David "Ike" Eisenhower (October 14, 1890 – March 28, 1969) was an American army general and statesman who served as the 34th president of the United States from 1953 to 1961. During World War II, he became a five-star general in the Army and served as Supreme Commander of the Allied Expeditionary Force in Europe.

Fidel Alejandro Castro Ruz (13 August 1926 – 25 November 2016) was a Cuban communist revolutionary and politician who governed the Republic of Cuba as Prime Minister from 1959 to 1976.

John Fitzgerald Kennedy (May 29, 1917 – November 22, 1963), often referred to by the initials JFK and Jack, was an American politician who served as the 35th President of the United States from January 1961 until his assassination in November 1963.

Roger Bruce Chaffee (February 15, 1935 – January 27, 1967) was an American naval officer and aviator, aeronautical engineer, and NASA astronaut in the Apollo program.

Virgil Ivan "Gus" Grissom (April 3, 1926 – January 27, 1967) was a United States Air Force (USAF) pilot and a member of the Mercury Seven selected by National Aeronautics and Space Administration's (NASA) as Project Mercury astronauts to be the first Americans in Space.

Edward Higgins White II (November 14, 1930 – January 27, 1967) (Lt Col, USAF) was an American aeronautical engineer, U.S. Air Force officer, test pilot, and NASA astronaut.

Richard Coleman (February 14, 1944 – July 18, 2003) was a research chemist with the USDA Agricultural Research Service, an environmental consultant, and a dynamic advocate for Florida's environment. He served on the board Florida Sierra Club, and as executive director of Florida Lake Management Society. He was instrumental in the restoration of the Kissimmee River and the protection of the Green Swamp.

Kenneth Morrison (April 1, 1918 – March 2011) was a naturalist and writer, 25-year director of Bok Tower Gardens and Mountain Lake Sanctuary in Lake Wales, Florida, founder of the Ridge Audubon Society, Green Horizon Land Trust, Florida Conservation Foundation, and co-founder of Florida Bipartisan Civic Affairs Group and the Defenders of Crooked Lake. He was President Emeritus of Florida Audubon Society and on the Board of Trustees of Defenders of Wildlife and The Nature Conservancy's Florida Chapter.

Helen Morrison (February 18, 1919 – March 31, 2018) Educator and environmental advocate, developed one of the first state-funded pilot conservation programs to expose countless school children to the wonders of the outdoors. She was a co-founder of the Florida Bipartisan Civic Affairs Group and worked tirelessly in opposition to the Cross-Florida Barge Canal, and for protection of the Green Swamp and the Everglades. She was active in the establishment of Tiger Creek Preserve, Lake Kissimmee State Park, and the Ridge Audubon Nature Center.

Sara Barnes (lifespan unknown) was a resident of Longwood, Florida. She was charged with igniting the fire that destroyed "The Senator," believed to be the tallest tree in the eastern United States.

About the Author

Robert James Connors was born in Chicago, Illinois, the eldest son of a CTA train motorman. He was raised in Florida and began work as a newspaper carrier at age eleven and joined his school newspaper in high school, where he displayed his passion for the written word. He was hired as a full-time news reporter before his graduation, only later enrolling in Barry University to study English.

An avid amateur historian, journalist, editor, and author, he has more than 1,000 published human-interest stories, features, and commentaries.

Connors is an experienced public speaker, a former Florida county commissioner, and self-taught speaker of Italian. He has served as an invited guest speaker (in both English and Italian) at military commemorative events in Italy, recognizing the service of American and Allied veterans of World War Two in the Liberation of Italy from the Nazi/Fascists.

Besides his deep fascination with history and writing, Robert leads efforts to restore historic Frederick Law Olmsted Jr. landscapes with Lake Wales Heritage, a Florida not-for-profit community organization. He also enjoys hiking, birding, sailing, and surfing. He resides with his wife, Susan, in Lake Wales, Florida.

Follow Robert on Twitter: @R_James_Connors